BLOOD BOND:
A HUNDRED
WAYS TO KILL

BLOOD BOND:
A HUNDRED
WAYS TO KILL

WILLIAM W. JOHNSTONE
with J. A. Johnstone

PINNACLE BOOKS
Kensington Publishing Corp.
www.kensingtonbooks.com

PINNACLE BOOKS are published by

Kensington Publishing Corp.
119 West 40th Street
New York, NY 10018

PUBLISHER'S NOTE
Following the death of William W. Johnstone, the Johnstone family is working with a carefully selected writer to organize and complete Mr. Johnstone's outlines and many unfinished manuscripts to create additional novels in all of his series like The Last Gunfighter, Mountain Man, and Eagles, among others. This novel was inspired by Mr. Johnstone's superb storytelling.

All Kensington titles, imprints, and distributed lines are available at special quantity discounts for bulk purchases for sales promotions, premiums, fund-raising, educational, or institutional use. Special book excerpts or customized printings can also be created to fit specific needs. For details, write or phone the office of the Kensington special sales manager: Kensington Publishing Corp., 119 West 40th Street, New York, NY 10018, attn: Special Sales Department; phone 1-800-221-2647.

PINNACLE BOOKS and the Pinnacle logo are Reg. U.S. Pat. & TM Off.
The WWJ steer head logo is a trademark of Kensington Publishing Corp.

ISBN-13: 978-0-7860-2813-9
ISBN-10: 0-7860-2813-0

First printing: November 2012

10 9 8 7 6 5 4 3 2 1

Printed in the United States of America

ONE

In September 1880, some of the most dangerous men in Tombstone, Arizona—meaning some of the most dangerous men in the world—undertook a desperate mission of mercy into Mexico. It began in Cactus Patch, a small town some miles northeast of Tombstone.

Too much whiskey, too much smoke in the air, too many losing hands of poker: Bob Farr had had enough of all three. He pushed his chair back from the card table and stood up. Three men remained seated: Joe Spooner, Don Brown, and Lee Lindsey.

"Where you goin', Bob?" Joe Spooner asked.

"Get me some air," Farr said.

"Going back to the ranch?"

"No, just stepping outside to clear my head. Maybe a break will change my luck."

It was a friendly game of poker. The four men had been playing for small stakes. But even small stakes are big when you don't have much money.

Ranch hands like Bob Farr and the others worked hard for low wages.

Bob Farr went to the front entrance of Shorty Kirk's small saloon. He pushed open one of the double doors, went outside. He was in his early twenties, of medium height, slim, wiry. Farr was a clean-lined, clean-cut young fellow.

He felt slightly sick at his stomach. The whiskey wasn't sitting right, but then, Shorty Kirk's whiskey was none too good.

A fan of murky yellow light shone out through the saloon doorway, spilling across the ground. A line of horses was tied up at the hitching post at the front of the building. Bob stepped to the side, away from the door. Sweat misted his face. He leaned against the wall, tilting his head back, closing his eyes.

The earth moved beneath him. He had the spins. He opened his eyes, straightening up. That worked a little better for him. Not much, but better.

Bob rubbed his face, trying to restore some feeling to it. He wiped his sweaty palms off on his jeans.

It was about ten o'clock. The night air was fresh after the smoky stuffiness of the saloon. Bob Farr breathed deeply, filling his lungs with it. After a while, the queasiness went away.

Somewhere across the street, a dog barked. Bob looked around. Cactus Patch was a mighty small town, more of a crossroads with a handful of buildings scattered around it. Some were adobe, others wooden frame, log cabin, or sod dugout.

Cactus Patch lay on a shelf at the foot of the west

slope of a mountain overlooking Sulphur Spring Valley in Pima County, southwest Arizona Territory. Its nearest neighbor was Tombstone, whose silver-rich earth had birthed a roaring mining boomtown.

Unlike many villages and settlements which had lately sprung up around Tombstone, Cactus Patch long predated the silver strike. A freshwater spring sited near a mountain pass brought it into being decades earlier, a vital part of the area's traditional cattle- and sheep-raising culture.

It featured a trading post, café, and two saloons, largely serving the small ranches in the gorges and side canyons honeycombing the foothills. It survived, but never flourished. Its growth was held in check by the Apaches, a dread power in the land until recent years, and still a threat.

A three-quarter moon hung midway between the eastern horizon and the zenith. The big, bright, orange-yellow September moon sailed through thin, hazy clouds.

Shops and stores were closed, dark, as were most of the dwellings. Cactus Patch folk were early risers, up and doing well before dawn. Inside the saloon were a handful of men—the poker players and a few solitary drinkers.

The street was bright where moonlight shone down on it; shadows were black dark. Stray breezes lifted off the western flat, blowing through the pass.

A girl ran out of an alley into the middle of street. She stopped, looking around, as if uncertain of which way to turn.

She was young, slim, with gently rounded curves

outlined against a thin dress. Long pale hair streamed down her back. She breathed hard, panting, gasping.

She seemed played out. She lost her footing, tripped, and fell sprawling into the street, in a tangle of arms and legs. The ground was hard, stony. She cried out.

She raised herself up, looking back the way she had come, toward the alley on the east side of the street. Moonbeams fell on her, lighting her up in a silver wash. She looked about fifteen. Her face was the face of fear, dark eyes wide and staring, mouth gaping. She seemed unaware of Bob Farr's presence.

There were few females in Cactus Patch, and even fewer young, good-looking ones. Bob knew them all by sight, and this wasn't one of them. She was a stranger.

Where had she come from? This was hard country, thinly populated, and no place for young women to be traveling alone by night. Or in the daytime, either.

The girl rose, swaying, stumbling. Her thin dress was torn in more than a few places and showed a lot of leg: long, slender calves and rounded thighs.

A man came out of the alley, rushing to her. She gathered herself to run, but he was on her before she could make a break.

He was a big man, solid, thick bodied, a full-grown adult. Even by moonlight you could see he was some twenty years her senior. Mean faced, too.

He wore a white five-gallon hat, black vest over light-colored shirt, and chaps over denims. Shirt-sleeves were rolled up past the elbows, exposing brawny forearms. A belt gun was holstered low on his right side, his spurred boots showed sharp-pointed toes. A short dog whip hung by a thong from his left wrist.

He caught the girl by the arm, causing her to cry out in pain. She struggled to break free. He pulled her back, lifting her off her feet and flinging her to the ground. He loomed menacingly over her, his shadow falling across her.

"Got ya, you blamed hellion! Give me a good hard run across half the county," he said, snarling. "No little bit of a gal gives Quirt Fane the slip! I'll learn ya what happens to runners—"

He lashed out at her with the short, thin whip, the lash curling around the curve of her hip. She shrieked, her voice weak, quavery. "Help! Help me, somebody, please—"

He slipped his hand free of the short whip's looped thong and clubbed the girl with the pommel's knobbed end, clipping her neatly behind an ear. The move, brutally efficient, was carried out with smooth, practiced ease. The girl fell unconscious.

Generally, on the frontier or elsewhere, it is wisdom not to interfere between a man and a woman. Bob Farr had once seen a saloon girl fly into a fury, trying to claw the eyes out of a deputy who had just cold-cocked the pimp-husband who'd been slapping her silly, slamming her with brutal open-handed blows that rocked her head from side to side, leaving her face swollen, and red-raw. It had been a lesson to Bob about the virtue of minding one's own business.

But a decent, red-blooded young fellow such as he could only stand for so much.

This was no lovers' quarrel, nor even some particularly fierce example of harsh family discipline. This was way out of line. Something was wrong here—bad wrong.

Bob would have acted sooner if he hadn't been more than a little drunk. And from the time the girl had run into view and the man clubbed her down, everything happened so fast.

Quirt Fane stood with his back to him. Bob pushed off from the wall, starting forward. He moved quickly, long striding, light-footed. He was on the man before the other was aware of his presence.

The big hombre outweighed Bob Farr by fifty, sixty pounds. Bob grabbed him by the shoulder hard and spun him around. His right fist came up from hip level, striking out.

Knobby knuckles connected with the point of Quirt Fane's chin, a powerful blow that landed right on the button with an audible thud. Quirt rocked back on his heels, knocked flat to the dirt street. The whip fell from his hand, the hat from his head.

Quirt sat up, blood trickling from the corner of a split, now-fat lip. He shook his head to clear it.

The girl stirred, moaning as if in the throes of a bad dream.

Quirt remembered his gun and reached for it. Bob Farr stood over him, hand resting on the butt of a holstered gun. "Try it," he said.

Quirt Fane thought better of it. Instead, he raised the hand to his swollen jaw, rubbing it. "Back off, cowboy."

"Like hell!" Bob said.

"You don't know what you're mixing into," Quirt said warningly, voice thick with menace.

"You tell me," Bob suggested.

"You're in over your head. Get out while you still can."

"You're the one who's flat on his ass on the street."

"Lucky punch. You hit me when I wasn't looking."

"A mite different from beating up some pore little ol' girl, ain't it?"

"What's it to you? She's my woman. Don't go mixing in what don't concern you."

"Funny, she don't seem willing," Bob pressed.

"Fool gal gets some crazy notions sometimes. I got to knock sense into her," Quirt said.

"Maybe you need some sense knocked into you."

"And you're the one who's gonna do it, huh?"

"Looks like."

"You figured wrong, sonny. Dead wrong." Fane then spoke as if to someone behind Bob Farr:

"Take him, Dorado!"

Bob smiled thinly, with contempt. "That dodge's got whiskers—"

He was brought up short by the sound of a gun

hammer clicking into place. The soft scuff of shoe leather against street grit sounded behind him.

"You're covered, amigo," a voice said, with a thick accent.

Bob was mousetrapped and knew it. Quirt wasn't alone; he had a sideman who had come up through the alley. Quirt was grinning now, an ugly grin that did not bode well for Bob Farr.

Bob stepped back and to the side, looking behind him.

Quirt's sideman stood in the mouth of the alley: Dorado.

A black bolero hat topped a raw-boned, hollow-eyed face. The hat had a gold-colored hatband. Black hair parted in the middle fell to jawline length. He had dark shiny eyes, high cheekbones, and a mustache with the ends turned down framing the mouth.

A gun held at hip height was leveled on Bob Farr, a golden gun. It gleamed with an unearthly glow in the moonlight.

It was El Dorado, "the Golden Man," a Mexican bandit with a golden pistol. Bob had heard of him. Who hadn't? A gold-crazy bandido who decked himself out in gold ornaments: earrings, rings, bolo tie holder, belt buckle. And a golden gun—solid gold.

"Where are the horses?" Quirt Fane asked.

"Tied to a tree in back of the buildings," Dorado said. He looked down at the girl sprawled motionless in the street. "What happened to her?"

"She's all right. She started hollering. I had to quiet her."

"You can carry her, too."

Quirt picked himself up, dusted himself off. He slipped the whip handle thong around his left wrist, and pulled on his hat.

"And this one?" Dorado asked, indicating Bob Farr with a lazy wag of his gun.

"I'll take care of him myself," Quirt said ominously.

A man came out of the saloon: Pace Hutchins, one of regulars. "Coming back in, Bob? Hey! What's going on here—?"

Pace fumbled with his gun. Dorado fired first, the blast shattering the stillness of the night. Pace crumpled, falling backwards through the swinging doors into the saloon.

Bob Farr saw his chance and took it. A slim chance, a long shot, but better than nothing. His hand plunged for his gun.

Quirt lashed out with the whip, striking Bob across the face, going for his eyes. Bob turned his head away, raising his left arm to ward off the blow.

The girl was awake. Maybe she'd just come to, or maybe she'd been shamming for a while, playing possum. She jumped up and ran, angling across the street.

Bob Farr drew. Dorado shot him in the back. Bob staggered forward. Quirt's gun was in his hand. He fired into Bob's middle at point-blank range. Bob folded, dropping.

Others in the saloon rushed to the door, shouting. Somebody shot at Quirt, and missed. Quirt blasted back, scoring on someone inside, but he couldn't see whom. A pained outcry was choked off.

Quirt looked away, for the girl. She was far up the other side of the street, running fast. He swung the gun toward her but an outburst of shots from the saloon forced him to turn his attention in that direction.

"Dorado, don't let the girl get away! Shoot her if you have to—"

Bullets tore the air around Quirt and Dorado, too close. Those in the saloon could shoot, too. Dorado ducked back into the alley, out of the firing line. He reached around a corner of the building, laying down covering fire for Quirt.

"Let's go, Quirt! *Vámonos!*"

"The girl—!"

"Forget her, save yourself!"

Gunfire from the saloon was getting hotter. Cursing, Quirt bent low, almost doubled, throwing lead as he scrambled for the alley.

He ducked into it just before Shorty Kirk cut loose at him with a shotgun blast. Quirt reached safety just in time. He followed Dorado to the far side of the alley, making a beeline for where the horses were tethered.

Men poured out of the saloon just as Quirt and Dorado were riding away. They fired at the fugitives, but they were too far away. The outlaws were swallowed up by darkness.

The regulars at Shorty Kirk's saloon took stock. Joe Spooner had been drilled through the arm, a clean shot that missed the bone and vital blood vessels. Pace Hutchins had been tagged in the side and thigh. He nearly bled to death before the thigh wound was staunched. A long recovery lay ahead, yet he would live.

But Bob Farr was dead.

Two

"This is the showdown. Let's see what you've got."

It was the final call at the Oriental Saloon. Dawn was breaking and a marathon all-night poker game had reached its climax.

The big players were seated at a round table in the gaming room, a space separate from the saloon proper. The scene had the bleak aspect of sunrise elbowing aside the revels of the night.

Life was lived at a fever pitch and death was always near at hand in Tombstone in Arizona Territory. Tombstone, boomtown! A fortune of silver ore lay below the surface of the earth; a fortune in silver had already been pried out from underground. Fresh fortunes remained to be found and taken. Riches were being extracted daily.

Even now, the morning shifts at the big mines such as the Tough Nut and the Contention had already been several hours on the job. Rock-hard miners labored in shafts and tunnels beneath rock-hard earth.

Working underground with pick and shovel was one way to gather riches; working the honey traps of Tombstone was another. The town was top-heavy with saloons, brothels, and gaming places. The gambling halls ranked high and low, from bucket-of-blood dives in canvas tents to pleasure palaces like the Oriental, located on the main thorough-fare of Allen Street.

For the Oriental, the dawn hour was ebb tide. The regular customers had long since cleared out. The saloon girls had gone to bed—not to ply the harlot's trade, but to get good day's rest before sun-down spelled the start of another working day.

Now, apart from the poker players, only a hard-core element remained of spectators determined to watch the high-stakes game reach its finish. They were staffers mostly, house men, barkeeps, faro dealers, even a few saloon girls.

All kept their distance—a respectful distance—from the big-money players. "Not safe to crowd the players at that table," a barkeep said, "they're a touchy bunch."

Among the players, Sam Two Wolves held three of a kind: three queens, a four, and a three. Like the others, he played his cards close to the vest, literally.

Heaped in the center of the green baize table was the pot, the treasure all were playing for. It anted up to over four thousand dollars, cash money.

Play had ebbed and flowed since the early evening hours, gold coins and greenbacks passing back and forth across the table. A night of intent play had unwound into dawn, culminating in this, the final hand. The showdown.

It was as if the game existed by night to be banished by the light of day, like some ghostly phantom. Now the time had come to show what was on the other side of the cards.

Those still in at the last hand: Sam Two Wolves, Wyatt Earp, Johnny Ringo, and Buckskin Frank Leslie.

They were names well-known thoughout the West and beyond, all skilled and deadly practioners of the Way of the Gun.

Others sat at the table, some no less renowned: Matt Bodine, Curly Bill Brocius, Morgan Earp. They had been in the game earlier, but had been busted out or folded their hands. They stayed to watch the last turn of the cards.

Sam Two Wolves was a man of two worlds, half red man and half white. His father was a Cheyenne Indian, his mother a onetime New England schoolmarm. His copper-hued, beardless chiseled face showed dark eyes, high cheekbones, and a hawklike nose. He wore white man's garb—a button-down long-sleeve shirt and denims. He was armed with a holstered belt gun and a knife.

But then, who didn't go armed in Tombstone? From preachers to prostitutes, everyone in town carried a firearm. Even respectable ladies went about with a derringer hidden in a beaded reticule handbag.

More unusual was the fact that Sam Two Wolves sat with his back to the front entrance. Nobody wanted to sit with their back to the entrance, not since Wild Bill Hickok had done so in a card game in Deadwood and been shot in the back. Yet Two Wolves occupied that universally unpopular seat, unconcerned. He had someone watching his back.

That someone was Matt Bodine. Thirty, lean, rawboned, handsome, and clear-eyed, wearing two guns on his hips, that was Matt Bodine. He and Sam Two Wolves were friends, partners, and more: They were blood brothers, Brothers of the Wolf.

Their sacred pact had been sealed in blood in boyhood days, when they were both growing up in the Northern Range, uneasily straddling two societies, that of the white man and the Cheyenne Indian.

But that fragile separate peace with the outside world came crashing to an end in July 1876. The annihilation of General George Custer and his 7th Cavalry regiment by the forces of Sitting Bull and Crazy Horse at the Battle of the Little Big Horn meant the end of the way of life shared by the young Brothers of the Wolf.

To stay in their homeland would compel them to choose sides in the war between the reds and the whites, fighting to a bitter end. Abandoning home and ranch, the Brothers went into self-imposed exile, far from their home grounds. The West was big enough for them to make new lives in.

Sam Two Wolves and Matt Bodine were fighting men, shootists, and adventurers. Fighting men, not outlaws. They were resolved to stay "on the side of the law," more or less. It was sometimes a shifty, slippery borderland, in a world where the unjust too often bent the law to their own devices and those outside the law often had their own peculiar brand of integrity.

Yes, Sam Two Wolves could rest easy knowing that Matt Bodine had his back, just as Matt was secure in the same confidence.

Two Wolves wielded a deadly gun, filling graves on Boot Hills throughout the West. Matt Bodine was a gunman of an even higher order of magnitude, with a lightning-fast draw and unerring accuracy. His bullets hit their mark as surely as a compass needle points north. He took his place in the front rank of such fabled gunhawks as Wes Hardin, Billy the Kid, Mysterious Dave Mather, Sartana, Colonel Douglas Mortimer, and Johnny Cross.

Few were his equals. Yet, now, at the card table, sat not one or two but possibly three gunfighters who were or might be his match. They were Johnny Ringo, Wyatt Earp, and Buckskin Frank Leslie.

Fate, fortune, or a combination of both had brought such masterful gunhawks together in Tombstone at the same time. Unlikely though such a concentration might seem to later ages, the history books will affirm the truth of such a gathering.

Tombstone was where the action was, the bonanza boomtown with fortunes waiting to be made. Its proximity to the Mexican border was a factor, too. Borders mean smuggling, gunrunning, robbery, rustling. Tombstone's badmen liked to say they worked "a two-way street, running north and south."

One who well knew the truth of that statement was Ringo. John Ringo, thirty-six, first made a name for himself in Texas's Mason County War. A natural-born loner, he was a man of few words—brooding, a thinker. To the amazement of his associates, he actually read and enjoyed books!

A handsome man with dark hair and hooded eyes, Ringo could be likeable enough when he tried, but he didn't try too often. He was a heavy drinker in a time and place where drinking to excess was not the exception but the rule. He was touchy when sober (which was rare enough), but when he was in his cups, he had a hair-trigger temper. Not long ago in the Tombstone area, he had shot and killed a man who refused his offer of a drink of whiskey. He was a dead shot and lightning-fast draw with the twin ivory-handled .44s worn on his hips.

Ringo had many acquaintances, few friends. His closest friend in all the world also sat at the table: Curly Bill Brocius. Curly Bill had a big black mop of curly hair, a big mustache, and a big, friendly grin. He was genuinely good-natured, which only made him more dangerous. He could genuinely like a man, yet kill him at the drop of a hat, if needed. A solid gunman with plenty of sand, he did not rank among the killer elite of gunfighters.

He was a rustler, robber, outlaw. He and Ringo were the undisputed leaders of a loose-knit gang of over half-a-hundred rustlers and outlaws known locally as "The Cowboys." The band numbered many Texans, Southerners, and ex-Rebels—or, rather, not so ex-, even though fifteen years had passed since war's end.

Seated across from Ringo at the round green table was a remarkable man who in many ways was Ringo's opposite—yet perhaps not so opposite as that, despite surface appearances.

He was Wyatt Earp, the keystone arch of the fighting Earp clan. His older brother Virgil was assistant deputy sheriff of Pima County, the vast tract of land in southeast Arizona Territory of which Tombstone was a part.

Wyatt, thirty-one, was tall, athletic, clean lined, with fair, almost blondish, hair and mustache. His eyes were icy: "Gunsight Eyes." He had been a shotgun messenger and range detective. As a fighting lawman in the wild and woolly cow towns of Ellsworth, Wichita, and Dodge City, he'd made the peace and kept it—at gunpoint, as needed. Even his enemies acknowledged his fearlessness.

Wyatt was not so wedded to the law that he hadn't had run-ins with it himself. The big iron on his hip was a Colt Peacemaker, a weighty piece useful both for shooting and clunking heads. Wyatt did plenty of both. He held down the post of assistant deputy sheriff in Tombstone. The job didn't pay much. He beefed up his finances by working as a Wells Fargo shotgun messenger and card slick.

His long-fingered cardplayer's hands were no less gunfighter's hands, uncallused by hard work. Wyatt liked to dude it up, dressing like a townsman, with a long-tailed black coat, fancy brocaded vest, white shirt, and string tie.

There was no love lost between Wyatt and Ringo. Bad blood? Not necessarily, not yet. But hard feelings. They'd crossed trails before. In Wichita, Wyatt had rousted and pistol-whipped friends of Ringo's. Strictly in the line of duty, Wyatt's defenders said, but the Cowboy faction saw it differently.

"Ringo's always half on the prod anyway, Wyatt's more even-tempered—he don't gun a man less'n it's needful. Needful for him, that is." So said Frank Leslie, another cardplayer sitting in on the last hand of this marathon poker game. But he didn't say it there and never said it to Wyatt's face.

Nashville Franklin Leslie was better known as Buckskin Frank, due to his penchant for wearing fringed leather vests and jackets. He had been an Indian scout for the army, gambler, brawler, shotgun messenger, gunman and, of all things, a wizard bartender. He made a dazzling show out of building and pouring drinks and was much in demand by the high-line saloons of Tombstone. He didn't go looking for trouble, but it seemed to find him, not least because of his habit of romancing other men's attractive wives.

It was estimated that he'd killed between ten and fifteen men in gunfights. Was he as fast and deadly as Matt Bodine, Ringo, or Wyatt Earp? None of them pushed too hard to find out.

Beside Wyatt and seated at the big table was younger brother Morgan Earp, twenty-four.

In all, a tableful of Tombstone's rising men. Some played for the fun of a sociable game; others were out for blood—not just at the card tables, either. Now came the last hand, for a $4,000–plus pot.

It was down to Sam Two Wolves, Ringo, Wyatt, and Buckskin Frank. The others at the table had either thrown in their hands or sat it out.

"Show."

Cool, nonchalant, professional, Wyatt showed his hand. "A straight. Can you beat it?"

Sam Two Wolves responded in kind. "Three ladies." Three queens.

Morgan Earp started. He began swearing under his breath, not so far under that it couldn't be made out. He swore violently, feelingly, with real emotion. He was a good-looking youngster, the handsomest of the Earp brood, though his face was now ugly with passion.

"Hell, Morg, the way you're carrying on, one'd think it was your money that was lost," Wyatt said mildly.

"All you Earps share and share alike," Ringo said.

"Yes and no." Wyatt was noncommittal.

"If one of you gets a job with Wells Fargo, another does. If one of you gets a lawdog's post, the others wind up as special deputies," Ringo went on.

In fact, that's what Morg was, a special deputy.

Ringo held his cards in his right hand, pouring from a bottle with his left. It was one of many such bottles he'd consumed this night. He threw in his hand. "That beats me."

He had two kings, and two aces.

Curly Bill exploded in amazement. "Two pair?!

You threw in all those hundreds of dollars and try to get away by bluffing with a lousy two pair?!"

"Thought it was worth a try," Ringo said, shrugging. "Nothing ventured, nothing gained."

"That's a mighty big bluff!"

"Who knows? Might've pulled it off with deeper pockets."

"What're you holding, Frank? Show," Wyatt said.

"Why not? You paid for a look-see," Buckskin Frank said. He had three jacks, two deuces. "Full house."

Morg resumed swearing. Frank's big hands reached out to rake in the pot. Matt and Two Wolves exchanged glances as Frank gathered up the cash.

"Oh, well. Hard come, easy go," Matt said, sighing.

"Couple years' wages for an honest cowpoke," Curly Bill said.

"Honest cowpoke? You got any?" Morg cracked.

"Nothing but. Got about a hundred or so," Bill said. The Cowboys, of which he and Ringo were the head, were cutthroats. Ringo laughed.

"That's Tombstone for you, men. Get rich quick, get dead faster," Buckskin Frank said.

The game was over. Chairs were pushed back from the table, their occupants rising to stretch out. Groans sounded as muscles stiff and sore from sitting hunched over a deck of cards all night got a workout. Weary eyes were rubbed, gaping mouths yawned.

"Aren't you gonna give us a chance to get even?" Morg demanded of Frank.

"We all agreed that was to be the last hand, Morg," Wyatt said.

"You'll get your chance to get even. Always another game somewhere," Matt Bodine said cheerfully.

Buckskin Frank paused. "I'm game for another hand, if you boys are."

Sam Two Wolves laughed. "You cleaned us out."

"You could put up your claim on Spear Blade Spur. That ought to be worth a couple of hundred dollars," Frank said.

"I'll give a hundred more than anything he offers," Wyatt said quickly.

"Not tonight, hoss. I got the dollars," Frank countered.

"We turned down two thousand from Johnny Behan for that claim last week," Two Wolves said.

"Tsk-tsk. And here I thought ol' Johnny B. could hold his liquor. He must've had a skinful to make that offer. I'd've jumped at it, if I was you."

"You're not me, Frank," Two Wolves said, smiling.

Matt chimed in. "That claim's proving out rich. Assays high."

"Mebbe. If you found a lode and not a surface vein that'll peter out after a few hundred dollars' yield," Frank said.

"Must be worth something for an ace gambler like you to take an interest in it," Two Wolves said.

"Like you said, I'm a gambler. Sometimes I like to play a long shot. Besides, you boys ain't miners.

I can't see you grubbing around in the hard rock away from the sun. All that grubbing in the dirt with pick and shovel . . ."

"We're not afraid of hard work, Frank."

"I ain't afraid of women, but that don't mean I want to get married. If you change your mind about selling, let me know. I'll take the claim off your hands out of friendship, the spirit of good fellowship."

"You're all heart, Frank," Matt said.

"The bidding is always open," Sam said. "Bring plenty of cash."

"I've got plenty of cash, but I think I'll hold on to it for a while longer," Frank said.

Ringo and Curly Bill stood off to one side. Ringo had a big grin, puzzling Bill. "Damned if I can figure out what you're so happy about, John."

"At least Wyatt didn't win," Ringo said.

Milt Joyce, owner-proprietor of the Oriental, joined the group of cardplayers. He was bright-eyed even after an all-nighter. "Buy you boys a drink?"

They took him up on his offer, filtering out of the gaming area into the saloon. Boot heels and leather soles sounded loud amid the unnatural hush of the big hall. The large, now nearly-empty room held the eerie air of a public space deserted in its off-hours.

A couple of saloon girls roused themselves from the sidelines where they'd been half-dozing. They had bold eyes, red-lipped mouths, masses of long hair, smooth white shoulders, full bosoms. Their seductive figures were wrapped in satin and lace, ruffles and frills.

Impelled by an irresistible instinct, they battened on big winner Buckskin Frank.

"Milt's looking to get back some of his money," Matt said, his elbow nudging Sam Two Wolves in the ribs.

Frank was squeezed between a big blonde and a redhead, with others crowding in. "Now, girls, don't grab, there's enough of me to go around," he protested weakly.

"Buy me some champagne, Frank, honey," one lovely cooed.

"Why not?" He bought a bottle for each of them.

The other cardplayers went to the bar where a barkeep was setting up the drinks. Sam Two Wolves was thirsty. He didn't drink much while gambling, wanting to keep a clear head. *For all the good that did me tonight,* he thought sourly.

Now he needed a boost, a bracer, for the ride out to the claim at Spear Blade Spur. The barkeep filled a whiskey glass and Sam Two Wolves drank deeply.

Matt set down an empty glass, the barkeep refilling it. He and Sam had a couple more drinks and said their good-byes.

"Stick around and have some breakfast, men. We'll go get us some steak and eggs," Curly Bill said.

"Sounds great, but we've got to go check on our claim. Won't do to leave it unattended for more than a day or so, not with all the claim jumping that's been going down lately," Matt said.

Ringo stopped drinking long enough to opine, "You don't sound worried."

"We know how to deal with claim jumpers," Sam said.

"Hah! I bet!" Curly Bill laughed.

Matt and Sam said so long and went out. The sun had been up an hour or so. It had been cool at night, almost chilly, but it was hot now. Before too long it would be hotter still. Tombstone was in high desert country. Like Denver, it was a mile-high town, its elevation above sea level.

A pinched-faced youngster in a white bib-front apron leaned on a broom, sweeping away dirt from the boardwalk sidewalk in front of a dry goods store. A couple of men on horseback rode past, raising thin clouds of dust, fine as mist, brown mist.

There were several decent livery stables in town. Sam and Matt put up their horses at one such place on Fremont Street between Third Street and Fourth Street. It was a decent-enough outfit, quiet, workmanlike. Nothing about it would make it stand out or have anybody give it a second thought.

O.K. Corral was its name.

Matt and Sam got their horses and rode out of town.

THREE

Tombstone stood atop a flat-topped rise of Goose Flats. A valley spread out for miles below. Sam Two Wolves and Matt Bodine rode together side by side down the slope, to a tablelike prairie. They angled southwest. The claim at Spear Blade Spur was some miles southwest of town.

Long purple-blue shadows of early morning slanted across the valley floor, dwindling as the sun rose higher in the east. Matt rode a handsome gray with fine lines and a wicked gleam in its eye. He and Sam could handle the animal, but others?— look out! Sam rode a bay with a reddish-brown mane—a scrappy, fast-cutting cow pony.

There was good grazing land around Tombstone, but not in this quarter of the plains. Rivers and streams shunned these flats. Grassland thinned, soil becoming sandy, stony, and arid. Here, vegetation gave way to the mineral kingdom. Boulders and rock outcroppings studded this waterless expanse.

Rock ridges, fin-backed and saw-toothed, humped up out of the ground. Ridges unrolled in long lines of gently swelling hills, like waves upon the sea. Their eastern slopes were bright with sunshine. Masses of upthrust rock carved up the tableland, laying down the outer ramparts of what soon became a maze of canyons.

Dry washes honeycombed the flat. Rock formations showed stacked multi-colored strata, rippling bands of red-brown-charcoal gray contrasting with tan and sandy soil.

The plain was fringed with a thin scrum of greenery. Cactus abounded: clumps and beds of prickly pear and catclaw, low, stout barrel cactus, upright saguaros standing sentinel, some eerily man-shaped.

Hard stony ground was blanketed by a layer of finely-powdered gray alkali dust and grit. Matt and Sam set their horses at a walk to keep the dust from being kicked up. The two frequently looked back to make sure they weren't being followed.

"Lots of bad hombres in town," Matt said.

"And outside it," said Sam.

On they rode to their claim on Spear Blade Spur. They didn't talk much.

Unlike townsfolk, they didn't have to be running their mouths all the time. Hunters know the virtues of silence and they were hunters born and bred. They were at home in the desert. The desert affects men in different ways. Anxious types frequently chatter away, making noise in a futile attempt to push back the great silent immensity of vastness that dwarfs man and his works.

Sam and Matt rode on in silent communion with Nature and each other. The steady stride of their high-stepping horses laid down a soothing rhythm. There were soft creakings of saddle leather, the chirp and flutter of tiny birds sheltering in the bare branches of gnarly dwarf trees and bushes.

There was grandeur, as rocky cliffs thrust up, rising hundreds of feet. The vista was scenic, deadly. Omnipresent was the threat of the Apaches with Victorio now on the warpath. The braves who'd attached themselves to Victorio were a hardy, wide-ranging bunch of desert raiders. Small bands might separate themselves a hundred miles or more from the main body to rejoin them later.

"He's supposed to be in Mexico," Sam said.

"Sure, but does Victorio know that?" Matt asked, half-joking.

There were roads, dirt roads, and horse and game trails inscribing a thin tracery across the dizzying space of the flat.

An undulating rock curtain, snaking north to south, was actually the eastern face of a minor mountain range. It seemed solid only from a distance. Up close, lofty cliffs revealed themselves to be shot through with gaps, openings that were passes and canyon mouths.

Toward mid-morning, the duo neared Spear Blade Spur. They never approached it by the same route twice in a row. Not that the claim was secret or hidden. It couldn't be, not in a town as mineral mad as Tombstone, where everybody and his brother ran a sideline seeking a silver-rich bonanza.

But Sam and Matt constantly varied the course of their arrivals and departures. Manhunting is like hunting any other game. The hunter looks for patterns of behavior in the prey, using them to stalk and slay. They weren't going to make it easy for hostile interests to track their comings and goings to use against them.

Spear Blade Spur was located on the western slope of the range. The duo came from the east, entering a mountain pass. The pass ran roughly east to west. Its far end would put them at a point a quarter-mile north of the claim.

The pass was twisty, snakelike. It was filled with cool blue shadows. In several places it ran north and south, always ultimately returning to its east-west course. At one point, it brought Matt and Sam to the eastern face of the rear wall of the box canyon housing their claim. The canyon mouth opened on the west, on the opposite side of the range.

The outer wall of the box canyon was about a hundred-and-fifty feet high.

Gaps and notches opened in the top of the wall, some considerably deep. A line of smoke rose above the wall, lifting skyward, feathering into a thin haze in the heights. The air was still, with barely the breath of a breeze to disturb the smoke. Sam and Matt halted, looking at the smoke.

"Uninvited guests," Matt said at last, breaking the silence.

"If they're uninvited, they can't be guests," Sam sensibly pointed out.

"No, but we'll give them a warm welcome anyway. Wonder what they've got planned for us?"

"I'll find out."

Some time later, from out of the west end of the pass came a lone rider, Matt Bodine. Sam Two Wolves was nowhere in view.

Matt rode out on the flat, turning left, south. A number of rocky arms and buttresses thrust out from the cliffs to the desert floor. Matt rode clear of them, coming to a wedge-shaped formation shaped roughly like the blade of a spear: Spear Blade Spur.

South of it lay a canyon stretching east deep into the rocks, a box canyon. It was shaped like a land-locked cove. Inside, a long, gentle slope rose to an elevation of a hundred feet, cresting in a half-moon-shaped shelf whose broad end faced outward.

The claim diggings were sited up on the shelf. Beyond rose a curved wall sealing up the canyon, the same notched wall whose outer face was accessible via the pass.

There was no sign of smoke now. Nor should there be. Matt had taken his time swinging wide west on the flat before curving back in toward the canyon. Plenty of time for the interlopers to get rid of the fire and hide themselves.

Matt came on into the canyon, eyes restlessly

scanning the scene. As he neared the foot of the slope, his skin felt like a tautly stretched drumhead.

Much of the canyon was still in shadow. Even without the touch of animating sunbeams, mineral-rich rocks flashed and glinted with fugitive gleams. He started his horse up the slope, hoping the unseen lurkers wouldn't just blast him.

He thought they wouldn't. Crooks are lazy. They'd rather have him deliver himself right to their doorstep (his doorstep actually, his and Two Wolves's), rather than gun him down from a distance and have to get off their lazy asses to rob the corpse and round up his horse.

Crooks are cruel, too, more often than not. They'd want to revel in having a victim in their power, so they could gloat over it and play cat-and-mouse games with human prey.

Crooks were pretty damned predictable, mostly. Still, it wouldn't do to underestimate them. You never know when you meet up with a tricky one.

One thing was sure, though. The intruders were not Apaches. When they were laying for you, you didn't see them unless they wanted you to.

The gray climbed up the slope, and Matt looked for signs. He saw plenty of them. The trespassers couldn't have left more evidence of their presence if they'd tried. The places where they'd used broken branches from bushes and shrubs to erase the tracks of their horses were almost more obvious than the tracks themselves would have been. Broad, swirly, smoothed-off bands of sand and dirt were rarely found in nature.

The gray crested the slope, coming onto the shelf, a semicircular bowl or disk. It was several hundred yards long and stretched seventy-five yards back at its widest.

A freshwater spring bubbled at the base of curved rock walls, yielding a thin trickling stream that wandered along the floor of the bowl. There were ankle-high patches of dark green grass. Stunted dwarf mesquite trees, a little larger than bushes, clung to narrow rock ledges along the inner rock wall.

An open-sided wooden shack with a flat, slanted roof sat on the shelf, facing west. Matt and Sam hadn't been working the site long enough to build a more permanent structure. They'd been too busy digging for silver ore.

Shafts were sunk in the rock walls, seeking silver-rich veins. Mounds of rock fragments, tailings, were piled high, like heaps of stony gray skulls.

The ears of Matt's horse stood up straight. Nostrils flaring, the gray breathed gustily. Matt patted its muscular neck, stroking and smoothing it, murmuring soft sounds of easement.

The gray knew of the lurkers, sensing their presence. It smelled them maybe, them or their horses. There were places on the shelf to hide horses, behind wagon-sized boulders and thick lines of scrub pine.

Matt heard the metallic clicking of a rifle being levered, jacking a cartridge into place. Gunfire cracked, a bullet whipping past his head.

It was a warning shot. If the shooter had wanted

to hit him, he would have. The gray started, not violently. A horse of Matt Bodine's soon became used to gunfire. If the gray trembled, it was from eagerness; if it desired to run, it was not to flee but to charge.

Matt was statue still in the saddle as the claim jumpers came into view Instead of melting into the shadows, they emerged from them. They were ranged in a loose arc at the opposite end of the shelf.

Matt was grim faced, impassive. He kept his hands clear of the twin Colts holstered at his hips. Even the fastest draw can't clear leather in time to beat already drawn guns.

The claim jumpers were a rowdy bunch, frayed, dirty, down at the heels. He knew them. Some of them he'd seen around Tombstone. They were part of the New Mexico crowd, outcasts and fugitives from that state's Lincoln County War, where Billy the Kid and his cohorts were making life hell for the big cattle ranchers who ran the territory.

When things got too hot in Lincoln County, a sizeable bunch emigrated to Tombstone, where they had fast-graduated from public nuisance to menace.

The trespassers came forward, guns in hand, swaggering. They were grouped on a ledge which raised them to eye level with Matt on horseback.

Their names were Justin Vollin, Dick Buttolph, Mick McGarren, Doug Chasen, and Hake Craney.

Justin Vollin was more tinhorn than cowboy, a gunslick but no great outdoorsman. He held a smoking rifle in both hands. He must have been the one who had fired the warning shot at Matt.

Beside him stood his longtime pard, his partner in crime, Dick Buttolph. Six-and-a-half feet tall, he wore a black, high-crowned hat with flat round brim, a single eagle feather sticking up straight out of the hatband. A big-bore .44 revolver was in his hand.

Mick McGarren showed carrot-colored hair, jug ears, a freckled horse face, and pipestem limbs. His thumbs were hooked in the top of a gun belt bearing twinned holstered sideguns.

Hake Craney was an older man, hatchet faced, beady eyed, with a thick brushy salt-and-pepper mustache.

Doug Chasen stood near the shack, where he'd been holding the gang's horses, reins gathered in his red-knuckled fists.

"Well, Bodine!" Justin Vollin crowed.

"That's Bodine? He don't look like much," Chasen said.

"You'd change your tune fast enough if he had those guns in hand, Doug," said Vollin.

"But he don't. And he ain't gonna get the chance, either."

"You're on private property, boys," Matt said.

That got a laugh from the intruders.

"Private property, huh? Yeah—mine," Vollin cracked.

That got a bigger laugh, except for Mick McGarren, unamused, who said, "Ours."

Vollin frowned, not liking being called on that particular possessive pronoun.

"Why waste time jawing? Shoot him and be done with it," Hake Craney complained. Hake Craney was the celebrated Dakota back shooter.

"Slow down, Hake, I'm calling the shots around here," Vollin said.

"Call 'em, then. Finish it so we can get back to town. I'm thirsty, and we done run out of whiskey."

"Somehow I can't see you as a prospector, Vollin," Matt said.

"You're the prospector, I'm the claim jumper," Vollin said smugly.

"Why don't you shoot?" Craney urged.

"Because I want to know where his redskin pard is. Everybody knows they string together. Where Bodine is, the Injun can't be far off."

"You don't know how right you are, Vollin," Matt said.

"Start talking before I start shooting pieces off of you, Bodine. Where's your red-ass buddy?"

"If I told you, you wouldn't believe me."

"Try me."

"He's behind you."

Outlaw laughter came again, raw and jeering.

"That'd be a pretty good trick," Vollin said, snickering.

"It is," Matt said. He raised his voice: "Best get to it, Sam, before Vollin gets off a lucky shot."

"Luck's got nothing to do with it—it's called skill," Vollin said, swinging the rifle toward Matt.

Matt was in a tight spot, but he hadn't shown

himself to the claim jumpers simply to get slaughtered. It was in the nature of a diversion while Sam Two Wolves got into place and got his ducks all lined up in a row.

One of the horses held by Doug Chasen was restive, jerking its head up and down. Doug changed his grip, moving it higher on the horse's reins. He glanced up as he did so.

What he saw gave him a violent start, but not quickly enough to stop Vollin from tightening his finger on the trigger of the rifle leveled on Matt.

"End of the trail," Vollin breathed—and then the top of his head exploded.

The Brothers of the Wolf were cautious men. It helped keep them alive. Part of that was scouting the terrain.

Spear Blade Spur's box canyon had no back door. Not to horsemen, that is. A rider could approach from only one direction, west. The curved wall at the eastern end closed it off, boxing it in.

But the east wall was open to a man on foot. Sam and Matt knew this, because they had previously scouted all possible avenues of entrance and exit.

Earlier, then, coming through the mountain pass, Sam had closely eyed the notched outer wall. It looked accessible, and was. He climbed the wall from the east, using outcroppings and ledges as stepping-stones. He slipped through a notch in the wall to the other side, into the box canyon.

It was a most useful escape route, in or out. Now,

this day, he put it to use again. He tied up his horse to a tree at the base of the wall, slung his rifle across his back by a strap, and started scaling the east face of the cliff while Matt rode west through the pass.

It was an easy climb. For most of it, all he had to do was walk up, hopping from ledge to ledge, like mounting a crude giant stairway. Only a few places required him to pull himself up to the next hand-hold or foothold. Luckily, Sam had no fear of heights.

The sun was high. The rocks were hot, hot to the touch. Sam was not impervious to pain; he felt it the same as anybody else. But he just put it out of his mind, the Cheyenne way.

Presently, he reached the base of the deepest notch, a plunging V-shaped gap in the curved rock wall. He stepped through it, crossing to the far side.

He looked down into the box canyon. The base of the shelf was some forty feet below. The interlopers were bunched up there, five of them, hiding from Matt until he could ride up the slope to them.

Sam could have picked them off with his rifle, but he held his fire. It was better to wait until Matt was in position. That was the plan. Else, one or more of the bushwhackers might escape.

The claim jumpers' attention was focused outward, west, on Matt. As Sam had often noted in the past, people don't look up. White people especially.

Sam eased down from the base of the notch into a square of shadow on the west side of the wall. He hunkered down there, becoming one with the rocks.

He was more concerned about the horses than their owners. Animals are sensitive. But as he was aloft, his alien man-scent could not reach them. He was silent, with no betraying footfall to alert them, nor a pebble fall, and no dislodged dust. He climbed down the broken rock face, getting into position.

Matt rode into view, topping the slope, riding deeper onto the shelf. Matt did not tilt his head to look up, avoiding tipping the claim jumpers to Sam's presence. Sam waved, alerting Matt that he was in position.

The ploy played out as planned. The claim jumpers, certain that they had got the drop on Matt, emerged from their hiding places as he neared, stepping into view.

Vollin, their leader, at the fore, leveled a rifle. He did most of the talking, plenty of it. He and his bunch were arrogant, contemptuous, secure in their power. They were so sure of themselves that some of them didn't even bother to draw their guns.

Matt came on, nearing, closing the distance to where his six-guns could be brought into play.

Sam assumed the kneeling shooting position: rifle shouldered, elbow of left arm resting on the bent knee of his left leg, weapon tilted downward. Not the easiest of shots.

Firing downward could be tricky, but he was a sharpshooter.

The claim jumpers were working themselves up to the kill, not that they needed much encouragement.

Sam lined the rifle's top sights up on the back of Vollin's head.

The horses were bunched up, due to their reins being all gathered together in Doug's hands. The animals were uneasy under the crowding. Maybe the human bloodlust was getting to them, too. Though, with this bunch, they should have been used to it.

The animals sidled against one another, jostling, pawing the ground. A horse lurched to one side, jerking its head up.

Doug Chasen, jerked off-balance, tightened his grip, moving it higher on the animals' reins. He glanced up, seeing Sam, then choking out an inarticulate outcry.

No whit distracted, Sam squeezed the trigger. The rifle barked, simultaneous with the top of Vollin's head exploding as the bullet drilled down through it.

Brain and bone fragments spewed, stinging the two bracketing Vollin—Dick Buttolph and Mick McGarren.

Instant brain death resulted for Vollin, suppressing a reflex trigger pull. Vollin was gone, his body so much inert directionless meat. The corpse pitched forward, falling on its face.

Matt threw himself to the right, off his horse, diving headfirst to the ground.

Pandemonium! Matt's gray horse upreared, rising on its hind legs. Buttolph and McGarren fired blindly, jerking the triggers of their guns.

They both missed Matt by a mile, and missed his horse, too.

Matt hit the ground with a jolt, cushioned somewhat by grass and dirt. He rolled sideways away from the gray, getting clear of its hooves. Getting his feet under him, he rose in a half-crouch, filling his hands with both guns.

He cut loose with the gun in his right hand, putting two shots into McGarren's belly. McGarren fell backwards.

Buttolph banged away at Matt, missing. Matt turned the Colt in his left fist on Buttolph, shooting him in the chest one, two, three times.

Buttolph swayed as slugs tore into him, shattering his chest. Yet somehow he managed to stay on his feet, backpedaling. He tried to lift his gun, but it was heavy, too heavy. He fell down.

Hake Craney had his gun in hand but the gray horse was between him and Matt Bodine. Cursing, Craney scuttled about, angling for a clear shot.

Sam shot him. The rifle round struck Craney, drilling him. Craney reeled, toppling sideways.

Doug Chasen let the gathered reins of the horses fall when the first shot was fired. He drew— then had to scramble to one side to avoid being trampled by the horses, some of whom surged forward.

A roan sideswiped him, slamming him against the cliff. He fought to keep hold of his gun, fought to stay on his feet and avoid falling and going under the horses' trampling hooves. They were not running yet, because they did not have enough room to run. Chasen flattened against the rock wall as horses rushed by him, scattering.

When they were clear of him and he of them, Chasen pointed his gun upward, seeking a clear line of fire on Sam Two Wolves high up on the rock wall. An outcropping spoiled his aim.

Chasen stepped out, away from the cliff for a better shot. He walked right into a bullet from Matt Bodine's gun. The impact swatted him like a fly. He was thrown backwards, slamming into a flat-faced boulder.

His legs folded, bending at the knees. He slid down the smooth rock face, the exit wound in his back leaving a bloody vertical smear.

He sat down, hard. He nodded, head tilting forward, spilling the hat from his head. It rolled on the brim, downhill, curving to one side in a half-circle before coming to a stop.

Matt rose, holding two leveled guns hip high. A puffy cloud of gun smoke hung in mid-air around him. He stepped through it, and the cloud broke apart.

The claim jumpers' horses had scattered to the far end of the shelf, not descending the slope. That would make it easier to round them up.

Matt's gray was nearby. He whistled and it came to him. The horse nudged him affectionately with its muzzle, nearly knocking him off his feet. Matt rubbed the gray's broad forehead. The gray liked having its head rubbed.

Sam stuck his head over a ledge, looking down. "You all right, Matt?"

"Just fine. You?"

"I'm good," Sam said, climbing down the rock wall. A man's-length from the ground, he hung by his hands and dropped down, landing lightly on his feet. He looked at the dead. "Who are they?"

"Some of that New Mexico crowd, from Lincoln County," Matt said. "Few if any of them actually hail from New Mexico, though. Most are guns from Texas and the Southwest. They went up to Lincoln to fight in the range wars there, between Chisum and the other big ranchers. The ones on the losing side are clearing out. A lot of them—too many—have been turning up in Tombstone. They're responsible for most of the claim jumping that's been going on here lately, killing prospectors and filing title to their digs."

"Somebody ought to clean up on them," Sam said.

"This is a pretty good start."

Hake Craney raised himself on his elbows, gun in hand. Matt fired from the hip, seemingly offhandedly, nonchalantly. Craney's round came a split-second later.

Matt's round tagged Craney smack in the middle of his face, finishing him. Craney's slug went wild, becoming a lead smear on the rocks.

"He was playing possum," Matt said, a bit sheepishly.

"He's playing dead now," Sam said.

Matt released the cylinder of his gun, extracting empty brass. He spilled them into his palm, pocketing them for reloading later. An avid hand loader, he constantly experimented with gunpowder mixtures, grinds, and weights. He fed fresh bullets into the chambers, leaving the one under the hammer empty as a safety precaution.

"I reckon Mr. Bonney owes us a favor now," he joked.

"William Bonney? Billy the Kid? How do you figure?" Sam asked.

"He scared Vollin and his pards out of Lincoln County. He had a big mad on them for killing one of his pards. We killed them, so . . . he kind of owes us one," Matt said.

"Better check your figuring. From all I've heard, the Kid's trouble, pure poison, to friends and foes alike. He's got no good sense. If he likes you, you can get dead just as fast as if he doesn't. Faster, maybe. Devil take Billy and his favors."

"There's something to what you say," Matt conceded.

Sam stood with hands on hips, eyeing the property. "Lot of bodies. Now we've got to get shut of them."

Matt stretched, stifling a yawn. "I'm bushed. It can wait till tomorrow."

"Not in this hot sun it can't. Those bodies'll go to rot and ruin fast," Sam pressed.

Matt made a face. "That's a fact. Can't be fouling our own nest. That's just like crooks, putting honest folks to pains cleaning up their messes."

"Maybe they're worth something to the law. Wanted—a bounty on their heads," Sam ventured.

"I misdoubt me that they're wanted in Tombstone, the county or the territory. If they were, they would have been bagged long ago, what with all the hungry lawmen we've got around here. Particularly those ambitious Earps," Matt said.

"They're money hungry, all right," Sam agreed. "They can sniff out a bounty like nobody's business."

"These varmints might be wanted for something back in Lincoln County," Matt suggested tentatively.

"Everybody in Lincoln County's wanted for something. Trouble is, you've got to be there to collect. I've had enough of range wars to last me for a while," Sam said definitely. "The horses should be worth something."

"And, brother, we can use every cent. Our funds have sunk mighty low since you backed those three queens with a fistful of hundred-dollar bills."

Sam sighed. "Well, let's get to the chores."

"First things first. After all that excitement, I could use a drink," Matt said. He went into the shack, prowling around. After a moment, he came out, red faced, agitated.

"What's wrong?" Sam asked.

"They drank up all our liquor, the dirty so and sos!" Matt fumed.

"They sure needed killing," Sam said sadly.

* * *

Sam went to get his horse. It was easier to climb the canyon wall and descend the far side to where he'd left the bay, than to ride one of the other horses out on the flat and through the pass to retrieve the animal.

Matt rounded up the claim jumpers' horses. They were all hitched to a rope line by the time Sam returned.

Matt and Sam searched the bodies, turning out their pockets and pokes. A distasteful task but necessary.

"It'd be a hell of a note if one of them had a pouch full of gold or a wad of greenbacks and we missed it and somebody else found it, the coroner or undertaker or whoever," Matt reasoned aloud.

"To the victor belongs the spoils, eh?" Sam said.

"That's right," Matt said, after thinking about it. "We killed them fair and square and anything they got's owing to us."

The combined total of the claim jumpers' pickings yielded thirty-seven dollars in cash and coin, and a couple of pebble-sized silver nuggets.

"Every little bit helps," Matt declared.

"I'm not arguing," Sam said.

"We didn't come off so badly for a day's work. Their guns're worth something. So are the horses and saddles."

"We're alive, too."

"Yes, there's that."

FOUR

Matt Bodine and Sam Two Wolves rode into Tombstone in late afternoon of the same day. They headed a pack train of corpses. The claim jumpers' bodies were tied facedown across the backs of their horses. The horses were strung out in file at the end of a lead rope secured to Matt's saddle horn.

The blood brothers took an out of the way route into town, to minimize the sensation. Five dead at a go was a lot for one day, even in Tombstone. The route kept to the side streets and quiet corners. But it was daylight and Tombstone was a busy town so, even with all due discretion, the event was sure to be noticed.

It attracted a lot of attention and favorable response. Nobody had any use for claim jumpers. Even the other claim jumpers were glad to be rid of the competition.

The gunfight at Spear Blade Spur was destined to have its thunder stolen by an even more spectacular occurrence. Sam and Matt were unaware of this twist of fate when they reined to a halt in front of the sheriff's office.

The sheriff was the county peacekeeper. The building housed administrative offices and a jail. It had an abandoned look to it. Nobody was around the premises, not even the idlers and loafers usually found loitering around the front steps.

"Looks closed," Sam said.

"Maybe the sheriff's taking a nap," Matt suggested.

"I'll see," Sam said, stepping down from the saddle. It was a hot day but the sheriff's office's front door was closed. He tried the doorknob. It wouldn't budge. "Locked."

He knocked on the door. No response. He knocked harder, hammering door panels with his fist. The door was built solid, to guard against jailbreaks, lynch mobs, and such. Sam could hear the banging echoing inside. If anyone was there, they'd have heard it.

He went to a window. It was covered on the outside with a barred iron grating. The window inside was open. The shade was pulled down. Sam reached through the bars, lifting the shade and looking within.

The front office area was dark with brown shadowy gloom. A thin line of sunlight slanted through a narrow crack in a window curtain. The ray slanted across the space, falling on a brass spittoon and making it shine like gold. Dust motes floated in the beam.

"That's odd—nobody's home," Sam said, rejoining Matt.

"Maybe they went to dinner," Matt said.

"Kind of early for that." Sam climbed into the saddle. "Where to now?"

"Let's try the marshal."

The sheriff handled county business and the marshal handled town business. A U.S. federal marshal was assigned to the district, too, handling Arizona territorial business, but he operated out of the capital city of Prescott.

Sam and Matt rode on, leading the string of death's pack train through the streets to the town marshal's office in Tombstone jail.

Fred White was marshal. The Citizen's Committee had gotten him appointed to the post. Deputy marshal was John Behan, a friend of Ringo's and a favorite of the Cowboy faction.

A gallows dominated the square fronting the jail. It was newly built, with raw yellow, unpainted fresh lumber planks and boards. A steep narrow flight of steps led to an eight-foot-high square wooden platform set on a scaffold framework. Atop it rose an upright wooden construction shaped like an upside-down L. From it would hang the condemned man. A hinged trapdoor in the middle of the platform would help drop him into eternity.

Between the gallows and the corpse-carrying horses, the setting had taken on a eerie, offbeat air.

Matt got down this time, Sam staying with the horses. Matt entered the jail. Behind a beat-up wooden desk sat Assistant Deputy Hubert Osgood, hunched over some paperwork. Osgood was the third man from the top on the marshal's office totem pole. He was tall, reedy, and storklike. His hat was pushed back on his head. He was chewing on the end of a pencil. He frowned fiercely, as if engaged in heavy thought.

He wasn't much of a lawman, but he had a lot of relatives in town who voted.

Matt cleared his throat. Osgood started, looking up. "Oh. It's you," he said without enthusiasm. He knew well of Matt Bodine and Sam Two Wolves. Gunmen of their stature were not necessarily beloved by the law in Tombstone. Or the law anywhere else, for that matter.

"What do you want?" Osgood asked dismissively. A thought struck him and he changed gears, showing genuine interest. "Wait a minute, wait a minute! Is this about the holdup?"

"What holdup?" Matt asked.

"Don't tell me you ain't heard about the holdup? Where you been? Everybody's heard about the holdup!"

"I just got into town."

Osgood rose, holding on to the edge of his desk with both hands. The cords on his neck stood out like big bunches of telegraph wires. He quivered with excitement. "They done robbed the Wells Fargo wagon today!"

"You don't say," Matt said, impressed.

"Hit the wagon on the San Pedro Valley Road! Killed Myles Cooper riding shotgun and wounded driver Walt Simms. Got away with twenty-seven thousand dollars in silver bullion—twenty-seven thousand dollars!"

"Who did it?"

"Who knows? It's a mystery. They were masked, all three of them. They're killers, whoever they are, killers! Gunned Cooper down like a dog and shot Simms without giving him a chance to surrender."

"Too bad."

"Murdering bastards," Osgood groused. "They were laying for the wagon at the top of the grade. Horses just naturally run slow by the time they reach the summit. Going a few miles an hour, no more. Outlaws came out from behind the trees and lit into the guards. Poor devils never had a chance.

"Lem Tolliver rode by around noon and came across the driver, Simms. He was still alive somehow. Bled white—be a miracle if he pulls through. Lem run Simms into town. Bullion was long gone, of course. All twenty-seven thousand!"

"The bandits couldn't have gotten far, not with twenty-seven thousand dollars in silver bars," Matt said thoughtfully. "That's a heavy load. It's sure to have slowed them down."

"They knew what they were doing, the cunning devils!" Osgood cried, shaking a bony fist in the air. "They stole the wagon, too! Did you ever hear of such brass-bound gall?

"Marshal White and the sheriff whipped up a big posse and set after 'em. Johnny Behan went along, the Earps, and Doc Holliday, too," he went on.

Matt whistled. "Whew! That's a lot of firepower."

"For all the good it'll do 'em. Robbery was an hour after sunup and Lem didn't bring Simms into town until two, two-thirty this afternoon. Got themselves a good half-day's head start. Time a-plenty to divvy up the loot and run it into the hills on horseback—twenty-seven thousand dollars!"

Osgood fell back in his chair, spent, exhausted by his storm of emotion. He mopped sweat off his brow with a bandana folded into a sodden fabric square. He looked feverish, haunted.

After a moment, he seemed to recover somewhat. His eyes came into focus. He took notice of his surroundings. He stared at Matt as if he'd never seen him before.

"Something you want, mister?" he asked dully.

"Well, yes, now that you mention it," Matt began.

Osgood wasn't listening, his attention was elsewhere. The front door was open. Excited-seeming citizens could be seen passing back and forth in front of it, collecting into a crowd. The sightlines prevented Osgood from seeing the pack train of death standing out in the street.

Osgood, irked, got up from behind his desk. "What's all that commotion?"

He started across the room.

"That's what I wanted to talk to you about," Matt said, following the assistant deputy marshal.

Osgood went outside, squinting against bright, hot, late-day sunshine. He glanced at the string of horses, then caught sight of the corpses.

He reeled as if thunderstruck, prominent Adam's apple bobbing in a long, scrawny neck as he gulped, swallowing hard. "Lord awlmighty! Slaughter at wholesale!"

The lawman's narrow-eyed gaze darted from the dead men to Matt and Sam, and back again. Recollecting his professional duties, he demanded, "Who done it?"

"We did," Matt said, indicating himself and Sam. "It was self-defense," Matt added quickly. "They're claim jumpers. They tried to kill us. It was them or us. We did what we had to do."

The dead were an unlovely sight, blank eyes bulging, mouths gaping, limbs already stiffening and contorting. Osgood tried not to stare.

"Who are—er, who were they?" he asked.

"Justin Vollin's bunch. Some of that Lincoln County crowd," Sam volunteered.

"Is that so?" Osgood said, interested in spite of himself. He forced himself to take a closer look. "Huh! Yeah, that's Vollin hisself. Shot in the back of the head. Hmmm."

He eyed Matt and Sam, suspicion smoldering behind those glassy orbs. "That don't look right!"

"We hit them from both sides, got them in a crossfire. It was five against two. We had to even up the odds," Matt said.

"No law says we have to take a gang of murdering thieves straight on, face to face," Sam chimed in.

Osgood weighed the point. "Huh. I suppose that's all right, then. Them New Mexico boys are all no-goods, troublemakers. Vollin was one of the worst. Used to sass me when I was making my rounds on duty, give me a lot of smart back talk to make me out a fool in front of folks. . . . Tried to jump your claim, you say?"

"That's right," Sam said.

"Could be they're the ones been shooting up the prospectors in the hills lately. Killed seven, eight of them this month."

"Could be," Sam allowed.

Osgood shook his head. "What a day! So much killing—too much killing. Whole danged territory's going to hell in a handbasket!" Having reached the end of his energy and interest in the matter, he turned and started to go back inside.

"Hey, wait a minute!" Sam called after him. Osgood halted, fidgeting.

"What about them?" Sam asked. "We brought them in. We want to get them off our hands."

"I don't blame you. I would, too," Osgood said.

"What're we supposed to do with them?"

"You got me there."

"You're the law in town," Sam pointed out.

Osgood shook his head. "Nope. I'm the town law, Tombstone town. Your claim's at Spear Blade Spur, you say? That's outside city limits. Marshal's got no jurisdiction there. It ain't none of our affair. Sorry." He didn't sound sorry.

"That's county business," Osgood went on. "A matter for the sheriff. Run them over to him—and quick. I'm getting kind of sick at my stomach looking at them. Move 'em out pronto."

He went back inside. Sam stared in disbelief.

"I'll work on him some more," Matt said quickly.

He entered the jail, relieved to find that the door had not been locked against him.

Osgood stood at a filing cabinet in the corner, rummaging through an open drawer. He took out a brown bottle and glass and sat down behind the desk. He set bottle and glass down on the desktop, looking up at Matt Bodine with no love.

"You again? We're done, son," Osgood said.

The glass was dirty, giving him no pause. Osgood uncorked the bottle, filling the glass to the brim with amber liquid. The fumes stung the inside of Matt's nose and made his eyes burn, and he was standing on the opposite side of the desk. He leaned back. It helped a little, not much.

Osgood did not offer to share. That was fine with Matt. Osgood drank half the contents of the glass, draining it as if it were colored water. He shuddered once. He closed his eyes, orbs bulging like walnuts against quivering eyelids.

Matt looked around. The office took up the front of the building. The cells were in back—iron cages with a grid framework. No partition separated office and cells. Matt could see into them.

In the nearest cell, a man lay on his back on a wooden pallet with a razor-thin mattress. He was dark-haired, swarthy, about thirty years old. Mexican, most likely, Matt guessed.

The prisoner lay with one leg on the bunk, bent at the knee. The other stretched off the side of the bunk, foot on the floor. His head was pillowed on an arm folded under it. He scrutinized Matt, dark eyes alive with curiosity in a masklike face.

This must be Gila Chacon, Matt realized with a start, the condemned man for whom the gallows waited.

Osgood stirred, opening his eyes. A red flush overspread his bony, balding head from scalp to chin, giving an illusory glow of good health. "You're still here? If you won't go away, I'll keep on drinking. Then it won't matter if you're here or not."

"Your problem's not going to go away so easily," Matt began.

"Your problem, not mine," Osgood said. He drank again from the glass.

"Our problem—I'm making it your problem, too."

Osgood choked, coughing. His face was lobster red. When he coughed it turned a dark beet-red. A moment passed before the coughing fit subsided.

"Don't get tough with me, sonny. I'm an officer of the law. I'll throw you in jail," Osgood warned.

"Not tough, just realistic. My pard and I don't intend to sit around playing nursemaid to a string of dead men until the sheriff gets back to town," Matt said.

"Should've thought of that before you killed them," Osgood said, snickering.

"You trying to be funny?"

Something in Matt's no-nonsense demeanor thrust through Osgood's alcoholic haze, chilling him to the bone.

Osgood held up a hand palm out, a placatory gesture. "I didn't mean nothing by it. I was just saying it's your misfortune and none of my own, as the song goes. Even if I wanted to help you, I can't. It's sheriff's business. He don't like it when the marshal steps on his toes."

"He won't like it if we dump the bodies on his doorstep and walk away from it,"

Matt said.

"You wouldn't dare!"

"No? What are you going to do, arrest me? That won't get the bodies moved."

Osgood got to thinking. "Waaaal," he drawled, "you could run them over to the coroner. Dead folks rightfully come under his jurisdiction. Or you could try the undertaker. He buries the bodies for town and county both. He might take them off your hands if he can figure how to get somebody else to pay the weight.

"Yes, I'd say the undertaker's your best bet. What the hell? It's in his line of business after all."

"I knew you'd come up with something if you tried. If it works, I'll bring you a bottle of something better than that rotgut you're drinking," Matt said.

"Always glad to help out. That's what I'm here for. Sorry I can't do more to help you boys out, but I've got to stay here and guard the prisoner. He's got a date with the hangman come Saturday and I've got to mother-hen him till Marshal White comes back."

"Should be a big show," Matt said dryly.

"Oh, they'll be coming from miles around to see the bad man swing," Osgood enthused.

Matt went out. A fair-sized crowd had gathered to gawk at the corpse pack train. On the sidewalks along both sides of the street, people paused to stop and stare. Others came out of stores and shops for a look-see. There were off-shift miners, burly, powerfully built men in shapeless hats, overalls, and work boots; along with cowboys and ranch hands, tinhorns and town dwellers, fancy ladies and freckle-faced kids.

All kept their distance from the dead.

From random street chatter he overheard, Matt got the idea that the New Mexico ruffians were fairly well detested, with Justin Vollin and his bunch coming in for more than their share of abuse.

Of course, that last might have been because Vollin's gang was unable to revenge insult with injury.

"What next, Matt?" Sam asked.

"The undertaker awaits."

FIVE

Fritz Guthrie made his living on the in-betweens. His house stood off by itself on a lot between the business district of Tombstone and the residential area. His trade put him in intimate contact with the living and the dead. Fritz lived and worked in a two-story, wooden frame house. The house was isolated, alone.

Fritz Guthrie was the undertaker of Tombstone—and business was good.

Like other towns on the boom, Tombstone had a thriving real estate market, with choice lots in town at high prices being traded and sold many times over by speculators, but nobody was in any hurry to make their home or business in close proximity to the undertaker.

The house was divided into two sections. The ground floor was devoted to business, while the living quarters were upstairs. A long wooden shed in the backyard served as workshop and storage area.

Set off from it to one side was a kind of carriage

house/barn where horses were stabled and a long black hearse was stored, held in reserve for higher-priced funerals.

Sam Two Wolves and Matt Bodine had received a ready welcome from the undertaker, who proved most receptive to their proposition of deriving some mutual benefit from the final disposition of the late Justin Vollin and friends.

The bodies had been unloaded from the horses and taken into the long shed that served as a work-shop and storage area. Matt, Sam, Fritz, and Jason Cobb, the undertaker's assistant, all pitched in to carry the bodies into the shed.

The horses were tied to a rope line strung be-tween two trees behind the barn, where they grazed on weeds and tall grass growing wild at the edge of the property.

The shed's long walls were lined with wooden worktables. The tables had two levels, allowing one body to be laid out on top and another on the lower level. Four bodies were placed on the tables, and the fifth was placed on a wheeled cart not unlike a hospital gurney.

Fritz Guthrie in no way resembled the popular conception of what an undetaker should look like. He was not gaunt, pale, thin, skeletal, or funereal. He had an air of distinction. He looked like a bank president or a politician of the statesman variety (a breed then, as now, in sadly short supply).

He was tall, heavyset, with a handsome head of glossy silver hair worn brushed back from the temples, and a neatly clipped mustache. He wore a white shirt, maroon tie and vest, and gray pants. Before joining in the heavy lifting, he had removed a charcoal-gray coat and rolled his shirtsleeves up to the elbows. His hands were covered in thin, wrist-length work gloves.

His assistant, Jason Cobb, was black bearded, thick set, and dressed in brown. He didn't say much, speaking only when he was spoken to.

Fritz eyed the bodies with keen professional interest. He stood beside the remains of Justin Vollin, bending over him to examine the head wound.

"Interesting angle of entry for the bullet—unique. Shot virtually through the top of the head. That's something you don't see every day," Fritz Guthrie said.

"I was up on a rock ledge shooting down at him," Sam said.

"Umm. Must have been a difficult shot."

Sam smiled, shrugging. "Harder on him than on me."

Fritz moved on, crossing to the other side of the shed, where Dick Buttolph lay stretched out on a worktable. "That's a big one! Looks like he would take a lot of killing . . . and he did. Three shots in the chest . . . two in the heart, either one would have proved fatal. The third is just an inch or two off to the side. All three shots are placed in a tight pattern; you could fit all three in the width of a man's palm," Fritz said.

He left off looking, straightened up, and turned to Matt. "Your friend was the rifleman, so you must have been wielding the pistol. Remarkable shooting, young man."

Matt wasn't paying attention. He was staring at the tools laid out on an instrument tray: hacksaws; circular saws; keen-edged, wide-bladed knives that looked like butcher's knives; long, thin, whippy blades that looked like filleting knives; slim, sharp-pointed, shiny probing tools; and even what looked like a meat cleaver.

Sam elbowed Matt in the ribs. Matt came out of his reverie, and realized that Fritz had been speaking to him. "Sorry, my mind was elsewhere," Matt said.

"I said, that was remarkable shooting, such a close placement of all three rounds in the target area," Fritz said.

"Oh . . . thanks."

"Think nothing of it. Considering the circumstances of being involved in a desperate gun battle, you certainly exhibited an admirable degree of coolness and self-possession, to get that kind of accuracy with a handgun."

"Nice of you to say so." Matt brightened. Compliments were always welcome, even from an undertaker.

"A simple statement of fact," Fritz said.

"Don't get too swelled up, Matt—you missed the heart with one shot," Sam said slyly.

"I did? Let me take a look at that," Matt said. He went to stand beside Dick Buttolph and examined the wounds, frowning at the single entry wound standing several inches apart from the twin bulletholes placed side by side in the heart area. "Huh. Well, I'll be darned," he said, mouth turning down at the corners.

"I wouldn't let it bother you; it's outstanding shooting," Fritz said.

"I can do better," Matt said, silently vowing to spend more time on target practice in the future to hone his skills to an even higher degree of accuracy. It made a difference somehow, knowing that there was an appreciative audience for his work.

Fritz Guthrie was now examining Hake Craney.

"You could have done better with that one, too, Matt," Sam said. "You didn't kill him on the first try. It took two times for you to kill him dead." He was engaging in some good-natured ribbing and that's the spirit in which Matt took it.

"Things were kind of hectic for a moment there. I neglected to dot my i's and cross my t's," Matt said.

Fritz peered at the bullethole in Hake Craney's skull, the one that had finished him off. "Dead center in the forehead. The only other time I've seen a shot like that, it was done by John Ringo— and the man he shot wasn't shooting back at the time."

"He didn't even have a gun in his hand, if that's the hombre Ringo killed for refusing to take a drink with him," Matt said.

All Tombstone knew that story. Ringo had been drunk and on the prod, like usual, only more so, and the unfortunate fellow to whom he offered a shot of whiskey had preferred to stick to his glass of beer. In the West it was considered an insult to refuse a man's offer of a drink, and the other man had been wearing a gun, so the coroner's inquest found nothing on Ringo and let him go free.

Fritz pulled off his gloves, putting them on the instrument tray.

"Seems like you can tell the difference between a hole made by a gun and one made by a rifle," Sam said.

"Oh, yes. When you've been in the business as long as I have, you can tell these things at a glance," Fritz said.

"You must get a lot of practice, working in Tombstone," Matt said.

"I see death from gunshot wounds pretty much on a daily basis, including Sundays," Fritz said. "Also stabbings, beatings, bludgeonings, axe murders, you name it. Not to mention deaths from chronic illness, acute alcoholism, exposure to the desert sun, blood poisoning, the last stages of syphilis, mining accidents, tramplings by horse or cattle, run over by coach or wagon, fire, drowning. The only thing I rarely or ever see is death by old age.

"There's a hundred ways to kill in the West—and a thousand ways to die."

The undertaker picked up his jacket from the hook on which he'd hung it, draping it across a forearm. "We're done here. Look after things, Jason. You know what to do."

"Yes, sir," the assistant said.

Matt, Sam, and Fritz went out of the shed. "It's about time for my afternoon pick-me-up," Fritz said. "Join me in a drink?"

"Don't mind if I do," Sam said.

"And how!" Matt seconded.

They crossed the yard toward the back of the house. "Damned decent of you to take those fellows off our hands," Matt said.

"Think nothing of it," Fritz said expansively. "They were killed in the county and it's the county's responsibility to see that they're interred properly. Can't have a lot of cadavers lying about littering up the landscape. It's not hygienic.

"I doubt any friends or relatives will claim the bodies or sponsor a full-dress funeral, so they'll all probably wind up on Boot Hill. Still, Jason will pick up a few dollars for planting them in their graves, so it's not a total loss. Lord knows the county can afford it, with all the taxes they've been assessing the citizenry lately."

"Maybe the outfit at Waco's will pay for the funerals," Matt said.

"Eh? How's that again?" Fritz asked.

Matt quickly explained about the Vollin gang being exiles from Lincoln County. "The New Mexico crowd hangs out at Waco Brindle's saloon. That's a dive over to the south side of town."

"I know of it. More than a few of their regulars come my way," Fritz said dryly.

"Vollin's gang is supposed to be pards of Waco. Maybe he'll spring for a proper sendoff."

"Soliciting for trade is a bit out of my line, I'm afraid. Besides, I have a feeling that Mr. Brindle and company may not be the best of credit risks," Fritz said. He looked blandly at Matt and Sam, though there was a twinkle in his eye. "In fact, I wouldn't be at all surprised if those fellows aren't with us for too much longer here in Tombstone, if you catch my meaning. And I'm sure you do."

"You may be on to something there," Sam said.

"It's not a sure thing, but that's the way to bet it," Matt agreed.

They entered the house through the back door, into a kitchen. It was small, clean, and neat. Fritz said, "I've got company, so if you'll excuse me for a minute while I go upstairs. . . ."

"We don't want to put you to any trouble," Matt said.

"No trouble at all. I'll be right back."

Fritz climbed a back staircase, disappearing in the upstairs area. Sam and Matt could hear him speaking to another party, but they couldn't make out the words. Fritz reappeared at the head of the stairs. "Come on up, gentlemen."

Matt and Sam went upstairs. The surroundings were bright, comfortable, cheery. At the end of the hallway a right-hand door opened into a well-furnished room. There was a writing desk, several handsome brown-leather-cushioned armchairs, and a wall lined with bookshelves. A Persian or Turkish carpet with intricately wrought dark blue and red designs covered the floor.

"My study. Make yourself comfortable," Fritz invited.

Sam and Matt sat down. Their host crossed to a sideboard, reaching for a crystal decanter. "Brandy?"

Brandy was fine with Sam and Matt. Fritz filled

three glasses, raising his in a kind of toast. "Here's to good health, and fine living."

"And dying of old age," Matt said.

They drank up, draining their glasses. Sam smacked his lips. A pleasant warmth bloomed in the pit of his stomach, racing through his veins. "This is good brandy," he said.

"Have another," Fritz offered. His guests were quick to take him up on it.

"Very good brandy," Sam said, after his second.

"Glad you like it," Fritz said, smiling, genial. The brandy had put some red color in his cheeks. He was not shy about passing the decanter around to his visitors, and was no slouch in sampling its wares himself. The general mood grew ever more genial.

Matt peered over the top of his brandy glass. "If you don't mind me saying so, Mr. Guthrie—"

"Call me Fritz."

"Sure, Fritz. I just want to say, you do pretty well for yourself, and just as good for your guests."

"Thank you."

"Fine brandy, Fritz, damned fine," Sam said.

"Help yourself to some more."

"Much obliged."

They all had another round.

"I like to surround myself with the good things of life," Fritz said. "You may have heard the biblical quote, 'In the midst of life, we are in death.' For myself, I believe, in the midst of death, I am in life. Why not enjoy that life to the fullest?"

They had another drink on that one. Presently, there came a knock on the door. "Come in," Fritz said.

The door opened. Standing in the doorway was a beautiful woman, about twenty-five. Champagne-colored hair was pinned up in great masses at the top of her head. She had deep blue eyes, a pert nose, and a luscious, full-lipped red mouth. Her physique was more than a little sensational. She wore a blue satin dress and white gloves. She stepped into the room.

Being the gentlemen that they were, Matt and Sam rose to their feet. Sam removed his hat; seeing him, Matt did the same.

"Come in, Yvonne," Fritz said, all smiles. "Yvonne, may I introduce Mr. Matt Bodine and Mr. Sam Two Wolves? Gentlemen, this is my friend Miss Yvonne Duval."

"Pleased to meet you, ma'am!" Matt said enthusiastically.

"Delighted!" said Sam.

"The pleasure is all mine," Yvonne cooed.

She held out a hand. Matt shook it, holding it as lightly in his hand as if it had been an eggshell. She pressed his hand warmly, her smile widening. When it was Sam's turn, he took her hand and raised it to his lips, kissing it.

"Enchanté, mademoiselle," Sam said.

Yvonne's eyes sparkled. "You are gallant, monsieur." She turned to Fritz. "Sorry to dsturb you when you have company, Fritz, but I really must go. I have a dinner appointment I must keep."

"Quite all right, my dear. I'll have Jason get the buckboard ready."

Matt spoke up. "We've taken up enough of your

time, Fritz, your time and your hospitality. So we'll be on our way."

"Thanks for everything," said Sam.

They excused themselves, again thanked their host, said their good-byes, and exited. They went out the back door into the yard, and crossed to the horses. Sam untied the rope from the trees, lining up the string of horses.

Matt finished tightening up his horse's saddle girth. He looked up at the house, at a curtained window on the second floor. "Nice fellow," he said.

"Nice lady," Sam said. They busied themselves securing the extra horses to a lead rope. "That Yvonne is sure something," Sam ventured.

"I'll say," Matt agreed. "I reckon after handling dead folks all the time, Fritz likes to get his hands on a nice warm body once in a while."

"I know the feeling. I wouldn't mind getting my hands on that warm body myself!"

"Where'd you learn that hand-kissing stuff, you son of a gun?"

"Benefits of a college education."

"I knew it had to be good for something," Matt said. "You know, I've seen that gal around before— she's not the type you forget—but I just can't remember when."

Sam laughed. "Sure you have. She works at French Marie's."

French Marie was a brothel keeper who ran one of the best, high-class houses in Tombstone. Her proud boast was that every girl in her employ came from France. In practice, that meant that all the ladies in her stable could fake a French accent that would more or less pass muster this side of St. Louis.

Matt smacked his palm against his forehead. "I knew I'd seen her before!"

"Sure, she was down in the parlor with the rest of the girls the last time we were there," Sam said.

"Say . . . I didn't go upstairs with her that night, did I?"

"No, you were with Louise."

"Louise . . . ?"

"The little brunette with the big—"

"Oh, yeah, now I remember. Louise. Ooh-lah-lah!" Remembering, Matt got a silly smile on his face. "If I'd been with Yvonne, I'd remember. I never get that drunk!"

"Not usually," Sam said. "Come to think of it, I've got a pretty nice glow on now. That sure was good brandy."

"Let's get these horses over to the corral and see what kind of a price they'll fetch," said Matt, all business now.

"Don't get your hopes up. Whatever it is, it won't be enough for a night at French Marie's," Sam said sadly.

After taking on a load of high-line brandy—an overload, even—Matt and Sam were feeling no pain. Maybe the alcohol brought their belliger-ence to the fore, or maybe it was an ornery streak asserting itself but, whatever the reason, they were minded to beard the foes in their own den.

Earlier, on the way to the undertaker's, they had ridden past Waco Brindle's saloon where the New Mexico crowd roosted. None of the regulars were out front and the duo rode by wihout incident.

Now, on their way to the corral to dicker over the price of horseflesh, they detoured so they would once more pass by Waco's.

The lead rope to the string of five horses was tied to Sam's saddle. Matt rode beside him. They rode south, down the middle of the street. Anybody that came along could go around them or press the point, they didn't much care which. Nobody came along.

They entered a seedy, rundown area on the outskirts of town whose shacks, cribs, and dives were outnumbered by vacant, weed-grown lots.

Ahead, on the left-hand side, stood a ramshackle, one-story, wooden frame building. Its warped boards were unpainted. The roof pole sagged in the middle, the ends of the roof higher than its midpoint. No sign proclaimed that this was "Waco's," the bucket-of-blood saloon and robber's roost run by Waco Brindle. A line of horses, most of them stolen no doubt, was tied to a hitching post in front.

Matt and Sam came on. "Some folks would say we were looking for trouble," Matt said.

"Well, aren't we?" Sam asked.

"Not me. I just want to know where we stand with this New Mexico outfit. I killed Justin Vollin—"

"I killed him," Sam corrected him.

"We killed Vollin and his gang and if his pards don't like it, it's just too damned bad. We weren't looking for trouble—they came to us. They came on our land without a by-your-leave and tried to jump our claim."

"I'm not arguing."

"I won't be buffaloed by any back-shooting Lincoln County trash. If they want a fight, they can have it and I don't mean maybe."

"Uh-huh. Better to come at them now than to let them call the tune."

"Damned right, Sam."

Waco's was noisy, its thin walls seeming to shake from the drunken clamor within. Sam took his gun out of the holster and tucked it into the top of his pants on the left side, worn butt out. He found a cross-belly draw quicker than reaching for a holstered gun on his hip, when he was on horseback.

On foot or in the saddle, Matt liked having two guns on his hips, his usual way.

Rawhide thongs were looped over the top of the hammers to secure the guns in their holsters. Matt thumbed them free, clearing them, readying the guns for fast action.

Waco's showed no porch, no boardwalk sidewalk. The structure was plunked down in the middle of the dirt. A couple of idlers sat on the ground in front of the saloon, leaning against the wall, smoking and chatting. One whittled away on a stick with a pocket knife. They glanced up to see who was coming.

Matt and Sam walked their horses at a slow,

steady, deliberate pace. The idlers stood up. One ran inside the saloon.

After a pause, a half-dozen or more tough-looking hardcases came shouldering out the door, ranging themselves in front of the building. They were gunmen, or at least they fancied themselves as such. The weapons were worn low on their hips, some tied down. They showed a lot of hard eyes, grim faces, and tight-set mouths.

A drunk stood in the doorway, bracing himself against the frame to keep from falling down.

Matt and Sam drew abreast of the ranked gunmen. Sam was closer to them. Matt reined in first, letting Sam get a length ahead before halting, so neither of them would be in the other's way and they'd both have a clear field of fire.

"You know who we are, and we know who you are," Sam said. "Any complaints?"

The drunk in the doorway was bulled aside as Waco Brindle came through. The drunk staggered and fell. Waco took a few steps forward.

His body was the size and shape of a hogshead barrel with arms and legs stuck on it. His head sat on his shoulders seemingly without the interposition of a neck. His scalp was shaved close to blue-black stubble. A big black mustache had upturned tips, like the handlebars of a bicycle. His small round eyes were red, bloodshot.

One of the gunmen spat on the ground. Sam fixed him with a cold, hard eye. The other looked away first.

"Whadda' ya want?" Waco growled.

"Vollin's over to the undertaker's, along with his pards," Matt said.

"So what?"

"Just thought you'd like to know, in case you feel like financing the funeral."

"Why should I? They ain't nothing to me," Waco said. "Neither are you, the both of you."

"They tried to jump our claim. They left across their horses," Matt said. "These are their horses. We're keeping them."

"Any objections?" Sam demanded loudly.

The gunman who'd spat squared his shoulders, hand straying toward his gun butt.

"I wish you'd try it," Sam said, more softly now, almost caressingly. "I surely wish you would."

The other seemed game, and the confrontation hung suspended in the balance for a timeless time, ready to tip either way—

"Back off," Waco said out of the corner of his mouth. His man seemed unsure whether to reach or stand down.

"Back off, I said!"

The gunman deflated, shoulders sagging. His hand sank slowly to his side.

"This ain't the time or the place," Waco said.

"You let us know when it is the time and the place," Matt said.

"You said your say. All right. I'm a busy man. I got me a business to run. I ain't making any money standing out here in the hot sun listening to you jawing," Waco said. "Anything else, Bodine?"

"Just this—anybody tries to jump us winds up facedown across their horse. We'll keep the horse, too."

"Those are some nice horses tied up at the hitching post," Sam said. "Bet you couldn't find a title or bill of sale for a one of them."

"No bet, Sam."

"I heard enough. I'm going inside," Waco said. "Come on, men, the house's buying." He turned and went inside, not looking back. The drunk who'd been shoved out of the doorway was right on his heels. The rest of the group silently filed into the saloon.

"What I thought," Matt said, laughing softly. He nudged his horse's flanks with his heels, starting forward. Sam did the same and they rode on.

They were pitched to the highest levels of alertness for any untoward sound: the click of a hammer being thumbed back, a window opening, a stealthy footstep. None came. They rode on without incident. When they were out of pistol range, Sam whistled soundlessly and said, "Whew!"

"Hell, if they were any kind of gunhawks, they'd never have got run out of Lincoln County," Matt said.

"They're not done yet."

"Neither are we."

Six

Assistant Deputy Marshal Osgood vented a long, heartfelt groan. "You again!"

"Glad to see you, too," Matt Bodine said brightly.

"Who's glad?"

"You, when you see what I've brought."

Osgood sat behind the desk in the marshal's office. Matt crossed to him. Osgood's eyes were half shut, dull, gummy with sleep. Matt guessed he'd been napping.

Osgood eyed the package held in Matt's left arm. His slitted eyes brightened. "What you got in the bag?"

"Token of appreciation." Matt put the brown paper bag down on the desk, reached inside and pulled out a bottle of whiskey, setting it down in front of Osgood.

Osgood's gaze fastened on the bottle. He licked his lips. "Who's that for?"

"You."

Osgood's hand shot out for it, abruptly stopping

short several inches from the bottle. That must have been when the second thoughts kicked in. "What do you want?"

"What makes you think I want anything?" Matt asked.

"Quit pulling my leg. Nobody does something for nothing. You must want something. What?"

Matt tried to look impressed. "Good thinking. With a brain like that, you'll make marshal in no time."

"I'm happy where I am, thank you very much," Osgood retorted.

"One good turn deserves another. You gave me a good steer when you put me on to the undertaker. Fritz Guthrie took the bodies off my hands, and he'll bury them for the county. I said I'd bring you a bottle of something if things worked out. I'm a man of my word."

"Well, good!" Osgood remained sceptical, suspicious. His hands resting on the desktop near the bottle trembled slightly. "That's it? Nothing else?"

"What else could there be?" Matt asked innocently.

"You ain't killed nobody since I last saw you?"

"Nope."

"That's a relief. No special favors you want?"

"Not a one. Go on, drink up."

"On the understanding that this is purely a gesture of goodwill and don't oblige me nohow no way to nothing, not-a-thing, no ifs, ands, or buts about, no fine print—I'll take it."

Osgood grabbed the bottle with both hands, like he was afraid it might get away from him. He wrenched the cork free. He raised the bottle to his mouth, thought better of it, and put the bottle down. He opened a drawer in the desk—the top drawer—and took out a glass tumbler. It was the same glass he'd used earlier. Matt recognized the smudges and stains.

Osgood filled the glass almost to the brim. Gripping it with both hands, he brought it to his mouth and drank deeply. When he set it down, less than a mouthful of whiskey remained in the glass.

He sat upright in his chair, perfectly still, not even blinking. A tinge of color brightened his sallow complexion. After a pause, he opened his mouth and said, "Ahhh."

"You're welcome," Matt prompted.

Osgood stared uncomprehendingly at him for a few beats before he got it. "Thanks," he said grudgingly.

"Don't mention it," Matt said, feeling pretty sure that Osgood wouldn't.

Osgood poured another one. Matt got a wooden chair out of the corner, set it down in front of the desk, and sat down.

"What're you doing?"

"I'm a sociable man, Deputy. I hate to see a man drink alone. Believe I'll join you."

"That's what I was afraid of." Osgood brightened. "Only got but the one glass."

"That's okay, I'll drink out of the bottle," Matt said.

"You would." Osgood started in on his second glassful. "Not bad, though. Pretty good stuff."

It was plain red whiskey, the cheapest stuff that was halfway drinkable that Matt could find. He'd picked up a couple of bottles on the way over.

Sam was at the corral horse-trading with the owner over the lot of five horses. He was a better horse trader than Matt. Matt was a horseman born and bred, but Sam really knew his horseflesh. It was like that for them with guns, too, only the other way around. Sam was a good gunman, a crack shot, but Matt was a wizard with the plowshares.

Besides, Matt didn't have the patience for bargaining with horse dealers. When the dickering went on too long, Matt either got irked or disgusted, and wound up taking the dealer's price or walking away. Not Sam. He took a positive pleasure in outwaiting the other party, wearing them down until they caved.

Matt reached for the bottle. Osgood flinched, but managed to control himself. Matt took a swallow. The stuff jolted him. Compared to Fritz Guthrie's brandy, this tasted like rusty, filthy drainpipe water laced with strychnine.

A expression of canny shrewdness came over Osgood's face. "Say . . . ain't that another bottle I see peeping out of that bag?"

"No hiding anything from you, is there, Deputy? That must come from being a trained lawman."

"I'm getting along."

"How's the manhunt going? Any leads on the Wells Fargo robbers?"

"Nary a word," Osgood said. "The Wells Fargo agent posted a five-thousand-dollar reward for whoever finds the silver bullion, though."

Matt laughed. "Only five thousand for a twenty-seven-thousand-dollar haul? Hell, I'll give six thousand!"

"You ain't got six thousand dollars," Osgood said with grim relish.

"Too true." Matt felt sorry for himself. No $6,000 for him. He took a swallow of red-eye. He could have gotten the same effect by running his head into the wall, he decided, and it would have been easier on his stomach, too.

Osgood drank from the glass, Matt from the bottle, the level of whiskey steadily declining. The whiskey didn't taste so bad to Matt. It must be getting to him.

"Those Vollin jaspers were a pretty bad bunch," Matt began, too casually.

Osgood froze, holding the glass halfway to his mouth. His head was bowed, chin on chest. He looked up at Matt out of the tops of his eyes. "Uh-oh! I seed it coming! I knew you wanted something."

"It won't cost you a red cent," Matt said.

"Good, I can't afford a red cent, not on what the town's paying me." Osgood took a drink. "Here it comes."

"Vollin must have been wanted for something. Him and his pards."

Osgood shook his head, sure, certain. "Not in Tombstone. Not in the county or the territory."

"What about New Mexico? They didn't spend all their time in Lincoln County going to prayer meetings and singing songs in the choir," Matt pressed.

"I wouldn't know."

"Don't you check the Wanted circulars?"

"Sure—when I can. You know how many circulars we got piled up from all over the West? Back East, too? Stacks of 'em, stacks and stacks."

"Maybe you could take a look at them, see if our boys were posted somewhere with a bounty on their heads," Matt suggested.

Osgood looked indignant. "What do you think I am, anyway?!"

Matt had definite opinions on that score, but maintained a diplomatic silence.

"I'm only one man here. With everybody else out on posse, I got the whole town to keep the peace in," Osgood said. "They're working me to death!"

"You haven't moved out of the jailhouse all day," Matt pointed out.

"'Course not. Folks got to know where to find me if trouble breaks." Osgood leaned back with a self-satisfied smile, as if he had just won a point.

"And don't forget the prisoner—a dangerous killer and condemned man who'd try anything to slip the noose. Why, his compadres could be laying up somewhere in town right now, waiting for a chance to make their move. I got to stay alert. They ain't gonna catch Hubert Osgood with his head buried in a pile of paperwork."

"Okay, okay," Matt said, sighing.

"Let's get down to brass tacks. Them stacks of paper is recent circulars from all over," Osgood said, indicating a square-topped wooden table against the wall. It was covered with packing crates stuffed with papers and documents. More crates, similarly stuffed, lay on the floor under the table. "You want to look 'em over, you can."

"That's something, anyway." Matt got up, and went to the table. He reached for the nearest crate and pulled out a double handful of papers, loosing a cloud of dust. He blew the dust off the papers he was holding and began thumbing through them.

He quickly discovered that there was no rhyme or reason to the arrangement of the papers, no pattern. They were Wanted dodgers and circulars from all over the West, from St. Louis to Sacramento, from Sioux Falls to San Antonio. Some had reproductions of photographs of the wanted; most were drawings. Together, they made up a rogue's gallery, as Matt noted while leafing through them:

"Wanted for murder, bank robbery, rustling, rape, horse theft, counterfeiting—and those are just the charges against one man!"

He shuffled more papers. "White slavery— train robbery—gunrunning—selling whiskey to Indians—smuggling . . ."

The papers were dusty, grimy, smudged, dog-eared. Some were dated from last month, others from last year. The dust tickled Matt's nose. He fought to keep from sneezing. A fast-growing pile of discards mounted up.

Matt pulled one circular, holding it up. "You can throw this one away. He's dead."

"Says who?" Osgood demanded.

"Me. I shot him myself," Matt said. "It'll go faster if you help."

"I might, after I crack open that second bottle."

"There's still some left in the first."

"It's getting mighty low. Makes me kind of anxious. Hard to concentrate."

"Help yourself."

Osgood eagerly pulled the bottle from the bag and opened it. Matt picked up a double armful of papers, carrying them to the desk, setting them down. Gray dust puffed up from the pile into his face, causing him to sneeze.

"God bless!"

The voice came from one of the cells in back, the one adjacent to that of the bandit Gila Chacon.

"Quiet! Don't start cutting up now," Osgood said, over his shoulder. "Don't make me come back there."

A figure, big and bearlike, rose from a cot and shambled to the front of his cell. He gripped the bars with both hands, pressing his face between them. "Is that my old pal Matt Bodine?" he asked.

Matt craned his head, trying to see the speaker. "Who's that?"

"Polk Muldoon," Osgood said sourly.

"It's me, sure 'nuff," the prisoner said.

Matt went into the cell area. It smelled bad. He wrinkled his nose, glad for the dust which partly blocked it up.

The prisoner was large sized, thick bodied, big bellied. He was fifty years old.

A pear-shaped head sat on a pear-shaped body. He was hard though—even his fat was hard fat, with plenty of muscle beneath. His weathered face and hands were seamed and cracked like old saddle leather. He had thinning wispy hair, an iron-gray beard, and a thick-featured, good-natured face.

He looked like an aging but still vigorous working cowhand, which indeed he was—among other things. The other things were what put him behind bars, Matt thought.

"Polk Muldoon! What're you in for?"

"Well, Matthew, I ain't rightly sure. I got drunk last Saturday night and I don't remember too much after that."

Osgood stood at the head of the aisle, glass in hand, facing the cells. His other hand held the bottle at his side, holding it by the neck. "I'll tell you what he did. He got blind, stinking drunk for starters. He tore up Dyker's bar, wrecked the place. That was after he beat a couple of miners senseless. Big, tough, pick-and-shovel men."

"They was prodding me, I do recall," Polk said.

"Is that all he did?" Matt asked.

"That was just the warm-up," Osgood said. "After that, Mr. Muldoon here shot up a couple of stores on Fifth Street, shooting out the front windows. They was closed for the night, so no one got hurt. Blind, stinking drunk though he was, he managed to find his way to Miss Laverne's sporting house. When the doorman wouldn't open up, Muldoon tore the door off its hinges and bulled his way in. A tinhorn in the parlor room threw down on him but Muldoon shot first."

"Kill him?" Matt asked.

"Shot him in the arm."

"Hell, I thought they was three fellows reaching on me," Polk said.

"I believe that's how you seed 'em," Osgood said. "You was trying to set the place on fire when Miss Laverne conked you on the head with a solid brass spittoon, and knocked you out."

"I still got me an almighty big lump, too," Polk said, rubbing the top of his head.

"You're lucky she didn't bust your skull wide open and spill out what little brains you got, she was so mad. You done tore up her prize player piano."

"That doesn't sound too bad," Matt said. "He didn't kill anybody."

"Not for lack of trying!" Osgood declared.

"What're you keeping him locked up for?"

"He's got to pay damages, which are gonna be considerable. And he ain't got no money. Which means he's gonna have to do a stint working for the city on a chain gang. Be working well into next year afore he's paid his debt."

"Anything you can do to help me out, Matt?" Polk asked meekly. "I'd surely appreciate it."

"You gonna pay his fine?" Osgood said, sneering.

"How much?" Matt asked.

"Five hundred dollars."

"That's awful hard," Polk said in a small voice.

"Sam and I are low on funds right now, Polk,

awful low. Once our claim starts paying off, I'll go your fine but, to be honest, that seems like a long way off right now."

"That's all right, Matt, don't trouble yourself."

"That could change anytime if we sell the claim. The ore assays high, the vein looks rich, but we don't have the funds to develop it properly by ourselves yet. . . ."

"Wouldn't do you no good if you had the dollars," Osgood said. "Marshal Fred's got a big mad on Muldoon and ain't letting him get off the hook. He's bound and determined to see he pays the full penalty of the law.

"Ya danged fool! Why'd you have to go and pick Miss Laverne's place to tear up? Don't you know she's the marshal's special lady?"

"I was drunk. I wasn't thinking. . . ."

"You'll have plenty of time to think it over now. At least six months, I'd say."

"Sounds like you had yourself a big night, Polk."

"I reckon. Wish I could remember more of it. It's a hard life full of troubles, Matt."

"Maybe you'd like to trade places, amigo?" The voice came from the adjacent cell, Gila Chacon speaking.

"No, thanks!" Polk said swiftly.

Osgood came down the aisle swaying. "You'll be getting out of jail come Saturday, Mex. All the way to the gallows. After that, your troubles'll be over."

Gila Chacon was silent, smiling.

"What'd he do?" Matt asked.

"Shot three men dead. They was Mexes, same as

him, but that don't matter. We still got laws in this town against killing folks, even Mexes," Osgood said.

"They came to kill me," Gila said to Matt. "You have an honest face, hombre. Perhaps this will be of interest to you. I have an enemy back home where I come from."

"Where's that?" Matt asked.

"Pago." Gila pronounced it "pah-go." "Pago, in the state of Sonora."

"I've heard of it." Not good things either, Matt thought.

"My enemy is a rich and powerful man. He hates me and would do anything to kill me—anything but face me himself. He sent *pistoleros*, paid assassins, to do the job. They were slow and their aim was bad. I was fast and my aim was true."

"He told that story to the jury and they wasn't buying," Osgood said.

"Sounds like self-defense," Matt said judiciously.

"He was riding a stolen horse when he was caught. We hang horse thieves here in Tombstone."

"Partic'arly when the horse belongs to Judge Randall," Polk said.

"It was a handsome horse," Gila said, smiling sadly.

"You'll swing for it," Osgood said.

The street door opened. Sam Two Wolves came in. "Matt Bodine around?"

"Back here, Sam," Matt called.

Sam crossed the office and went down the aisle between the cells. He seemed excited, pulsing with barely contained energy. "Hey, Matt, I've been looking for you—"

He broke off when he recognized the occupant of the cell. "Polk! What're you doing here?"

"It's a long story, Samuel."

"I'll tell you later," Matt told Sam.

"Come on, let's take a walk," Sam said.

"I just started looking through the Wanted notices for the Vollin gang," Matt said. "It's a big job. I can use your help with it—"

"It can wait till later. Something's come up. It's important, Matt—business."

"If you say so." Matt turned to Osgood. "I've got to go now."

Osgood frowned, pressing his lips together in a tight line. "You ain't taking the bottle with you?"

"You keep it," Matt said.

The frown smoothed out. "That's all right, then. You just go about your business."

"I'll be back later," Matt said.

"Bring another bottle when you come," Osgood said.

"Say, how 'bout a taste of that there red-eye?" Polk asked.

"Be serious," Osgood said.

"I could use some myself, señor," Gila said.

Osgood snorted.

"Surely you would not deny the simple request of a condemned man?"

"No? Try me."

"Give them a drink, Deputy, both of them," Matt

said. "Give them a drink, and when I come back, I'll bring two bottles."

"How do I know you're good for it?"

"Hell, I already came across with the whiz when I didn't have to. I'll be back to visit my friend Polk anyhow. You can trust me."

"I reckon one little drink wouldn't hurt 'em," Osgood said grudgingly—it was like pulling teeth from him.

"If they don't get it you can say good-bye to the next two bottles."

"Dang it, I said I'd come across, didn't I?"

"Thanks, Deputy, I knew I could count on you. I'll be along directly," Matt said. "See you later, Polk. Maybe we can do something to make your stay here a mite easier."

"You know where to find me," Polk said cheerfully.

"Sit tight, Polk."

"What else can I do, Sam?"

Matt and Sam went out.

"You're in an all-fired hurry, Sam. What's the big rush?"

"We've got an appointment with greatness."

SEVEN

Night had come to Tombstone. Sam Two Wolves and Matt Bodine stood outside the Hotel Erle, the best hotel in town, and there were some fine hotels in town.

Speculators had found it profitable to build and operate high-toned hostelries to accommodate the ever-growing number of wealthy businessmen and entrepreneurs who flocked to the boomtown to cash in on the silver bonanza.

The Hotel Erle was located on busy, bustling Allen Street, Tombstone's main thoroughfare, in the heart of the lively commercial district. It stood between Fourth Street and Fifth Street, on the same stretch of prime real estate as the Cosmopolitan Hotel and the Occidental Hotel, two other outstanding establishments.

Farther along the street was the Oriental Saloon, site of the recent high-stakes poker game featuring some of Tombstone's most celebrated citizens.

Wyatt Earp was a professional gambler at the Oriental when he wasn't attending to his law enforcement duties. That was where he made his real money. Oriental owner, Milt Joyce, had recently cut Wyatt in on a percentage of the profits of the gaming room, a plum prize for the most ambitious and dangerous member of the Earp clan.

Now Wyatt, and brothers Virgil and Morg, were out of town on the posse hunting the Wells Fargo robbers, along with the sheriff, Marshal Fred White, Deputy Marshal Johnny Behan, and a number of Tombstone's top guns.

Sam and Matt had made almost two hundred dollars this day selling off the Vollin gang's horses, guns, and saddles. After leaving the marshal's office, they went to a dry-goods store to buy some new clothes, following which they went to the bathhouse to get cleaned up—a telling sign of the importance of their upcoming meeting at eight. They put on their new clothes and left their old ones wrapped up in a brown paper parcel, held in a bin under the front counter for later retrieval.

A stop at the barbershop for a haircut and shave further spruced them up. Sam kept his hair shoulder length, but he cleaned it up by having the edges trimmed. They ducked into a café for something to eat. The food worked on Matt's stomach something like a blotter, soaking up much of the booze he'd taken on at the marshal's office. The steam and hot bath earlier had already sweated much of the alcohol out of his system, for which he was grateful. He'd been feeling a bit unsteady, but now he was back on an even keel.

At the time of twenty minutes before eight o'clock, the duo arrived at the Hotel Erle. Their appointment was at eight o'clock. The scene was alive with lights, color, people, movement.

The Hotel Erle was two stories of white-painted wood ornamented by a variety of Gilded Age architectural embellishments: newel posts on staircase bannisters, scrimshaw decorative moldings and cornices, gables, and dormers. The ground floor was edged on three sides by a verandah, the second floor by a balcony.

The double-door entrance was topped by an ornate stained-glass fanlight. Backlit by bright lobby lights, it threw a scattering of rainbow highlights on Sam and Matt standing at the foot of the front stairs.

Matt finished smoking a cigar, tossing the butt into the dirt street. He brushed some few specks of dust off his shoulders, straightened out his lapel, and hitched his guns on his hips so they sat just right, gun butts level with his fingertips. Not that he anticipated using them at this upcoming meeting.

But he and Sam had more than a few enemies; this was Tombstone, where danger and sudden death might come anytime, from any direction.

Sam similarly performed a last-minute overseeing of the fine details of his personal appearance.

"We're early," Matt said.

"That gives us time for a word with Buckskin Frank, who tipped us to this deal," Sam said.

"Time for a drink, too."

They climbed the stairs, crossed the verandah to the entrance, and went inside into the front hall. The interior blazed with light, reflections glimmering on brass and bronze fittings and dark wood paneling. Men's starched shirtfronts, cuffs, and collars gleamed white and shining. Women were gowned in outfits with plunging necklines that bared smooth shoulders and deep cleavage, luscious flesh all cream, pink, and ivory.

A wide central staircase led to the second floor. To the right was the front desk and a restaurant. To the left was a lobby, beyond which lay the bar.

People came and went, hotel guests and visitors, restaurant and bar patrons. A lot of business deals were done in the lobby and barroom. The men looked prosperous, well fed; the ladies, well dressed and well turned out.

The lobby featured big overstuffed armchairs and divans. Globe lamps sat on drum tables. The hardwood floor was richly carpeted. In the spaces between carpets where the floor showed, honey-gold-colored wood showed, waxed and polished to a lustrous shine.

Some men smoked cigars. No ladies smoked, not here. Even in the free and easy West, it was thought improper for women to smoke in public, if at all.

Matt and Sam went through the lobby into the barroom. A long bar stretched along the rear wall. It was a stand-up bar with a brass rail along the foot, no chairs or stools. Tables and chairs were grouped around the space. There was a good-sized crowd, some hotel guests, some not. Most looked to be of the business class.

Among the men there were less belt guns to be seen on average than on the streets of Tombstone. Some carried concealed weapons, no doubt. Others relied on their wits, well-stuffed wallets, or both.

One of the barmen was Frank Leslie, clad in a trademark fringed buckskin shirt. He was armed. A gunman of renown such as he must go armed at work or play.

Buckskin Frank was considered a popular local character and he played the role to the hilt. He made a show out of tending bar, tossing empty glasses into the air and catching them behind his back, pouring drinks from a height into glasses without spilling a drop, and suchlike dazzling bits of business. He had fast hands, an asset in both his trades of gunman and bartender.

Seeing Matt and Sam approaching, he finished the drink he was making and handed it to a patron with a flourish. He spoke to the other bartender on duty, telling him he was going to step away for a moment. He wiped his hands on a hand towel and came out from behind the bar, crossing to Sam and Matt.

They shook hands. "You two look all duded up," Frank said.

"We want to make a good impression," said Sam.

"You want to make a good impression on the colonel, you've got to show him how he can make some money. A whole lot of money."

"That's what we're here for," Matt said.

"The colonel's looking forward to meeting you. He made a point of saying how much he wanted to meet some of the famous gunmen of Tombstone, so naturally I thought of you," Frank said.

"We're not so famous," Matt said with a show of modesty.

"No, but the other famous gunmen are on the Wells Fargo posse," Frank fired back.

Matt gave him a dirty look. "What's the matter, weren't you famous enough for him?"

"He's already met me. Besides, I don't have a silver claim—you do."

"Tell me, Frank, did you know Colonel Davenport was coming for a visit when you tried to buy our claim this morning? You don't have to answer that, I already know the answer. Of course you did. You work here at the hotel, so you know when important guests are coming."

Buckskin Frank was unabashed. "Business is business, Matt. You can't blame a man for trying. With those poker winnings in hand, I tried to make hay while the sun shines. Guess I got a little carried away. But I'm making amends by steering you to the colonel."

"And we appreciate it," Sam said.

"I gave you a big buildup with the old boy, telling him about some of your adventures. He's mighty keen on meeting real Westerners."

"It might have helped if you gave the claim a big buildup," Matt said.

Frank held out his hands palms up, shrugging in

a kind of gesture that said, what-can-I-do? "I know you boys can shoot. I don't know that your claim's a silver mother lode."

"You thought enough of it to try to buy it."

"I'm a gambler, remember?"

"That's water under the bridge," Sam said, wanting to smooth things over.

"My sentiments exactly. Time to move past that. Sell the hell out of the claim to the colonel and good luck."

"Thanks, Frank. Anything we should know about the setup before we walk in?"

"Colonel Davenport's got an assistant with him name of Stebbins. A private secretary or bookkeeper or something, he keeps an eye on the colonel's money for him. He's a real tight ass and a cheapskate. He squeezes a dollar so hard the eagle screams. You could be giving away solid silver bars and he'd still say nay. He don't tip worth a damn neither, the waiters and chambermaids tell me."

"We'll keep it in mind. Anything else?"

"The colonel's got another fellow traveling with him, kind of a mysterious hombre. Name of Markand. Not a moneyman. He's an agent for a European arms maker. Got some kind of invention he's touting to Davenport, trying to get him to invest. Some kind of fancy gun or something, but that's all I know."

"Foreigner?" Matt asked.

"No, he's American. Creole from New Orleans, but he's been around. Looks like he can take care of himself in a pinch," Buckskin Frank said.

He changed the subject. "How about that Wells Fargo robbery! That sure was some sweet haul."

"Twenty-seven-thousand dollars," Matt said.

"I'd like to get my hands on that!"

"Who do you think did it?" Sam asked. "You get around, Frank. A bartender hears all kinds of things on the grapevine. Any ideas who the robbers are?"

"It happened an hour after sunup. I was with you at the time. So I know you didn't do it and you know I didn't do it. Ringo and Curly Bill were there with us, so that lets them out. Otherwise, they'd be the logical choice."

"We know who didn't do it. Who did?"

Buckskin Frank looked around to make sure no one else was within earshot. "I'm not making accusations, mind, and you didn't hear it from me, but it sure would be interesting to know where Doc Holliday was when the bullion wagon was hit."

"Doc's on the posse hunting the robbers," Matt pointed out.

"What of it? The posse didn't go out till two in the afternoon, if not later. Plenty of time for Doc to get back to town and set up an alibi.

"And here's another thing: The robbers burned down Cooper, the shotgun messenger, right straight off and tried to kill driver Simms, too. Cooper and Simms both know Doc pretty well. Could be they recognized him even with a mask on, or Doc thought they did, so he decided to take care of them permanentlike."

Matt looked thoughtful. "I'm not saying Doc

wouldn't do it if he had the chance, but what about Wyatt Earp? Doc's his right-hand man. I've got no love for Wyatt, but I can't see him tieing into something as raw as this. . . ."

"Wyatt looks the other way when it comes to Doc. There's a lot about Doc Holliday that Wyatt don't know because he don't want to know," Frank said.

At the bar the bartender gestured to Frank, motioning for him to come over. "I jawed long enough. I got to get back to work," Frank said.

"We better get moving, too, or we'll be late for our meeting," said Sam.

"You don't want to do that. Davenport's supposed to be a stickler for punctuality."

"One thing puzzles me," Matt said. "You never gave away something for nothing in your life, Frank. What's in it for you for steering us to the colonel?"

"Just doing you a good turn. If you close the deal, you might do me one by paying me a finder's fee."

"Now it makes sense."

"If it's a go, we'll cut you in for a slice, Frank," Sam said.

"I knew I could count on you. Good luck, men. Let me know how it comes out." Buckskin Frank said so long and went back behind the bar.

"Frank's a slippery cuss. He's probably got it rigged for Davenport to pay him a finder's fee if the deal goes through, too," Matt said.

"Let's not keep the great man waiting," said Sam.

* * *

Colonel Davenport's room was upstairs, on the second floor: Room 208, the so-called Presidential Suite, best room in the house. Sam and Matt stood outside the door. Sam knocked on it.

The door opened almost as soon as Sam finished knocking, as though the person within had been standing there waiting. Beyond the threshold lay a short narrow vestibule opening on a large drawing room.

The doorkeeper was lean and lank, with bony shoulder knobs, elbows, and knees.

Thin, spidery, colorless hair webbed his high-domed head. His face was long, mournful, with close-set eyes, turnip-shaped nose, and a tight mouth pursed in an expression of disapproval. He was clean-shaven, but with prominent "mutton chop" side whiskers.

He wore a black frock coat, stiff white collar, and a gray-patterned cravat.

"Matt Bodine and Sam Two Wolves to see Colonel Davenport. We're expected," Sam said.

"Come in, please," the doorkeeper said. They went in.

"I am Arnholt Stebbins, Colonel Davenport's confidential assistant," the doorkeeper said.

"Glad to know you," said Matt.

"Quite. This way, please."

Stebbins turned, moving forward. Matt was glad he hadn't expected a handshake. Stebbins probably would have ignored it and that would have been irritating. He and Sam followed Stebbins into the drawing room. Other rooms opened off it to the left and right.

The drawing room was large, expansive, well appointed and furnished. Framed engravings of the Capitol building and White House hung on the walls. A sideboard was well stocked with an array of bottles holding a variety of whiskeys and wines. Cigar smoke hung heavy in the room. The windows were open and the curtains parted, but it was a still night with barely the breath of a breeze.

Two men stood standing and talking, with well-filled glasses in hand, puffing away on fat, aromatic cigars. One was white-haired with a white mustache; the other, a younger man with black hair and finely cut features.

"Colonel Davenport, this is Mr. Bodine and Mr. Wolves," Stebbins announced with a show of formality.

"Two Wolves," Sam corrected him.

Stebbins looked like he'd been told his fly was open. Matt toyed with the idea of doing just that, to see his reaction, but he stifled the impulse.

"The name is Sam Two Wolves—Mr. Two Wolves," Sam said.

"Whatever your name is, I'm damned glad to meet you," the white-haired man said, stepping forward.

He was sixty-five, short, with short, neatly parted snowy hair, tufted white eyebrows, a bushy white mustache, and shiny pink skin. He looked well set up in the ways of good living, comfortably padded, custom tailored.

He was Colonel Holland Davenport, celebrated plutocrat and promoter. He'd achieved some minor success as a Union Army commander in the War Between the States. Since then, he'd been a banker, Wall Street financier, railroad builder, bridge builder, and mighty master of several million dollars.

The front man for a group of Eastern money brokers, he was making a grand tour of the Southwest in search of investment properties, concentrating on mining and timber holdings.

Tombstone was in need of an infusion of large outside capital. A large fortune in silver ore lay beneath the ground, but it would take a small fortune to develop it properly.

The hard rock mining required to wrest the ore from below required heavy earthmoving equipment and a legion of men to work the diggings.

The local prospectors and speculators who found and claimed the deposit sites simply didn't have the money to haul out the ore in a big way, loosing a flood of Eastern bankers and moneymen to remedy the lack.

Earlier today, Buckskin Frank Leslie had sought out Sam Two Wolves, finding him horse-trading at the corral. He alerted Sam that Davenport was in town and staying at the Hotel Erle where Frank tended bar. Davenport's fascination for Western gunfighters was well-known, giving Frank a wedge to arrange a meeting between the colonel and the duo.

Davenport reached out to shake Sam's hand. The colonel's hands were smooth and uncallused, but his grip was strong. He shook Matt's hand, too.

"Allow me to introduce an associate of mine, Mr. Remy Markand," Davenport said.

Markand, forty, was several inches above medium height, with an athletic build.

He had black hair, blue eyes, and a black Vandyke mustache and goatee. His hair had blue highlights. It was so shiny, it looked lacquered. His skin was bronzed, weathered, the skin of an outdoorsman. His eyebrows were arched in the centers and his goatee came to a sharp point, giving him something of a Mephisto look. A good-humored Mephisto, with a quick, friendly smile.

Like Matt and Sam, he wore a gun. It was worn on his left hip in a gun belt made of fine reddish-brown Moroccan leather—he was a left-hand draw, a fact duly noted by Sam and Matt, whose livelihood and lives depended on noting such important details.

Markand and the duo shook hands all around. Markand's grip was firm, dry.

"A historic encounter," Colonel Davenport enthused, "the Brothers of the Wolf meeting the Panther of the Atlas!

"Yes, I'm well acquainted with your background, gentlemen. One white boy, one red, both raised among the Cheyenne, the Brothers of the Wolf. Blood brothers and fighting men, roaming the West in search of adventure!"

Actually, Sam was born of a Cheyenne warrior

and a New England schoolmarm, making him half-white and half-red, but both he and Matt independently decided it was more politic not to correct the colonel in his outburst of enthusiasm.

"It's my distinct pleasure to present you to Captain Remy Markand, late of the French Foreign Legion, whose bold exploits against the Riffian Berbers and the Blue Men of the Tuareg in the colonies of Algiers and Morocco earned him the sobriquet 'Panther of the Atlas Mountains.'"

"That was long ago and far away, Colonel," Markand said with a small smile.

"Valor lives forever, my fine young sir, as you and Messers Bodine and Two Wolves will come to realize in the future, if you don't already."

"In this day and age it seems one is only as good as his next exploit," Markand said.

"Well put. Doubtless more exciting adventures lie in wait for all three of you."

"I hope not. I could use a rest from being shot at."

"I know what you mean!" Matt said feelingly.

"What're you drinking, men?" Davenport asked.

"Whiskey!" Sam and Matt said simultaneously.

"Hop to it, Stebbins, serve them out. We've got some thirsty men here. Markand and I could use another round, too."

Stebbins hovered over the sideboard, pouring the drinks: whisky for the duo, bourbon for Markand, brandy for Davenport.

"A toast, gentlemen," Davenport said, hoisting a glass. "Adventure!"

Sam's idea of adventure was somebody else having

a hell of a tough time a thousand miles away, as a wise man once said (he forgot whom). He kept his thoughts to himself. Sam didn't want to tell his war stories; he wanted to pitch the Spear Blade Spur claim. The subject would have to be introduced with some finesse, he realized. Hard-charging tycoons like Davenport weren't in the habit of being led around by the nose—or even being interrupted, for that matter.

He and the others drank up, draining their glasses. Stebbins hovered around the edges, not drinking. He refilled the glasses.

"I want to hear all about your thrilling exploits, shooting your way across the map from Hell to Texas—"

"Sometimes there's not much difference, Colonel," Matt said.

"Eh? What? How's that again?"

"Not much difference between Hell and Texas."

Davenport barked a laugh. "Ha! A jest! I get it— I've been to Texas, ha-ha! And I'm destined to spend the afterlife sizzling on a hot spit in the Other Place, if you believe my critics! Personally, I don't even ignore them. Have a cigar, Bodine."

"Thanks, Colonel."

"They're Cubans, Monte Cristo, specially cut, cured, and hand-rolled to my specifications. Have a cigar, Two Wolves."

"Thank you kindly, sir." Sam held the cigar under his nose, rolling it in his fingers. Its fragrant aroma tantalized his senses. Stebbins held out a lit match and Sam and Matt puffed away, lighting up.

"Damned fine cigar, Colonel," Matt said.

The foursome smoked and drank for a bit before Colonel Davenport started up again. "You Brothers of the Wolf being fighting men, I've got something to show you that'll fill you with awe and wonderment— awe and wonderment, I say!

"Or, rather, Markand will say. He'll do the talking— it's his baby."

"Hardly that, Colonel Davenport. I'm not the inventor, merely the sales agent for the North American region. I will concede that nothing sells like sincere admiration, and I have all that and more for our product," Markand said. "I'm a true believer in the Montigny Mitrailleuse."

He pronounced it "mon-tee-nee mit-ray-yoos."

Matt and Sam exchanged blank glances. "I don't know the name," Matt said. Not only did he not know the name, he doubted he could pronounce it correctly. "Is it some kind of gun?"

Colonel Davenport convulsed with mirth, his face reddening. "Is it some kind of gun? That's a good one, eh, Markand? Is it some kind of gun— why, it's the very devil of a gun, Bodine, the very devil!

"But seeing is believing. What say you give them a peek, Markand?"

"I'd be delighted, Colonel. If you gentlemen will come this way," Markand said, crossing the drawing room and passing under an archway. The others followed. Beyond the arch lay another room, part of the suite. Its far wall had several windows in it that opened on a balcony and, beyond that, Allen

Street. The windows were open. Shadowy figures could be seen on the balcony.

Sam began, "Men outside—"

"They work for me," Davenport said, "standing guard over the Mitrailleuse. Can't risk a hotel sneak thief making off with the mechanical wonder of the age!"

"A wise precaution," Sam said.

"Colonel Davenport leaves nothing to chance," Stebbins said primly.

The room was a dining room, its centerpiece a large, sturdy table covered with a white linen tablecloth. Instead of being set with plates and cutlery, the table served as a platform for a unique piece of weaponry.

It was the height of incongruity, this futuristic armament laid out for display on a white-covered dining table. The piece was all gleaming curves and sharp edges, reflected lamplight glimmering along its shiny surfaces.

Matt and Sam moved in, circling the table to eye the piece. A three-foot-long metal cylinder was mounted on a tripod stand. One end of the cylinder was encased in an oblong housing or shell, taking up one-third of its total length; the other two-thirds consisted of the cylinder itself, a pipe barrel six inches in diameter. The muzzle was covered by a metal disk sieved with several dozen regularly spaced holes.

A square plate hung down from the underside where the barrel met the oblong receiver box. The bottom of the box was supported by a short, thick, vertical rod girded round with wheels and springs. The rod fitted into a housing at the top of the tripod. A curved handle rose vertically out of the top of the rear of the housing.

"I give you the Montigny Mitrailleuse," Markand said, beaming, a proud papa presenting his pride and joy.

"Looks like a vest-pocket Gatling gun," Matt said.

Davenport said. "Hear that, Markand? 'A vest-pocket Gatling gun!' Not bad, eh? He's got you there!"

"In truth, it is not unlike a Gatling gun, though profoundly improved, lighter, more portable," Markand said. "At the home office, we like to call it a *machine gun.*"

"A machine gun!" Sam breathed, realizing the implications of the concept—of the piece.

Matt, fascinated, lightly fingered the many bores in the circular muzzle disk. "These bores—they're each part of a separate barrel."

"Correct," Markand said. "The cylinder holds thirty-seven barrels inside. They are connected to this metal plate"—here, he indicated the square-shaped case, not unlike a cigarette case in size, which fit into a receiver below the cylinder, where it met the oblong housing—"this plate, which holds thirty-seven cartridges. The cartridge plate can be quickly removed at the press of a button, extracting an empty plate and loading a full one.

"The Mitrailleuse is a multi-barreled, man-powered piece. The gunner turns this hand crank to fire the weapon. A switch permits either single-shot firing or a single tremendous volley.

"In either case, the effect, I assure you, is formidable—devastating."

"Markand is the North American sales representative for the arms maker," Davenport said. "What say you, men?"

"One of the damnedest things I've ever seen," Sam said. Despite the whiskey he'd drunk, he felt cold sober.

"It sure does beat all, if it does what you say," Matt said.

"It does all that and more," Markand said.

"I'd buy one right now, except I can't fit it in my holster," Matt joked weakly. He was transfixed, mesmerized by the machine. Guns were his vocation and his avocation, his livelihood and his ruling passion.

"I'm going to put on a demonstration tomorrow. I invite you both to attend as my guests," Markand said.

"I accept," Sam said gravely.

"I'll be there. I wouldn't miss it," Matt said.

"I knew you fighting men would appreciate the piece. I'm thinking of acquiring the North American rights for my combine," Davenport said. "But speaking of acquisitions, I'm given to understand that you men have some sort of a proposition for me—something about a silver mine claim?"

Sam and Matt had difficulty getting their heads

out of the machine gun to pitch the prospects of Spear Blade Spur.

Sam came to himself first. "You're a business-man, Colonel, and time is money, so we'll get right to it. As you said, seeing is believing. Why don't you show him the samples, Matt?"

"Huh? Oh, right." Matt shook his head as if to clear it. Reaching into the inside breast pocket of his jacket, he took out a cloth pouch. Opening its draw-string mouth, he upended it, emptied its contents on the white-linen covered tabletop, spilling out a handful of silver nuggets. They rattled like dice, coming to rest in the shadow of the machine gun.

The silver-rich nuggets had been cleaned and polished for presentational purposes. They scintil-lated, striking glints and glimmers of reflected lamplight.

Precious metal exerted its age-old lure on the company, fascinating them. Davenport, Markand, and even Stebbins moved closer, crowding the edge of the table for a better look.

"Samples from our claim at Spear Blade Spur," Sam said. "We'll give you a copy of the assayer's report, but I'm sure you'll want to have your own people run the tests on it to prove it out."

The noise level on the street outside was rising markedly. Davenport glanced toward the windows, frowning.

"Handsome specimen," he said, picking up a nugget between thumb and forefinger and holding it up to the light.

"There's more where that came from," Matt said, speaking up to be heard over the racket coming from Allen Street.

"How much more?" Davenport asked.

"Remains to be seen," Sam said. "We're prospectors, not miners. We've struck a vein that could be the leading head of a lode, but we need funds to do the extraction and better see what it is exactly we've got."

"Are you interested in acquiring a partner or selling the claim outright?"

"It's negotiable. Why not come out to Spear Blade Spur and see for yourself? Bring your people, your geologists and engineers. We've got nothing to hide. We're an open book—"

Allen Street was in an uproar. People milled around in the street, buzzing and shouting.

"What the devil is all that fuss?" Davenport snapped.

"I'll see what it is, Colonel," Stebbins said, going to a window. He ducked down, sticking his head outside.

Two armed guards in civilian clothes stood at the balcony rail, staring down into the street.

"You men there! What's happening in the street?"

"I don't know, Mr. Stebbins," a guard said. "Looks like a riot is breaking out!"

EIGHT

Skeets Boyar was a singing cowboy. There was nothing unusual in that. Most folks sang, in church and as a social pasttime. Many cowboys sang, especially while night-herding during long cattle trail drives.

Cattle are spooky critters. It doesn't take much—a coyote's howl, a gunshot—to set them off running on a wild panicked flight, creating a dangerous and costly stampede.

Dangerous, in that men and horses can go down under the thundering herd to be trampled to death; costly, because some of the fear-maddened critters are liable to run off the edge of a cliff or into a ditch, breaking their fool necks.

Or they'll just run themselves out for miles until they drop from sheer exhaustion, having worked off in the process pounds of flesh that have been fattening up all season—and cattle is sold by the pound at the trailhead.

Cowboys learned that singing aloud while

patrolling the herd had a pacifying effect on the stock, helping the animals get used to the presence of the humans and soothing their anxious nerves. So, many cowboys whiled away the night hours warbling tunes, popular songs, folk ballads, and the like.

Skeets Boyar was different. He had a good voice and genuine musical talent. He played a sweet, lyric guitar.

It was about eight-thirty that night at Ben Burnham's Big Sky Saloon, located on a side street at the edge of Tombstone town. It was a companionable meeting place offering decent whiskey and beer at a reasonable price, straightforward and with no frills.

Genial (but fast-shooting if riled) owner-host Ben Burnham dispensed drinks from behind a trestle-table bar. There was sawdust on the floor. The barmaids were a bit frayed at the edges but not bad looking, especially once you had a couple of drinks in you. The Big Sky was a favorite of the Cowboy set; Ringo and Curly Bill often held court here when they were in town, as they were now.

The saloon was doing a lively business this night, the absence of the sheriff and his deputies and the much-despised (by the Cowboys) Earp brothers contributed to a celebratory mood. Patrons were packed two-deep at the bar and all the tables and chairs were filled. The overflow crowd stood at the rear of the building, whiskey glasses and beer mugs in hand.

At the opposite end of the building, a raised

platform served as a kind of stage. Skeets Boyar sat there on a chair, singing and strumming on a Mexican guitar.

Skeets was the unofficial Cowboy troubador, and like most of his fellows, a roper, wrangler, all-around cowhand, and sometime rustler and smuggler. Like them, he thought nothing of wearing his hat indoors and wouldn't be caught without it. He was young, fresh faced, overdue for a haircut and shave. His clothes were worn and faded, his gun belt leather was weathered, but his holstered six-gun looked shiny new and well tended.

Skeets played Mexican style, without a pick, using all five fingers of his strumming hand on the strings. It was a good guitar, with multicolored bands of inlaid wood and a rich, resonant tone. Skeets got a big sound out of it.

He played the old standards, trail laments like "Streets of Laredo," and sprightly upbeat tunes like "Git Along Home, Cindy, Cindy."

He performed purely for the fun of it, his pay only the pleasure of his friends and the free drinks Ben Burnham set him up to by way of recompense.

His listeners were carried away on a melodic carriage of notes and chords.

Flint-eyed hardcases couldn't help but set booted feet tapping away in time with frisky tunes, while more than a few fancy ladies and saloon girls got misty eyed during the soulful ballads.

Among the appreciative audience were Johnny Ringo and Curly Bill Brocius. They sat up front at

one of the best tables in the house, along with some
of their inner circle, fast guns and faster women.

Ringo's current lady friend clung to his arm; Bill
sat between two femmes, an arm around each of
their shoulders while they snuggled in tight. Arlene
was with Ringo; Ginny and Sue cuddled up with
Curly Bill.

Arlene was in her late teens, with short, dark
reddish-brown hair cut in bangs over a heart-
shaped face. Her features were finely made, but
her dark blue eyes were hard and there was a bitter
twist to her provocatively shaped mouth. Her slim
figure was exquisite.

Sue was short, petite, and busty, with chestnut
hair curling up at the edges in a lip at her shoulders. Ginny was a big blonde, green eyed, creamy
skinned, high breasted, and long legged.

They were grouped at the head of the long table,
with some sidemen and their lady friends ranged
along the table's long sides. The tabletop was
crowded with glasses and mugs, half-full bottles,
and a growing crowd of empties.

Ringo sat slouched back in his chair, long legs
extended. His eyes were hooded, and the corners
of his lips quirked upward. He seemed to be enjoying himself. He was about as relaxed and happy as
he ever got, which wasn't much.

He was a man with a lot on his mind. No one
knew what was haunting him, not even Curly Bill,
his best friend. Bill never asked, either. Maybe that's
why he was Ringo's best friend.

Curly Bill's nature was different. He was an

easygoing sort when he wasn't crossed. His eyes now glimmered, his face was red and shining, strong white teeth flashing in a big grin.

Arlene clung to Ringo like a starfish gripping a clam whose shell it's trying to pry open. She chattered away nonstop. When her talk managed to catch his attention, Ringo looked bored or irritated. The longer she went on, the more boredom gave way to irritation.

Arlene was one of those who paid little or no attention to the effect they have on their auditors. Being one of the best-looking women in town, she was used to having men hang on her every word. She had little use for talking to other women, and they gladly reciprocated her indifference.

"I picked you out of all the rest, John. A lot of men would give plenty to be in your shoes, to be with me," she said, a refrain she had repeated several times before noticing that Ringo made no reply. "Don't you think I'm pretty? I said, don't you think I'm pretty, Johnny?"

"Sure, sure," Ringo said, nodding absently.

"Do you know how lucky you are, to have a beautiful woman like me?" Arlene took a drink. That was the only time she stopped talking, to take a drink. "Buy me another one, Johnny."

"You've had plenty."

"I want another."

"Where do you put it all?"

She gave him a dirty look, and swore. "You should talk!"

"I can hold my liquor," Ringo said.

"So can I. I'm fine, perfectly fine."

"You think so, huh?"

Arlene changed tack. "That Kate Elder isn't so much." Kate Elder was a hard-drinking, fiery-tempered whore with whom Ringo was carrying on a casual, on-off affair. Right now it was off, so he was keeping company with Arlene.

"Do you think she's pretty? She's not as pretty as me. Don't you think that I'm prettier?"

"I'm trying to hear the music," Ringo said, giving her a hard look.

Arlene was not one to take a hint—not when she was in her cups, which was most of the time "She's old. She's got a lot of miles on her, been over a lot of bad road."

Ringo looked steadily at her, a red flush creeping up from his neck, overspreading his face. A warning sign, to those in the know.

Arlene knew, but chose to ignore it. "Kate belongs with a busted-down drunk like Doc Holliday—"

"Don't you ever shut up?"

Arlene flinched. She switched from complaining to whining. "You're mean. Why can't you be nice to me? Sherm McMasters is."

"You like him so well, why don't you go with him? Then I wouldn't have to listen to you running off at the mouth," Ringo said.

"You're mean. How come you're so mean?"

"Too many women like you."

Arlene teared up, lower lip quivering, chin trembling. She blinked repeatedly through watery eyes, studying Ringo. He studiously ignored her.

Up front, Skeets Boyar finished his current tune with a flourish. His listeners clapped and whistled their approval, some stamping their feet. They called out requests: "Old Dog Trey," "Arkansas Traveler," "Yellow Rose of Texas," and many others.

There was a lull. Ringo called out for "Shenadoah."

"No sad songs please, it makes the gals blue and they get behind on their serving," Ben Burnham called out from behind the bar—joking, but meaning it, too.

Ringo cut him a side glance that would have chilled the blood of even the toughest hombres.

"'Course, if that's what you want, Johnny, we'd all love to hear it," Burnham said quickly, white faced.

"Don't shoot ol' Ben, John. Who'll pour the drinks?" Curly Bill cracked.

That broke the tension, getting a laugh all around, even warming to a degree Ringo's icy hauteur.

"'Shenandoah' it is, folks," Skeets said cheerfully. Apart from everything else, the tune was a favorite of his.

He launched into that song of the wide blue Virginia river and the wayfarer who's left behind a long-lost love, playing and singing it sweetly and plaintively, lacing it with a lyrical Mexican flavor.

Ringo listened, transfixed. He had a look on his face like some believers get when they're in church. Even Arlene knew to keep her mouth shut.

Suddenly, a meaty palm heel hammered open a swinging door, as a newcomer burst into the saloon. Sawdust on the floor muffled but could not silence the clatter of big booted feet hurrying across the room to the front.

Ringo's head whipped around, his long-necked head bobbing like a striking rattlesnake's, to pin the intruder with a forbidding glare.

Skeets Boyar kept on singing and playing as if there'd been no interruption, staying on pitch and never missing a note.

Ringo was wild of eye, grim of aspect. Curly Bill fastened a hand on Ringo's upper arm, the arm of his gun hand, which had gone to the ivory-handled grip of his holstered Colt. Only Bill could have gotten away with it, or would have dared.

"Whoa, John, that's Jeb Harris. Jeb—a friend of ours," Curly Bill said, soft voiced, and persuasive. "Look at him, he's all worked up—something's wrong."

Jeb Harris, the new entrant, was a disorderly character at the best of times, which this obviously was not. He was ungainly, big gutted, with a soft moon face, and moist dark eyes bulging behind oval lenses of wire-rimmed spectacles.

His eyes widened farther still when he saw how Ringo was looking at him, but he pressed on, making his way to the table. Ringo's sixth sense for trouble kicked in and he held his hand.

Jeb Harris was a member in good standing of the Cowboy crowd. Urgency now oozed out of him like sweat on a quarter-horse pulling a plow during the dog days of August. Falling under the glare of Ringo's evil eyes, he froze, fleshy face paling despite the flush of recent exertion.

"Lord, Johnny, you should see your face! You look like you want to kill me!" Jeb Harris said.

"You better have a damned good reason for busting in on the middle of Skeets's musicale, else I'm gonna peel the bark off of you," Ringo said. "What is it? What do you want? Spit it out and make it quick."

"You better come with me, John—you, too, Bill."

"What's got you in an uproar, Jeb?" Curly Bill asked.

"Come quick, there's trouble over to the jail-house!"

A crowd milled around the front of the Tombstone jail, site of the marshal's office. More people were arrowing toward the scene by the minute, clustering together, rubbernecking, buzzing. A rising moon caused the gallows to throw long shadows westward across the square.

A wagon and horse team stood outside the jail-house, showing the effects of a long, hard ride. The horses stood in the traces, heads bowed, sagging at the knees—winded.

They were dusted with alkali, the dust mixing with glossy sweat to form a ghostly paste. The wagon was powdered with the stuff, as was the man who sat slumping upon the driver's seat, smoking a handmade cigarette.

Someone handed him a canteen. He stubbed the cigarette out on the seat. He took off his hat, poured water into it, and upended the contents on top of his head, wetting it down and washing away much of the dust. He wet his bandana, mopping his face as clean as he could. A youthful face was revealed, grim, haggard with fatigue. Eyes stared off into the distance, reddened from sun and grit.

Ringo and Curly Bill plunged into and through the crowd. Resentment at their vigorous approach was swiftly self-stifled when they were recognized: "Who you pushing?—Oops! Er, sorry, Mr. Ringo, Mr. Brocius, didn't know it was you!"

Curly Bill got a good look at the driver, and said, "Lee! Lee Lindsey!"

The driver shook off his blank stare, looking around to see who was calling him by name, and spotting Bill and Ringo surging to the fore. Lee Lindsey (for it was indeed him) climbed down heavily from the wagon. Unsteady on his feet, he gripped a sidewall for balance.

Ringo and Bill made their way to him. Lindsey started toward them, stiff-legged, staggering. He stumbled. Ringo and Curly Bill caught him, keeping him from falling.

"Don't mind me, boys, I'm tuckered out," Lindsey said.

"What're you doing here, hoss? Thought you was over to Cactus Patch," Curly Bill said.

"I was. Me and Don Brown rode a long way fast to find you."

"Where's Don?"

Lindsey indicated the jail. "Inside, with the girl."

"What girl is that?" Ringo asked.

"She's at the heart of it. It's murder, boys, murder and worse."

"Who got killed?"

"Let me go, I can stand now," Lindsey said. They released him.

Lindsey made his shaky way to the back of the wagon. The tailgate was down.

Inside, on the wagon bed, covered by a dark green horse blanket, lay the unmistakeable outline of a human body. A hand protruded beyond the blanket's edge. It lay palm up, fingers curling, stiff, chalk white.

"Who is it?" Curly Bill asked.

"Bob Farr," Lindsey said, his face anguished. He and Farr had been great friends, partners.

Bill swore. Ringo reached into the wagon, turning the blanket down, exposing Farr's head, shoulders, and chest. His eyes were closed. They had been closed for him by one of his handlers. His pale, bloodless face was carved into a mask of shocked surprise.

"He was shot in the back," Lee Lindsey said, his voice breaking.

Curly Bill continued venting a string of muttered obscenities.

"Who did it?" Ringo asked, intent.

"Dorado, the Mex bandit with the golden gun," Lindsey said.

"I've heard of him. I always thought that golden gun story was a legend."

"It's not, and he wasn't alone."

"Who else?"

"Quirt Fane."

Curly Bill stopped swearing. "I know Quirt. He should've been killed long ago."

"He's got his time now," Ringo said. "Him and Dorado both."

The Citizens Committee had been instrumental in having Fred White appointed marshal of Tombstone. They represented the mine owners, leading merchants, and big ranchers. But there was an election coming up and if White wanted to stay marshal, he needed a majority of votes.

The townsfolk's allegiance was split between the big business faction and the Cowboys. The small shopkeepers, mine workers, and small ranchers tended to side with the Cowboys. They didn't much care if the big ranchers lost stock to rustlers and they resented the heavy-handed methods of the sheriff and his deputies, the Earps, in laying down the law.

Marshal White had to walk a fine line between the businessmen and the Cowboys.

Deputy Johnny Behan was an outright Cowboy partisan. Assistant Deputy Hubert Osgood took his cue from Behan, a canny politician and rising man in town. Osgood played to the Cowboys, especially with Marshal White out of town on a posse chasing the Wells Fargo robbers.

Now present in the marshal's office were Osgood, Ringo, Curly Bill, Lee Lindsey, and Don Brown.

Rumors and wild tales about the incident in

Cactus Patch had spread like wildfire in Tombstone, causing the occupants of the hotels and saloons of Allen Street to take to the street to hear the latest news.

It was their excited clamoring which created a hubbub in front of the Hotel Erle, interrupting Matt Bodine and Sam Two Wolves as they pitched their silver claim on Spear Blade Spur to Colonel Davenport.

Davenport, himself, took an interest in the case, not enough to cause him to bestir himself forth from the Hotel Erle, but enough to send his representatives Arnholt Stebbins and Remy Markand to the jailhouse to investigate. Davenport's millionaire status ensured that Assistant Deputy Osgood was most attentive to his wishes.

The Brothers of the Wolf, themselves intensely curious about the incident, attached themselves to Stebbins and Markand, using them to gain entry to the marshal's office.

Harry Woods, editor of the pro-Cowboy newspaper *The Nugget*, gained access to the scene.

Also there were Lee Lindsey and Don Brown, who'd been there for the shootout in Cactus Patch and had brought eyewitness Linda Gordon to Tombstone.

Sam and Matt stood off to one side, eyeing Ringo and Curly Bill—who were eyeing them. "What're you doing here?" Matt asked.

"Bob Farr was a friend of mine," Ringo said.

"Mine, too," said Bill.

"He was shot in the back," Ringo added, his tone of voice boding ill for the perpretrators.

"Sorry," Sam said. What else was there to say?

"Yeah, well, somebody's going to be a whole lot sorrier," Bill said. "What brings you here?"

"Good citizenship," Sam said.

"We like to help people," Matt said, open faced, showing every sign of meaning it.

"That what you were doing when you shot Justin Vollin?"

"He tried to jump our claim, Bill."

"And the rest of his gang?"

"Them, too."

"Well, you made a clean sweep of it."

"Nice of you to say so."

Ringo said, "Waco Brindle's making noises about evening up on you two."

"Is that right? He didn't show much fight the last time we saw him," Sam said.

"Waco's a bag of wind. He's a yellowbelly," Matt said.

"Maybe we better talk to him again," said Sam.

"Watch out—he's a back shooter," Curly Bill warned.

"I hate back shooters," Ringo said feelingly. "They don't deserve to live."

Deputy Osgood came over to them. "Hush up now, the gal's gonna tell her story." He looked over the four of them, sour faced. "This is law-enforcement business. You don't belong here. By all rights, I should put you out."

"You would if you could." Bill laughed.

Osgood pointedly ignored him. "I might need to call on you all to help out the law, what with Marshal Fred and the sheriff and them all out on the trail of them stage robbers. But no cutting up now, hear?"

"We're here to help out," Matt said.

"Uh-huh," Osgood said. "Where's them two bottles you promised?"

"I didn't forget. Things got kind of busy in the rush. I'll bring them along later, honest."

"See that you do."

The center of interest and the focus of all eyes was Linda Gordon, the young woman who'd fled Quirt Fane and Dorado at Cactus Patch. She sat in the marshal's chair, the most comfortable chair in the office. It had been moved out from behind the desk and put to one side of it.

Those present grouped around her. Linda Gordon was sixteen, medium height, and weighed about one hundred and ten pounds. Her long blond hair was the color and texture of pale yellow cornsilk, spilling across her shoulders and down her back. Dark brown eyes contrasted with her fair hair and complexion. She was slender, but nicely rounded where it counted.

One of the women at Cactus Patch had fitted her out with a clean dress to replace her torn and dirty garments. She still wore her original shoes, a pair of lace-up, flat-heeled ankle boots.

Linda bore the marks of her ordeal, her well-tanned face showing exposure to the fierce desert sun. Her skin was peeling, her pale lips were cracked and parched. Her face and arms were scratched, bruised.

She had a firm mouth and a prominent, out-thrust chin, a family trait she'd inherited from her father, Mal Gordon. There was strength in her, strength buttressed by the freshness and vitality of youth. She sipped water from a tin cup, moistening her cracked lips.

Nugget editor Harry Woods had strengthened it with a dash of brandy from his ever-ready pocket flask, to brace her up. Woods prompted her in telling her story, Assistant Deputy Osgood's people skills being somewhat lacking, especially when it came to eliciting confidence and candor from young women.

"You're safe here, among friends. No one can hurt you now," Woods said. "I hate to bother you after all you've been through. But the sooner we know what we're dealing with, the sooner we can get to work to do something about it.

"Lindsey and Brown here told us some of it, but you're the only one who knows the whole story. The only one who can tell it all."

"I'll tell. They did all they could to stop me from talking. Nothing could stop me now," Linda Gordon said.

NINE

This is the tale told by Linda Gordon:

Land! Free land! Prime real estate located in the Sacramento River valley of the Golden State of California! Rich bottom land, loamy black, well watered. Just throw handfuls of seeds upon the earth and sure enough, in due season, up sprouts massive crops of vegetables: red-ripe tomatoes, squash, beets, corn, wheat, you name it.

No savage Indian tribes lurking omnipresent to fall on the hapless yeoman farmer.

No need to wear a gun while tilling the fields. No fear of leaving wife and children unguarded back at the farmhouse, at the tender mercies of murdering savages.

The price? Best of all: free! Each tract of land is there for the taking, for the bold venturer with energy and gumption enough to stake his claim and make it his.

Public land, by virtue of a new Homestead Act

passed by a bountiful government on behalf of its land-hungry masses!

So read the promotional literature on the handbills and proclamations circulated throughout the nation to pubicize the offering of a new Homestead Act.

It looked like a lifeline to Malcolm "Mal" Gordon, a stubborn, hardworking man who'd suffered more than his share of bad luck and hard times.

To his wife he said, "This is our big chance, Fran, and not a minute too soon, now that the lode's played out and the town's gone bust."

He wasn't talking to convince his spouse, Frances Gordon, who, being married to an inflexible hardnose like Mal, required her to be even more long suffering than he. Perhaps he sought to convince himself. What she thought didn't matter, once he'd made his mind up. A man followed his own counsel only, for good or ill—that was the gospel according to Mal Gordon.

The Gordons—Mal, wife Fran, and daughter, Linda—made their home in Bear Paw, a mining boomtown on the front range of the Rockies near Denver, Colorado. Gordon was not a miner but a farmer. Miners have to eat, though, and Gordon farmed a piece of land outside Bear Paw, raising crops to sell in town. Then the silver lode played out and the boom went bust

"Most of the miners have already moved on, and only the diehards are left. Bear Paw's gone belly-up.

It'll be a ghost town soon. No miners, no market for our crops. The nearest market's down on the flat. It wouldn't pay to haul them down there. The wear and tear'd kill off the horses, leaving us worse off than we are now," Mal said.

"We have to move on in any case. We can't survive another winter in the mountains. This way, we have some place to move to," he went on, off on another tirade.

"Now, Mal Gordon is nobody's fool. I've got sense enough not to believe a lot of pie-in-the-sky promises. But the fact is that the land is there in Sacramento. The government's making it available to homesteaders. I've seen the proclamations and so have you. And whatever it is, free California land's better than what we've got to look forward to here. All we've got to do is get there and take it."

"California's a long way off, Mal," Fran said wearily, sighing. She did a lot of sighing. Being married to Mal Gordon was a wearying thing. "We've got to cross the mountains, then the desert, then more mountains before we get there. . . ."

"Nobody said it's going to be easy. If it was, they wouldn't be giving the land away. But it can be done. It has been done, by men not as good as me, lots of them. It's being done every day. It's not like the days of 'forty-nine. The trail's blazed, well-known. And we won't be alone. Others from Bear Paw are going, too, our friends and neighbors—"

"Friends, Mal?" Fran said, a bit sharply.

Mal colored, his face reddening. "Neighbors,

anyhow. At least they're not strangers. No crooks or malingerers . . . not much, anyhow."

So it was. It was a done deal. There was no other choice, not really. Bear Paw was already close to being a ghost town. There were no jobs to be found in Denver, Colorado Springs, or wherever. Not for Mal Gordon. He was a farmer born and bred. Farming was what he did and that's all there was to it. If he couldn't farm here, he'd farm somewhere else, on the far edge of the continent in the Sacramento River valley, if need be.

Henry McGee was mayor of Bear Paw, when there'd been a town to be mayor of. He was white haired, beak nosed, and spry. Abigail was his wife. Their kids were long grown up and scattered across the country raising their own families now.

McGee had a plan, which he pitched at a meeting to the last handful of settlers still residing in Bear Paw:

"In numbers there is strength; in union there is strength. We shall go to California together. We know each other, know there are no thieves and cutthroats among us."

That was a big worry about hitting the trail, the danger of falling among thieves and cutthroats, a very real danger. Not to mention wild Indians, including the dread Apaches, whose lands they must cross.

McGee roped eight families into his plan. They sold their possessions to raise money for the trip, buying wagons, horses, provisions. July was their departure date. A late start, but it couldn't be helped. It took that long for the experts to confirm that the silver lode which had made the town was well and truly finished.

The pilgrims crossed the mountain passes, descending the western range to the flat. They followed the old Santa Fe Trail to Taos in New Mexico Territory, and were joined by several wagons of emigrants along the way.

From Taos, they set forth on the Overland Stagecoach route, winding southwest. It would ultimately take them through Arizona and Nevada territories, across the Sierra Nevadas into California.

McGee and the Bear Paw folks hoped to attach themselves to a larger wagon train for the rest of the journey. But few wagons were going west that season. Apache war chief Victorio had jumped the reservation earlier in the year, taking hundreds of his braves with him.

The braves had unleashed bitter guerilla warfare throughout their onetime home grounds in Arizona and New Mexico. In less than a year, they had slain close to one thousand white settlers—men, women, and children.

Many in the Bear Paw group were for stopping or turning back. But there was no real alternative. There was nothing to go back to and if they stopped, they'd eventually run out of supplies and starve.

Besides, the word was that Victorio and his tribe had fled south, into the Sierra Madres in Sonora, Mexico. The emigrants pressed on.

A day's trek outside Lordsburg, the wagoneers made camp, bedding down for the night. The following dawn revealed that they'd been hit by horse thieves, who'd stolen a string of the animals undetected. It spelled disaster for the victims, left without enough horses to make proper teams to haul their wagons.

McGee managed to persuade the others to donate a horse or two each to make up the difference so their fellows could proceed. It was a tough sell, but he managed to make the case by mid-morning. As they were about to apportion the horses out to the victimized families, a stranger appeared.

The newcomer was an emigrant like themselves, driving a Conestoga wagon. He was not alone. With him was a woman and another man. Trailing his wagon was a lead rope to which was secured a string of horses—the same horses that had been stolen the night before.

The stranger hailed them, pulling up at their camp. "Howdy, folks. I'm Al Jensen. This here's my wife, Carol, and my nephew Sonny Boy," he said.

Al Jensen occupied the driver's seat of the wagon, his big-knuckled, oversized hands holding the long reins of his team. He was in his mid-forties, tall, with long limbs. His curly salt-and-pepper hair was textured like sheep's wool. Tricky mutton-chop side whiskers came down his cheeks, arching into a mustache and beard. His worn oval face was tobacco colored from sun and weathering. Warm moist brown eyes nestled in rings of laugh lines.

His hat had a round-topped crown and broad flat brim, like a preacher's hat. A big-caliber Colt, holstered in an old leather rig, was worn on his right hip.

Seated beside him was his wife, Carol. She was about thirty. A big, floppy, colorless sunbonnet covered much of her face and head. Reddish-brown hair was tied up at the back of her neck. Her skin was a metallic golden brown. She had wide dark eyes, sharp cheekbones, sunken cheeks, and a full-lipped mouth turned down at the corners.

A lightning-bolt-shaped scar zigzagged along her left cheek, perhaps explaining why she sought to conceal her striking good looks under the sunbonnet. She seemed sullen, uncommunicative. A drab, shapeless Mother Hubbard shift and flat-soled, mid-calf, lace-up work boots completed her outfit. The baggy dress covered, but could not conceal a ripely curved physique.

Nephew Sonny Boy sat astride a roan gelding that was deep chested and strongly made.

Sonny Boy, too, was deep chested and strongly made. He was in his late twenties, with black hair, green eyes, thick features, strong jaw, and dimpled chin. Broad-shouldered and narrow-waisted, he wore twin guns strapped down.

McGee and some of the men went to the wagon. Mal Gordon hadn't lost any horses himself. He just wanted to establish the Bear Paw emigrants' right of ownership at the start.

Indicating the string tied to the rear of the wagon, he said, "Those're our horses, mister!"

"I know. I saw them when you were passing through Lordsburg yesterday," Jensen said. "I meant to introduce myself then and see if I could tie in with you, but a wagon wheel needed fixing and we were delayed.

"Some fellows tried to steal out horses early this morning. Sonny Boy and me opened fire on them and laced into them pretty good and they broke and run."

Sonny Boy nodded and smirked, green eyes twinkling.

"Must've been the same bunch that hit us," Henry McGee said. "What'd they look like?"

"Didn't get too close a look at them. There was three of them. Mexes or 'breeds, I'd say. I think we hit one. There was blood on the ground. When they ran, they lost this string of horses. We rounded them up. We didn't chase them—didn't want to leave the missus alone, though Carol can take care of herself," Jensen said. "She's a danged good hand with a Winchester, ain't you, dear?"

Carol nodded.

"We were lucky to come out of it as well as we did. Thought we recognized the animals as belonging to you all," Jensen said.

"Uncle Al's got an eye for horseflesh," Sonny Boy chimed in.

"We're following the westward trail same as you folks. I figured we'd run into you sooner or later. Glad it was sooner. A man can't afford to lose a horse out here."

"Ain't it the truth!" said Ames Sutton, one of those who'd fallen prey to the thieves.

"Help yourself. I know you'll be glad to get your animals back."

The emigrants were relieved that Jensen wasn't going to make any fuss about ownership. Others might not have been so broadminded, instead applying the principle of "finders keepers," in which case things might have gotten ugly.

The owners untied the rope, leading the string away. "You sure are a lifesaver, mister. We'd have been in a mighty tough spot if you hadn't come along now," Henry McGee said.

"Folks have got to help out their neighbors on the trail, that's how I see it," Al Jensen said.

"Me, too, but it ain't everybody you find who feels that way. The fire's still going. Step down and have some coffee with us."

"Don't mind if I do. Me and Sonny Boy'll come along. Carol'll stick with the wagon. She ain't hungry anyway."

Presently, Jensen and Sonny Boy sat on the ground near the fire, drinking black coffee out of tin cups. McGee and some of the Bear Paw men joined them.

"Where you bound, Mr. Jensen?" McGee asked.

"California—and call me Al."

"Glad to, Al. I'm Henry McGee. Unity is strength, I always say. We'd admire to have you folks join up and travel with us for the rest of the way."

"To tell the truth, Henry, I was hoping you'd ask.

This is mighty lonesome country for three people and a wagon."

Al Jensen, Carol, and Sonny Boy joined the Bear Paw wagon train. Jensen proved to be a sociable fellow, a companionable fellow traveler. He threw himself into the life of the emigrants without overstepping his bounds. He was ever ready to pitch in, lending a helping hand.

Never at a loss for a cheerful comment, quip, or pleasantry, he was a quick study, quick to learn the names and kinship of the wagoneer families. He liked people and they liked him. Even Mal Gordon warmed to him, in his grudging, guarded way. Linda Gordon thought Mr. Jensen was "nice."

Al Jensen's outgoing personality was balanced by the reclusive nature of his mate. Carol Jensen kept to herself, not exactly shunning the society of the other wives and mothers, but not seeking it out, either. She wasn't one to coo over the youngsters, whose energetic antics she tolerated with tight-lipped taciturnity.

Some of the wives thought she was unsociable because of the scar on her face, that it made her self-conscious around other people.

Sonny Boy was physically strong, a crack shot, and a fine horseman, three attributes respected by the men of the caravan. Sometimes he drank too much, causing his Uncle Al to have to rein him in with a sharp word several times. When tipsy, Sonny Boy was an amiable buffoon, clumsy but harmless, or so it seemed.

After several days travel southwest along the trail,

the wagon train stopped at Buckdun Station, a stagecoach way station and flyspeck town grown up at a crossroads where a spring bubbled forth out of the rocks.

The wagon train halted to water the horses and take on fresh water supplies for the next leg of the trip.

Al Jensen took Henry McGee off to one side. Jensen's manner was excited seeming, confidential. He spoke in a hushed voice. "Know who's eating lunch in the station dining room, Henry? Sime Simmons!"

"Don't believe I know the name, Al. . . ."

"What! Never heard of Sime Simmons, the famous Indian fighter and scout? Why, he's one of the best-known and most-respected hombres this side of the Rocky Mountains!"

"Is that a fact?"

"I hope to hell it is. He's led wagon trains without number westward through the Sierras to California without losing a man or a horse. Knows every pass and water hole along the trail. We'd be sitting pretty if we could hire him on as guide."

McGee looked doubtful. "We don't have much money, Al."

"Me, neither. Who does? But that works both ways. Simmons may not have much money. Maybe we can get him on the cheap. Guiding a wagon train's a whole lot safer and easier than hunting Apaches."

Some of the other men on the wagon train broached the same idea to McGee. Seemed Sonny

Boy had sung the praises of Simmons in their ears. Several of them came together to persuade McGee.

"It won't cost anything to ask," Karl Haber said.

"You're a good man, McGee, but you ain't no wagon master and you never been west on the trail before. I'd rest easier if we could depend on a professional who knows his business," Jack Collins said.

Sime Simmons was in his late forties, gray at the temples, with a gray-speckled, sharp-pointed spade beard.

"He's no youngster. He must be good to have lived so long, with the life he's led, the places he's been," wagoneer Burt Rowley said, low voiced and intense, urging McGee to approach the scout.

Simmons had gray eyes, high cheekbones, and a wide face. He wore a flannel shirt, and a brown, fringed rawhide vest, red bandana, black denims, and cowboy boots. He wore a gun on his right hip; a gun belt was worn over his shoulder, hanging a second gun butt out under his left arm. Two men were with him, hard-bitten frontier types.

McGee cautiously sounded out Simmons about a job as scout, Simmons expressing guarded interest without committing himself. He pointed out that he was traveling with two sidemen, partners, whose interests must be taken care of.

Porgy Best had oily black hair combed in a rooster-tail haircut with long sideburns. Mort Donegan had close-cropped blond hair and beard. His hair was so pale and yellow it was almost colorless.

Long-slitted yellow eyes were set in a long, seamed face.

McGee stressed that neither he nor his fellows had much money.

"I can see that," Simmons said dourly. "Tell you what I'll do: What you ain't got in money I'll take in horses. Once we reach Sacramento, you folks won't need all your horses. Make up the difference in pay with horseflesh. I'll take care of my pards.

"Fact is, I been eating red dirt and chasing Apaches—and being chased by them—for too many years now. I been thinking of starting me a horse farm and California looks like a good place to set down in."

A price was set and mutually agreed on, and the deal was made. The wagon train left Buckdun Station with Simmons riding point, sided by Best and Donegan.

"I feel better knowing those three are with us in case we run into trouble along the way," Burt Rowley confided to his wife, Colleen.

"Me, too," she said in heartfelt sincerity.

The convoy made its way south by southwest through New Mexico into Arizona.

Brown-and-black mountains and yellow sands gave way to gray-black mountains and red dirt.

The wagon train made camp for the night in Yellow Snake Canyon, a half-mile north of the trail. A twisty, narrow cut, it was bordered by sharp-edged, razor-backed rock ridges. Its red-brown-yellow floor was boulder studded and thick with cactus. A sweet scent of wild-growing aloe permeated the site.

"We're in Apache country," Sime Simmons said, "Victorio's land. Victorio and most of his bucks are down in Mexico, but that don't mean some of the war parties ain't gone north on their own to do some raiding. This is a box canyon, so we can only be approached from one direction. The canyon mouth is easily held.

"There ain't been no Apache sign in these parts all summer and I don't expect to run across any of them red devils now, but it pays to take all due precautions. Me and the boys'll be keeping watch all night, so don't you folks stay up fretting and worrying. Get a good night's sleep—we got a big day ahead tomorrow."

"Don't nobody go a-wandering, not with all them snakes around in the rocks," Porgy Best added. "They don't call this Yellow Snake Canyon for nothing—them snakes is rattlers."

"Stay together, sleep in your wagons and you'll be fine," Simmons said.

Linda Gordon didn't stay in her wagon, not all night. She woke up an hour or two before dawn. She had to answer a call of nature. She didn't want to leave the wagon, but there was no help for it.

She wore a nightdress. She pulled on a pair of boots and slipped out of the back of the wagon without waking up her folks, Mal and Fran.

The moon was low and there was plenty of moonlight to see by. She stepped carefully, afraid of stepping on a rattlesnake. Her ears were pitched for the telltale sign of a reptilian rattle. She didn't want to go far from the wagon.

A few men were standing and talking around the campfire, which had burned low: Sonny Boy, Sime Simmons, and his two sidemen. Linda was embarrassed to have them see her going to do her business, so she kept the wagon between herself and them.

A man-high rocky outcropping was a stone's throw away. She went to it. She didn't want to climb over it for fear of stumbling over a rattlesnake den in the rocks, so she went around it, behind the back of it. The scent of aloe tasted sweet in her nostrils.

She did what she had to do and started to head back. Hoofbeats sounded—riders were approaching the mouth of the canyon.

Apaches!

Linda opened her mouth to scream a warning, but before she could do so, the men in the camp started shouting and shooting off guns.

Sonny Boy had a gun in each hand. He was holding them pointed up in the air and firing them off one by one, whooping and hollering as he did so.

Karl Haber stuck his head out the back of the wagon. "What is it? Indians—?"

Sonny Boy shot him. Karl Haber fell back into the wagon.

A horrible mistake, thought Linda, frozen in place, peeking around a jagged rock edge. Sonny

Boy must have lost his head and shot Mr. Haber by accident—

Shrieks sounded inside the tentlike covering of the Conestoga, the screams of the Haber females, Karl's wife, Lilli, and his two daughters, Gretchen and Eva.

Lilli Haber popped up in the back of the wagon, clutching the top of the closed tailgate, screaming Karl's name. Seeing Sonny Boy standing nearby with a smoking gun, she cried, "You killed my husband!"

"I killed you, too," Sonny Boy said, coolly and deliberately shooting her.

Linda was so close she could hear the thwack of the bullet impacting flesh.

Lilli Haber's body bowed backwards. Her tight grip on the tailgate kept her from toppling over. She opened her mouth. Dark liquid—blood!— spilled from her mouth, staining the front of her nightdress.

Sonny Boy shot her again. She collapsed, falling across the tailgate, upper body draped across the top, head and arms hanging down toward the ground. Inside the wagon the Haber girls were screaming and crying.

A half-dozen riders came tearing into camp, reining in hard just short of the wagons grouped in a circle. They whooped and shouted, firing their guns, venting fierce bloodcurdling howls and yips. They weren't Apaches, though, not even Indians. They were white men.

Henry McGee jumped down from his wagon, six-gun in hand. He wore a pair of pants and was bare from the waist up and barefoot. A big belly hung over the top of his pants. He darted into the circle of firelight, eyes wild, looking this way and that, trying to make sense of things.

"Henry! Over here!"

McGee looked around to see who'd called his name. It came from Al Jensen, seated on the driver's seat of his wagon fully dressed and with his hat on.

McGee darted toward him. "It's an attack, Al—!"

Jensen pointed a gun at McGee and fired. McGee was hit, and he lurched. He wavered like a flame in a breeze. The gun fell from his hands. He clutched his middle with both hands where he'd been hit.

He dropped to his knees, shocked, disbelieving. Jensen fired two more shots into him.

"Al," McGee whispered, dying. He fell face forward into the dirt.

Lon Brumm and Chris Hooper, two young bachelor farmers who'd come out from Nebraska to Bear Paw and shared a wagon on the trip west, climbed down from their wagon and started shooting at Jensen, banging away at him. They were no good with guns, all their shots going wild.

Someone stepped into view from behind a nearby wagon and opened up on them.

Muzzle flares underlit the shooter's face, revealing Sime Simmons, his eyes and mouth slits. He looked infinitely cruel, vicious.

Chris Hooper was hit, spinning sideways, falling. Lon Brumm shouted, blasting away at Simmons. Simmons put a bullet in him. Lon Brumm staggered. Simmons fired again, felling him.

Chris Hooper was on his hands and knees, feeling around for the gun he'd dropped. Finding it, he straightened up, only to be slapped down by a bullet from Al Jensen's gun.

The riders who'd stormed into the canyon jumped down from their horses, running around the wagons, circling them. They thrust gun hands inside the overarching canvas tents, shooting every male Bear Paw emigrant they found, man and boy.

One of the newcomers stuck his head in the back of the Gordons' wagon. Fran Gordon screamed. The raider fired, silencing the scream.

A tremendous boom followed, the shooter's head exploding. Mal Gordon jumped down from the wagon, double-barreled shotgun in hand.

Mort Donegan shot him. Mal Gordon dropped. Mort moved off in search of other prey.

Mal Gordon wasn't dead. He rose shakily, clutching the shotgun in one hand. He spread his feet wide apart, bracing himself to keep from falling. He gripped the shotgun in both hands, swinging it toward Mort Donegan's back.

Donegan prowled around, too intent on finding fresh prey to realize that imminent doom loomed behind him.

A rifle cracked, once, twice, three times. Each time

it fired, Mal Gordon shuddered, hit. The reports sounded quickly, one after the other, one, two, three.

Mal Gordon dropped.

Linda stuffed a fist in her mouth to keep from screaming.

Carol Jensen stood there, holding a leveled Winchester hip high, a tendril of smoke wriggling from the barrel.

Mort Donegan saw her, and waved, shouting, "Thanks!"

"When you shoot a man, kill him!" Carol said.

"Next time I will!"

"Be more careful or there won't be a next time."

"Yes, ma'am," Donegan said, laughing. He went off, looking for more emigrants to slay.

This was no battle; it was a massacre punctuated by sporadic, largely ineffectual gunfire from those attacked.

The enemy within were Al Jensen, Carol Jensen, Sonny Boy, Sime Simmons, Porgy Best, and Mort Donegan.

The enemy without were the six riders who'd come storming into camp, minus the one whose head had been blown off by Mal Gordon.

Who were they, what did they want? They acted like a pack of crazy killers, Linda thought.

They went from wagon to wagon, killing the males where they found them and dragging out the females. Women and girls were herded shrieking and sobbing around the campfire.

The gunmen took orders from Al Jensen, who

was not shy about giving them. Al and Carol went among the females, selecting out all the wives, mothers, and older women, leaving behind the teenagers and young girls.

Al Jensen stood in a posture of dominance over the youngsters, hat tilted back, hands on hips, booted legs spread wide.

"You belong to Black Angus now," he sneered.

Linda Gordon knew what she had to do. Her parents were dead. There was nothing she could do to help the other girls. It would only be a matter of time before Al Jensen or one of the insiders who'd traveled with the wagon train noticed her absence and set the others searching for her. She couldn't stay where she was. The night sky was lightening and the sun would come up soon.

While the gunmen led the women away, she sneaked out from behind the rock outcropping where she'd been hiding. One of the riders had hitched his horse to a rear wheel of the Gordons' wagon. Bent low, almost double, she snuck over to it.

Linda was trembling so hard she almost couldn't stand. She panted, unable to catch her breath. The horse was a big black. It snorted as she neared it, going around behind it. The bulk of the wagon mostly screened her from view of those inside the circle.

She picked at the reins, knotted around a spoke of the rear wagon wheel. The knot fought her and she broke a nail trying to pick it loose. Biting her lip, she plucked at the reins. Suddenly, the knot came undone.

Linda fisted the reins, turning the horse, walking it away from the wagon. She expected an outcry any second, but no one had yet noticed her.

The women were dragged away kicking and screaming out of the circle of wagons into the restless dark beyond the firelight.

"You know what to do," Al Jensen called to the men taking the women away.

"Sure—like always!" one shouted back.

Linda gripped the pommel, climbing into the saddle.

The women and the men herding them were swallowed up in darkness. After a pause, wails and cries of horror sounded, drowned out by a fusillade of gunfire.

Linda kicked her heels into the horse's flanks, urging it forward. This animal was used to running. It dug dirt and lunged forward, coursing ahead.

When the guns fell silent, the women weren't screaming anymore. The men returned, alone. The horse's hoofbeats were loud in the sudden silence.

"One's getting away—stop her!" somebody shouted.

Men ran after Linda, but she had a good head start. She hunkered down low in the saddle, leaning far forward over the horse's muscular crupper, bent legs hugging its surging flanks.

Shots sounded, bullets streaming past her on all

sides. Darkness hid her and the shooters couldn't see to hit her.

"Get her! Don't let her get away!"

She got away, galloping out of the canyon south across the flat. She crossed the dirt road of the east-west trail, continuing south. She knew from conversations she'd overheard the night before that Tombstone lay some miles to the south. She rode on.

When it was light, Linda looked back and saw two black specks in the distance, pursuing her. All the long day she played cat-and-mouse with the hunters, trying to lose them. Her evasive course often detoured her miles alternately east, then west and back again in a zigzag course down what she would later learn was the Sulphur Spring Valley.

More than once she thought she'd lost her pursuers, only to find the duo once more inexorably on her trail. Sun beat down on her, squeezing the moisture out of her trembling form.

Sometime in late afternoon, she seemed to have lost her pursuers. Sundown came, bringing welcome relief from the naked sun's burning rays. Night fell, and she became lost, riding around in the dark without a clue for some hours.

Moonrise brought the key to her salvation. She knew the moon, like the sun, rose in the east and set in the west. She pointed the horse's head toward where she thought south lay and continued onward.

Later that night, she was unsure when, a patch of light appeared on a hillside to the east. The lights of a town. It was not Tombstone as she'd hoped, but, as she would eventually learn, Cactus Patch.

She rode to it. The horse was on its last legs, panting, unsteady. It had gone without water all day into the night.

Linda reached the outskirts of town. She dismounted, hitching the reins to a bush. She staggered on foot into town.

She almost stumbled into Dorado and Quirt Fane, lurking, waiting for her. She didn't know who they were, but she knew what they were: hunters, bloodhunters dogging her trail.

Having lost her earlier, they must have headed toward the nearest town, knowing that if she saw its lights, she'd make for it. Cactus Patch was that town.

She fled, evading their clutches. A desperate burst of speed propelled her as she darted up and down side streets and alleys at the edge of town. Giving them the slip, she made her way to the main street.

Only she hadn't escaped. Quirt Fane loomed up out of the night, grabbing her. She was lashed and then clubbed into semi-consciousness.

Bob Farr stepped in, trying to help. Shooting broke out. Linda Gordon took her chance. She jumped up and ran for her life.

Return fire from Shorty Kirk's saloon drove off Quirt and Dorado. Bob Farr was dead, another man was badly wounded.

Linda emerged from hiding, falling into the arms of her rescuers.

TEN

Linda Gordon was emotionally and physically exhausted from her ordeal.

Telling her story to those gathered in the marshal's office had left her weak, drained.

"She needs rest and lots of it," *Nugget* editor-publisher Harry Woods said.

"She needs justice," Matt Bodine said, glowering, "and she'll by God have it, as long as I've got a breath in me." His fighting blood was hot, and he was burning to hit the vengeance trail.

Linda looked up at him from where she was sitting, a look of mingled gratitude and appeal in her eyes.

"Colonel Davenport is taking a personal interest in the girl," Arnholt Stebbins said. "He's arranged for a room for her at the hotel. A doctor is there waiting to look after her. We'll need a carriage to take her to the hotel."

"I'll have one of the boys scare one up," Deputy Osgood said.

He was thrilled that Davenport was taking an interest, and not just because the colonel was a millionaire (though that didn't hurt). This was a big thing being dumped in his lap and he was on the lookout for anybody he could slough off some or all of the responsibility onto.

Osgood went outside and hustled up one of the hangers-on to fetch a carriage.

A number of private carriages for hire plied the streets of Tombstone, cruising for fares. It was part of the bustling, hustling commerce of a twenty-four-hour boomtown.

A short time later, the carriage arrived, a four-seater open cab drawn by a single horse. Stebbins and Markand would escort Linda Gordon to the hotel.

Sam put a hand on Stebbins's arm, leading him aside. Stebbins frowned, pinched face expressing distaste. He stared down his long, pointed, turnip nose at Sam's strong copper-colored hand gripping his upper arm.

Sam let go, having no desire to maintain physical contact with Stebbins any longer than necessary.

"What?" Stebbins demanded, his manner that of a man in a hurry too busy to bother with trifles.

"Tell Davenport to put a couple of guards on the girl, men who can take care of themselves and know how to handle a gun," Sam said. He pitched his voice low so Linda would not overhear, not wishing to further disturb her.

"Is that really necessary?" Stebbins said, his

raised eyebrow and sceptical tone implying it was anything but.

"I wouldn't say it if I didn't think it was. Angus Jones—alias 'Black Angus,' alias 'Al Jensen'—is one of the worst bandit chiefs in the territory. He's got a gang of killers at his beck and call. His spies and contacts are everywhere, including right here in Tombstone. Linda Gordon's testimony can put a noose around his neck for the killings at Yellow Snake Canyon, but only if she lives to get to trial," Sam said.

Sam was a patient man who took the trouble to explain things to others less quick on the uptake. He did not suffer fools gladly, but he suffered them. That's why he was bothering to explain the facts of life to Stebbins, because a pinch of foresight now might well spare a pound of grief later.

Stebbins was inclined to make light of the possible threat. "Surely the danger to the girl is past, now that she's safe in town."

"What makes you think so?" Sam countered.

"Why surely, with all these people around, no one would try to harm her—"

"Who's going to stop them? Osgood? The rest of the lawmen are chasing the Wells Fargo robbers, and there's no telling when they'll be back. Black Angus sent Quirt and Dorado after the girl, two of his best men. He might be anywhere, outside town with the rest of his gang, maybe. You're new to these parts so you may not appreciate the seriousness of the matter, but I warn you: don't underestimate Black Angus."

Stebbins looked eager to be anywhere else than here, having Sam Two Wolves giving him an earful. "I'll take it under advisement," he said, fidgeting.

"Don't take it under advisement—do it," Sam insisted. "The colonel's got plenty of bodyguards along, from what I saw at the hotel. It'll be easy to assign a couple to Linda.

"You're a bookkeeper, Stebbins, a man who appreciates the importance of the bottom line. Well, here it is: Like you said, the colonel is taking an interest in the girl. Where'll that leave you if something bad happens to her right under your nose, especially after I've warned you to take proper precautions?"

"I see what you mean," Stebbins said icily. "Everthing will be done to assure Miss Gordon's safety."

"I'll hold you to it, and I mean just that—I'll hold you to it," Sam said. "Lord help you if something happens to that girl, because I surely won't." He let Stebbins be on his way, satisfied he had hammered some sense into the man's head.

Stebbins and Markand escorted Linda to the carriage. Harry Woods went with them. He would stay as close to Linda as possible—he knew a big story when he saw it. And right now, he had an exclusive on it. Rival editor John Clum of the pro–big business, anti-Cowboy *Tombstone Epitaph* newspaper had so far been left out of the running.

The four of them got in the carriage, which set off for the hotel.

Matt Bodine collared an idler loitering outside, a youngster with whom he had a passing acquaintance.

He gave him a five-dollar gold piece and sent him off to the nearest saloon to fetch some bottles of whiskey.

Matt, Sam, Osgood, Ringo, Curly Bill, Lee Lindsey, and Don Brown made themselves comfortable around the office.

Curly Bill commandeered the marshal's chair, the comfortable one, settling himself into it. Osgood scowled, but made no effort to stake his claim to it.

"A hell of a thing," Lee Lindsey said, "a hell of a thing." Everyone nodded agreement: It was a hell of a thing.

"I didn't bring it up when Linda was here," Don Brown began, "but we sent a couple of riders from the Patch to Yellow Snake Canyon, for a look-see. Pete Green and Nick Fargo. Good men, fast riders. They took a string of extra horses along, in case there were any survivors."

He shook his head. "Nary a one. They were all stone dead, men and women. Pete said it looked like all hell. Some had been finished off execution-style with a bullet to the head. There was a couple of youngsters, even, boys no more than five years old, with their brains bashed against the rocks. What kind of man kills a five-year-old boy?"

"Men, hell! They're a pack of mad dogs," Curly Bill said.

"Black Angus must've gone plumb loco," Lee Lindsey said.

"Not hardly," Matt Bodine said. "Mean as a poison snake, sure, but not crazy. He and his gang are slave hunters. They wanted young girls to sell and they took them. They killed everybody else. If the boys had been old enough to take care of themselves on the trail, the slavers would've kept them along—they could always be sold as field hands or house boys. But kids that young need looking after and Jones couldn't be bothered."

"You talk like you know something about the game," Bill said.

"Sam and I tangled with slave hunters once before," Matt said.

"Looks like we'll be tangling with them once again," Sam said. "You can see how Jones worked it. Slavers are always on the lookout for fresh prey. The wagon train was fresh meat. Maybe spotters put Jones on to them, maybe he had the trail staked out waiting for something like them to come along.

"His gang stole the pilgrims' horses. Then Jones comes along the next day with the ponies in tow, playing the part of Al Jensen, Good Samaritan. That's how he ropes them in. He and the woman and Sonny Boy join up with the emigrants. That puts him in position to size up their strengths and weaknesses, find out what kind of firepower they're packing, who'll show fight and who won't.

"At Buckdun Station they meet up with Simmons, accidentally on purpose. Simmons and his two sidemen ride along and that puts five enemy guns in the emigrants' camp."

"Six," Ringo corrected. "The woman Carol is a killer, too. She gunned the Gordon gal's pa." He lit a cigar.

"Six," Sam agreed.

"Sime Simmons has sunk mighty low," Curly Bill said. "I knew him back in the day. He was always hard and with no give in him, but I never figgered him for no woman-killer or nothing like that."

Sam went on. "The ambush was set for Yellow Snake Canyon. That's where Black Angus made the strike. The rest of the Jones gang must've been nearby, waiting for his signal. Yellow Snake Canyon is a good place for a massacre. It's well off the trail. Nobody goes there—it's full of snakes. The killings might've gone undiscovered for a long time and nobody would have known Black Angus was responsible."

Ringo stood leaning against the wall, puffing his cigar, blowing smoke rings.

"It was pure blind luck that Linda Gordon got away," Don Brown said.

"Good luck for her and bad luck for Angus Jones," said Curly Bill.

"A lot of men are going to die because of that turn of fate," Ringo said. "Starting with Dorado and Quirt Fane."

The boy came in with a bag full of whiskey bottles. "Keep the change," Matt told him. The boy said thanks and went out. A bottle was opened and drinks were poured. There weren't enough glasses and tin cups for all, so some drank straight from the bottle, passing it around. It emptied fast and another was opened.

Ringo amused himself between drinks by blowing smoke rings at Osgood when he wasn't looking.

"Where'll they sell the girls?" Lee Lindsey wondered.

"Not in the territory," Osgood said definitely, stating it as fact. "No house or crib, no matter how low, would take the risk. It's a hanging offense, sure. Can't keep something like that secret, for somebody'd be bound to talk. The whoremongers would never reach trial—they'd be lynched outright. Nobody in these parts would stand for something that raw!"

"It won't be in these parts," Sam said. "Slavery may not be legal in Mexico, but it's alive and well and that's a fact. The border is near. Jones'll take them south to be sold into some Mexico City bordello or to a rich *padrón* on a rancho deep in the interior."

"Makes sense," Osgood said, nodding.

"That's where we'll find them," Sam said.

"And we will find them," Matt seconded.

"That's mighty tall talk," Osgood said doubtfully, "a tall order."

"It can be done," Matt said. "Black Angus can be found; he'll leave a trail. About a dozen slavers and how many girls—?"

"Seven," Don Brown said. "We've got a list of their names and descriptions from what Linda told us."

"All that killing for seven girls," Lee Lindsey marveled.

"They'll fetch a high price. Seven girls, and maybe a few more they picked up along the way.

Them and the slavers—they'll leave a trail, all right," Matt said.

"If they leave a trail, I can pick it up," Sam said flatly.

"We know they set out from Yellow Snake Canyon," Matt went on. "Linda Gordon survived to tell the tale and put a name on the slavers. That'll set them running, no shilly-shallying around. They'll make a beeline for Mexico. There's only a few places where they can cross the border with captive girls in tow and wherever they cross they're sure to be noticed. If we hurry, we can pick up their trail and catch up to them before they sell the girls off—maybe."

"Jones may make another try for Linda," Sam warned. "Not himself, he's too well known to show his face in Tombstone. But there's plenty in his gang who'd do the job."

Osgood took notice. He looked disturbed, agitated. "You reckon?"

"One person and only one can put Black Angus in Yellow Snake Canyon and that's Linda Gordon. Without her to point the finger, there's no case. Jones is not the man to leave any loose ends," Sam said.

"Hell, he's already wanted throughout the territory for robbery and murder and a list of crimes as long as both your arms. Why would he bother about this one?"

"You said it yourself, Deputy: This is mighty raw, even for an outlaw or murderer like Black Angus. Killing women and children and selling young girls into whoredom is the sort of thing that sets a fellow an appointment with Judge Lynch. If Jones is ever taken alive, there's always a chance that his gang'll bust him out of jail or his lawyers will win an acquittal. But not if he's taken out of jail at night by a citizens' uplift committee to be hanged by the neck from a sour apple tree."

"Huh!"

Ringo blew another smoke ring at the deputy. Osgood turned his head in time to catch the smoke ring full in the face. It broke apart, getting in his eyes. "Now cut that out, Ringo, dern you!" Osgood said, rubbing his eyes to clear them.

Ringo smiled. "I don't know about playing white knight or Sir Galahad. But Bob Farr was a friend of mine. If I've got to go through Angus Jones and the rest of them to get to Dorado and Quirt, why then, so be it."

"That goes double for me," Curly Bill said.

"Saving the girls has got to be our top priority," Sam said.

Ringo showed a quirked smile that was unreadable. It might have signalled agreement, disagreement, or that he was thinking about some altogether different matter.

It might have meant many things or nothing.

"Time is all important," Matt said. "Best to strike while the captive girls are all bunched together. Once they're sold off and separated, we'll have seven trails to follow, instead of one."

"I'd surely like to go with you boys, but I can't," Osgood hedged.

"Nobody's asking you to."

"Right now I'm the only law in Tombstone."

Ringo drew his gun, holding it up in plain sight. "Here's the only law I need," he said.

"We don't need no tin star to give us his blessing. We can handle it ourselves," Curly Bill said.

"Plenty of tough hombres in town, enough to form a posse to get after Black Angus," said Matt.

"Now don't take it like that, fellows," Osgood protested. "I got responsibilities, I can't just light out—"

"Why don't you go to Yellow Snake Canyon? You ought to feel right at home there, with all them other yellow snakes," Bill cracked. Ringo blew another smoke ring at the assistant deputy.

"Mexico's a big country," Osgood argued. "Once them slavers cross the border, who knows where they'll be?"

"I know," a voice said, a voice unheard from till now in the conversation.

It came from behind the office, from the first cell to the right of the center aisle—

The voice of Gila Chacon. He stood pressed against the near wall of his cage, facing the office, his hands at shoulder height, each gripping a vertical iron bar.

"Shut your mouth, Mex!" Osgood shouted, red faced, blustering. To the others he said, "He don't know nothing. He's talking big, trying to get hisself off the hook—"

"I wonder," Sam said thoughtfully. Something in the bandit's tone had rung with a note of conviction, of simple truth.

It must have struck Matt the same way. "Let him talk. It won't hurt to listen," he said.

He crossed to the rear of the office, where he could see Gila Chacon better. "What is it you know, or think you know?"

"I know where Dorado is going," Gila said.

That got Ringo's attention. He pushed off with his shoulders from the wall where he'd been leaning, to turn and face the bandit. "Where?"

Gila smiled slowly, showing a mouthful of yellowed teeth in a wide Cheshire Cat grin. "What is in it for me?" he asked.

Curly Bill took that wrong, nostrils flaring, neck swelling. "You go to the hangman with all your teeth and no bones broken."

"It takes more than that to frighten Gila Chacon," the bandit said, his grin undiminished.

"Pshaw!" Deputy Osgood made a dismissive gesture, scoffing. "He's just talking, running his mouth in hopes of saving his worthless hide. He's got nothing!"

Gila shrugged. "In a matter of such importance I would think that you would at least try to find out if my words are true . . . which they are, I assure you."

"Prove it," Curly Bill said. Ringo stood silent, listening attentively.

"I could not help but overhear the tragic tale of the so-unfortunate señorita Linda."

Gila pronounced it "Leen-dah." "She spoke of the woman who called herself 'Carol,' who has a scar like a zee running down the side of her face,"

Gila said, his index finger tracing a zigzag course caressingly along his left cheek.

"So?" Bill said.

"That scar—I put it there. Do not think ill of me for it, señores. She was trying to kill me at the time."

"I'm listening," Matt said, prompting him to continue.

"Her name is not Carol. It is Carmen—Carmen Oliva. She is the half-sister of the Golden Man, El Dorado," Gila said.

"Now I'm listening," Ringo breathed, moving closer.

"They have the same mother, Carmen and Dorado—a whore—and different fathers. Both bastards. They have the same color hair, reddish-brown, like old dried blood. A color which suits them."

Sam turned to Lee Lindsey and Don Brown. "What color hair did Carol have? Did Linda say?"

Lindsey shrugged. Don Brown said, "If she did, I didn't catch it."

"Ask her," Gila said. "Women, girls, they notice such things. It is important to them. Ask her, she will tell you it is so."

"We will if it's needful," Sam said. "Say Carol is Carmen Oliva, Dorado's sister. What of it?"

"There is more. You, señor, the man with the honest face," Gila said, speaking to Matt. "We spoke earlier today. I told you of my home of Pago, in Sonora."

"That's right, you did," Matt said.

"Carmen, Dorado, and I all come from Pago. We

grew up together. Once we were all great friends. With Carmen and I, it was more than friendship. She was my woman—my wife.

"I spoke, too, of my enemy in Pago, who sent *pistoleros* to kill me—which is why I am in this stinking jail. Don Carlos is his name—Don Carlos de la Vega. He is a big man, the master of Pago. The *padrón*. A rich man. Carmen preferred him to me. She betrayed me. They tried to kill me.

"I escaped, but not before my knife marked Carmen with the scar. Don Carlos did not want her after that. She was very unhappy, but she got over it. She is a great whore, is Carmen. She has been with many men. She met her match in the outlaw Jones— Black Angus, you call him. Now they are lovers.

"How did Don Carlos get rich? I will tell you, señores. He is a slave trader, the biggest in Sonora if not all Mexico. His men search the land for fresh young girls. Virgins, innocent, untasted. Stolen away from their families, never to be seen by them again.

"Jones and Carmen—and Dorado—they are slave hunters for Don Carlos. They take the captive girls to the great slave market at Pago, to be sold at auction at the opera house. It has a name: '*La Casa de las Lloronas*,' the House of Crying Women. It is where the Apaches, the *bandidos*, and the gringo slave hunters bring their captive women and girls for to sell.

"At the end of the summer raiding season, buyers come to Pago from all over Mexico—from Mexico

City, Guanajuato, Tlaxcala, Vera Cruz, Durango, many more. Some come from as far as Guatemala and Salvador. Pimps, procurers, whoremongers, madams of high-priced bordellos, *padrónes* from lonely ranchos in the hills, and others worse—far worse. All come to the slave auction, and they pay in gold. For them it is like going to market to buy cattle. Young virgins bring the best prices and and gringa virgins bring the highest prices of all.

"The House of Crying Women in Pago. That is where you will find Jones, and Dorado, and the captive girls of whom the Señorita Linda spoke," Gila finished.

"A fine tale," Sam said, "but how can you prove what you say?"

"At my trial, such as it was, I told of Don Carlos sending men from Pago to kill me. Ask him, he was there," Gila said, indicating Osgood.

"Sure, he told some cock-and-bull story about the men he killed. I didn't pay it no never mind and neither did the jury," Osgood said.

"Did he testify about any Don Carlos?" Sam asked.

"He might have. I don't recollect."

"Look at the trial records and you will see that what I say is true," Gila pressed.

"Maybe he did name a certain Don Carlos, but so what?" Osgood fired back testily. "He was found guilty of stealing Judge Randall's horse and duly sentenced to hang. He sure didn't say nothing about no captive gals or slave auction, believe you me."

"It did not affect my defense, so I did not bring it up."

"That's mighty slim," Matt said. "Got anything else to back it up?"

"There is the matter of knowing Carmen's hair color without the Señorita Linda having spoken of it," Gila said.

"If Linda Gordon says this Carmen or Carol has red hair, that would be something in your favor. A small something," Sam said. "You might have met Carmen before or picked up some gossip in the cantinas. It proves nothing about Black Angus taking the girls to Pago."

"You are a hard man to convince, señor," Gila said, sighing.

"You're trying to save your neck, so you'd say anything."

"There are other Mexicans in town, and many of them, I know. I was among them before I was caught and put in jail. Ask them about Don Carlos and the slave market of Pago; some of them are sure to know the truth."

"We will. Anything else?"

Gila shugged. "I could tell you much more about Carmen and Dorado, but it would prove nothing about them taking the girls to Pago. I can think of two ways to prove the truth of my words. Catch one of Jones's men and make him talk."

"Easier said than done. We don't have any Black Angus men."

"You might, if they come to kill the girl."

"That's one way, maybe. An awful iffy one. What's the other?" Sam challenged.

"Why, it is simplicity itself. Take me with you to Pago. If the girls are there, set me free and I will help you. If I lie, kill me and be done with it," Gila said, smiling.

"You'd like that, wouldn't you?" Osgood said, laughing derisively. He turned to the others. "Hell, you don't believe this jumped-up chicken thief, do you? He'd say anything to keep from hanging."

"Parts of his story make sense. It explains why Dorado's teamed up with Black Angus and Quirt Fane," Matt said.

"Aw, bosh!" Osgood spat.

"It might be true and it might not be. It's worth checking on, the parts that can be checked," Sam said. "Ringo, you and Bill have spent some time in Mexico. This ring any bells with you?"

"I've never been to Pago. You, Bill?" Ringo asked.

"Not me, John. I've heard of it, though. A big market for white slaves, they say."

"I've heard that, too, but that's all I know."

"Women stealing is out of our line. It's a filthy game and we wouldn't have nothing to do with it," Curly Bill said to the others.

"Which leaves us pretty much where we started," Sam said. "Still, it's a lead, no matter how slim. What say we head over to the hotel to have a word with Linda Gordon, Matt?"

"I'm game."

"I've got some amigos over to the Mex side of

town. Ringo and I'll prowl the cantinas, see what we can pick up on the grapevine. Okay with you, John?"

"Sounds good, Bill."

"Lee and I'll tag along if you boys don't mind," Don Brown offered.

"Glad to have you," Curly Bill said.

They stirred, readying to go out, all but Osgood. "You can go off on a wild goose chase if you want. I'm gonna stay right here. And right here's where Chacon's gonna stay, till the hangman calls for him."

"Let's go, time's a-wasting," Matt urged.

"Do not delay, señores," Gila cautioned. "The auction in Pago comes soon."

"When?"

"This coming Saturday, I believe."

"Haw! If that don't tear it—!" Osgood exploded. "The slave auction is Saturday, same day he's slated for a hanging! If that don't prove to you fellows he's talking out of his hat to save his miserable hide, nothing will!"

"You will see that I speak the truth, and then you must come to Gila. I know Pago and its wicked ways. I have many friends there. You need me as guide. Without my help, you will never get within a mile of the auction at La Casa. You will succeed only in going before a firing squad. You need me, hombres."

Curly Bill grunted. "And all we got to do is set you free?"

"*Sí*, a fair trade. Better—my life for seven young lives. A poor sinner for seven *pobrecitas*, seven poor, innocent, young girls. And the lives of the men you seek, Dorado and the man Quirt Fane, the ones who killed your friend."

"If you speak truly, Gila, we'll be back," Matt said.

"And if you're lying, I'll be back, too, to peel the hide off a' you," Curly Bill said.

The six exited. "The Mex kind of sounds like he knows what he's talking about," Don Brown ventured.

"My amigos over to the cantinas'll tell if he speaks the straight of it," Curly Bill said.

"I hope so," said Sam. "We better find out one way or the other—and quick."

ELEVEN

Matt and Sam headed for Allen Street, while the others went off to Tombstone's Mexican district. Low clouds bottomed the sky, hiding moon and stars. The air was heavy. It felt like it was going to rain.

The crowd had cleared out of Allen Street, but the Hotel Erle was still crowded. Sam and Matt entered. The lobby and bar were packed with people talking over the night's events:

"Ain't it a shame about them pore gals?"

"It's a damned outrage!"

"I'm scared! What if the slave hunters come to Tombstone?"

"If they do, they'll have a hell of a time finding a virgin—oww! What'd you go and slap my face for, Myrtle?"

"There's nothing funny about woman stealing!"

"I'll make it up to you—let me buy you a drink."

"Well—just one . . ."

The duo went to the front desk. Manager Mark Fredericks was on duty behind the counter. "Howdy, Mark," Sam said.

The manager nodded.

"What room's the Gordon girl in?"

"I'm not supposed to give that information out—"

"It's all right, we're with Colonel Davenport," Matt said, lying quickly.

"Oh. Well, if that's the case, I'm sure it's all right. Room two-oh-seven, across the hall from the colonel's suite."

"Thanks."

"But you can't go in. The church ladies have the girl in tow. Mrs. Sanderson and Mrs. Whiteside. Couple of battle-axes, if you ask me," Mark Fredericks confided.

"Matt'll get along fine with them—he's righteous, too," Sam said.

"A fine man, that Colonel Davenport," the manager said, "a great man!"

"A rich man," Sam said. He and Matt turned, went to the lobby, pausing at the foot of the grand staircase. "You go and talk to the girl, Matt. I want to look around, see what I can see."

"Okay, Sam."

Matt climbed the stairs to the second floor, crossing the landing and going down the hall. Wall-mounted globed gas lamps were cones of amber light alternating with bands of muddy-brown shadows. The lamps' glow fluttered and vibrated, a faint whooshing noise of gas pouring through wallpipes into the fixtures.

The long carpeted corridor was lined with room doors on either side. Room 207 was near the landing, on the right-hand side of the corridor.

A gunman sat in a chair outside the door, one of Davenport's men. Matt recalled seeing him earlier, hovering around the fringes of the scene in Davenport's suite. Stebbins must have taken Sam's warning to heart about setting guards on Linda, Matt was pleased to see.

The guard had short-cropped hair, a neatly trimmed mustache, and a wide, flat, level-eyed face. He wore a black broadcloth suit, knotted black ribbon tie, white shirt, boots. A six-gun was holstered at his side.

"Bodine, with the marshal's office," Matt said, taking the initiative. "Deputy Osgood sent me to ask the Gordon girl a couple of questions. You saw me before when my partner and I met with the colonel in his suite."

"I remember you. I'm Riker, one of Davenport's men."

"Glad to know you."

"Go on in, if you can get by those two old biddies in there. The doc's in there, too."

Matt reached for the door handle. Somebody turned it on the other side, opening the door outward.

Dr. Willis came out. A well-respected Tombstone medical man, he had gray hair, gray tufted eyebrows, a gray mustache, and a long, seamed, suntanned face. He carried a black doctor's bag in his hand.

He knew Matt. Matt hoped Willis wouldn't inadvertently tip Riker that he, Matt, had a thin connection at best with the marshal's office.

"Hello, Matt."

"Howdy, Doc. How's Linda Gordon doing?"

"She'll be all right. She's suffering from the effects of shock and exposure, but she's otherwise unharmed. She's young and strong; the young have great recuperative powers. What she needs now is sleep, lots of it."

"I need to talk to her. It'll only take a minute."

Willis opened his mouth to make what Matt was sure would be an objection, so Matt said swiftly, "A single question, Doc, just one, but it's important. I came over from the marshal's office to find out something. It could be important to helping out those other girls, the ones who got took."

"Under the circumstances, I suppose I'll have to say yes," the medic grumped.

"Thanks, Doc."

Willis stepped back inside, Matt following. The hall door opened on to a tiny anteroom with wood-paneled, shoulder-height wainscoting, and above that, burgundy patterned wallpaper to the ceiling.

At the far end of the anteroom stood a second door, closed. Female voices could be heard behind it.

"Better let me go first," Dr. Willis said, easing past Matt. He knocked sharply once on the door panel, opened the door, and let himself in without waiting for a by-your-leave. He eased the door partly closed behind him.

He talked to those inside. A woman answered him back, and he said something else and then opened the door. "Come on in, Matt."

Matt entered a bedroom. Within were Linda Gordon, a pair of Tombstone matrons, and the doctor.

The room was large. A bed stood against a wall to the left, a writing desk stood at the opposite end on the right. There was a chest of drawers with an oval mirror mounted on a stand atop it, and a couple of comfortable armchairs. Light was provided by a wall gas lamp and a portable lamp set on the nightstand on the left side of the bed in which Linda lay.

Mrs. Sanderson and Mrs. Whiteside stood hovering over Linda. They were fiftyish, the wives of well-to-do businessmen. They were leaders of the church ladies' auxiliary do-gooding society and a pair of eminently respectable dowagers.

Mrs. Sanderson was short, pigeon breasted, with a massive swelling bosom; Mrs. Whiteside was built like a fence post. They looked at Matt like he was something the cat dragged in.

Matt touched the tip of his hat, self-conscious. "Howdy, ladies."

Mrs. Sanderson sniffed. Mrs. Whiteside said, "You don't belong here."

Dr. Willis stepped in. "I explained that you'll only be a minute and that you have my permission.

"Be quick about it, Matt," he added.

Matt went to Linda Gordon's bedside, standing

on her right. Linda lay sitting up in bed, her back propped up by pillows. Somewhere they'd found a long-sleeved, white cotton nightdress for her. Blankets and sheets were drawn up to her waist.

Matt took off his hat, holding it in front of him. "Hello, Linda. You remember me from the marshal's office?"

She nodded, wide-eyed, solemn.

"I need to ask you a couple of questions to clear up one or two points. I wouldn't be bothering you if it wasn't important. It could be a big help."

"I'll try," she said.

"It may sound silly, but it's not. It could help us get a lead on the outlaws and the girls they took. Here goes: The woman, Carol—what color hair did she have? Was she a brunette, or blonde . . . ?"

"Red hair. She had red hair. She kept it covered mostly with a hat or scarf, but I saw once when she was washing it in a basin. Red hair, not bright red or orange, but muddy. That's it, muddy. It was the color of the banks of the Red River, a kind of reddish-brown."

"That's fine. Now, did Jensen or Sonny Boy ever call her anything but Carol? Ever address her by any other name?"

Linda thought it over long and hard. "Not that I can remember."

"One more. What was she like? Apart from the scar, we know about that. But was she tall or short, thin or fat, fair or dark?"

"She came from Mexico, I think," Linda said. "That's what all the women from Bear Paw said, though some thought she was a 'breed. She looked Mexican, dark, kind of fierce looking in a way, apart from the scar. She had a good figure—the men couldn't stop talking about it.

"The damned fools," she added bitterly.

Mrs. Whiteside gasped. "Such language!"

"Now, now, Linda, I know you've been through a lot, but you mustn't say such words. It's not lady-like," Mrs. Sanderson chided.

Linda sat up straight, proud chin defiantly out-thrust, arms folded across her chest.

"That's good, Linda, a big help. Anything else you recall about Carol?"

"She killed my father."

"And the other two, Jensen and Sonny Boy. They ever say anything about where they came from, places they'd been, where they were bound? Things like that?"

"Al Jensen talked a lot. He was a great one for talking. But when you listened to it, he never said anything about himself, never gave away anything. As for Sonny Boy, he took his cue fom his uncle, if Jensen was his uncle. He never talked much except when he was drunk and then he talked a lot of silly nonsense, like a damned fool."

Mrs. Sanderson tsk-tsked and Mrs. Whiteside said, "Well!"

"That's all I can think of. Sorry I can't remember anything else," Linda said.

"You've been a big help, Linda. If anything else comes to mind, tell Colonel Davenport or Mr. Steb-bins and have them leave word at the front desk for

Matt Bodine—that's me. The manager'll see I get word," Matt said. "I'll be moseying along. I hope you get well soon. Again, thanks."

"I hope you find the outlaws."

"I hope so, too, Linda."

"I hope you kill them."

The church ladies gasped.

"Kill them all, Jensen and Sonny Boy and Carol and the whole filthy bunch of them," Linda said.

"If I find them, I will. And I'll sure try to find them—that's a promise," Matt said.

"I believe you."

"Good night, Linda. Try and get some rest." Matt stepped away from the bedside. "Good night, ladies."

"Good night," Mrs. Sanderson said frostily, while Mrs. Whiteside vented a heartfelt "Hmmph!"

"'Night, Doc."

"Wait up, Matt, I'll go out with you."

Matt and Dr. Willis went through the anteroom out into the hall, Willis closing the door behind him.

"Whew! I don't think those ladies liked me too well," Matt said, fitting his hat on his head.

"Hell, they haven't liked anything too well since Buck Buchanan was president back in fifty-six," Willis said. "That help any, what you got from the girl?"

"I think so. It confirms a key point of a story I'm checking. I'll know better later. That Al Jensen Linda spoke of, that's Angus Jones—Black Angus."

"I know," Willis said grimly. "Word like that spreads like wildfire. Going after that bunch, Matt?"

"I'm seriously studying on the subject, Doc."

"You'll go. You and Sam both. You're like fire horses—as soon as you hear the alarm bells you're up and running."

"I've killed better men for less," Matt admitted.

"This scum needs killing," Willis growled, angry, red faced under his deep bronze tan.

"I'll tell you who is on their trail: Ringo and Brocius. Jones's men killed a friend of theirs, shot him in the back."

"That'll give Black Angus some sleepless nights," Willis said. Then he added, more seriously, "Watch yourself, Matt. Be careful out on the trail."

"I can take care of myself, Doc."

"It's not only Jones you have to look out for—it's Ringo, too. He's a strange one, surprisingly decent one day and a half-crazed killer the next, with no rhyme or reason for his moods except that he's a bad drunk, and he's drunk most of the time.

"I once had occasion to be in a saloon with him where he bought me a drink. Needless to say I accepted gratefully and returned the favor by buying him one, too. Believe it or not, he's an educated man, a reader, knows Shakespeare and the classics."

"He should get along with Sam then. Sam's a great one for reading, too."

"From what I've heard, Ringo doesn't much get along with anyone, except for Brocius and a few others. Riding with him is like playing with dynamite."

"I'd rather ride with him than have to ride against him," Matt said, grinning. "I've got to be on my way, Doc. Going downstairs?"

Willis shook his head. "I'm going to nip next door for a word with Davenport. He's footing the bills for Linda Gordon, medical bills, lodging, the works. Maybe I can wangle a snifter or two of that good Napoleon brandy he keeps out of view."

"The colonel's a pretty free-handed host. It's that Stebbins you've got to watch out for," Matt laughed.

Willis went across the hall and knocked on the door of Room 206. The door opened and Stebbins let him in. Matt stepped back, out of the sight lines so Stebbins wouldn't see him. He wasn't in the mood for Stebbins or Davenport right now.

He looked down the long hall, toward the rear of the building. "There's a back stairs there at the end of the hall. Might not be a bad idea to set a guard on it," Matt said to Riker, sitting beside Linda Gordon's room door.

"Good thought. I'll pass it along," Riker said.

"See you," Matt said. Riker nodded.

Matt went to the landing, looking down at the ground-floor lobby. He didn't see Sam. He went downstairs, into the bar. Plenty of people were there but Sam was not among them. Buckskin Frank Leslie was still on duty tending bar. Matt went to him.

"Drink?" Frank asked.

"A quick one," Matt said.

Frank poured a shot and Matt downed it, liking the fiery warmth rushing through his veins.

"Seen Sam?" Matt asked.

"I was just talking to him."

"Where'd he go?"

Frank shrugged. "We were talking, just chewing

the fat, when he broke off and said he'd see me later. I thought he saw somebody he knew and went to speak to him. Seemed perfectly natural so I didn't give it a second thought. Besides, I had some customers to take care of. Ain't he around?"

"I don't see him. Did you see who he spotted?"

"I wasn't looking." Frank gave Matt a shrewd, sharp glance. "Any trouble?"

"I don't think so."

"Sam didn't seem upset or excited or nothing. 'Course, he's a hard man to read—that poker face of his don't crack too much. He said he had to take care of something and he'd see me later."

"When was this, Frank?"

"No more'n ten minutes ago."

"Forget it, it's probably nothing," Matt said. He reached into a breast pocket of his shirt, feeling around for a coin. "How much for the drink?"

"On the house."

"Thanks," Matt said. He went to the front desk. "Sam leave any messages for me?"

"No," the manager, Mark Fredericks, said. "Haven't seen him."

Matt said thanks and went out. He stood on the broad front porch, standing beside one of the uprights supporting the front balcony. He let his eyes become accustomed to the dimness. Allen Street was not dark, not with all those hotel and saloon front windows ablaze with light.

Matt scanned up and down the street, looking for Sam, not finding him. He was not particularly worried. Sam was a tough customer and not one to be easily taken. Matt was more puzzled than anything else.

Maybe Sam had been called away, or maybe he was on the scent of big game. It remained to be seen which.

Matt went down the front steps into the street. He went to the corner of Allen and Fourth Street, peering into front windows and along the boardwalk sidewalks, looking for Sam, and not finding him.

Working back along the other side of the street, he made his way to Fifth Street, again experiencing no success in finding Sam. He started to turn back toward the hotel to wait for Sam there, when he caught sight of something across the street on the corner.

An orange dot showed in the dark recessed doorway of a shop that was closed for the night. The glow was at head height, brightening, then dimming.

It was the lit end of a cigar being smoked, the smoker's features being wanly underlit, heavy-featured with shadow, outlined with orange highlights. Matt recognized the other man, and went to him. "Ringo," he said.

"You've got good eyes, Bodine," Ringo said.

"Any news? Anything breaking?"

"Not at my end. Sorry. I left Curly Bill and the others working the cantinas, looking for word about Chacon and Dorado and all. Bill's a sociable cuss. He knows everybody and likes to talk to people."

"But not you, eh, Ringo?"

"Generally no. Bill'll get more out of them without me hanging over his shoulder glooming things up. Some of those Mexes figure I've got what they call the *ojo malo.*"

"'The evil eye,'" Matt said. "Those folks run to superstition some time."

"Yes and no. I'm not sure but what there might be something to what they say," Ringo opined.

Matt thought the same, but kept it to himself. "Seen Sam?"

"No, is he missing?"

"Well, he wandered off about ten minutes ago."

"I got here about five minutes ago. I got to thinking about what you two said about Jones's men making a play for the girl and figured I could do more good here, laying back out of sight and keeping an eye out for them."

"There were no shots or dead bodies around so I guess you didn't see them."

"Got me figured out pretty well, don't you, Bodine?"

"I wouldn't presume on that score, Ringo."

Ringo chuckled. "Maybe your pard got on the trail of something big."

"Maybe," Matt allowed.

Ringo finished his cigar, tossing the stub into the street. "Hell, I'm no good at playing a waiting game. Let's mosey over to the Big Sky for a drink. I could use one. Bill's supposed to meet me later when he's done making his rounds."

"All right. Let me leave word for Sam." Matt motioned to one of the many street urchins loitering on Allen Street, gesturing for him to come over.

The boy darted to them. He was about ten, needing a haircut, and dressed in ragged clothes.

"Go into the Hotel Erle and tell the man behind the front desk that Matt says to tell Sam to meet him at the Big Sky Saloon." Matt had the youngster repeat the message to show he'd gotten it right.

"Don't let anybody put you out of the hotel until you give the clerk the message."

"Mister, nobody puts me out less'n they can catch me first and that takes some doing!"

Matt gave him a half-dollar. "Thanks!" the boy said, taking off at a run, angling across the street to the hotel. "Spunky kid," Matt said.

"He'll need it in this town," Ringo said.

"Let's walk."

"Hell, yes! I'm not paying some cabman to ferry me a couple of blocks across town, not when I've got two good legs."

They went east, walking along the south side of Allen Street. The thoroughfare was quieter this side of Fifth Street. There were some cheaper, less brightly lit hotels, a boardinghouse for "respectable" women, and some stores and shops that were closed for the night.

"How'd you make out at the hotel?" Ringo asked. Matt said that Linda Gordon had described Carol/Carmen as a redheaded woman, most likely Mexican.

"That's a point in Chacon's favor," Ringo said.

"It's a slim lead, but there's something about Gila that makes me suspect he's telling the truth. Call it a hunch. It's a fact that he was telling me about Pago earlier today, long before Linda showed."

"Curly Bill's got a lot of Mex friends, especially among the señoritas. If there's anything to Chacon's story, Bill will ferret it out. Folks just naturally tend to like him, like talking to him. Bill's a likeable cuss," Ringo said, "not like me."

A man stood on the corner of Fifth and Allen, watching the two. Their backs were to him, so they were unaware of his presence.

Matt and Ringo turned right on Sixth Street, going south. The man on the corner turned, hurrying south on Fifth Street. His horse was hitched to a rail near the corner. The man untied the reins, gathered them up, and swung up into the saddle.

He rode south to the intersection of Fifth and the next cross street, Toughnut Street. He halted, sitting his horse there, looking east, waiting.

"It'll make things a whole lot easier if Gila is telling the truth. Easier, but not easy," Matt said.

"We can hash things out at the Big Sky, start making plans," Ringo said. "I figure we'd best hit the trail no later than sunup tomorrow."

"I agree. We're going to have a problem with Osgood. He won't let Gila go, even if we need him."

"If we need him, there won't be any problem. You let me handle the deputy."

Matt cut a sharp side-glance at Ringo. "No killing, mind."

Ringo laughed. "That pissant? I wouldn't waste a bullet on him. All I have to do is say 'boo' to Osgood and he'll fall over in a dead faint."

Sixth Street was dark, and largely deserted. A breeze lifted from the east. "Nice night," Ringo said.

It started to rain. "Maybe you do have the evil eye," Matt joked.

The rain came down lightly, like mist, a thin warm drizzle that blurred the scene and threw haloes around the street lamps. Matt and Ringo turned left on Toughnut Street, going east.

The rider rode to the street below and parallel to Toughnut, spurring the horse to a run east.

East of Sixth Street lay Tombstone's red-light district. There were blocks of wooden frame houses serving now as sporting houses. Matt and Ringo's route largely skirted the south fringe of the district to avoid being importuned by the numerous street-walkers working the area. The Big Sky Saloon was southeast of the red-light district, in an enclave of bars, dives, and gin mills.

Matt and Ringo entered a border zone between the red-light district and the saloons. It comprised several square blocks of warehouses and storehouses, now closed for the night, a kind of no-man's-land.

They came to a cross street. In the next square south stood a half-dozen or so men on foot, along with a rider, the watcher who'd been dogging Matt since Allen Street.

The group fell into step with the duo, exiting the square into the cross street, where they were screened behind a row of buildings.

Matt loosed the rawhide loops securing the tops of his guns in the holsters

"Trouble?" Ringo asked, knowing the answer, a

faint smiling playing around the corners of his lips. He hoped it was trouble; he'd be disappointed if it weren't.

"The Lincoln County crowd have a mad on against Sam and me for ventilating some of their compadres. It might not be too healthy for you to be seen walking with me," Matt said.

"Ringo walks where he pleases. I've got a few enemies of my own in town. Maybe they're some of mine."

"We'll find out soon enough."

From a distance came the sound of running feet, a fair number of them. Matt and Ringo had reachd the middle of the block. Suddenly, the square ahead to the east filled with a knot of men, the group that had been pacing them along the parallel street south.

They stood blocking the way, facing west, facing Matt and Ringo.

The two halted. A sound behind them made them look back. A second group appeared in the square at the opposite end of the street, closing it off.

"More company," Matt said.

"We'll make a party of it," Ringo said.

"You don't have to mix in. It's not your fight."

"Don't talk stupid. I can't back out now, even if I wanted to. And I don't want to."

The group in the rear fanned out, moving forward, walking east along the middle of the street. Their pace was measured, deliberate, ominous.

Matt and Ringo both wore twin guns. They fisted

their weapons, leveling them, looking around for the best place to make a stand.

A stone's throw east on the north side of the street there was a gap between two warehouse buildings, an alley. Somewhere in the alley a coyote yipped.

"Coyote in the alley? Hell, no! That's no coyote," Ringo snarled.

"It's not—it's Sam," Matt said, grinning.

"You sure? I'd hate to go into an alley and meet the wrong coyote," Ringo said.

"That's the right coyote. It's a signal we've used in the past," Matt said.

"Then what are waiting for? Things are about to get hot out here on the street—let's go!"

The street was ill lit, and dim; what little light there was reached only a few feet into the alley. Beyond that, the alley was black dark, with a faint glow at the opposite end where it opened on Tough-nut Street.

Matt and Ringo ducked into the alley. It was eight feet wide, hemmed in on both sides by ware-house walls two-stories high. They crouched low to present less of a target to anyone shooting blindly into the alley.

Motion stirred within the darkness as a manlike form separated itself from the shadows to loom up before Matt and Ringo. "Psst! Matt!" it said.

"Don't shoot, Ringo, it's Sam," Matt said. He stumbled over a body which he hadn't seen where it lay sprawling on the ground. He tripped, almost falling before he recovered his balance. He swore under his breath.

"He was waiting here with this," Sam said, holding a double-barreled shotgun.

"Who is he?" Matt asked.

"One of the New Mexico crowd. So're the ones out in the street. Waco's with them."

They spoke in low voices. "Where'd you disappear to, Sam?"

"Tell you later. The hombre on the ground was waiting for you. The plan must have been to stampede you into the alley, straight into a load of double-ought buck."

"He dead?"

"No, I snuck up on him and knocked him out."

"Should've killed him, the bushwhacking bastard," Ringo said. He planted a vicious kick to the side of the head of the unconscious man. There was a sharp snapping sound.

"I think you broke his neck," Matt said.

"Hope so," Ringo said.

He peeked around the corners of the alley mouth, keeping watch. Men with drawn guns advanced from both ends of the street, closing in on the alley. They moved slowly, warily.

"They're holding off, like they're waiting for something," Ringo said.

"They're waiting for the bushwhack kill, so let's not disappoint them," Sam said.

Matt got the idea. He shouted, "No— No, don't—!"

Sam triggered a double-barreled shotgun blast harmlessly into the air. It sounded like a thunderclap exploding in the alley. Matt suddenly silenced a choked outcry, cutting it off in mid-screech.

Playing along with the subterfuge, Ringo shouted triumphantly, "Got 'em!"

Shouts and whoops came from the street. Sam broke the shotgun, shucking out the spent cartridges and loading up with some fresh ones. "The ambusher had a pocketful of shells. Let's put them to good use."

He stepped forward, outlining his silhouette in the alley mouth but hanging back so his face and form were hidden in shadow. "I got 'em!—both of 'em!" he cried, making his voice gruff, unrecognizable.

A couple of gunmen nearest the alley straightened up, starting toward it. "Nice work, Clem!" said one.

Another blurted, "Wait, that ain't Clem—"

The trio was bunched up in front of the alley mouth, facing it. Sam cut loose with both barrels, the blast ripping into them. Two men were hammered flat, mortal shrieks of agony sounding as their bodies thumped down to the hardpacked dirt of the street.

The third caught the edge of the fan, pellets peppering his side. He reeled, staggering, spinning, shrieking. He triggered a shot by reflex, the bullet going wild.

Sam stepped back into the alley, standing with his back flattened against a wall as he broke the smoking shotgun and reloaded.

Matt and Ringo were already in action, sheltering

behind their respective corners of the alley mouth, reaching out to shoot around them. Matt knelt on one knee, turned to the east, where dark outlines of figures shifted and darted, spectral in the thin, misty drizzle.

Two men scrambled across the street, from its south side to its north side. One had a broad-brimmed hat and two guns; the other had one gun and wore his pants tucked into the tops of his boots.

Matt loosed some shots at them as they ran for cover. A slug tagged the one-gun man; he fell, spilling into the street, and lay there cursing and writhing.

Two-Gun reached the safety of a deep-set doorway. He blasted away at Matt, firing high, bullets tearing into the sharp-edged corner of the building behind which Matt knelt. Splinters and wood chips flew, Matt squinting to protect his eyes.

Two-Gun leaned farther out of the cover of the doorway, angling for a better shot at Matt. Matt shot him in the leg. The leg folded, toppling Two-Gun sideways to the plank sidewalk, which he hit with a crash.

He dropped one gun, but held on to the other. He lay on his side, raising himself up on an elbow, and shooting at Matt. Matt's next shot hit him in the head, sending his hat flying up into the air.

Ringo stood beside the wall, shoulder touching it, body turned at an angle. His arm was extended like that of a duellist, gun barrel protruding beyond the wall's edge as he coolly fired into a knot of figures clustered together west of the alley.

Ringo plinked away target-shooter style, picking off the foe one by one. They separated, scattering. Those on the wings of the group went to cover, while those in the center fell to rise no more.

No matter where they were, those on the street dodged for cover, throwing themselves into doorways, huddling behind abutments or the roundness of decorative half-columns on building façades. Others, caught out in the open with no shelter nearby, flattened themselves, lying prone on the ground or sidewalks. They returned fire, joining in concert and beginning to really pour it on.

Gunfire filled the street with a tremendous racket, cataracts of noise. Six-guns popped like strings of firecrackers, muzzle flares thrusting spears of red-yellow light that laced the gloomy haze of drizzling rain. The growing number of wounded shrieked and cried in pain and fear.

A couple of gunmen at the far ends of the street exercised the better part of valor by discreetly absenting themselves from the melée, slinking off into the night.

"They're stalled for now—let's vamoose," Sam said.

"You go. I'll lay down some covering fire," Matt said, proceeding to do so.

Sam and Ringo withdrew, easing back into the depths of the alley. They halted just short of where the opposite end of the alley emptied out on Toughnut Street.

Cradling the reloaded shotgun in his arms, Sam gingerly peeked around the corner of the north alley mouth, surveying the street. He looked right and left, east and west.

Toughnut Street seemed clear. This stretch of it was largely shuttered and closed by night and the lightly falling rain had discouraged pedestrians from taking the air. Mainly though, Tombstone folks knew to make themselves scarce when gunfire erupted, a too-frequent occurrence in the boomtown.

The entire incident of gunplay thus far had barely taken more than two minutes, if that, from the first shotgun blast to the current blistering exchange.

Matt faded back to join Sam and Ringo at the north end of the alley. The trio peeled out of the alley to the left, west, removing themselves from the line of fire of bullets sent down the passageway. They stood with their backs against the wall of a warehouse, facing north, but alert for trouble from any direction.

The cessation of gunfire coming from the alley caused the attackers to take heart and recover some of their nerve. They closed on the south alley mouth, throwing lead into its dark corridor.

Streaming rounds tore through the opposite end, tearing up some building fronts on the north side of Toughnut Street. It was a futile discharge, harming no one.

"Follow them! Don't let them get away!" came the cry from among the New Mexico bunch. Foot-falls pounded in the alley, clattering, rushing north, coming near, nearer—

Sam pivoted, facing into the alley with shotgun leveled. He loosed both barrels into an onrushing handful of foes, four or five of them. They ran headlong into a withering scythe of twelve-gauge shot that chopped them in the middle, felling them.

Some were killed straight off; others were badly wounded. The alley mouth filled with gun smoke.

No sooner had he fired than Sam dodged back, shielded behind the corner.

Gunfire tore into the spot he had just quit.

Three men stood at the east end of Toughnut Street, shooting at Sam, Matt, and Ringo.

One was an oversized individual with a barrel-shaped torso, a ten-gallon hat, and grotesque woolly chaps. Even in silhouette, the signature out-line of Waco Brindle was unmistakeable. Waco, owner of the saloon that bore his name, was ring-leader of the transplanted New Mexico bunch.

His massive form took up much of the open space at the end of the street. He held a repeating rifle at hip height, levering it, pumping out rapid-fire rounds. He bellowed as he fired, shouting out a string of garbled, furious obscenities. He had the alley mouth in range, but Sam had sidestepped out of the way and Waco's rounds missed him.

Raging still more incoherently, Waco swung the

rifle muzzle to the side, tracking Sam, hot rounds reaching for him.

Matt squeezed off three shots in quick succession, planting them in the center of Waco's torso. Waco reeled with the impact, swaying. His rifle fell silent as he ceased levering out shots. Tree-trunk legs were planted wide apart, helping to keep him on his feet after sustaining the mortal wounds.

The two gunmen bracketing him on either side opened fire. Sam released the empty shotgun, pulling his gun. It cleared leather and barked a shot that drilled one of the gunmen before the empty shotgun hit the ground.

Ringo shot the other, who threw his arms up over his head, spun around, and fell, measuring his length in the dust, where he lay unmoving.

Waco was still on his feet. Matt and Sam threw another volley into him, their guns bucking, spitting fire and hot lead.

Waco fell backwards, crashing to the ground. He lay there on his back, face up, motionless, inert—stone dead. His huge form looked like a particularly large bump in the road.

So ended Waco Brindle. The rest of his bunch, what was left of them, had no more appetite for fight. Silent guns were stuffed into holsters as their owners hurried away, hurrying to Waco's saloon to plunder it and drink up all his stock of beer and whiskey.

It was raining harder now.

"Let's get out of here. I don't want to have to

explain this to the law, when the sheriff gets back to town," Matt said.

Sam and Ringo agreed. The three of them melted away into the night, even as the first eager curiosity-seekers began thronging to the scene. They wove a wide and circuitous course down the backstreets and side alleys, distancing themselves from the scene of the gun battle.

"Now that we're clear, Sam, tell me how you came to be in the alley in time to save our bacon," Matt said.

"When I was in the Hotel Erle barroom, I spotted Sid Felder trying to look like he belonged there. Sid's a longtime Black Angus gang member," Sam began.

"Your hunch was right," Ringo said, "about Jones making another try for the girl."

"Looks like, considering Felder was prowling around the same hotel that Linda Gordon's in, on the very night she arrived in town," Sam went on. "He was with some other fellow I didn't recognize, a sneaky-looking stringbean kind of hombre. They were going out of the barroom when I saw them. I don't think they saw me.

"I tried to follow, but there were too many people in the way and, by the time I reached the lobby, they were gone. I went outside in time to see them turning the corner on Fourth Street, going north toward Fremont. I ran after, but when I reached Fourth Street they were nowhere to be seen. I prowled around the saloons there for some time to see if I could raise them, but no luck.

"I went back to the hotel, saw you and Ringo standing on the corner of Fifth Street. You started toward Sixth Street. A man stood there watching you go, one of the bunch we bucked earlier today at Waco's. I hung back, waiting to see what he'd do. He got on a horse and rode down Fifth Street. I ran after. No question he was dogging you. He followed you on the next cross street down. He stopped a couple of times to see which way you went, so I was able to keep up with him.

"He met up with a half-dozen or so men on the street below Toughnut. I doubled back to Toughnut, going east. I figured on turning right at the end of the street and going south to intercept you. Halfway across the block I saw the alley. It looked like a good shortcut. I was lightfooting it down the alley when I came across the shotgunner. Nobody had to draw me a picture to tell me what that was all about.

"I knocked him out, grabbed the shotgun, and went looking for you. I stuck my head out the alley, saw Waco's men closing off both ends of the street, and knew they were springing the trap. I gave out with our old coyote call to get your attention—the rest you know," Sam concluded.

"You boys handle yourself all right," Ringo said.

"You're no slouch with the plow handles yourself," said Sam.

"Thanks for tying in with us, Ringo. That was a tight squeeze. Don't know how it would've gone without your guns siding us," Matt said.

"What else could I do? I had to throw in to save my own neck," Ringo said.

"Thanks all the same. I owe you one."

"That goes for me, too," Sam said.

"Help me get Dorado and Quirt Fane and we'll be even up," Ringo said.

Matt laughed. "Hell, we'd do that anyway."

Their long, meandering route had delivered them in sight of the Big Sky Saloon.

"Maybe Bill's back with some news," Ringo said. "In any case, we can get out of the wet and have us some drinks."

"We've got some planning to do," Matt said.

TWELVE

It stopped raining around midnight. An hour or so later, Ringo and Curly Bill rode up to the jailhouse. They had two extra horses with them.

A blurred, fuzzy moon played peekaboo with low-hanging cloud cover that was starting to come apart at the seams, letting thin sheets of moonlight shine through. Rainwater dripped from the gallows, pattering on the ground below.

Ringo and Bill tied up the horses and went in the jail. The door wasn't locked.

Assistant Deputy Osgood sat upright at his desk, rigid, his hand on a gun which lay on the desktop. He relaxed visibly when he recognized the visitors, the quivering tension going out of him, mostly.

He took his hand off the gun. A bottle and glass stood on the desk, too. He poured a drink, draining it in one gulp. "Ain't you ever heard of knocking?" he demanded.

Ringo ignored him, and Curly Bill just laughed.

"Easy does it, Deputy. You're wound up tighter than the mainspring of a Swiss watch," Bill said.

"There's some mighty funny business going on tonight. Unfunny funny business," Osgood said. "I been chasing around half the night cleaning up after that big killdown over to Toughnut Street."

"Don't blame me, I was at the Toro Loco cantina when it happened. I got a roomful of witnesses who'll swear they saw me there, too," Bill said.

"Witnesses," Osgood said, sniffing, "Mexes."

"Who the hell else you expect to find in the Toro Loco cantina—Swedes?" Bill said, venting his big booming laugh.

"You can't hang that one on us," Ringo said. "What do we care if Waco Brindle and his Lincoln County pards have a falling out and shoot each other full of holes?"

"What're you getting yourself in an uproar over Waco and the rest of them skunks for?" Curly Bill asked reasonably. "You ought to be glad they're headed for Boot Hill. Claim jumping will decline overnight by a hundred and ten percent in these parts."

"I got a feeling Matt Bodine and his Injun friend are somewhere at the bottom of it. I'm sure of it. They killed the Vollin gang and Vollin and them were thick with Waco," Osgood said.

"The great detective," Ringo sneered.

"Why don't you ask them about it, instead of grousing at us?" Curly Bill said.

"I got better things to do than chase after them two, Bill."

"Like what? Kill another bottle?"

"Now that you mention it—yeah."

"We'll help."

"I'm doing fine by myself."

"I can see that. There ain't much left."

While Curly Bill was bantering with Osgood, Ringo went around to the side and lifted the whiskey bottle. "Hey! Just a danged minute now," Osgood squawked.

"Relax, you'll live longer," Ringo said. He took a long pull from the bottle, making a face. "Damn, that's lousy."

"Why do you drink it then?" Osgood said.

"It's the only bottle to hand. Why do you drink it?"

"Same reason," Curly Bill said, snickering.

"Want a taste, Bill?"

"I don't mind."

Ringo tossed the bottle to Curly Bill, who caught it. Bill drank deeply. Ringo wandered behind the marshal's desk, eyeing the cells in the rear of the building.

There were no lights in the densely shadowed area. What dim illumination there was came from lamps burning in the front office.

Gila Chacon lay on his back on his bunk, one arm folded under his head, pillowing it. One leg was bent at the knee, the other extended off the edge of the bunk, reaching down to the floor. His face was turned to the front office, impassive, dark eyes watchful. Ringo gave him a slight nod, and Gila bobbed his head equally slightly in response.

Polk lay on his bunk, snoring, with a hat over his

face. He snored loudly and intermittently, by fits and starts.

A third prisoner, a miner who'd beaten his common-law wife to death with a ball-peen hammer, lay on his side, face to the wall.

"This is lousy," Curly Bill said, setting the bottle down on the desk. Osgood grabbed it, holding it to the light. "I left you some," Bill said.

"A mouthful," Osgood said, sullen. "What do you want, anyhow? You got a reason for being here except to mouth off and drink my whiskey?"

"We're here to do you a favor," Curly Bill said.

"That's a good one, a real knee-slapper," Osgood said. "Since when are you boys in the favor-doing business?"

"Since Bob Farr got killed," Ringo said. "We're here to take the *bandido* off your hands."

"Thought it was something like that," Osgood said, smug. "You ain't doing me a favor; you want me to do you one."

"Have it any way you like. We want Gila Chacon."

"Not a chance," Osgood said, shaking his head.

"We got some new evidence in the Black Angus case," Curly Bill said. "I been asking around and it turns out everybody knows about Gila and Don Carlos and Carmen. Everybody in Mex town, that is. It's a real famous love story or hate story, call it what you will. They even wrote songs about it.

"Everybody knows about the slave auction in Pago, too, and how Don Carlos runs it. All you got to do is ask the right folks, they'll tell you."

"It's a sure bet Black Angus is taking those girls

to Pago to sell," Ringo said. "A sure bet Dorado and Quirt Fane'll be there, too."

"It's a sure bet that Gila Chacon won't be there," Osgood said. "You two want to go to Pago to kill Dorado and Quirt, why you go right ahead. Nobody's stopping you. Chacon stays here."

"What the hell? It's not as if other prisoners haven't 'escaped' from this jail before," Curly Bill said, beginning to show signs of irritation. "I could name more than one hombre who bought his way out of here."

"I don't know nothing about that," Osgood declared, clearly uncomfortable with the line the conversation was taking. "I ain't saying it's so, but I ain't saying it ain't so. I just plain ain't saying."

"If the marshal was here, he'd do it," Curly Bill said.

"If Johnny Behan was here, he'd surely do it," Ringo added.

"Well, they ain't here. If you feel that way about it, you can just wait till they get back and ask them," Osgood said.

"We're in a hurry," Ringo said.

"Think of them poor little gals. They're in a mighty tough spot. Their folks dead—kilt; captives of a band of cold-blooded killers carrying them off to what they call 'a fate worse than death.' No hope, no help in sight, not knowing if anybody is even aware of their plight."

"You ought to write for the *Nugget*, Bill, you're piling it on so high," Osgood said. "Put yourself in my place. In case you ain't noticed, this Chacon ain't no ordinary prisoner. He's a killer, slated to hang come Saturday. He ain't here for to get his neck stretched, folks are going to be mighty sore and looking to take it out on the man responsible and that ain't gonna be me." Osgood's face was set in hard, unyielding lines.

"Save your breath, John, he's mule stubborn," Curly Bill said, disgusted. "When he gets that way, there ain't no making him see reason."

"What'll you bet?" Ringo said, picking up Osgood's gun and pointing it at him. It was all done in one seamless fluid motion: Ringo's hand was empty, at his side; an eyeblink later, the gun was in his fist, leveled on the deputy.

Gila got to his feet, and Polk Muldoon stopped snoring. Osgood goggled, then gulped, swallowing hard. "Now hold on, Ringo—"

"Some folks just won't listen to reason," Ringo remarked conversationally to Curly Bill.

"Quit your fooling, Ringo," Osgood blustered. "You ain't gonna shoot me—"

Ringo thumbed the hammer back with a click. "I killed Lou Hancock because he made the mistake of insulting me by refusing my offer to buy him a drink. Believe me, Deputy, when I tell you that I wanted him to take that drink a whole hell of a lot less than I want Gila Chacon.

"Now come around from behind that desk and don't cut up and you might come out of this alive."

Osgood rose, doing what he'd been told. He stood with hands up, face even more sour than usual, and looking more than a little bit sick, too.

Curly Bill set to work. He didn't need to be told what to do. This wasn't his first jailbreak, either busting somebody out of jail or busting out himself.

He picked up the jailer's big key ring from where it was hanging on a peg on the wall and went to Gila's cell, fitting the oversized key in the lock, unlocking and opening it. The cell door swung open with a creaking and Gila stepped out, long, slitted, not-so-sleepy eyes glinting. He nodded to Bill, saying, *"Gracias, amigo."*

"We ain't amigos yet. Whether we are or not remains to be seen, so don't you go cutting up none, neither. I reckon you could still travel with a bullet through the elbow or kneecap," Curly Bill said.

Polk Muldoon was sitting up on his bunk with his hat on his head and his feet on the floor, eyes shining. The remorseful miner stiffened, but remained steadfastly oblivious of all that was going on, keeping his face to the wall.

Ringo marched Osgood at gunpoint to the *bandido's* now-empty cell. "This is what we call a 'transfer of custody,' Gila. Instead of being his prisoner, you're mine."

"As you wish, señor. Anything to get out of this filthy hole."

Ringo poked Osgood's back with the muzzle of the pistol. "In you go, Deputy."

Osgood stepped into the cell. Curly Bill slammed the door shut, locking it.

"This is a switch, me locking up a lawman. That's a horse on you, Deputy."

"Let's go," Ringo said.

Polk Muldoon jumped up. "Hey, fellows, how about taking me with you?"

Ringo and Curly Bill exchanged glances. "What do you say, Bill?"

"Polk's a good ol' boy. It's a shame to let him set in here and rust. He can shoot, too."

"What do you say, Polk? Feel like taking a ride down Mexico way?"

"Ringo, I'd ride to hell for a hot coal to light my see-gar with, if'n it'd git me out of here."

Curly Bill unlocked the cell door, letting Polk out. "Hallelujah," Polk said.

"You're making a big mistake, Muldoon," Osgood said.

"The biggest mistake I made was getting caught. That won't happen again."

"You're riding to your death in Mexico, all of you. What can a handful of you do against a whole army of slave hunters?"

"Now you just hesh up, little deppity, and try them iron bars on for size."

"'Stone walls do not a prison make, nor iron bars a cage,' the poet said—but that's not the way to bet it," Ringo said.

"What the hell are you talking about, John?" Curly Bill said, puzzled, frowning.

"Never mind."

"You got to stop reading all them books. It ain't healthy. Makes you talk crazy."

Ringo, Curly Bill, Gila, and Polk went into the front office.

"*Por favor*, señores, my gun. It has been with me

for a long time. I would hate to lose it now, when I shall soon have need of it."

"I'd like to hold on to my hogleg, too, Ringo—it suits me," Polk said.

"Where do they keep your guns?"

"Locked up in the side drawer of the desk, the big one on the right, like a locker drawer," Polk said, indicating it.

Curly Bill went to Osgood, holding the key ring up in front of his face. "Which key opens the drawer, Deputy?"

Osgood was silent. "If I have to shoot the lock off, a ricochet might hit you right between the eyes," Ringo said to Osgood.

"The small shiny steel key," Osgood said, pointing it out.

Curly Bill separated the key from the others and fit it in the locked drawer of the desk. It was a locker-like cabinet, its rectangular hinged door opening outward. Within lay a heap of gun belts and knives.

Bill hauled out an armful and dropped them on the desk. "That one there, in the buscadero holster," Gila said, eagerly reaching for it.

Ringo pointed the pistol at him, wagging it chidingly. "Uh-uh. No guns for you, not yet. Maybe when we get to know you better. You take it, Bill."

Gila's gun was a long-barreled .44 in a soft leather holster, Mexican buscadero style. The gun belt was buckled closed. Curly Bill looped it over his left shoulder. "I'll take real good care of it for you," he told Gila. "You won't be needing it just yet."

"Tombstone is a dangerous town, señor."

"You won't be staying long. We'll be leaving soon."

"The sooner, the better."

"Okay if I get my gun?" Polk Muldoon asked.

"Help yourself," Ringo said.

Polk picked up a well-worn gun belt with an equally well-worn Colt .45 in the holster. He buckled it low on his hips, below the swelling bulge of his big gut. "First time I've felt fully dressed in a coon's age."

Ringo used a pencil to scrawl something on the back of a Wanted circular.

"What's that, John?" Curly Bill asked.

"A receipt."

It read:

> Received one prisoner.
> *(signed)*
> **RINGO**

Ringo read the message aloud to the others. "That makes everything nice and legal." He left the receipt on the desk, pinning it down with Osgood's pistol. He and the others went out, making for the horses.

"Them two's my horse and Ringo's. Mount up on the others."

"I see you brung a horse for me. You must've been almighty sure of yourselves," Polk said.

Ringo shook his head. "We were sure of you."

They untied the horses and saddled up.

"A few minutes ago, I was in an iron cage under

the shadow of the gallows. Now I am a free man with a fine horse under me," Gila said.

"A philosopher, eh?" Ringo said.

"Life sure is funny," Polk Muldoon wheezed.

"Two philosphers," said Ringo.

They readied to ride. "No tricks, *bandido*," Curly Bill warned.

"Even if I was so ungracious as to turn against my saviours, I have no desire to be shot," Gila said.

"Keep thinking like that and we'll get along fine."

Off they rode.

THIRTEEN

Three a.m. The dead of night hour, halfway between midnight and dawn.

Tombstone was quiet as it ever got, which was not necessarily so quiet. Beneath the surface of the earth mining went on without slackening, the night shift of the big mining concerns going about its digging, tunneling, rock breaking, and clearing. The business of extracting silver ore from below was a twenty-four-hour endeavor.

A number of saloons, gambling halls, and brothels continued to operate, though even the appetites of the flesh seemed to slow and ebb at this bleak hour—the hour when, according to doctor's reports, most sickly patients expire.

Clouds had broken up and scattered, baring the moon and stars. There was a freshness and softness to the air which the moisture of the rain had brought. The moon was bright and shining; the eternal stars glittered.

A handful of drunks wandered the streets, singly

and in combination, some silent, others loud and rowdy. There were no lawmen to crack down on them.

The jailhouse stood stolid and foursquare, seemingly undisturbed, though from time to time muffled shouting and wall banging were heard to emanate from the rear of the building where the cells were.

There was little traffic on foot or horseback in the area at this hour. If any passersby heard the outbursts, as a penned Assistant Deputy Osgood sought to attract help, they ignored it and moved on.

Allen Street was more or less deserted, save for the infrequent comings and goings of various night owls.

The Oriental Saloon and several similar establishments were still doing some business, but the numbers of gamblers, drinkers, and skirt chasers had dwindled down to a hardcore few.

Lights showed in the front of the ground floor of the Hotel Erle, and behind the curtained windows of some of the guest rooms, but most of the building was dark. The restaurant and barroom were closed; the lobby was abandoned save for a lone occupant, the house detective, who sat in a deep-cushioned armchair reading a weeks-old copy of the *Tombstone Epitaph* newspaper and smoking a cigar. From time to time, he restored his spirits by nipping from a pocket flask of liquor.

Hotel manager Mark Fredericks had retired for the night and gone to bed. The front desk was being held down by Dewey, the night clerk, a soft-faced, lumpish man-boy. He sat dozing perched on a stool behind the desk, an elbow on the countertop, upraised palm supporting the side of his head. His face was flushed, his mouth open, and a thread of spittle wetted his chin.

The second floor was still, quiet. Two of Colonel Davenport's men were posted in the hall as guards.

Dean Duane sat outside the door of Room 207, Linda Gordon's room. He had replaced Riker, who'd gone off shift at midnight. Wes Crawley guarded the door to the back stairs at the far end of the corridor in the rear of the building. The long corridor was straight, allowing the two men to keep each other in view.

Dean Duane was square built, with a thick, straight torso. He was hatless and wore a lightweight gray suit, white shirt, and black tie. Crawley was similarly attired. Davenport liked his bodyguards to dress like businessmen so they'd be properly attired for his world of banks and boardrooms.

Duane wore a short-barreled .45 revolver, holstered butt out and worn high on his right hip, up near his waist. He sat in an armless straight-backed chair, rising from time to time to yawn, stretch, and pace the floor to relieve the strain of sitting for so many hours.

The corridor was unpeopled, apart from the guards, but not unquiet. There were the creakings of the building settling on its foundations, the murmur of voices behind closed hotel room doors, the rushing hiss of gas funneling through pipes to fuel the wall lamps.

A little after three, the rear door opened, and a man stepped inside. Wes Crawley rose, facing him. Duane turned his head, looking down the hall to see what it was all about. He stirred with interest. Any interruption to the monotony of guard duty was welcome diversion.

The newcomer was a tall thin man wearing a white, bib-front kitchen apron. He held a serving tray in both hands. On it was a coffeepot, and some cups and saucers. Duane's mouth watered. He hungered for a taste of some strong black fresh brew.

The waiter or kitchen help, for so the newcomer most obviously seemed to be, held the coffeepot by the handle in one hand, balancing the serving tray on the upraised palm of his other hand.

He poured a cup of coffee. Crawley took the cup and saucer and sat down. He held the coffee cup in one hand, while his other held the saucer on top of one of his thighs. He nodded to Duane, grinning. His atttitude said: This is all right.

Crawley sat drinking coffee while the waiter came up the hall to Dean Duane. The waiter was a regular beanpole, thought Duane. He was balding, with a thin, horseshoe-shaped fringe of brown hair framing a shiny, gleaming scalp. Beneath the white bib apron, he wore a faded, red flannel shirt and striped gray trousers tucked into knee-high boot tops. Shirtsleeves were rolled up to the elbows.

He held the tray in front of him in both hands. On it, he had placed the gleaming, silver-plated coffeepot, some cups and saucers, and some white folded linen napkins.

Dean Duane rose, the full rich aroma of coffee tingling in his nostrils. His stomach rumbled.

"Compliments of the hotel, sir. The manager thought you might like some coffee," the waiter said.

"I sure would!" Duane enthused.

The waiter shifted his grip, balancing the tray on an upraised palm. He poured coffee from the pot into a cup, filling it. There was no cream, nor sugar. In the West, men took their coffee hot, black, and strong.

Duane took a cup in hand. The cup was a big over-sized mug, a man-sized cup of coffee. Duane took a sip, tasting it. "That's good," he said. "Thanks."

"You're welcome, sir."

Duane sat down, steaming coffee cup in one hand, saucer in the other. The waiter hovered around, standing so that he blocked Duane's view of Crawley.

The coffee was hot. Duane sat there sipping it. The waiter stood in place, not moving on. Duane frowned. What was he waiting around for, a tip? Fat chance!

He looked up at the waiter. "Something you want?"

"Perhaps you'd care for a napkin, sir. Don't want to risk staining your clothes," the waiter said.

"Good idea."

The waiter's bony hand reached under a folded napkin on the tray, coming out with a derringer. He pointed it at Duane's forehead. His body was turned so Crawley at the other end of the hall could see nothing amiss. The derringer was a pearl-handled, double-barreled, over-under job bearing two shots with two triggers.

"Blink and you're dead," the waiter said.

He stepped back, turning his head so he could see Crawley and Duane at the same time. His body screened the derringer from Crawley's view. He nodded several times. Crawley thought he was nodding at him and raised his cup in a friendly salute.

Crawley was unaware that the rear door was open a crack. Somebody stood behind the door looking through the crack, watching for the go-ahead signal, which had now been given.

The door opened and a man came out, a short, slight man holding a big knife. He came up behind Crawley and slashed the knife across his throat, cutting it. Blood jetted, the knife wielder nimbly stepping back to avoid it.

Cup and saucer fell from Crawley's hands, dropping to the carpeted floor, which muffled the noise of their fall. Crawley clasped both hands to his throat, making choking noises. His legs straightened, jerking.

The knife man stepped in, thrusting the blade into Crawley's heart. It was a fatal blow, bringing instant death. Crawley stiffened, then slumped, sagging. It all happened very quickly and with minimal disturbance.

"Good Lord!" Duane said, gasping.

"Shut up," the waiter said. "Do as you're told and you'll get out of this alive. Otherwise, you'll get what your friend got."

He was the "stringbean" whom Sam Two Wolves

had seen earlier that night in the hotel barroom with Black Angus gang stalwart Sid Felder. His name was Preston "Slim" Giles.

The role of waiter came easily to him because he'd been a waiter once, some time back when he was serving an Iowa prison term for armed robbery. He was competent and well-spoken and he'd been made a trustee, serving the warden as his personal valet and manservant. It was an easy job and he'd done his time without a hitch. But that was long ago.

A third man entered via the rear door: Sid Felder, thorough-going badman and long-time Angus Jones associate. A burly man, he had wavy black hair with a widow's peak, thick black eyebrows, and mustache. He wore a six-gun in a black leather holster.

The knife wielder was Tom Bardo, a Missouri outlaw. He was slight, sharp featured, with a pointed nose and chin. He had long stringy hair and a wispy mustache and chin whiskers. He wore a gun, but the blade was his specialty.

Slim Giles motioned with the derringer. "Either barrel could blow your brains out, so don't try anything funny," he warned Dean Duane. "Set the cup and saucer down on the floor. Good. Stand up."

Duane rose shakily, his complexion leaden under a sheen of cold sweat. Slim set the tray down on the flat seat bottom, keeping Duane covered with the derringer. He stepped in, pressing the barrels to the side of Duane's head while reaching under the guard's coat to pull the gun from his holster.

Stepping back, he leveled both guns on the guard. "Turn around and face the wall."

Duane turned in time to see Tom Bardo holding the rear door open while Sid Felder hooked his meaty hands under Wes Crawley's arms and dragged his corpse through the doorway onto the landing. "Don't kill me . . . please," Duane breathed.

"Shut the hell up."

Duane stood facing the wall to the left of the door to Room 207. Slim pocketed the derringer, transferring Duane's short, stubby, solid-built, big-bore revolver to his right hand. He crashed the gun butt against Duane's skull, clubbing him behind the back of his ear.

Duane grunted, sagging at the knees. Slim struck again, harder. Duane's eyes rolled up in his head, whites showing. He started to fold up.

Slim's free hand collared him at the back of the neck. He was thin but wiry, with surprising strength. He eased Duane down to the floor in a heap. Duane was limp, a deadweight.

Slim looked around warily. All was clear, with nobody sticking their head outside their room door to investigate. Just as well for them because if they had, Slim would have blown it off for them.

Sid Felder and Tom Bardo came down the hall, guns in hand. Bardo was slight and wore moccasins, his passage raising barely a whisper. Felder was big, and heavyset, but lightfooted, moving as stealthily as Bardo.

Felder reached for the door handle of Room 207, his gun leveled hip high. The door was un-locked, handle turning under his hand. He eased the door open. Within, the anteroom was empty, a table lamp burning. The bedroom door was closed.

Felder stepped back, making eye contact with Bardo. "Take care of the girl and anybody with her," he rasped, low voiced. "Try not to make any noise, but shoot if you must. We'll blast our way out of here if we have to."

Bardo nodded, pale eyes shining. His knife was in a sheath worn under his left arm. It had antler-plated handles, a foot-long, razor-sharp blade, and a wicked, slightly curved point. He'd wiped it clean after using it on Crawley, but some red spots showed on the guard and handle.

He padded into the anteroom, noiselessly. Felder stood outside the room door, looking in, watching him. Slim Giles stood with gun drawn, serving as lookout.

"Go with Bardo," Felder whispered.

"What for? He knows what to do. He needs no help from me," Slim said.

"He likes to use that knife too much. Make sure he finishes the gal off fast with no nonsense. I'll keep watch."

Slim swore, but moved to obey. He entered the anteroom. Bardo had the bedroom door open a hand's-breadth and was looking in as Slim's shadow fell on him.

Bardo looked over his shoulder, face alive with unholy delight. "Room's dark, the gal's alone, in bed sleeping."

He holstered his gun and drew his knife, its mirror-bright surfaces gleaming with reflected light.

"Sid says finish her off fast," Slim hissed.

"Sure, sure," Bardo muttered, opening the door.

Slim stayed behind. He was a robber, gunman, and killer, but even he drew the line somewhere. He didn't have the stomach to watch Bardo at his work.

Bardo eased sideways through the partly opened door into the dark bedroom. The sole source of light was lamplight from the anteroom. Bardo moved deeper into the room, out of Slim's sight.

After a pause, there were the sounds of a slight disturbance, one that might have gone unnoticed except for those like Slim who knew what to listen for. A soft scuffle, the sound of a blow, a stifled gasp—silence.

Slim waited for Bardo to emerge, his pounding heartbeats measuring out the time.

It seemed like a long time but Slim reckoned that was just nerves. More time passed, while Slim fidgeted.

"Psst!" That was from Sid Felder in the hall, glaring into the anteroom. He scowled, thick eyebrows frowning fiercely. "Hurry up!" he urged in a hoarse whisper.

"Bardo's still in there," Slim said.

"What's the stall?" Felder asked.

Slim shrugged, holding his palms up in an I-don't-know gesture.

"Get him," Felder said.

"I don't want to get him riled," Slim said, looking

hapless and helpless. "He's real mean with a knife in his hand—"

"What do you think I sent you in for, to wring your hands? Get moving and haul his ass out of there!"

"Oke," Slim said. He tiptoed away, walking on the toes of his boots, giving him an unnatural stilted gait, at once both sinister and comic.

Felder found nothing to laugh about. He stood there fuming, trying to watch in two directions at the same time, the room and the hall.

Slim listened hard. It was mighty quiet in the bedroom. He opened the door wider, stepping inside. "Bardo?"

No reply.

Light shone through the doorway, laying a yellow oblong on the floor. The rest of the room was very dark. Slim's eyes had trouble adjusting to the dimness. An angle of light fell on a brass bedpost at the foot of the bed.

He moved toward it, out of Felder's view. He stumbled over something on the floor, and fell, dropping his gun. He fell amidst a tangle of limbs. Not all the limbs were his own.

He recoiled, gasping, rising to hands and knees. A puddle of warm liquid lay where his palms pressed the floor. He felt around for his gun, touching a body. He groped it, feeling around its contours with fear and frenzy fast rising in him. This was not the flesh of a young female, this was the body, the corpse, of a male:

Bardo!

Slim's hands were sticky with wetness. The stuff had a metallic, coppery scent he knew full well— blood!

Slim cried out. He jumped to his feet, rushing the door. All thoughts of the girl, gun, and the gold that was going to be paid for this little job of murder flew out of his head, replaced only by a blind instinctive need to flee this dark room and its bloody corpse.

Felder saw Slim reel into view, framed in the bedroom's open doorway. Slim was terrified, fear stricken. He looked like he was going to scream. Felder could have killed him for that.

Slim gripped the doorframe with both hands to steady himself. He threw himself forward. Bloody red handprints marked the white door molding where he'd held it.

From the shadows of the room, something came flashing through the air, whirling, pinwheeling— what was it?

It struck Slim a stiff blow in the back, thudding home, bowing his torso forward and out. He shrieked in mortal pain and terror, the cry falling to a thick, choking gurgle.

Slim staggered forward as if struggling against hip-deep mud, seemingly expending an awesome effort to advance each single step. He reached around behind him to his back, as if groping for something.

Even as Felder watched openmouthed, the light went out of Slim's bulging eyes, orbs glazing over in death. Slim was dead on his feet. He pitched face forward, crashing to the floor.

A war hatchet lay buried deep in his back between the shoulder blades. He'd been *tomahawked.*

Spooked, Felder fired a blast through the open bedroom door, gun bucking and roaring in his hand.

The echoes of the gunshots faded, replaced by hollow laughter sounding from within the bedroom, mocking, disembodied.

Felder had had enough. His nerve broke. He jumped back as if scalded. He spun toward the rear of the building, ready to race to the end of the corridor, down the back stairs and away—

Only to come face to face with Matt Bodine. Matt was in the corridor, coming on with drawn gun, barring the way to the back stairs and escape.

Felder swung his gun up, cursing, and firing. Matt's gun was already on target. Felder's shot missed. Matt's didn't.

A bullet tagged Felder high on the right side of his chest, below the collarbone. A second and third round ripped into his right shoulder, shattering the bone. Felder screamed, gun falling from his dead hand. He fell, too.

Matt stood in the middle of the hallway, gun leveled at the hip, gun smoke hazing his form.

Whatever else he was, Felder was still game. He crawled across the floor, sobbing and squirming, clawing for his gun with his good left hand. Matt shot him in the hand, blowing off some fingers, sending them flying.

Felder lay on his side in a fetal position, legs together, bent at the knees. He hugged his maimed hand to him, his right arm limp, unresponsive and useless.

Matt approached, bending at the knees to scoop up Felder's gun. He circled past him, looking into Room 207.

Sam Two Wolves was in the anteroom, hunkered down beside Slim. His gun was in his holster, un-fired. He'd done for Bardo and Slim with his toma-hawk.

He and Matt had laid a trap for Felder and his sidemen. Linda Gordon was safe in another room. She'd been moved earlier to Room 204, which had a connecting door with Davenport's suite.

Remy Markand and Riker were in there guarding her, with Mrs. Sanderson present as chaperone—social proprieties must be observed, no matter what kill-happy characters might be on the prowl.

Matt and Sam had come up with the scheme ear-lier still, after meeting with Ringo and Curly Bill at the Big Sky Saloon.

Curly Bill's friends and informants at the canti-nas had come up with plenty of evidence to corrob-orate Gila Chacon's story about himself, Carmen, and Don Carlos of slave auction infamy. It seemed a sure bet that Black Angus would press on to Pago to sell the captive girls there.

The adventurers needed Gila's services as guide in order to mount a proper rescue effort. Ringo and Curly Bill had volunteered to spring Gila from jail.

"We've got nothing to lose, we're already on the wrong side of the law." Curly Bill grinned.

"Besides, Deputy Johnny Behan'll square it for us when he gets back," Ringo said. "Fred White's had a bellyful of being marshal—he's not going to stand for election. Behan's the power in that office and a sure bet to win when he stands for marshal come November.

"You two have already got an in with Colonel Moneybags, so you might as well work it for all it's worth. We'll fetch the *bandido.*"

Matt and Sam went to the Hotel Erle for a private conclave with Davenport. They pitched him their plan, and he went for it. Linda Gordon was quietly moved into Room 204, the room switch being kept secret from all but a handful of insiders.

Sam kept vigil alone in Linda's previous room, waiting in darkness. Matt patrolled the hotel, watching for assassins by night.

It was later learned that Sid Felder and his two accomplices broke into the hotel through a side window on the ground floor sometime around two-thirty, entering unobserved, undetected. They made their way to the kitchen, empty and untended, where a pot of coffee was customarily kept on a hot plate for the use of the night clerk and staff members on the night shift.

Sid Felder came up with the plan to gain entry to Linda Gordon's room by disguising Slim as a kitchen staff member. A number of aprons hung on a hook in the kitchen. Slim donned one, checking that the coffee was hot and readying the serving tray, including the derringer hidden under napkins.

The trio climbed the back stairs, Felder and Bardo lurking on a lower landing while Slim entered the second floor through the rear fire door. While he distracted Crawley, Felder and Bardo sneaked up the stairs, opening the door a crack and watching for Slim's signal. Slim nodded emphatically and repeatedly, signalling that he had Duane under the gun. Bardo came through the door and swiftly cut Crawley's throat.

That was where the plan had gone awry. It was the X factor, the unknown variable that confounds all planning.

The trap got back on track when Bardo and Slim entered Room 207. Instead of a teenaged girl lying helpless in bed in a dark room, the killers had found Sam. He lay on his back, long hair streaming across the pillows, a thin blanket covering him to the neck.

An arm was at his side, tomahawk in hand, hidden under the blanket.

Bardo had gotten quite a surprise as he leaned over the bed knife in hand, ready to make the fatal strike. He fell to the tomahawk chop.

Sam slipped out of the bed on the other side, crouching in a far corner, watching while Slim stumbled around in the dark. Sam had his night eyes and saw clearly as Slim fell over the body, making the horrified discovery that it belonged to Bardo.

When Slim fled, Sam threw the tomahawk, taking him expertly in the back. . . .

Now, Sam took hold of the wooden shaft of the

steel-bladed, double-edged tomahawk, wrenching it loose from Slim's corpse. He had to yank hard, as it was in deep. It came loose with a wet scrunching sound. He used Slim's shirttails to wipe the blade clean.

"What're you trying to do, save on bullets?" Matt joked.

"Just trying to be quiet. I didn't want to wake anybody up," Sam said, sticking the tomahawk in his belt.

"That didn't work out so well."

Sam joined Matt in the hallway. The second floor was in an uproar. Sid Felder sat on the floor with his back against the wall, sobbing and groaning.

Hotel guests had stayed safely behind locked room doors during the gunplay, but they were all coming out to gaze and gawk now. Remy Markand was there, gun at his side. Riker stood in the doorway of Room 204, wanting to see what happened, but unwilling to leave Linda Gordon's room unguarded.

Colonel Davenport was there in his nightshirt, a pair of hastily thrown-on trousers underneath, his feet shod in bedroom slippers. He was bright-eyed and alert, seemingly not a bit sleepy.

Arnholt Stebbins was there, too, his sole concession to the informality of the late hour being that his jacket was off and the knot of his tie loosened.

A number of Davenport's guards thronged the scene. A couple of them were assisting Dean Duane, who'd come around to consciousness after being knocked out. He was dazed, groggy, bleeding from a head wound. They helped him to his feet, leading him into Davenport's suite to lie down and rest while waiting for Dr. Willis, who had been summoned.

"You've got a man on the back stairs landing, dead. I saw him when I came up," Matt said.

Several guards went down the corridor to investigate, finding Wes Crawley's butchered corpse where Felder and Bardo had hidden it.

Matt and Sam went to Sid Felder, looming over him. He sat there shivering, trying to shrink into a small package. His eyes teared, his nose ran, and he gasped through gritted teeth, rolling his eyes from the pain.

Matt kicked him sharply with the toe of his boot to get his attention. Felder looked up, mouthing obscenities.

"Well, well, Sid Felder. So you managed to take him alive," Sam said mildly.

"The hard part was not finishing him off. Polecats like Sid were made for Boot Hill," Matt said. "You know us, Sid, Sam and me."

"Yeah, I know you, you bastards," Felder muttered.

"Actually, both our mothers were married, which I'm sure is more than you can say," Sam returned.

Felder told them briefly what they could do with their mothers.

Matt tsk-tsked. "You've got a nasty mouth, Sid. Better be careful nobody cuts your tongue out."

"Don't do that—he's got to talk."

"Thanks for reminding me, Sam. Oh, well, I'm sure there's other parts we can cut off if it's needful," Matt said.

"Misguided folks who think being an outlaw is some big, bold, romantic thing should see you now, Sid. Look at you: all shot up, fingers shot off, lifeblood leaking all over the place, snot dripping out of your nose—you're a mess," Sam said.

Felder had two words for him.

"Where's Black Angus, Sid?" Matt asked.

"Who?" Felder said, laughing hollowly.

"Jones left Sid here to die while he went to the slave auction in Pago," Matt said.

"Never heard of it," Felder said. Through a supreme act of will, he forced his lips upward into a twisted grin, leering up at them.

"Better take him where nobody can interfere. You know how tenderhearted some folks can be, even with a sidewinder like Sid," Sam said.

"Room two-oh-seven should fit the bill. There's already two bodies in there," Matt said.

"Good idea," said Sam. He bent over, taking hold of one of Felder's feet while Matt grasped the other. Together, they dragged him kicking and screaming along the corridor toward Room 207.

Witnesses looked on aghast, quickly moving out of the way. Matt and Sam hauled Felder into the anteroom, Matt freeing a hand to slam the door shut behind him.

They straightened up. Felder lay sobbing and gasping on the floor.

Matt toed his boot under Slim's corpse, flipping it over on its side and rolling it against a wall, out of the way. "That gives us some room to work," he said.

He went down on one knee beside Felder, gripping an ear between thumb and forefinger and twisting it to get Felder's attention. Felder bellowed in pain. He let go finally and Felder stopped hollering.

"Listen up, Sid. You know us and you know we don't play," Matt said. "I'm going to ask you one more time: Where's Black Angus Jones?"

"In hell with your mother—"

Matt rocked him with a backhanded slap that made Felder see stars. Blood trickled from smashed lips.

"You would have it the hard way, Sid," Matt said. "Okay, Sam—scalp him."

"I know just the thing," Sam said. He went into the bedroom.

"You're bluffing," Felder said.

"You think so," Matt said pleasantly.

Sam returned, holding Bardo's knife. "This should do the trick."

"You can't scare me—"

"I don't want to scare you, Sid, I want to scalp you," Sam said. He hunkered down beside Felder on the side opposite from Matt. "Nice hair, Sid, good and thick. Your scalp will look good hanging on the reins of my pony."

"You go to hell!"

"Better hold him down, Matt. This is going to hurt and I don't want him thrashing around. It might make the scalp come off uneven."

"Makes sense," Matt said. He planted a knee on Felder's left shoulder and chest, pinning his upper body to the floor.

Felder started yelling. Sam crouched over him,

knife in hand. He touched the tip to the upper left corner of Felder's forehead, right below the hairline. The wicked-sharp tip pierced the skin, drawing a ruby droplet of blood.

Sam drew the tip of the knife slowly along Felder's forehead, its course paralleling the hairline, leaving a red razor line of blood to mark its progress.

Felder kicked and screamed, hysterical. Matt was hard-pressed to hold him down.

"Quit all that thrashing or you'll lose an eye along with your scalp," Sam said, speaking loudly to be heard over Felder's squalling shrieks.

Outside in the hall, bystanders stood wide-eyed and staring as screams rang behind the closed door of Room 207.

"What are those two up to? Go see what they're doing, Stebbins," Colonel Davenport said.

"Yes, sir." Stebbins went to the door, opening it and looking in.

He saw Matt and Sam holding Felder down on the floor, despite Felder's fear-maddened efforts to break loose. Sam's face was a study in deep concentration as he drew the knife blade along Felder's hairline, marking a red line of blood.

Matt looked up, and barked, "Get out!"

Stebbins jumped back, shutting the door.

"What's going on in there, Stebbins? Speak up, man, don't shilly-shally. I can't hear you!"

"Er—arh—ahem! It looks like they're, uh, they're *scalping* that man, sir!"

Colonel Davenport slammed a fist into his palm,

exultant. "By heaven! Those are the men to lead my rescue mission into Mexico!"

In Room 207, Sid Felder sobbed hysterically. "I'll talk, I'll talk! I'll tell you anything you want, only don't scalp me, please, don't scalp me!"

Sam and Matt exchanged glances. "You're not funning, Sid? You'll tell us what we want to know?" Sam asked.

"Yes, yes, oh, Lord, yes. Only please don't scalp me, please—"

"Just like I thought, a yellowbelly," Matt said disgustedly.

Ten minutes later, the door of Room 207 opened, Matt stepping into the hall, the focus of the eyes of the onlookers gathered there. "He talked," Matt said.

"Did you—did you scalp him?" Colonel Davenport ventured, all quivering eager expectancy.

"Didn't have to, he spilled his guts without it. He's still in there babbling away," Matt said.

"No scalping? Damnation!" Davenport thundered. "What a disappointment! His scalp would have made an unforgettable souvenir of my Western trip!

"Oh, well, I suppose it couldn't be helped," he said, sighing.

FOURTEEN

Black Angus Jones and his gang were taking the seven young female captives from the Bear Paw wagon train to Pago in Sonora, Mexico. With them were five other girls they'd abducted along the way. The females were being transported by wagon—wagons looted from the sack of the Bear Paw caravan.

The gang moved out from Yellow Snake Canyon the morning of the raid, heading south. Angus Jones was unhappy—to put it mildly—with Linda Gordon's escape from Dorado and Quirt Fane. He sent Felder, Slim, and Bardo to Tombstone to silence her.

Meanwhile, he and the gang kept pushing south to Mexico.

Felder and the others were supposed to meet Jones in the town of Fronteras across the border in Mexico. Jones had some business to take care of there. He was not staying overnight, but would only be in Fronteras for a few hours before resuming the trek. If Felder and his sidemen missed Jones in Fronteras, they would catch up with him in Pago.

Pago was about sixty miles south of the border, located in the Sierra Espinazo del Diablo, the mountain range known as "the Devil's Spine." The isolated mountain town was a safe zone for outlaws, Mexican or American, as long as they were connected to the slave trade.

Don Carlos de la Vega was a power in that part of Sonora. Pago and its surrounding area was his own. A private army of gunmen enforced his will and law.

He was in cahoots with Captain Bravo, commanding officer of a body of troops garrisoned in Pago.

Bravo's men patrolled the outlying roads and trails, providing some protection against Victorio and his outlaws, who had taken refuge in Sonora's Sierra Madre mountains, of which the Espinazo was a small part.

This much and more Matt Bodine and Sam Two Wolves learned from Sid Felder. Dr. Willis grudgingly patched up Felder, grumbling, "I don't know why I bother—I'm only saving him for the hangman."

"Hangman's got to make a living, too, Doc," Matt said.

Willis had taken the physician's oath to preserve life, even the life of a no-good such as Felder. He extracted the bullets, stemmed the bleeding, and bandaged Felder, who was then taken to jail.

Matt and Sam skipped that trip. They thought it politic to avoid encountering Assistant Deputy

Osgood, for reasons they kept to themselves. Plenty of volunteers were available to haul Felder off to jail.

The prisoner's armed escort discovered Gila Chacon gone, with a mortified Hubert Osgood occupying the bandit's cell. Everybody got a good laugh out of Ringo's written receipt for Gila— everyone but Osgood, that is. Osgood was released and Felder locked up.

"If we hurry with the trial, we can still hold a hanging on Saturday, with Felder taking Gila's place," somebody said. The others agreed that that was a fine idea. A lot of folks were looking forward to a hanging and it would be a shame to disappoint them.

A couple of men stayed behind at the jailhouse to help out Osgood. "Seeing as you're having trouble holding on to your prisoners, Deputy, we'd hate to see you lose this one, too," one of the helpers said.

"Have Ringo stick a gun in your face and see if you say him no," Osgood retorted angrily. Nobody faulted him there.

The consensus was that Ringo and Curly Bill had freed the *bandido* to guide them through the hazards of Pago to a showdown with Dorado and Quirt Fane, killers of their pal Bob Farr.

Wheels were turning in Tombstone, things were happening despite the late night hour. Hastily called meetings and conferences were held at the Hotel Erle, where Colonel Davenport held court. Runners were sent around town to knock on doors and wake men up, citizens whose services were needed pronto. Word raced along the grapevine that something big was in the offing.

The result was that a group of bold, hard gunmen gathered at the O.K. Corral at first light.

Night was on the wane, the overarching vault of sky fading from blackness to a rich purple and royal-blue color. The moon hung low in the west, and the sun had still not shown in the east.

Lanterns hung on posts were pale yellow blurs floating amidst a sea of blue shadows. Smeared along the eastern horizon was a patch of ghostly brightness that was the forerunner of sunrise, that first light called by whites the "false dawn" and by Indians the "Wolf's Tail."

Present at the scene were those Brothers of the Wolf, Matt and Sam. It was a sleepless night for the Wolf Brethren. Colonel Davenport had picked them to head an emergency rescue mission into Mexico to free the captive girls. A rescue raid.

The sheriff and marshal and their men were still out somewhere on the trail chasing the Wells Fargo robbers. Not that it mattered, the lawmen being forbidden by law from crossing the border and carrying out their duties in Mexico. They had no jurisdiction in Mexico, no authority to operate.

Such strictures would not have stopped such men as Wyatt Earp and his brothers Virgil and Morgan from taking off their badges and venturing south as private citizens.

But they and their cohorts were on the Wells Fargo posse and nobody in town knew where they were or how to find them.

Luckily, this was Tombstone, where there was no shortage of tough men who knew how to handle a gun. When the call went out for volunteers, the problem lay not in finding enough men for the job, it was in finding the right men from the many ready to offer themselves up for duty.

Civic responsibility, a passion for justice, and simple human decency were augmented by that surest of all motivators: gold. Each member of the raiding party would receive a hundred dollars payment in advance and another hundred on return.

The funds would be furnished by Colonel Davenport, who had also posted a ten-thousand-dollar reward for a majority of the captive girls. He was mindful that some of the captives might have perished or been sold off along the way to Pago. The reward would be divided by the surviving raiding party members on their return to Tombstone with most of the captives.

The Mine Owners Association of Greater Tombstone had hastily convened to pass a resolution offering a five-thousand-dollar reward based on the same conditions, no matter what the result, and fifteen-thousand dollars would be split by the surviving raiders on successful completion of the mission.

It was a dazzling sum. For though Tombstone was a boomtown where the lucky few struck it rich, the vast majority of cowhands and miners worked like hell to earn a five to ten dollars weekly salary.

A force of fifty first-rate gunmen could easily

have been recuited from those clamoring to serve. For tactical reasons, a smaller bunch was needed. And what a band they were.

Matt and Sam headed the group. Weaponeer Remy Markand was part of the party. The others were Hal Purdy, Ed Dane, Jeff Howell, Geetus Maggard, Dutch Snyder, Juan Garza, Pima Joe, and Vern Tooker.

Hal Purdy, a Texas gunslinger, was regarded as one of the fastest guns west of the Pecos—which meant one of the fastest guns anywhere. He often hired out as a range detective for the big cattlemen, tracking down rustlers and outlaws who preyed on the herds and eliminating them.

He was forty, fleshy but handsome, with thick black hair, a Greek profile, and thick lips. He wore slate-gray garments and a black ribbon tie, and was a right-hand draw.

"A top man, we're lucky to get him," Matt told Colonel Davenport.

"Ed Dane, too," Sam said.

"Let's hope they don't kill each other," Matt said.

Ed Dane, too, was a West Texas gunman from the Big Bend region. A few years younger than Purdy, he had wispy blond hair and blue eyes. He wore a wide-brimmed straw planter's hat to protect against the sun, and thin, wrist-length gloves on soft hands that did no work except gun handling.

A background virtually identical to that of Purdy's had fostered no affection between the two. They were bitter rivals, often in competition for the same jobs. Their skills being at the same level, a shoot-out between them would most like result in a mutual slaying, which was the main reason why their enmity had not yet boiled over into a showdown. But the clock was ticking.

Before taking them on for the raid, Matt had extracted a solemn promise from Dane and Purdy both that they would engage in no hostilities until the mission was done.

Geetus Maggard and Dutch Snyder were partners. They'd long worked both sides of the law, sometimes wearing a badge, sometimes riding the owlhoot trail—occasionally, at the same time, playing both sides against the middle.

Maggard was small, slight, wizened. He looked like a burnt-out cinder of a man, but could outride and outlast most other men on the trail. His two guns were worn low and tied down. He had a big voice and a short temper and the sand and skill to back his play.

Dutch Snyder was Maggard's physical and temperamental opposite. A head taller and some seventy pounds heavier than his partner, he was big, bearlike, with broad sloping shoulders and a barrel torso. He was easygoing and agreeable, especially for one known to have killed over a dozen men in fair duels: a laid-back gunman and killer.

Howling Jeff Howell, the Arkansas Razorback, was in his late twenties, of medium height and build. He'd been a deputy, army scout, shotgun messenger, and a gunman for the railroads. A rooster-tail hairstyle crowned a bony fish face with dark restless eyes. He was thin lipped, with almost no upper lip.

Juan Garza was of Mexican ancestry with some Indian blood. His family had lived in the Arizona region for two hundred years. He'd been a lawman, scout, bounty hunter. He'd spent much time in Sonora and knew it well. He was a top hand at packing horses for long treks, no mean skill, and one much appreciated by trailsmen. Fiftyish, he had iron-gray hair and mustache, misty, dark brown eyes, and a square-shaped torso. A dead shot with a rifle, he favored a sawed-off shotgun for in-close work.

As his name implied, Pima Joe was a member of the Pima Indian tribe. It was said of the Pimas that they were the one neighboring tribe feared by the Apaches. In any case, Joe had given them plenty of reason to fear him, having worked as an army scout in the territory for much of the previous two decades. He wore a round-top-crowned black hat with an eagle feather in the hatband.

Vern Tooker was another of the "Last of the Mountain Men," a hunter, trapper, Indian fighter, scout, roaming from the Northern Range to the Southwest. He was big and tough, his face and body well-scarred. A Sharps .50 long-rifle buffalo gun was sheathed in his saddle scabbard.

Such was the raiding party: Rough men who would rather kill than run. The O.K. Corral served as an assembly area. Tension was in the air, the raiders eyeing each other like a pack of tomcats in a midnight alley sizing up the competition.

A fair-sized crowd had gathered to watch from the sidelines: night owls winding down before going to roost, early birds stopping off on their way to work, miners coming off or going on shift, and suchlike.

Great effort had been expended to ensure the party got as early a start as possible.

The raiders all had their own mounts, but pack-horses were needed to carry supplies of water, food, ammunition. Other horses were collected to serve as spares.

Colonel Davenport was footing most of the bills, but civic-minded Tombstone merchants had opened stores and shops in the pre-dawn darkness to make up the supplies and rations needed, donating them gratis in most cases.

"Some of you might wonder why we're going with so few men," Matt said. "This raid calls for speed and surprise. The fewer men, the faster we'll travel. We've got to be in Pago by Saturday at the latest and a day sooner wouldn't hurt. With luck we'll make it there in two days hard riding, which puts us there Thursday.

"There'll be lots of strangers in town and plenty of gringos, so a group this size shouldn't attract much attention. Anything larger might put the slave masters on guard and make our job that much harder. There's enough willing in town to recruit a small army, but if we did, the slavers would just hide the girls where we couldn't find them. Or kill them outright to keep us from having them."

"I don't like going in blind. How can you be sure of knowing where the girls are?" Ed Dane asked.

"We've got a few ins in Pago. I'll tell you more

when we're out of town where there's less chance of unfriendly ears overhearing," Matt said.

He went on. "We've got to walk soft, move fast. Surprise—speed—hitting hard, that's the key to success. This isn't a a a military mission; it's a raid. More like a train robbery or robbing a bank."

"That ought to be right up our line, Geetus," Dutch Snyder joked.

"Shut your mouth, you damned fool," Geetus Maggard snapped.

"What for? We're not wanted for anything in Arizona."

"I like it better this way. The less men, the bigger the payday," Jeff Howell said.

"How're we supposed to bring the girls back? There's not enough horses," Juan Garza said.

"It'd be a tip-off if we rode in trailing a string of extra horses for the girls. Once we're down there, we'll get them the old-fashioned way: horse theft," Matt said. "We're going to shoot up Pago and grab the girls back. I don't reckon we can make Don Carlos any madder by stealing his horses.

"Any more questions? No? Collect your advance and we'll ride out."

"Sign your name or make your mark," Arnholt Stebbins said, moving among the men, requiring each of them to sign a receipt before paying out their hundred dollars in gold. He put the signed documents in a folder and put the folder in a slim leather portfolio.

"You took the gold, and you're in for the duration. I know what kind of men you are. You wouldn't have been picked if there was any worry about your taking off with the gold. Funny things can happen on the trail, though, so I give you all fair warning. If any man tries to quit before the mission is done, I'll kill him," Matt said.

"If I don't get him first," Sam said.

The men prepared to mount up. Remy Markand circled a packhorse to which had been affixed a wooden crate he'd had brought to the corral. He checked the ropes and the knots, making sure the load was sitting properly on the animal.

"You don't have to worry none about your gear. Juan Garza packed it and he's the best blamed packer in the territory," mountain man Vern Tooker said.

"What's in that box anyhow?" Jeff Howell wondered aloud, eyeing the crate, squinting at it from different angles.

"An equalizer. Something to even the odds against Don Carlos's men and the government troops," Markand said.

"Dynamite?"

"No. We thought of bringing dynamite along, but the heat and rough trail would make it more dangerous to us than to the foe."

"What is it then?"

"A machine gun."

Jeff Howell looked suspicious, sceptical, as if unsure whether or not his leg was being pulled. "Ain't no ways big enough for a Gatling gun."

"It's lighter than a Gatling gun, but with plenty of firepower," Markand said.

"How is it called?"

"A Montigny Mitrailleuse. Ever heard of it?"

"Heard of it? Mister, I can't even say it! But I know this: the fancier the brand, the poorer the grade of beef."

"You may be surprised," Remy Markand said, a slight smile playing around his lips.

In the corral's stable barn, to one side of the front double doors, a small office area had been partitioned off for business functions, record keeping, and the like. Arnholt Stebbins set a leather briefcase on a table.

He opened it, reached inside, and took out a well-worn gun belt with a holstered Colt .45 Peacemaker revolver. It seemed to have seen much use, but was serviceable. He buckled on the gun belt, settling it in place. His movements were skilled, sure.

He tucked the folder with the signed receipts into the briefcase, fastening it shut. He went out into the corral. He gave the briefcase to Colonel Davenport.

"Gad! I envy you, Stebbins, setting out on an adventure like this. If I were only ten years younger, wild horses couldn't keep me away," Davenport said.

"Of course not, sir," Stebbins said. "You'll find the receipts in the briefcase. All seems in order, and so, without further ado, I'll take my leave of you now, sir."

"Good man," the other said heartily, slapping him on the back.

"Thank you, sir."

Earlier, Stebbins had selected a horse. It was

saddled and ready to go. He unhitched it. Holding it by the reins, he led it to where the other saddled horses were massed.

Sam saw him and did a take. It took a lot to surprise such a response from Sam, but this development merited it. "What're you doing, Stebbins?"

"I'm coming with you."

Sam was too polite to laugh in his face. "You're not serious!"

"Ah, but Colonel Davenport is. I'll be bringing along a sizeable amount of discretionary funds and he insists that I accompany the expedition to see that his money is well spent. He also wants an eyewitness present to make a full report on how Markand's machine gun performs in the field."

"This is no job for a desk man. The ride alone's enough to ruin anybody but a seasoned horseman," Sam said. "Not to mention you've got a better than even chance of getting killed."

"I'll take that chance. Ten years ago when I first came out west, clerking jobs were few and far between. One took the work where it could be found. I was the original circuit-riding bookkeeper at all the big strikes: Cripple Creek, Leadville, Virginia City, Silver City, many others."

"Ever use that gun you're wearing on your hip?"

"Yes. Not lately, but I practice regularly to keep my hand in."

"Ever kill a man with it?"

"Two men, robbers. Really, Mr. Two Wolves, there's no point in arguing. What you or I want in the matter is unimportant. The colonel has his mind set on my making the trip. Take it up with him if you like, though I assure you that once he's made his mind up, he's as steadfast as a rock."

"You've got sand, Stebbins, I'll give you that," Sam said, shaking his head. "Not a lot of sense, maybe, but sand." He went to tell Matt the news.

Matt tried to talk Davenport out of it, but the colonel was adamant and unyielding. Matt returned, shrugging.

"I hope you know what you're doing, Stebbins. Every man's got to carry his weight on this go. If you change your mind or can't keep up, you'll be cut loose and left to your own devices, same as anybody else in this bunch," Matt said.

"I expect nothing less," Stebbins said stiffly.

"Welcome aboard then, and good luck. I admire your guts if not your good sense."

Yellow rays shafted fanwise out of the eastern horizon, heralding the sunrise. "Daylight's burning! Saddle up, men, and let's ride," Matt said.

The raiders mounted up, the corral gates were opened, and the men on horseback began filing out.

"Good hunting, men, and Godspeed!" Colonel Davenport said. Among the spectators, men cheered and the women waved and fluttered their handkerchiefs.

The column rode west to the end of the street, past the outskirts of town. Leaving behind the table of Goose Flats on which Tombstone town was set, the line of riders and their string of packhorses and spare horses descended the slope, moving south across the San Pedro Valley.

Lemon-yellow light filled the eastern horizon, the limb of the sun coming into view. Sunbeams shafted across the cactus- and boulder-strewn flat, causing the riders and mounts of the column to cast eerily elongated shadows stretching west for hundreds of feet.

With the sun came the first nagging pricklings of heat. The night had been cool, almost chill, as was the way of it in the high desert. The coolness ceased to exist with the advent of dawn. That, too, was the way of the desert.

The column angled southeast, away from the Tombstone Hills on its right. There was no need to send out scouts yet. The countryside was open in all directions, affording no cover for ambush. Though rash indeed would have been the bushwhacker who opened fire on this formidable outfit.

They rode on, the temperature climbing with the sun as it inched up the vault of sky. The riders began grouping together in twos and threes, according to the degree of affinity between them.

Matt and Sam rode together at the point, Hal Purdy riding up along with them. Remy Markand and Arnholt Stebbins rode side by side, with Ed Dane making up a third.

Markand and Stebbins had a mutual interest in Colonel Davenport and Dane was fascinated by the idea of the machine gun, pumping Markand with questions about it.

Dane and Purdy would've ridden with anyone as long as it wasn't with each other.

Partners Geetus Maggard and Dutch Snyder

were paired farther down the line. Howling Jeff Howell and Vern Tooker strung together. Each was a wild man in his own way: Howell the hellraising Arkansas Razorback and soft-spoken Tooker the veteran of countless brawls, knifings, Indian fights, and manhunts.

Juan Garza and Pima Joe rode at the tail of the column, where horseman Garza trailed the string of packhorses and spares, keeping an eye on the animals and their burdens. Garza and Pima Joe, both men of few words, seemed to take some enjoyment in each other's laconic company.

To the column's right, running north to south, stretched the San Pedro River, a scrub of greenery growing along its banks making a welcome change from the tan and sandy wastes sprawling on all sides.

The column angled south by southeast, away from the San Pedro, passing far-flung, isolated ranches. A blur in the southern distance gradually resolved itself into the figures of a group of mounted men.

"Riders up ahead," Hal Purdy said, frowning. "Three or four, I make it."

"Four," Sam said.

"They ain't hiding. They're showing themselves."

"It's okay, Hal, they're with us," Matt said. Sam turned in the saddle, telling those riding behind to pass the word along the column that the quartet ahead were friendlies.

Presently, the column approached a crossroads.

Waiting in the shade of a clump of mesquite trees were Ringo, Curly Bill, Gila Chacon, and Polk Muldoon.

The road east led to the McLaury brothers ranch. Siblings Tom and Will McLaury were in the inner circle of the Cowboy faction, friends of Ringo and Curly Bill. Ringo, Bill, Gila, and Polk had gone to the ranch after the jailbreak. Ringo and Bill had set the crossroads as their meeting place when they'd made plans with Sam and Matt last night at the Big Sky Saloon.

The four rode out to meet the column.

"They're going with us. Most of you know Ringo, Bill, and Polk. The *bandido* is from Pago, knows the ins and outs of it. He knows some folks there that'll help us out," Matt explained.

"Why trust him?" Hal Purdy asked.

"Don Carlos, boss of the slavers, is an enemy of Chacon's. He sent three men to kill him. That's why Chacon was caught and in jail, waiting for the hangman."

"I don't like it. What's to stop him from leading us into a trap or selling us out when we reach Pago?"

"My gun, Hal," Ringo said said smiling, but meaning it, too.

"That's good enough for me," Ed Dane said. If Hal Purdy was against something, he'd be for it.

"We're Chacon's best hope—hell, only hope— for tearing into Don Carlos and breaking his power. He needs us, and we can damned sure use him," Matt said.

"An excellent basis for trust, señor," Gila said.

"How's this affect the split of the reward, that's

what I want to know," Geetus Maggard said, scowling, his face bunched up like a clenched fist. "Four more slices of the pie mean smaller shares for the rest of us."

"Gila gets no share," Sam said. "There's a rope waiting for him in Tombstone and he can't come in to collect."

"Ringo, Bill, and Polk come in for equal shares," Matt said.

"Don't know as I like that," Maggard said.

"They run the same risks as the rest of us and come in for an equal payday. Fair's fair."

"For myself, I am glad to have these men with us. We need guns such as theirs," Juan Garza said.

"I've ridden with Polk and he's plenty salty. And I reckon everybody here knows what Ringo and Curly Bill can do," Vern Tooker said.

The others seemed to agree; in any case, no dissenting opinion was voiced aloud.

"I s'pose enough of us'll get killed to fatten them shares back up," Maggard said grudgingly.

"That's Geetus for you, always looking on the bright side," Dutch Snyder said, laughing.

Gila turned toward Polk. "We go into dangerous country, amigo. My gun?"

Sam and Matt exchanged glances, nodding. "Give him his gun, Polk," Sam said.

Polk Muldoon raised the flap of his saddlebag and pulled out Gila's gun belt and gun, handing it to him.

"*Gracias.*" Gila smiled, showing strong white teeth.

He fastened the belt around his waist, snugging it into place, settling the soft leather holster where it hung down from his hip.

"Ahh," he said contentedly, sounding like a man slipping into a hot bath. "I am going to reach for my gun now, to make sure it is in working order. I tell you this so none of you bad hombres gets the wrong idea. I would hate for there to be a tragic misunderstanding before we have a chance to get to know each other better."

"You sure would," Purdy said grimly.

Gila reached for his gun, slowly drawing it from the holster. Holding it so it wasn't pointing at anyone, he checked the action. Satisfied, he put it back in the holster.

"I could use a rifle, too. When someone shoots at you from a distance, it is good to be able to shoot back, no?"

"There's extra rifles on one of the packhorses. You can get one the next time we stop," Sam said.

"We are stopped now."

"What the hell," Matt said, "give him a rifle, somebody."

"I'll get one. I packed them so it's less trouble if I get it," Juan Garza said. He got down from the saddle, going down the line of packhorses until he found the one he wanted. Strong fingers plucked open knotted ropes, lifting the edge of a canvas tarpaulin.

Presently, Gila Chacon had a loaded rifle in hand. "Winchester! This is very good, señores." His saddle scabbard was empty. He filled it with the rifle. "Now, on to Pago, eh, *muchachos? Vámonos!*"

The four newcomers got into line and the column resumed its forward progress south. Hooves kicked up dust, its yellow plume marking their course. The sun rose higher. The dirt road arrowed across the prairie, narrowing to the vanishing point. The road to Mexico.

On they rode through the mounting heat of day. Shadows shortened. Small dusty lizards perched on rocks, panting, quivering.

The column passed Bisbee somewhere on its right, too distant to be seen. The last of the sparsely scattered ranches had been left behind hours ago. Brief stops were made to water the horses and give them some moments rest, before the trek was resumed once more.

The naked sun turned the sky a seething yellow-white. Buzzards circled in the heights, soaring on the thermals, dipping and gliding.

The flat began to rise, outcroppings thrusting into the open, black-brown rocks lifting themselves from sandy yellow-gray soil. Sunbaked ground rang to the tread of hoofbeats.

Matt Bodine rode alongside Remy Markand for a while, studying the other out of the corner of his eye. Markand was an unknown quantity. At least, he knew how to ride. He seemed unfazed by the relentless heat.

"It's been a long time since I was in Mexico," Markand said presently. "Fifteen years. I was here with the Legion, the Foreign Legion, when Maximilian was emperor."

"That didn't work out so well," Matt said.

"For Maximilian, no. He died in front of a Juarista firing squad. A mad scheme, trying to install an Austro-Hungarian prince on the throne of Mexico. Only a maniac like Napoleon III could have conceived of it."

"You were a legionaire, huh? Tough outfit, they say."

Markand shrugged. "It suited me at the time. You may have heard what they say in the recruiting offices: 'You joined the Legion to die, and France will send you where you can die.'"

"But you didn't die," Matt said.

"I know. I daresay I was a great disappointment to them," Markand said dryly.

They rode farther along. "The landscape is much like that of Morocco, you know. Morocco and Mexico sit roughly along the same latitude line. Similar arid climate, similar terrain, stony desert and mountains," Markand said.

"No Apaches in Morocco, though," Matt said.

"Morocco has its own savage tribesmen: Riffs, Berbers, Tuaregs. . . . Fine horsemen, fine fighters. Torturers—God help you if they take you alive."

"What are you doing here, Markand? I mean, what's in it for you?"

"I'm a salesman for an arms maker. This is my chance to give a field demonstration of the Montigny Mitrailleuse. If Colonel Davenport likes the result, he and his associates may buy into the weapon's North American rights."

"That all of it?"

Markand shrugged. "Perhaps there is something

of what you might call desert hunger. I spend much time in banks, offices, and boardrooms. I hunger to experience desert and mountains, sun and stars."

Matt nodded. It was a feeling he could understand.

"Why are you here?" Markand asked.

"Sam and I have tangled with slave hunters before. I've seen their work, the bloodshed and human misery they cause. Anytime I can wipe a few of them off the face of the earth, I'll jump at the chance," Matt said.

"And to get paid for it is even better," he added.

FIFTEEN

The captives were at the end of their rope, almost. At the end of their chain, more accurately. They were fettered to an iron chain bolted to the floor of the covered wagon taking them to Pago in Sonora, Mexico.

The Black Angus Gang had two covered wagons filled with captive girls. The Bear Paw wagon train had not been the only target. They'd raided lonely ranch houses along the way to the rendezvous at Yellow Snake Canyon, killing all the inhabitants but the young female family members.

They'd robbed, too, but the loot to be found in such ranches was laughable, next to nothing. The girls were the loot; they'd fetch big money down Mexico way.

Angus Jones, Carmen Oliva, Sonny Boy Algar, Sime Simmons, Mort Donegan, and Porgy Best had insinuated themselves into McGee's westbound caravan. The rest of the gang, under the leadership of

Quirt Fane, brought an additional five abucted girls to Yellow Snake Canyon.

Once the Bear Paw emigrants had been wiped out, all but the girls, Jones had picked out three wagons in the best condition and had had them rigged for the trip south.

Precious human cargo was consolidated in two Conestoga wagons, while a third was filled with arms, ammunition, supplies, and whatever few meager items of value had been pillaged from the wagon train to sell in the *mercado*, the marketplace of Pago.

The more mature female chattels, in their mid to late teens, were kept in one wagon, the younger girls in another.

The senior girls had gotten their growth and were mostly full-bodied, vital, healthy young women in every respect, save for the fact of their being unmarried; this in a society where it was accepted as a matter of course that a maiden of fifteen was of a fit age to be a wife and mother.

The senior girls also posed the greatest threat of escape. To a slave master, disobedience is the greatest sin and escape the supreme act of disobedience.

The senior girls included Eva Haber, sixteen; Jenna Rowley, seventeen; Devon Collins, fourteen; and Priscilla Ard, fifteen. All were from Bear Paw. Chained with them were girls taken by the slavers on the road to Yellow Snake Canyon: Gail Merwin, eighteen; Rowena Whitman, fourteen; and Sherry Dubois, sixteen.

They sat on the floor of the wagon bed with their

backs to the long sides of the hopper, three on one side, four on the other. They were as seemingly wretched, miserable, and unhappy a lot of human beings as to be found under the Southwestern sun. A length of heavy chain was fastened to iron staples bolted to the floorboards.

Each captive had an iron cuff locked around her ankle, and a thinner length of chain securing the cuff to the massive main chain.

Such leg irons were easily acquired, being in wide use throughout the frontier; indeed, across the nation, being found in reformatories, jails, prisons, workhouses for debtors and the poor, convict labor gangs, and so on.

"That'll keep any of you little missies with rabbit blood in you from trying to take it on the run," said Jones Gang member Slicker Dupree, chortling when the captives were first locked in chains. "It's for your own good so you don't hurt yourselves. Where would you run to anyway, in this desert hell? You'd die from heat and thirst, if you was lucky. If not lucky, the Apaches would find you. . . ."

Sime Simmons drove the senior girls' wagon. He was the most dependable member of the gang where young female flesh was concerned.

Long years of backbreaking toil and unremitting danger for little return had left him with a cold heart. All he wanted now was to gain as much gold as he could while he was still strong enough to take it with his own two hands.

Black Angus could rely on Simmons not to assault one of the virginal captives, thereby drastically reducing her selling price at the slave auction in Pago. If any of the band outraged one of the girls, Angus Jones vowed openly to slay that man.

"Anybody ruins a gal is stealing money from the rest of us. I'll kill him, whoever it is. I'll cut it off at the root first, to teach the rest of you a lesson about the cost of not following orders straight down the line. It don't matter who it is or what they've been to me in the past. Friendship don't count when it comes to keeping faith with your fellow gang members—it's a matter of ethics," he said.

His woman, Carmen Oliva, rode up front on the wagon's driver's seat beside Sime Simmons. She smoked long, skinny, gnarly black cigars that looked like dried twigs and smelled like burning buffalo chips.

She was an unholy terror to the girls. When one displeased her—and it took very little to get on Carmen's bad side—a sullen glance, a too-slowness in carrying out a command being enough to trigger her volcanic temper—she set on the offender with the fury of a harpy. Carmen knew how to inflict pain without doing permanent damage, or leaving marks or scars that would knock down the victim's selling price.

The second wagon in the convoy held the younger girls, those in their early teens and below. From Bear Paw, they were April Collins, ten; Gretchen Haber, twelve; and Mandy Sutton, thirteen. The others were Emily Jane Bartlett, fourteen; and Dora Hernandez, thirteen.

Despite their tender years, they too would fetch top prices at Pago. Reflecting on their youth, Angus

Jones philosophized, "It's an investment, like buying a yearling calf. Wait a few years and they'll get their growth. In the meantime, they can make themselves useful helping out around the house—"

"The whorehouse, that is, aw-haw-haw-haw!" Sonny Boy Algar leered. His being a nephew and blood kin, Black Angus tolerated the interruption without clouting Sonny Boy.

"Somebody's got to build the fires and make the beds and wash the sheets and clean the slops and drudge away in the kitchen," Jones said.

The junior girls weren't kept in chains, most being too slender for leg irons, which tended to slip free of their ankles. No, each was fitted with a high, stiff, thick leather collar, like a choker collar, buckled and locked in place with a small padlock. A length of clothesline ran through rings in the collars binding them all together.

Moronically cheerful, oblivious as though he'd been struck by lightning, Slicker Dupree drove the second wagon mostly, sometimes being spelled by one of the others. Dupree's virtue lay in the fact that for him the word of Black Angus was absolute law.

Mort Donegan piloted the third wagon, the one containing supplies, arms, ammunition, and plundered loot. Donegan was grim, taciturn, and a stolid professional.

The convoy crossed the border, churning along the road winding through the northernmost mountains of the Sierra Madre Occidental, a line of 800-plus miles of mountain ranges known as the "spine of Mexico."

The mountains were made of volcanic rock,

spewed up from the internal heat below, molten magma upthrusting through earth's crust to cool into jagged peaks, pinnacles, promontories, and cliffs. They were honeycombed with *barrancas*, a twisty labyrinth of canyons, passes, dry washes, and river valleys.

In the north, the hills were home and refuge to the Yaqui Indians, fierce foes of the hated flatlanders of Spanish descent. They were also the redoubt of renegade bronco Apaches who'd jumped the reservations, now hiding out in the sierra from the armies of two countries, the United States and Mexico.

Jumbled adobe blocks and cubes that were pueblo villages nestled among the cliffs like crystalline rock formations.

Dangerous country, and its threat was infinitely magnified during the last year when fearsome Apache war chief Victorio fled the Arizona Territory reservation, taking his tribespeople south into the mountains of Sonora.

If the Sierra Madre was the spine of Mexico, Sonora's Espinazo range was the spine of the Sierra Madre. The locals had another name for it: the Spine of the Devil, or the Devil's Backbone.

The Black Angus gang regarded themselves as a rough bunch, hardcases who made way for no man, but they walked softly during their passage through the Espinazo en route to Pago. Apache sign was abroad: scourged pueblo villages, abandoned and depopulated, along with burnings and dead bodies.

The gang skulked as best they were able, creeping

cautiously along the trail, mounted men and wagons clustered together as if hunched up in expectation of a fearful blow that might land anytime without warning.

The outlaws' usual devil-may-care demeanor, laughing and scratching, drinking and joking, pranks and games of grab ass—were all gone now. They had vanished on first sight of a burned-out village and the mutilated dead bodies of men, women, and children littering the streets: Victorio's handiwork.

The badmen's narrowed eyes restlessly swept the landscape of rocky sierra and sunbaked plains, seeking the Apache. Faces were set in hard lines, their mouths tight, dry, their hands hovering near rifles and holstered guns.

"Keep your eyes peeled for 'paches!" Quirt Fane said.

"What good will that do? You won't see 'em until it's too late," Porgy Best gloomed. "You'll know they're there when the first bullet tears into you. You won't get no more sign than that."

"Grow yourself a pair, your guts are leaking down your leg."

"Shut your mouth, Porgy. That's defeatist thinking, bad for morale," Black Angus snapped.

In the wagons, female captives already stunned, shocked, and terrorized now had new reason to fear. Most of the girls were too scared to cry, as if tears and sobbing would call the savages down on them.

When one began whimpering, the others darted furious glances at her, hissing at her to shut up.

"They finally found something they fear more than us—the Apaches," Sime Simmons said. Carmen laughed, but it had a hollow sound.

"Trouble is, there's no way to sneak through this territory, not with two wagons full of kids. No back trail for smugglers or mountain goats that the Apaches don't know better," Quirt Fane complained.

"We got plenty of guns and some salty hombres siding us," Black Angus said. "If they come on us, we can still outgun the Apaches."

"One thing we got going for us. 'Paches won't want to kill any of the captives," Quirt said.

"Don't take no comfort from that," Porgy Best said. "Them red devils can shoot. They never have enough bullets so they know how to make every shot count."

"Cheerful cuss, ain't you?" Quirt said sourly.

"Damn it, Porgy, I told you to belay that defeatist bad-mouthing," Black Angus said.

The convoy was climbing a ridge, its crest screening what lay beyond. "Scouts are coming back, boss," Rio Jordan said.

Angus Jones raised a hand, signaling a halt. The tread of hoofbeats, pantings of teamed horses drawing the wagons, the rumbling of iron-rimmed, wooden wagon wheels, all such sounds were suddenly stilled.

Wailing winds could be heard whipping through

the pass under a hot high sun on a bright, blue sky day.

"Soldiers!" Earl Calder cried out, riding in after scouting ahead. "They're here, boss. On the other side of the hill, in the valley."

That was cheering . . . in a way.

"Don Carlos said troops would be guarding the road south into Pago, but I figured it was just talk. I didn't think they'd do it," Black Angus said

"Them Mexes can get off their lazy asses when there's gold in it," Rio Jordan said.

"Don't let Dorado hear you talking like that, he's mighty touchy," Quirt Fane cautioned.

"The hell do I care?" Rio blustered, but not before looking around to make sure Dorado was well out of earshot before he spoke.

"How many troops, Earl?"

"Looks like a couple dozen, boss."

Jones gave the signal and the convoy began moving ahead, cresting the ridge.

Beyond, the slope descended into a lens-shaped valley, its long axis running north to south. At midpoint of the flat, east of the dirt road on a flat-topped knoll, stood a ruined mission church.

A hundred years old, maybe more, it was made of stone and adobe. The roof had collapsed, and only parts of the walls were left standing. The structure looked like a brown sugar cube that had partly dissolved.

Clustered around it was a bunch of brown ants and tan stick figures. The ants were horses and the figures were men, soldiers. Government troops. They were grouped on a stony plaza aproning the ruined church. The convoy's arrival caused no small activity among the troops, setting them into swarming, seething motion.

Seeing the troops, some of the captives took heart. "Soldiers! They'll save us," one said.

"No, they won't, else we'd be running away from them, not to them," said another, a realist.

Troopers mounted horses and formed up, riding toward the convoy coming down off the hill onto the flat. Halting, they formed a wide crescent shape whose center was in the middle of the road.

"Now what do we do?" Slicker Dupree asked, shouting.

"Keep moving, nice and easy. Nobody do anything stupid, but keep your guard up," Black Angus ordered, his word going forth to the convoy.

A handful of soldiers rode out to meet them. At their head was a slovenly sergeant, thick bodied, big bellied, seeming as much outlaw as soldier. The same could be said of his troops, those riding forward with him and the rest staying behind. They were a scrawny, ill-fed, piratical looking group. Fodder for cannon, gallows, or firing squad.

"They got rifles pointed at us," Rio Jordan breathed.

"Easy—if they're planning a cross, they'll try to buffalo us first, flanking us for a clear field of fire to avoid hitting the girls," Jones said.

Dorado scrutinized the oncoming riders, relaxing to a degree, though still watchful. "It is well," he said. "It's that pig Sergeant Sancho. He knows not to go against Don Carlos. He knows better than to go against—Dorado."

Jones and Dorado rode forward, halting when face to face with Sergeant Sancho and his squad. Except for Sancho and a corporal, the soldiers gawked at the wagonloads of girls, craning for a better look. They shouted familiarly, making lewd remarks, and wet kissing noises.

"Shut your filthy mouths, you dogs," Sergeant Sancho said matter-of-factly, and the men fell silent.

Longish dark hair curled out from beneath Sancho's flat, short-billed cap. He was moon faced, with bulging pop eyes, thin mustache, and a double-chin. A jowly face was grizzled with a three-day growth of beard. His swelling belly strained the buttons of a tan military tunic.

Black Angus, Dorado, and Sergeant Sancho exchanged glances as knowing and jaded as that of three old bawds in a bordello of sin. Sancho nodded at them with recognition, but no joy.

"I know you," he said to Jones, "and you," to Dorado. "What are you doing with so much gringos?" he asked Dorado.

"Bound for Pago."

"Too much gringos," Sancho said. He shook his head dolefully, and spat into the dust.

"A man needs many friends," Black Angus said.

"And so many guns." The corporal tsk-tsked. He was undersized, weaselly.

"This is hard country," Jones said.

"Very hard, and bad—for some," Sancho agreed.

"Not for friends of Don Carlos, surely."

"You, gringo, are a friend of Don Carlos, eh?"

"As you well know, *sargento*, you've seen me in Pago before. Don Carlos is expecting us, and he'll be greatly disappointed if we're late."

"You bring pretty little young songbirds for to sing on the stage of his opera house, no?"

"That's right."

"Don Carlos does not like for strangers to have his name in their mouths, especially not when they're gringos. This is his land. You got a pass from him, maybe?" Sancho demanded.

Dorado had been watching the exchange with mounting irritation, eyes flashing, lips compressing into a thin line. He rested a hand on the butt of his gun, patting it significantly. "This is all the pass we need."

The corporal flinched, as if struck in the face. Coloring, he clawed for his gun. The golden pistol cleared Dorado's holster, filling his hand and pointing at the corporal's middle. The corporal froze.

Soldiers stirred, swinging rifles to cover Jones and Dorado and the convoy, working bolt-action levers.

Black Angus turned in the saddle, facing his men. "As you were, men, as you were! Nobody draw yet. We don't want to set off a whole shooting match here!"

Sancho smirked, seeming otherwise unexcited. He took off his cap, fanning his face, brushing away flies. "You want to kill my Corporal Cruz, Dorado?"

"He'll be the first, not the last," Dorado said. Corporal Cruz sat rigid in the saddle, upright.

"A good joke," Sancho said, chuckling throatily. "But do not kill him, please. He is not worth much, but I would not like to have to train another to take his place. I am a lazy man.

"Put up your gun, Golden Man. It's too hot to fight."

"Tell your men to put up theirs first."

"Why not?" Sancho said, shrugging. "Stand down, hombres!"

The troops obeyed, rifle barrels lowering with obvious reluctance.

"See? Nothing to worry about. We are all friends here. Now put away your gun."

"Tell that chicken thief of a corporal to take his hand away from his gun first," Dorado said.

"Do what the Golden Man says, Corporal."

"*Sí, mi sargento.*" Cruz complied, hand crawling away from his gun. Dorado dropped his pistol in the holster.

"You're a fair piece from Pago, *sargento*," Black Angus remarked, as if nothing had happened.

"We are on patrol, in search of Victorio and his bronco Apaches."

"Yes, I saw how hard you were looking for him," Jones said pointedly.

Sancho was a man who could not be insulted. A man of the world, broadminded, genial. "Catch the Apache? Try to catch the wind. Instead, we protect the road for travelers like you. The road is safe. Victorio fears us, he stays away. If you had met up with Victorio or his bravos we would not be talking now."

"We were lucky," Jones said, meaning it.

"Ah, but we have delayed you long enough with our foolishness. You may pass," Sancho said, gesturing grandly at the road south.

"*Gracias* . . . cigar?" Jones offered.

"Why not?"

Jones handed Sancho a cigar, the latter rolling it between his fat fingers. He held it under his nose, sniffing appreciatively. "Ah, fine tobacco, a good cigar, señor."

"Have another for later," Jones offered.

Sancho took it, saying, "I would rather have one of those *bonitas*, a pretty little *chiquita* to warm my bed at night."

"Come to the auction at Pago, and you'll have a chance to bid."

"I am but a poor soldier, señor. That is too rich for me."

Black Angus shrugged. "Is the road to town clear?"

"It seems to be. We were not bothered by the Apache on our way here. Victorio was last seen high in the mountains to the west," Sancho said, "but that means nothing. The Apache goes where he likes."

"We'll be moving on, then. We've still got a fair piece of ground to cover before nightfall."

"May God go with you, señor—that is, if He is to be found in this wilderness, which I sincerely doubt," Sancho said.

He shouted orders to his men, the crescent breaking apart in the middle, leaving the road south open and unbarred. "*Hasta luego, señor.* Perhaps we will meet again," the sergeant said.

Black Angus hoped not. He signalled the convoy to proceed. It lurched into motion, mule skinner whips in the hands of drivers cracking above yoked and harnessed teams. Wooden wheels clattered, churning up yellow-brown dust.

Sergeant Sancho and his squad turned aside, leading the rest of the troops back toward the mission.

The convoy rolled south. Sancho and Cruz sat their horses on top of the church knoll, watching the caravan pass.

"Dog of a Dorado! I should have killed him," Cruz said feelingly.

"You? You could not kill such a one in a thousand years," Sancho said, puffing on his cigar. There was no insult in his remark, merely a statement of fact.

"He's not so much. A bullet in the back, and it is done, he is a dead man."

"You know nothing of the Legend of the Golden Gun, then, eh, Cruz?"

"I know only that it is a waste of good gold, *mi sargento*. With so much gold, a man could have many pretty women and an ocean of tequila to bathe them in."

"No, no. The golden gun is accursed. When it was forged, the gunsmith melted down an old golden mask of the Aztecas, the Aztec Indians. A mask of one of the heathen devil-gods of old, a God of Death.

"Death and black magic, pagan sorcery— something of the death-god entered into the gun. It protects its owner against harm. No *pistolero* can defeat he who wields the golden gun. In exchange, the souls of those killed by the golden gun become slaves to the dark god."

"You believe that, *sargento?*"

"I neither believe nor disbelieve, Cruz. I relay the legend as it was told to me. There is more: It is said that the owner of the golden gun cannot die by gunfire. He must be killed by knife, noose, lance, fire, yes, even by bare hands—but not by bullets. That is part of the magic."

The corporal stroked his pointy chin, eyes narrowed with thought. "Even if it is as you say, there must be a remedy. A gun holds but six bullets. When it is empty, the owner must fall."

"Try if you dare, Corporal," Sancho said, "if you dare. After the auction, Dorado and the gringos will have much gold. They may pass by here. Perhaps we shall meet again."

"This is good thinking." Corporal Cruz grinned, showing yellowed horse teeth.

"That is why I am sergeant. We must keep an eye open for the Golden Man and his friends. The gringos will have to ride north sooner or later."

The convoy was a dwindling blot to the south, almost out of sight. Sergeant Sancho stubbed out the cigar butt against the pommel of his saddle, putting it away in a breast pocket for later. He took out the other cigar given him by Black Angus. He bit off the tip, spitting it away.

Corporal Cruz was quick with a lit match, holding the flame to one end of the cigar while Sancho puffed away. A haze of rich, aromatic tobacco smoke wreathed Sancho's head.

"Perhaps we will cross paths again, yes," he mused, "and if we do . . . We shall see, we shall see."

SIXTEEN

They came to Candido's. Candido's Cantina, in Fronteras, Mexico.

Fronteras was a border town, located not too far south of the dividing line separating Arizona Territory from the state of Sonora, the United States from Mexico.

Like most border towns, it was tough, rowdy, wide open, a meeting place of smugglers, rustlers, fugitives, and outlaws. Ringo and Curly Bill knew it well.

Most of Tombstone's Cowboy faction actually were or had been working cowboys, cowboys who'd jumped the fence between law and outlawry. Cattle rustling was their meat and potatoes, the heart and soul of their larcenous enterprise.

The Cowboys rustled livestock on both sides of the border, stealing stock in Arizona and selling it in Mexico, stealing stock in Mexico and selling it in Arizona. There was plenty of hijacking and robbery, too. Contraband was constantly being moved across the border: gold, silver, guns, women, and whiskey.

Fronteras was a place where deals were made, where horses and cattle were bought and sold. There were a number of corrals and stock pens where animals could be held and transferred with no questions asked. Fronteras put the buyers and sellers together. By nature it was a magnet for bad men and outlaws, a town whose only law was the gun and the knife.

Here information, too, was a commodity to be bought, sold, or traded: knowledge of what gangs were working in the region—who killed whom, who was double-crossing whom, the going rate to bribe government officials and army officers, hideouts and where to find them, and suchlike.

Commerce of this sort was a specialty of the house at Candido's Cantina. Of all the brokers in the latest word/news, few were better informed than the cantina's proprietor, "Candy" Candido himself.

To him came Matt Bodine and Johnny Ringo.

The Tombstone rescue raiders made brief camp at a secure and isolated spot outside Fronteras. They kept a low profile to avoid attracting notice of their descent into Sonora. Ringo and Curly Bill Brocius knew the campsite well. They had used it before during some of their own rustling schemes and deals. It was an oval park hidden among low, rounded, wooded hills. A stream ran through it and there was good grazing grass for the horses.

"We'll be in Fronteras just long enough to make

some contacts and pick up some intelligence about Black Angus and how things stand in Pago," Matt Bodine said. "Ringo, you know Candido best so you should be the one to meet him. I'll go with you to hold the horses and watch your back."

"Let's ride," Ringo said.

He and Matt rode into Fronteras, following an indirect route little traveled, one known to Ringo. They threaded narrow, dusty dirt streets through blocks of one-room, flat-roofed adobe houses honeycombed by corrals, huts, and backyard gardens.

Candido's Cantina was one such whitewashed rectangular cube. It had small square windows; its open front door was an oblong of murky blackness. It was aromatic with the scent of baked corn tortillas and coffee. A line of horses was hitched in front of the cantina.

Matt and Ringo rode around to the back of the building. They stepped down from the saddle, hitching their mounts to the top rail of a skeletal wooden-pole fence. "The horses okay here?" Matt asked.

"Anybody dumb enough to steal a horse from Candy's would be found in an alley with his throat cut, and everyone knows it," Ringo said.

"That'd be scant consolation if it left me without a horse."

"They'll be okay."

A massive, wide-bodied woman sat on a three-legged stool in the shade of a wooden awning overhanging the back door. She weighed about as much as Matt and Ringo put together. A golden moon face showed heavy-lidded, black-button eyes, a flat wide nose, and a tiny, puckered, cherub mouth.

Thick black hair tied up in a bun was held in place by a knotted strip of rainbow-colored cloth. She was adorned with oversized silver-and-turquoise earrings and a necklace made of the same materials. She puffed on a corncob pipe, and whatever she was smoking, it didn't smell like tobacco.

"*Hola.* I'm Ringo."

She looked up, eyeing him. Her eyes were very red. "I know who you are," she said in thick, heavily accented English.

"Tell Candy I want to see him."

"Tell him yourself," she said, indicating the back door. Matt and Ringo exchanged glances, Matt shrugging.

"*Gracias,*" Ringo said to the woman. She resumed puffing on her pipe. He and Matt went in.

Candy Candido was drinking tequila by himself in a back room. The room was warm and shadowy, filled with dark brown shadows like pools of warm muddy water. Candido was short and stout, of indeterminate origins and nationality. He had a wide, thick black mustache, jug ears, and a lot of chin and jaw. He wore a baggy white Mexican long-sleeve shirt, a thin reddish-brown leather vest that barely reached down below his armpits, white pantaloons, and sandals.

He and his two visitors sat around a wooden table on high-backed armless wooden chairs with woven wicker seats. "Who's your friend, Ringo?" Candido asked.

"Matt Bodine."

Candido's eyes flashed with lively interest. "So you're Bodine, eh? I've heard of you. Where's your Indian pard?"

"He's around," Matt said. Candido set out two glazed brown ceramic cups on the table, duplicates of the one from which he was drinking. He filled all three and they drank up, Matt repressing a shudder. It was strong stuff. Matt's face reddened. He broke a fresh sweat, shivering at the same time.

Candido refilled the cups. Matt drank his more slowly, taking small sips.

"I like good talk but I don't have time to sit around and chew the fat," Ringo began.

"In a hurry to kill someone, huh?" Candido asked, chuckling.

"Does it show that badly?"

"There's a kind of look you get when you're on the prod. Your face and neck swell up like a puff adder about to strike. Who's the lucky fellow?"

"Angus Jones."

"Black Angus," Candido said, nodding. "What've you got against him, Ringo?"

"Two of his men killed a friend of mine. Bob Farr—shot him in the back."

"Why don't you kill them then?"

"I will. I don't believe in doing things by halves," Ringo said. "Seen Jones lately?" Ringo asked.

"No—but I know he's been around, recent-like," Candido said.

"When?"

"Yesterday. I didn't see Jones himself, mind you. Two of his men, Donegan and Porgy Best. They came in here about sundown."

"What did they want?"

"They was looking to see which of the boys was around, searching for likely prospects, you see. Sax Everly, Nolan Hall, and Ian Pate rode out with them."

"Where'd they go?"

"Black Angus is a slave hunter, a woman stealer. Everybody knows that. They're going to the auction in Pago. It figgers he took on Sax and them as extra guns, gringo guns."

"Much traffic headed that way, Candy?"

"Buyers? None. Sellers? Some. Slavers bypass this town if they can. Too many bad boys here looking for trouble. They'd steal the women from the woman stealers if they could."

"What else do you hear?

"No buyers come through here, Ringo. The white slave traffic runs north to south, not the other way. The auction in Pago is a big thing. The town's big man Don Carlos puts on the dog for his guests. Like a fiesta."

"Except for the girls who get sold," Matt said.

"Well, yes, there's that," Candido conceded.

"Anything else I should know?" Ringo asked.

"Don Carlos is sitting on a powder keg from what I hear," Candido said. "He's greedy—well, ain't we all? But Don Carlos is overdoing it. His men harrow town and countryside for fresh young girls to sell to beef up his quota. A lot of bad feeling there. Not a townsman or peon who hasn't lost a female to the slavers.

"Don Carlos is safe as long as he's got Captain Bravo siding him. Bravo heads the Pago presidio, an army fort that's supposed to guard the roads south into the interior from Apaches, Yaquis, and bandits. Don Carlos cut him in on the slave trade profits, which are considerable."

"That's it, Candy?"

"That's all of it."

Ringo and Matt pushed back their chairs, rising. "We'll be moseying then," Ringo said. He set a couple of gold coins down on the table. Candido rested a meaty hand on them. When he lifted it, the coins were gone, disappeared into his fisted palm. *"Gracias."*

"One thing more, Candy. I'd take it poorly if you were to spread word that friend Bodine and I have been asking around about Jones."

Candido's shrug said, What can I do? "Information is my stock in trade, Ringo."

"Killing is mine. Keep your mouth shut, Candy— a word to the wise."

Candido paled beneath his tan. "Sure, Ringo, sure. You can count on me, you know that."

"What I thought," Ringo said. He and Matt went out.

Candido poured a cup of tequila, gulping it

quickly. After a while, some of the color came back into his face.

Why won't they just let Paco Maldonado be?! So Paco asked himself, half-awake, self-pitying. He sat in a corner of the Red Mill cantina in Fronteras at dusk, trying to sleep off this afternoon's drunk. His arms were folded on the table, pillowing the head which lay on its side atop them. A broad sombrero covered his head to keep out the light, such as it was, the light of dying day.

Someone was tugging at Paco's sleeve at the elbow—a persistent bastard who wouldn't leave him alone. He'd slept for a few fitful hours, drifting in and out of wakefulness, trying to stay submerged in sodden slumber. Now, this!

Groaning, mumbling, he was astir. "Go away, pest," he muttered. The *rudo* importuning him was not only pulling on his sleeve, but taking hold of his shoulder and giving it a shake. Paco tried to shoo away the pest, but whoever it was was out of the reach of his blindly flailing hand.

Paco's head raised, upsetting his precariously balanced hat and causing it to fall off the table. Paco cursed, his garblings unintelligible to any but himself. His gummy eyes flickered open.

He was in his early twenties, rawboned, thin faced, with high cheekbones and thick, matte-black hair reaching to his jawline. He wore a holstered gun and bandoliers across his chest, and a machete dangled by a rawhide loop from his belt. A repeating rifle stood near at hand.

Bleary, red-eyed, he peered at his tormentor as if through a smoke-fogged room. The room indeed was smoky with alcohol and tobacco fumes, but they were not the haze that veiled his gaze like drifting clouds; his was the haze of ebbing drunkenness. Paco rubbed his eyes to clear them.

His nemesis was a young boy, a street urchin solemn as an owl. He held Paco's hat, which he had caught before it fell to the floor, proffering it to Paco, who stuck it on his head at an off-angle.

"What do you want, insect?" Paco asked.

"The señorita," the boy said.

"Eh? What's that, what señorita?"

"The lady—her," the boy said, pointing to the entrance. A fine-looking young woman stood outside the entryway, looking in.

She had shiny, long black hair, bold dark eyes, a sweetly wicked face and shapely figure that was being shown off to best advantage by a low-cut white blouse and tight skirt. She beckoned, motioning Paco to her.

Paco stood up, still clumsy with the alcohol in him, accidentally overturning his chair. It fell back into the corner, which held it up at a tilted angle. He pulled his hat down tightly on his head to keep it from falling off—the hat, that is, not the head. Though, in his present condition, he felt in possible jeopardy of losing them both.

The boy stood in front of him blocking the way,

hand held out palm up. "The lady said you would pay me a coin for running the errand," he said.

Paco stared down at him foggily, swaying slightly. He dug a hand into his vest's side pocket, fumbling out a few small copper coins. He dropped one in the boy's palm. The boy darted away through the crowd and disappearred.

Paco glanced at the doorway. It was empty, the girl gone. He picked up his rifle and went to the door, walking heavily.

He stepped outside. Dusky purple shadows pooled at the edges of things. Above low rooftops the sky was dark blue with a handful of twinkling stars. Paco looked around for the girl. She stood on the other side of the small square formed by the intersection of two side streets.

Her back was to him. She looked over her shoulder at him, flashing him a come-hither look, a smooth curve of golden flesh bared by the scooped-out neck of the blouse. Inky black hair glided waterlike across her upper back and shoulders. She stood there waiting.

Paco was suspicious—it smelled like a trap. Who would set a trap for Paco Maldonado? He had many enemies on both sides of the law. Whatever else he was, thief, bandit, slayer, he was no coward. He crossed to the woman. "What do you want, *chiquita*?" he asked.

"From you, nothing." Her expression was cool, indifferent. She pointed down a side street "He wants to talk to you."

A lone man sat a horse a half-dozen paces away,

beside the wall of a house whose overhanging eaves shadowed his upper body.

"Who is he?" Paco asked. The girl shrugged. Paco's once-bleary eyes were in focus now, scanning the scene. He saw no sign of lurking ambushers hiding behind corners, in alcoves or recessed doorways. No telltale rifle barrels protruded from the roofline on either side of the street. It was just the lone man, the stranger.

If this was a conspiracy, the girl was not in it. Her massive and total indifference was proof of that.

Now, as to the stranger . . . He wore a broad-brimmed sombrero, the brim decorated with rebozos, little black pom-poms hanging on short strings along the rim of the hat. Generally, it was a somewhat ridiculous affectation on a man's headgear, clownish, but not on this hombre. He looked like a serious individual. The comical touch was more sinister than laughable.

A patterned blue-and-white serape, a long narrow blanket, was wrapped around his shoulders and upper body. The band of dangling rebozos partly veiled his eyes and the serape folds hid his lower face. A gun in a buscadero rig was holstered on his hip, and a repeating rifle was stowed in his saddle scabbard.

Masked? Well, many men of Paco's acquaintance had cause to hide their faces. He'd done it himself many a time, but usually only when pulling a job of crime. "What do you want, hombre? Do I know you? Show your face," Paco demanded.

A lamp was lit in a second-story room above the

side street, light shining down on the stranger. Moving easily, carefully, he lifted a hand to lower the serape folds, uncovering his face.

Gila Chacon!

Paco, shook, was neither so drunk nor shocked as to do something stupid like blurting out the other's name out loud. In outlaw circles, it was considered bad form and worse to be careless in saying another man's name out loud, for there are many reasons for wishing to go about unrecognized and incognito.

Gila tilted down the hat so that its broad brim once more threw his face into shadow, agitating the little black pom-pom rebozos so they swung back and forth.

Paco went to him. "Do I see truly, is it really you?"

"Where did you think I was, Paco, in a gringo jail?" Gila returned.

"*Jefe*, chief, I swear, me and some of the *muchachos* were going to ride north and break you out of jail," Paco said fervently, abashed.

"Like the gringos say, I'd hate to have to hang by the neck waiting for the likes of you to come to the rescue," Gila said.

"We had an escape plan, *jefe*, I swear on my mother—"

"Don't take your mother's name in vain—the poor woman already has too many gray hairs on her head from birthing a bad boy like you, Paco. As you can see, I freed myself. Gila Chacon waits on no man, nor needs to."

"But this is wonderful—!"

"*Sí, sí,* it's wonderful, *sí.* What of the rest of the gang? My Guardsmen, where are they?" The Guardsmen were Gila's inner circle, his lieutenants. Paco was one of them.

"Octavio, Felipe, and Bronco Duro are all in Fronteras with me," Paco said, naming the rest of the Guardsmen. "We're here to make a raid across the border into Tombstone, like I said—"

"Never mind about that now," Gila said, cutting the other short. "And the rest of the *muchachos?*"

"Most of them are in town. A few are at the hideout in Pago, hoping to rob some of the buyers of their girls of gold. Not many, though, since it's the rope or the firing squad if they're caught down there," Paco said.

"So much the better. Round up the three Guardsmen and have them round up the *muchachos.* Tell them to meet me tomorrow night at the hideout in Pago."

"You've got something planned for that pig of a Don Carlos, eh, *jefe?*"

"Something big, Paco, maybe the biggest job ever—one that will bury our enemies and make us a power in the land. The time is right to deal a death blow to our foes, Don Carlos, Sebastiano, Capitán Bravo, Sancho, Dorado and—Carmen.

"But we—you, me, all of us—must act fast to ensure that this golden opportunity for revenge does not slip through our fingers, nor the prey slip the noose. I know something about the noose,

Paco, having lived under its shadow for some time now. Too long.

"You were the first one of the gang I could find. I knew you'd be here in Old Fierro's cantina making yourself stupid with tequila, as you always do between jobs. He's the only one who'll give you credit when your gold's run out.

"The girl was just another whore picked at random, the first one who came by and fit my purpose. You were never one to resist the lure of a pretty face, and I don't care to show myself just yet. For now, it suits me to have others think me dead or waiting to swing at the end of a a gringo rope.

"Only you know that I'm alive. Tell the rest of the Guardsmen, but no others. You four have been running the gang in my absence and the *muchachos* will do what you say when you tell them to ride to Pago. Gather up the most dependable of our men, the tried and true *pistoleros* and stone killers. Don't bother with the hangers-on and camp followers. Don't bother with anybody that hasn't ridden with us before, only those with a price on their heads. Stay out of town and meet me at the hideout tomorrow night.

"One more thing. Pepe Herrera, is he still in Pago?"

"*Sí, jefe*, alive and uncaught, when last I heard. Don Carlos thinks he's loyal."

"Good. Let's keep him thinking that way. Don't try to contact him, Paco. I will get in touch with him myself. *Comprende?*"

"*Sí, jefe, sí!*"

"Tomorrow night, then." Gila turned his horse, riding up the side street and around a corner, making for the edge of town. Once clear of Fronteras, he put his horse to the gallop, the evening star glittering brightly in the west.

SEVENTEEN

South to Espinazo del Diablo, "The Devil's Backbone"

The jagged peaks of the sierra were like the ridged armor plates along the back of some monstrous thunder lizard from prehistory. Gray-black volcanic rock, spewed up from the bowels of the earth, had formed spiky, gnarly piles of crystalline blocks bristling with needles and pinnacles, throwing out winglike spurs and buttresses on all sides

The main route through the Espinazo was La Garganta, "The Throat," a long narrow gorge running north to south through the range. To the north, it was the gateway to Fronteras and the border; to the south, it opened on a sandy high desert plateau where Pago lay.

Running through the passage was the Camino Real, the old King's Highway, the royal road blazed north by the conquistadors three hundred years earlier when they set out from Mexico City into the remote fastnesses of what was now the great American Southwest.

La Garganta was the main route south into Pago, but not the only one. There were other, alternate routes more difficult of access, yet not impossible to traverse. One such was called The Goat Trail, lying east of La Garganta. When long ago they named it "The Goat Trail," its discoverers meant mountain goat. It was a trail on a narrow ledge winding high along the cliffs of the east face of the Espinazo. Swift death was the reward for a single misstep, for one wrong move would send man and mount plummeting to the rocks hundreds of feet below.

The Tombstone raiders took the Goat Trail the day after their brief stopover outside Fronteras. The line was strung out in single file along a ledge barely wide enough to allow the passage of horse and rider.

In some places it was needful to dismount and go on foot, leading the horses by the reins. Some of the horses who'd showed skittishness in the mountain heights had been blindfolded by strips of cloth tied over their eyes, to prevent them from seeing the vertiginous drop gaping to one side. Packhorses with the added width of supplies tied to sides and backs made the traverse even more harrowing.

Hundreds of feet above the ground, the rescuers threaded a narrow ledge contouring along rounded, curving limbs of rock cliff. Eagles glided by at eye level.

From time to time, a horse's hoof dislodged a loose stone, sending it over the edge. A long time passed before that rock hit bottom.

"One thing's sure: We can't come back this way,

not with the girls along," Matt Bodine said tightly as his horse picked its way along the ledge.

"No, on the way back we'll have to take La Garganta," Sam said.

The grudging, inching, breathless, cautious passage combined tedium and danger in equal measure, yet was finally passed by all without losing man nor beast. The Goat Trail sloped downward, gently descending as the eastern range subsided, its southern end shrinking into the sandy wastes of the Pago plateau. At last, the trail spilled out on flat ground.

"Now we'll have to be even more watchful," Sam said. Other people were the peril, not mountain peaks and sheer precipices, with the ever-present threat of Apaches, bandits, soldiers, snitches, and spies.

The Tombstone column angled southwest over a flat lava bed, leaving no tracks. Beyond it, they entered a lonely waste of sandy gray soil, dwarf pines, and scrub brush. No farmers, no human habitations were here.

On they rode, coming to a valley. Pima Joe went on ahead scouting, returning to tell that he'd seen a patrol of about a dozen soldiers camping on the bottom beside a stream.

"They come from the Pago presidio," Gila Chacon said, after sneaking forward with Sam and Pima Joe for a closer look at the troops, spying on them from behind a screen of brush.

"Some of Capitán Bravo's doing. Sometimes the peons of the countryside, the *campesinos*, come to Pago to try to rescue wives and daughters stolen by the slavers. The patrol is there to find and stop them. When they find them, they kill them. That stops them," Gila said.

The Tombstone trekkers swung wide around the encampment, avoiding detection by the patrol. They worked their way across the countryside, keeping to arroyos where they could, sheltering in those dry washes and riverbeds. They rode below the crest of ridges, careful not to skyline.

Shadows lengthened, the sun sank, and then it was night. The raiders crossed the plains east of Pago. The town lay on a rise, its spiky outline with its cathedral tower and domed opera house with turrets all a-glitter by starlight in the clear, dry, high desert air.

The moon had not yet risen.

Gila Chacon led the way, taking the Tombstoners to his hideout. They circled southwest below the town, then rode north, entering a hilly patch of ground bordering a mesa-studded plain.

Ahead rose a freestanding butte, whose rocky plateau was crowned by a dwarf pine forest. The spicy, tangy scent of pine needles and resin wafted on gentle night breezes. They advanced, with Gila pausing frequently to take note of local landmarks.

"Thought you knew your way around these parts," Geetus Maggard snapped.

"And so I do, angry little man with mouth so big, but the entrance is hard to find, especially at night. That is what makes it a good hideout," Gila said patiently, as if explaining things to a child.

From a distance the west face of the butte looked

like a solid rock wall. Nearing it, this proved to be an illusion.

The rock wall was jagged, irregular, thrusting out buttresses, spurs, and limbs. About one-third of the way north from its southwest corner was a rock spur forty feet high, its stepped face overgrown with trees and brush.

Gila pointed his horse straight at it and rode on, the others following. Their eyes now were all long-accustomed to darkness and the growing light of moonrise helped. But the Tombstoners would never have found the entrance by night, or even possiby by day, nor noticed that the seemingly solid spur with its heavily wooded face masked a gap in the rock, a cleft narrow at the opening and tall, high, and thick with brush.

The column halted. "I will go first. My compadres may be quick to fire. Wait for my return," Gila said.

He went ahead, brushes rustling as he rode between them. They swallowed him up, man and mount disappearing in the bushy cleft. The others waited, time seeming to stand still, each minute prolonging the suspense and working on their nerves. Hands rested on holstered gun butts and sheathed saddle rifles.

"Funny if Apaches found the place and are hiding out in there," Dutch Snyder said absently.

"We'll die laughing," Geetus Maggard returned.

Ten minutes passed. From somewhere deep within rock walls came the sound of an owl hoot, distant, disembodied, eerie.

"That's Gila," Sam said.

"How can you tell?" somebody asked.

"I can tell."

"Hell, you're just guessing," Maggard said. "I heard plenty of owls myself in my day and that sure sounded like one to me."

"No, that's Gila," Vern Tooker said. Pima Joe grunted, nodding agreement.

An answering hoot to the first call now sounded from somewhere deeper in the cleft. Five minutes more passed.

"Here he comes," Sam said.

"I don't hear nothing, not-a-thing," Maggard maintained.

But they all did a moment later: There was the click of an iron horseshoe stepping on rock, the sough of a horse moving through high bush and weeds, the rustle of brush, a twig snapping under hoof.

Gila emerged from behind the screen of brush.

"We was starting to worry about you," Dutch Snyder said.

"All is well, but there are only a few men there. My *muchachos* have not yet arrived," Gila said. "Come."

He turned his horse around and once more passed the brush screen, the others following one by one in single file. For the first fifteen or twenty yards the cleft was so tight that a rider could barely pass through without his mount scraping its sides on rock walls. The rocks were worn smooth, polished perhaps by the passage of many others stretching back through dim mists of time.

There was a smell of moisture, of green growing

things. The snakelike passage opened on a box canyon nestled in the heart of the butte. It was an oval park about one hundred yards on its long axis and forty at the beam.

A spring rose from among the rocks, spilling over into a thin stream trickling across the canyon floor. A small flock of sheep huddled together on a grassy patch.

A campfire burned. Around it stood an old man, a boy, and a scrawny sheepdog with its ribs showing.

The Tombstoners stepped down from their horses, looking around, stretching to relieve muscles tired and strained from long hours in the saddle. Some moved to water their horses.

The old man's name was Nando. He was white haired and white bearded, looking like a snowy owl, hooded dark eyes surrounded by white plumage. He held a wooden walking staff upright in one hand. He wore a grimy sheepskin vest, clean white shirt and pants, a rope belt and rope sandals. A machete was thrust through the rope belt to hang at his hip. Standing against a rock was his long rifle, an old-time, single-shot, smoothbore musket.

The boy was twelve years old, thin, dark-haired with wide dark eyes. He followed Nando around, standing a pace or two behind and to the side of the oldster.

Nando eyed the newcomers with no discernible sign of pleasure or welcome.

"These are friends," Gila said.

"Gringos," said Nando.

"They saved me from a hangman's rope, and will furnish me with a rope to hang Don Carlos."

"So! You are welcome, friends." Nando bared his white teeth in a grin, dark eyes alight with savage joy.

"My Guardsmen and the rest of the *muchachos* will be here soon."

"I will so tell the sentries, Gila."

EIGHTEEN

Sam Two Wolves and Remy Markand came to town, the town of Pago.

Pago was important culturally and commercially, having been founded three hundred years earlier. The first building to arise on the site was the presidio, a military fort of massive, Cyclopean stone-block construction built by Indian slaves and convict labor battalions. The presidio squatted on a rocky knob apart from the rest of the town, brooding over the flat plains trending northward to the mountains of the Espinazo.

Stretching across the flat was the Camino Real, the King's Highway connecting far-distant Mexico City in the southern interior to the great southwestern desert in the north.

Pago means "payment," and the town was well-named, for from earliest times royal officials and military commanders had collected tolls and taxes on all travelers passing by this way on the Camino Real.

The body of the town was set on a wide, low, flat-topped rise. Its central feature was the *zócalo*, the plaza, around whose square sides the main buildings had been raised, the heart of the old colonial administrative apparatus.

On the west side of the *zócalo* fronting east stood the cathedral, an ornate structure of ash-gray stone with lofty needlelike spires, flying buttresses, octagonal side chapels, pointed arches, steep slanted roofs, and elaborate, decorative stone carvings.

North stood the *Palacio*, the royal colonial administration's headquarters and now the seat of the district's government. It was a three-story office building housing a tribunal court, extensive historical archives, and the numerous small offices of an arrogant and overbearing bureaucracy.

The *zócalo's* east side held a row of commercial buildings, including an indoor *mercado*, or marketplace, and a selection of government-licensed shops and stores selling various high-line, expensive goods.

A wide, flat, square plaza, open on the south side, featured lines of temporary booths and stalls selling a variety of goods and foodstuffs.

The *zócalo* and environs comprised Old Town.

New Town lay north of and apart from the plaza. It was centered around that great architectural and cultural folly, the opera house. Built by Don Carlos's immediate predecessor and the cause of his ruination, the opera house was a grandiose baroque pile topped by a domed roof and four corner turrets, surrounded by gardens bordered by iron-spear fences and gates.

A wealthy residential section had grown up in the neighborhood, a tract of expensive houses bordered by high walls. Most of its denizens were newly rich, owing their affluence to the slave trade brokered by Don Carlos.

In the center of the plaza lay a fountain and basin. The fountain was broken and the basin was dry. At the basin's midpoint stood a pedestal atop which sat a monumental, cast-bronze statue of an armor-clad conquistador on a horse. Rider and horse faced north, the conquistador holding a lance. The horse reared up on its two hind legs. Time had weathered the bronze to a pale green hue and disrespectful pigeons had layered it with white guano.

At eight in the morning, Sam and Markand met their local contact, Pepe Herrera, at the fountain.

Herrera, a feisty bantamweight, seemed natty and dapper, though his clothes were frayed and threadbare and his boots wearing down to the uppers. He was medum-sized, thin, nimble, with sharp-pointed features and a hooked nose, wide expressive mouth, graying mustache, and chin whiskers. Deep-set eyes burned in a hollow-cheeked face.

He was one of a staff of temporary workers employed twice yearly at the opera house before, during, and after auction week. A Pago town dweller, he was maintenance man and handyman, a jack-of-all-trades.

He would arrange for Sam and Remy Markand to

take a guided tour of the opera house this morning. Pepe Herrera was one of Gila Chacon's contacts. He'd been put together with Sam and Remy by the bandit.

The Tombstone rescue raiders couldn't do their job blindfolded. They needed inside information, the layout of the opera house, locale of the captives, and disposition of enemy forces.

An underground resistance against Don Carlos and his slave hunters had long been building in Pago. The would-be rebels had penetrated the operation, planting their people inside. But so far they'd been unable to strike back effectively.

"Between Don Carlos and Capitán Bravo, they have us outgunned," Herrera told Sam and Remy.

"We've come to even up those odds," Sam said.

Markand would pretend to be a slave buyer, while Sam would pose as his bodyguard. Why Remy Markand? Because he was a French-speaking Creole from New Orleans who could carry off the imposture with style and steel nerves. He would pose as a whoremonger on the buy for fresh young virgins from Mexico. Cultured and educated, yet a one-time Legionnaire and fighting man, Remy could go among the well-heeled heels and pass as one of them. His background was exotic enough to make it stick.

Why Sam? Because like Markand he was not the stereotypical gringo. There were many gringos in Pago at the moment, most coming from the left-hand side of the ledger, the Dark Trail: slave hunters, gunmen, and bodyguards of top vice merchants.

Sam, as could be seen at a glance, was no ordinary gringo. Shoulder-length black hair, copper-colored skin, corner eye folds, hawklike nose, and beardless face marked him out as an Indian. Yet he was a university graduate, a man of great depth, fluent in Spanish and French, attributes which would enhance the reality of his role.

Had he been paired with Matt Bodine, the two might have been recognized as the Brothers of the Wolf who were fast becoming a legend of the West. But teamed with Remy, Sam's unusual presence would bolster the credibility of both.

What's more, Sam was a dangerous man, a cool-nerved killer with all weapons, including his feet and hands. He was walking into a snake pit; if anyone had the skills to go in and come back alive, he did.

Nando had gone into town before dawn, meeting one of Herrera's rebel agents who furnished him with a change of clothes for Sam and Remy, to buttress their roles as a New Orleans French Quarter vice lord and his lethally efficient enforcer.

Behind some bushes, Sam and Remy donned the garments, getting duded up in suits and ties. They kept their own boots, footwear being difficult to get sized right. Pants were worn over the boots. The worn and dusty condition of the parts that showed would back up their cover story of having trailed overland on horseback to attend the auction.

The jacket was tight around Sam's shoulders and the pants baggy at the hips, but the garments were new and expensive enough to enhance the masquerade.

Remy donned a white ruffled shirt with a black satin cravat and pearl stickpin. "We look a pair of fine fops," he said.

"I sure hope so," said Sam.

They kept their weapons, holstered belt guns. In addition, Remy had a sleeve gun hidden inside his right cuff and a derringer in his left jacket pocket. Sam had a long knife worn sheathed under his left arm and a second short thin throwing knife, little more than a sharp-pointed, keen-edged piece of stamped-out metal worn on a rawhide thong hanging down between his shoulder blades.

Nando escorted them to the southwest corner of the square, pointing out Herrera, who was crossing toward the fountain from the north. A bright clear day with a cloudless sky, it was already hot in the open sun but still cool in the shade.

Sam, Remy, and Pepe Herrera stood at the west of the *zócalo* fountain and basin, in the shadow of the conquistador's bronze statue. A number of idlers loitered in the plaza, most clad in elegant, expensive garments, well-to-do gentlemen and their ladies.

A few small knots of young, attractive, and well-dressed women with parasols were most likely fashionable prostitutes of the town. Uniformed soldiers with shouldered rifles stood guard outside the front entrance of the Palacio.

"Nice day," Sam remarked.

"You see that there are few townsfolk abroad enjoying this fine weather," Herrera said, his tone acid, withering. "Families lock up their daughters and stay closely by their sides when the auction comes around, afraid they'll be stolen and sold to Don Carlos to round off some consignment of flesh.

"But enough of an old man's bitterness. You speak Spanish?"

"Yes," Remy said.

"We both do," said Sam.

"That is good," Herrera said, switching from English to Spanish. "I speak some English, but for where we are going in the Casa it is best to speak Spanish, since everybody in Pago hates gringos as a matter of course."

"Including you?" Sam asked with a tight grin.

"I mean you no offense."

"None taken."

"I and my compadres welcome all freedom-loving men of good will who have come to help us in the struggle, no matter who they are or where they come from," Herrera said. "You come well recommended, if Gila Chacon vouches for you. Now to business. You have gold with you?"

"Some," Remy said, "enough for now." A pouch of gold nestled in his jacket's inside breast pocket, gotten earlier from Arnholt Stebbins to carry out the mission. It had been no mean feat to pry some of Colonel Davenport's gold from the "fighting bookkeeper," as Ringo had christened him. But it was a necessary prop and tool to carry out the masquerade.

Sam had the hundred dollars in gold he'd been

advanced at the start of the trek, with a bit extra besides.

"How much do you need?" Remy asked.

Pepe Herrera gestured as if brushing the idea aside. "No, no, the gold is not for me, but for *them*, for the slave masters. No one needs a special invitation to attend the auction. No, the ticket of admission is a pocketful of gold. Hard cash is the only bona fides required."

"I've got enough to make a fair showing," Remy said, "with more available for the auction if needed."

"Good! Shall we go?"

They crossed the plaza, going around the Palacio and continuing north on foot toward the opera house. The grounds were enclosed by an iron-spear fence eight-feet high. A cobblestone road led through the main gates, making a looping drive that curved through the gardens to the foot of the marble stairs, then back out again

"It was made so that the opera patrons could arrive by carriage to the performances. Never used, of course. No opera has ever been staged at La Casa. No touring company in the world will come to Pago, for fear that their prima donna sopranos and coloraturas will be stolen away and locked in a gilded cage like the veriest songbird," Herrera said.

The main gates were open. Inside the gateway on the left stood a guard box.

The guards were two of Don Carlos's *vaqueros*, his riders. They looked more like *pistoleros* than cattle tenders of the *ranchero*. They were armed with repeating rifles and gun belts.

"Good morning, men," Herrera said. One grunted in acknowledgment, the other nodded. Herrera swept through the gates without slowing and Sam and Remy kept right up with him.

"That was easy," Remy said.

"It gets harder at the opera house entrance. That is the real test," Herrera said.

The grounds had once been handsomely land-scaped, with lawns, box hedges, flowerbeds, straight and winding paths. There were pieces of marble statuary, nooks with stone alcoves, and small circular ponds.

All were long neglected now. The grass needed cutting, for it was ankle high. Weeds grew in the cracks between paving stones on the garden paths. The hedges needed trimming. The ponds were empty, dried up.

The opera house loomed ahead.

"That's one of the damnedest things I've ever seen. And to find it here in Pago, of all places," Sam marveled, shaking his head, half appalled, half bemused.

"It looks like a beached whale, a beached marble whale that washed up in the Espinazo," Remy said.

"We call it *La Casa de las Lloronas*," Herrera said.

"The House of Crying Women," Sam said, nodding.

"Yes, that is how we name it—in private behind locked doors and shuttered windows, to be free of the spies of Don Carlos and Capitán Bravo."

"That bad, huh? Are the spies so many?"

"Who can say? They don't wear signs," Herrera

said, shrugging. "That is part of the problem—trust. Who to trust? Is the man sitting at the next table in the cantina working as the eyes and ears of Don Carlos?

"That neighbor across the fence, the woman in the next church pew. The old lady peeking out from behind the curtains, is she a harmless village busybody or one of Don Carlos's spies? It's hard to tell. How can you be sure? Yet to pass a word in the wrong ear in the wrong place at the wrong time can mean death for the unlucky. Not the unwary, for all are on their guard. But the unlucky, for blind chance so often decides who shall live and who shall die."

"How do you know you can trust us?" Remy asked.

"How do you know you can trust me?" Herrera countered. "Perhaps even now I am the Judas goat leading you to the slaughterhouse, señores?"

"How, indeed?" Sam wondered.

An uncomfortable pause dropped into the conversation. Herrera's brittle laugh broke the tension. "Put your minds at ease, gentlemen, I am no traitor," he said.

Sam wasn't worried, not about Herrera betraying them. He prided himself on his ability to read people and all his instincts told him that Herrera was all right. And if by some fluke he were not all right, he would be the first to die. Sam would see to that.

"Don Carlos's men killed my brother when he protested the slave raids on the *campesinos*. They shot him down like a dog," Herrera went on. "Don

Carlos thinks I don't know the truth and I never let on that I do. That is how I have managed to worm my way into his confidence so now I am placed at the black heart of the slave master's operation, ready to strike."

As he spoke, Herrera's face remained carefully composed, with only a bitter twist at the corner of his mouth to betray the intense emotion dammed up within. His tone was casual, offhand, as if discussing some trivia of the day.

"I laugh at their jokes, grovel for their filthy money, and look the other way among their numberless infamies. All the time I am waiting, waiting for the day that I cast aside the mask and take my vengeance. The day when I become the worm that gnaws at the heart, the worm that kills."

"With any luck that day is about to dawn," Sam said. "Unsteady lies the head that wears the crown, the head of Don Carlos."

"May it be so, my friends. In any case, you come well recommended. You could not hope for a better sponsor than the Chacon," Herrera said.

"Being a bandit and cutthroat his references are impeccable, eh?" Remy joked.

"In Pago, yes. Gila Chacon is the one man those of us who hate Don Carlos and his works can be sure of. The Chacon will never turn his coat and become one of Don Carlos's creatures. There is no reconciling those two. Theirs is a peculiarly pure mutual hatred. They are locked in a blood feud which can only end with the death of one or the other, or both."

"Why do they have a big hate on for each other?" Sam asked Herrera.

"Gila is a *campesino*, a peasant. He comes from a long line of peasants bound to the Vega *estancia*, the estate. I speak now of the original Vega bloodline, the real one, not the newcomer who bought the title. The last of the de la Vegas went bankrupt after building the opera house. He died shortly after of taking poison—whether by his own hand or another's, who can say?

"He lived long enough to sell his lands and title to Carlos Mondregón, going so far as to adopt him, to ensure that the title and patent of nobility would pass directly to him. Old Vega was then so considerate as to conveniently die, permitting Mondregón to become the newly ennobled Don Carlos.

"When he made himself master of the *estancia*, Don Carlos began by showing the peasants that his was a new regime. He did this with violence and brutality, lavishly dispensed by his private army of *pistoleros* and thugs. Where his predecessor ground the peons fine, he ground them to dust. Many died by the shootings and beatings and torture, more by starvation.

"The males of the Chacon family butchered a Vega cow to avoid perishing for want of food. They took what meat they needed and gave the rest to their relatives and neighbors. To make an object lesson of them, Don Carlos killed all the male Chacons, from the oldest graybeard to the youngest babe in arms. The father and his two oldest sons

Don Carlos hanged, leaving them hanging until the flesh dropped from their bones.

"By sheer luck, young Gila was away from home when the *vaqueros* came for the others, and so he escaped. Don Carlos put a price on his head and a sentence of death on any who might aid the boy with food or shelter. But Gila did not die. Somehow, he escaped to run away and survive.

"He became an outlaw, a bandit. As soon as he was able, he began bedevilling Don Carlos: stealing his horses, rustling his cattle, shooting down his *vaqueros* whenever he could find them. The last of his line, and now the first when it came to deeds of blood and valor, Gila was acclaimed as The Chacon.

"Neither Don Carlos nor Capitán Bravo—then Teniente Bravo, Lieutenant Bravo you would call him—could catch him. He made fools of both of them. The clamor reached Mexico City, where Bravo's superior officers became displeased. They put a black mark beside his name in the official records, ensuring that Bravo would never rise higher than the rank of captain and never command a post more prestigious than the Pago presidio.

"This went on for some time. Then came the old, old story. The Chacon's woman was Carmen Oliva, a fiery beauty with a body made by Satan to lead the race of Adam astray. She was a faithless slut, a born whore—as much of a born whore as her vicious half-brother, Dorado, was a born killer. Carmen could be had by anyone for a few pesos or a cheap trinket. It was common knowledge known to all except the *bandido*, or if he knew, he was so besotted with her charms that he chose to ignore the truth. Carmen was not only his woman, she was his wife, married to him by a priest in a church.

"You can guess the rest. Carmen decided she was the Chacon's woman no more. She took up with Capitán Bravo first, but quickly moved on to better prospects: Don Carlos himself. She needed little urging to betray the outlaw for gold, baiting him into a death trap sprung by soldiers and the *vaqueros*. Yet somehow, the Chacon managed to break free, though not before being seriously wounded.

"That was some years ago. Since then, the Chacon has long since recovered from his wounds and resumed his career of banditry with a new gang somewhere a long way from here, though he sneaks into Pago from time to time to work some devilment on his old foe. No, he and Don Carlos will never rest until death writes *el fin* to the blood feud.

"Many of us hate Don Carlos and will not rest until he is destroyed. But we don't want to throw away our lives needlessly. Too many martyrs have already died in desperate ploys with little or no chance of success.

"Now it remains to be seen what you can do, señores. Show us how to do the deed in a way that will win and you will find us ready and willing to do what we can to help; aye, even at the cost of our lives. For be sure that there is no way you can throw down the challenge to Don Carlos without putting your own lives at risk.

"As, indeed, you do now," Pepe Herrera said, smiling thinly. "But now we are here at La Casa.

Best we speak of other things. You must be the rich, carefree whoremonger and his hired gun, while I embrace my role of grinning, fawning toady to a gang of pimps and killers."

The trio had halted some distance from the opera house while Herrera told his tale of blood, lust, and vengeance unslaked. They now resumed walking, closing briskly on the opera house.

"Puts a different slant on Gila, eh?" Remy remarked.

"Um," Sam said, noncommittal, thoughtful. But not so deep in thought as to be unaware of his surroundings, which he monitored with his senses heightened to their keenest pitch.

Well-dressed folk strolled about the grounds and gardens, taking their ease. They were obviously buyers in town for the slave auction. Most were men, but there were some women, whorehouse madams and procuresses. All were well fed proudly flaunting the accoutrements of prosperity, having achieved the good life by doing bad.

Some bared their evil nature openly stamped on face and form, with animalistic visages and twisted bodies. Others were handsome and attractive, beautiful and alluring. Some looked and dressed like respectable businessmen; others like racetrack touts. Pimps and vice merchants from the cities of the interior and the coasts often were dressed loudly, flashily, with showy hats, flamboyant cravats, and brocaded vests, thick gold chains, and diamond pinky rings.

The bodyguards almost always could be seen for

what they were—gunmen, *pistoleros*. They stayed close to their paymasters, but not too close. Some wore weapons openly in holstered gun belts; others concealed theirs under suit jackets and inside hip pockets where they made obvious bulges.

Noting their behavior, Sam faded back a pace or two, trailing Remy from behind and to the side. He, Remy, and Herrera crossed the curved drive fronting the structure. A brick apron led to a wide, curving marble staircase. Long shallow steps were arranged in tiers separated by wide landings. The trio climbed the stairs to the portico, passing between Greek–style Corinthian columns decorated with elaborate stonework.

They went under an overhanging pediment roof, out of the sunlight into the shadow. Several small knots of people stood scattered among the pillars, putting their heads together, talking among themselves. Some of the women gave Sam and Remy frankly appraising looks, liking what they saw.

Men, too, looked them over openly or with sidelong glances, seeing them as competition and wondering: how rich? How ruthless, dangerous? How much of a threat, if any, are they to me?

The *pistoleros* saw that the newcomers wore their guns openly and carried themselves as if they knew how to use them and wouldn't shy from doing so if challenged.

A central set of big brass double doors was propped open. Sam, Remy, and Herrera passed beneath an arched entryway into a high-ceilinged, vaulting lobby and entrance hall, the checkerboard marble floor echoing to their footfalls. It was cooler indoors, out of the sun.

A few paces beyond the entrance and to one side of it stood a uniformed doorman and two armed guards.

That the guards had been recruited from among Don Carlos's *vaqueros* was obvious from their prominent bowlegs, born from a lifetime spent in the saddle. They had shed sombreros, ponchos, and leather chaps for dark, short bolero jackets, white shirts, black string ties with silver-and-turquoise bolos, red sash cummerbunds, and black wide-bottomed pants over black boots. Impassive, stone-faced, they were armed with big-caliber six-guns and repeating rifles.

The doorman was decked out in ceremonial regalia like a Swiss admiral. He wore gold horsecomb epaulets over a black scissor-tail coat, starched white shirt, lace cuffs, red satin sash worn diagonally across his chest, and gray pinstripe pants.

His face suggested that of a pickled fish: tart, dour, with salt-and-pepper hair, hooded eyes, mouth downturned with deep lines at the corners. The picture was completed by stooped shoulders, a froglike paunch, and thin stooped legs.

Herrera held a hand up in greeting, the other nodding coolly in return. "Good morning, Álvaro."

"Pepe." The doorman looked questioningly at the two strangers.

"Buyers," Herrera said, not slackening his pace. Álvaro waved Remy and Sam through. The three started across the main floor, Herrera leading a pace ahead, angling now to the left.

"Hold up there! One moment, gentlemen, if you please!" Implicit in the sharply ringing command was its subtext: even if you don't please, halt!

A clerkish-looking fellow charged up to the trio, now halted. He was short, thin, with an oversized head sprouting a thatch of unruly black hair and a bristling black beard. A pair of wire-rim spectacles with thumbprint-sized, green-tinted lenses perched on the middle of a wide-bridged nose.

The armed guards posted near the entrance stiffened. They were blank faced, but paying close attention, ready to take their cue from the clerk.

Visitors in the lobby turned their heads, looking to see what the disturbance was all about.

"Sebastiano, Don Carlos's man. And nobody's fool," Herrera said to Sam and Remy in a rasping whisper out of the corner of his mouth.

"Would you gentlemen please step over to the side?" Sebastiano's command was couched in the form of a question

"What's all this?" Remy Markand inquired, looking supremely nonchalant. Sam was blank faced, watchful, as befitted a bodyguard, as well as his own self-contained nature.

"Please," Sebastiano said, gesturing to the direction in which he wanted them to go. The two armed guards came up behind Sam and Remy, who had to proceed as Sebastiano indicated or risk the guards colliding into them.

The two fell into step, good humored, easy. When

they were sufficiently isolated from the others in the lobby, Sebastiano circled around so that he was facing them. He had small, neat hands. He held them clasped in front of his belt buckle. The guards stood behind the duo.

"This is your first time at the exhibition," Sebastiano said. "I crave the privilege of making your acquaintance and examining your credentials. Entrance to these premises is restricted to members of the trade."

"Credentials?" Remy echoed, arching an eyebrow in mild query of his interrogator. "Sorry, but I didn't bring any of my sporting fillies with me to Pago. Seemed like carrying coals to Newcastle, no? This trip I buy, not sell.

"Credentials!" he snorted, shaking his head with amusement.

Herrera laughed easily. "I found these two strays wandering about the *zócalo* trying to find the opera house, Sebastiano, so I brought them here. I'm hoping to earn myself a finder's fee for steering these gentlemen to the merchandise."

"Looks like you've got competition," Remy said, eyeing Sebastiano with just the right amount of amused insolence.

"Our custom is reserved to members of the trade, a specialized clientele," Sebastiano continued, unfazed. "We reserve the right to refuse admittance."

"Kind of exclusive, ain't you, *amigo*?" Sam said, taking a step forward, the steely-eyed bodyguard taking his client's part in the dispute. The guards grumbled, stirring uneasily, edging forward, but still a long way off from being committed to action.

"Now now, Cherokee, no need for impertinence. This gentleman is only doing his job," Remy said, putting a brief but noticeable pause in his voice before saying the word "gentleman," as though there might be some slight quibble in ascribing that status to Sebastiano. But that he, Remy, was broad-minded enough to stretch the definition of the word to the man now confronting him.

Sebastiano picked up on it, a faint tinge of red coloring his cheeks.

"Yes, we know of the enterprise in Pago, even in the quaint little backwater from which I hail, a charmingly insignificant and unimportant provincial hamlet—New Orleans," Remy said. "Perhaps you've heard of it?"

"You are a long way from *los Estados Unidos*, señor," Sebastiano said stiffly.

"Quite, and I hope it doesn't prove to be a wasted trip."

"We shall see, we shall see. You are . . . ?"

"Monsieur Jules Duval, owner and proprietor of the House of the Rising Sun in the *Quartier Latin*— French Quarter to you."

"I know what the *Quartier Latin* is, sir."

"Then you know that the Rising Sun is one of the most expensive and exclusive pleasure palaces on the Gulf Coast, *monsieur*. My customers demand the best and are willing to pay for it. So am I. As you must know, there's a fast turnover in the trade. The patrons are always looking for something new. And what's newer and more precious in this wicked old world but innocence? Tender young flesh, unspoiled and new. For that I'll pay top dollar, provided it lives up to advance billing and is as advertised."

"The exhibition promises satisfaction guaranteed. We require the same of our clients—that they be what they seem to be."

"I could provide a dozen references from my colleagues in New Orleans. They'd be glad to vouch for me. Be sure to exercise discretion in wording your telegram inquiries, please."

"The nearest telegraph lines are in Mexico City. Perhaps one of the other buyers could vouch for you?"

"This is my first visit. The reason I'm down here is because I'm looking to develop new markets."

"Are there not young girls enough in your homeland to satisfy your needs?"

"Virgins? In New Orleans? Don't be ridiculous! After all, we can't just grab them off the street and carry them away like you do here."

"There's a little more to it than that, sir," Sebastiano said, coloring once more.

"Don't get me wrong, I don't speak ill of it. Quite the contrary. I admire what you've done here," Remy said. Reaching into his jacket's inside pocket, he took out his money pouch, loosening the drawstings and opening its mouth. He poured a quantity of gold coins into an open palm, the glittering golden disks jingling with their cheery music.

"I daresay my money is as good as any man's

here," Remy said, stray sunbeams glinting off the coins to underlight his face with golden highlights.

Sebastiano eyed the coins, little golden glints mirrored in the dark of his eyes. He breathed deeply, nostrils quivering as he came to a decision.

"Your credentials are impeccable, *monsieur*. Welcome to the Pago exhibition," he said, forcing a wintry smile.

"Delighted," Remy said, discreetly pressing several gold coins into Sebastiano's hand.

"That's not necessary, sir, but thank you," Sebastiano said, pocketing the money. "A bit risky traveling about Mexico with such a large sum."

"This? Pocket change," Remy pooh-poohed. "My real assets are being held in reserve for the auction. As for the danger, I can take care of myself.

"My associate Cherokee also protects my interests," he added, indicating Sam.

"Very good, *monsieur*. A pleasure to make your acquaintance," Sebastiano said.

He nodded to the two guards, making shooing motions with his fingers, as if brushing away insect pests. They withdrew, returning to their post inside the front entrance.

"The livestock will be available for viewing until sundown tonight, and all day tomorrow. The auction begins tomorrow night promptly at eight o'clock. And we do mean promptly at eight. In a moment, Pepe will show you what you want to see and answer any questions you may have," Sebastiano said. "Pepe, a brief word please."

He took Pepe to one side several paces away, out

of earshot of Remy and Sam, for an exchange of hurried, whispered conversation. Sebastiano did most of the talking, Herrera nodding in agreement.

"Good luck in tomorrow night's bidding, *monsieur.* May you find whatever it is that you seek," Sebastiano said.

"That is my fondest wish," Remy said, beaming with good fellowship.

Sebastiano went away, off on some private errand.

"What did he want?" Remy asked, low voiced.

"He demanded a cut of whatever you might pay me as a bonus," Herrera said. "Naturally, I agreed, though he did not offer to share any of what you gave him, nor did I ask him to. You see we understand each other very well, Sebastiano and I."

Herrera started off once again, Sam and Remy following. They crossed to a door on the far left. It opened onto the landing of a stairwell. A flight of stairs went up to a balcony, and another flight descended to an underground level.

They went downstairs, through a doorway at the bottom of the well into a long corridor that ran the length of the building. They traveled its length, emerging in the under-stage area, a maze of storerooms and side rooms at the rear of the theater.

The side rooms were the so-called green rooms, originally intended for the use of the members of opera troupes before, during, and after performances. No opera singer had ever graced the premises.

Here was where the captive females were now kept, held separated by groups in different rooms.

Apparently, the slavers found it easier that way to maintain control of both their human chattels and the prospective buyers examining them.

There was a gamy odor of flesh and soap, the smell of the sweat of fear gone cold on taut young bodies, stiff and angular with terror, mixed with a sharp chemical reek of ammonia and disinfectant.

The rooms were guarded on the outside by armed gunmen and on the inside by female enforcers, adult women in the trade, prison matron types mostly, strong, stolid, and unforgiving.

Remy and Sam made a point of visiting all the rooms in which girls were kept. They wanted to avoid betraying undue interest in the abducted American girls for fear of exciting suspicion in their keepers.

The mazy warren of rooms penned dozens, scores of girls, numbering in all somewhere between fifty and sixty.

Most were Mexican, their ages ranging from full-grown young adult women, through the middle teens and down to the barely pubescent. Many were very young. Their clothes had been taken from them and they'd all been uniformly outfitted in simple white shifts—sleeveless cotton nightdresses that hugged their ripening curves.

An atmosphere of misery, shock, and stunned resignation predominated among the captives, who wished for nothing more than to be anywhere else. They could look forward only to being sold on the block and condemned to a life of whoredom, an existence nasty, brutish, and short.

Many had seen family members brutally slain

during their abductions; some had been brutalized themselves. Few slave hunters were as greedy for gold as Black Angus was and exercised the restraint he did over his gang in keeping the girls inviolate to fetch the highest market price.

Pepe Herrera kept up a line of patter, flip, brittle, and intended to be amusing, or at least sound that way to anyone eavesdropping on him and his two companions. He was used to playing a part, putting on the mask every day to go among those he hated and wanted dead, pretending they were a fine bunch of coworkers and associates.

Remy and Sam went from room to room eyeing the "merchandise." Other buyers and groups of buyers were doing the same, weighing and judging which specimens they wanted the most and for whom they would pay the highest price.

It reminded Sam of nothing so much as a horse auction—he actually saw a number of canny buyers holding the jaws open of young girls to appraise the condition of their teeth. It was a mighty grim business made endurable only by the knowledge that he was working an agenda of his own, a hidden agenda that with luck would give slavers and buyers alike a *big* surprise.

The course of their inspection tour brought Sam and Remy to where the American girls were penned, seven from the wagon train and five others who'd been picked up along the way—twelve in all.

Sam knew the Bear Paw girls by Linda Gordon's description of their names, ages, and personal characteristics, a list he'd committed to memory:

Devon Collins, fourteen, her sister, April Collins, ten (*Ten!*, thought Sam, his blood coming to a boil); the Haber sisters, Eva, sixteen, and Gretchen, twelve; Jenna Rowley, seventeen; Mandy Sutton, thirteen; and Priscilla Ard.

He didn't know the names of the other five, and it would have broken character in his role of bodyguard to a New Orleans whoremonger to inquire, but memory of the girls' lost, haunted faces was branded into his brain.

They seemed to be in decent enough health, intact and relatively unharmed, at least physically—so far, that is.

They were policed by Duenna Dulce, a fearsome female bulldog quick to lash out with a leather strap at her charges for various real or imagined minor transgressions of attitude and deportment.

The captives huddled together in shared misery, some seeming to try to shrink in on themselves to avoid drawing the attention of oily buyers with icy eyes, lewd comments, and probing fingers.

Eyes were red from crying; faces looked prematurely aged, haggard with strain.

Sobs and whimpers drew menacing glares from Duenna Dulce and the imminent threat of harsh correction. The girls were terrified of her.

Due to the rarity in these parts of the trophy animals, the American girls drew much interest, even by those disinclined to buy because of high prices. Many wanted to have a look to satisfy their curiosity, their numbers requiring a traffic manager and waiting line.

Inspection done, Remy and Sam moved on to the next room to continue counterfeiting interest in the goods.

Remy had the harder part as the buyer. He had to take more of an active interest, playing out his role with vigor so no false note would be detected by Don Carlos's and Sebastiano's spies and eyes. Sam as bodyguard had an easier role to play, seeming to show his primary interest as that of protecting his principal.

Sam spent much time in a level-eyed survey of room guards and the buyers' personal gunmen, happy to see no one there that he knew, or that knew him. Gunmen are used to giving each other bad eyes, that I'm-your-pallbearer stare. It comes with the territory.

The *pistoleros* coldly and unsympathetically sized up each other for future reference.

Sam and Remy took note of the floor layout, the twistings and turnings of halls and corridors, the location of the rooms where girls were held—all the girls—the number and placement of the guards, how well armed they were, where positioned at which critical junctions, the location of entrances, exits, and stairwells.

Herrera led them through a doorway into a big room filled with machinery and rigged with rope lines like a sailing ship. "The under-stage area," he said.

The space was unguarded, empty of buyers. The vice merchants wanted flesh, not man-powered machines. Sam looked around with interest. The gear included block-and-tackle hoists, lifts, winches, capstans, and similar devices for getting performers, props, and sets onstage and offstage fast.

They did this by moving the stuff straight up and down. The high ceiling was actually the underside of the stage floor. It was divided into a gridded framework, with each individual square numbered and connected to an intricate framework of metal rods and gears.

Sam eyed the hardware. The devices showed every evidence of being properly maintained. They were clean, oiled, free of rust and dust. "The gear looks well-tended," Sam said.

"Oh, it's kept in fine working order," Herrera said. "The opera house was equipped with everything needed to stage a full-fledged performance. The lifting machinery was shipped to the port of Vera Cruz, transported to Mexico City, and then hauled overland by freight wagon to Pago.

"The pity of it is that it's never been used for what it's intended. No opera has ever gone up on this stage. But it still serves a purpose, in a way.

"At auction time, the separate lots of girls—'lot' being a term of art in the auction game to describe the property going up on the block for bids," Herrera commented dryly, "the different lots of girls are loaded on that stage elevator and lifted up onto the stage through those overhead trapdoors.

"It's designed to move big stage props and backdrops onstage fast. It makes for a spectacular effect: One moment the stage is bare of all save the auctioneer, the next a group of young lovelies comes up through the bottom of the floor, as if by magic. It always gets a great reaction from the crowd. The buyers love it."

"That lifting platform really works, then," Sam said.

"Yes. The rope hawsers on the lift run through a series of block-and-tackle winches rigged to a capstan. It's modeled on the same principle that lets a handful of sailors raise and lower a heavy anchor-and-chain. A few stagehands turning the capstan wheel can effortlessly raise and lower the platform," said Herrera.

"Those doors at the back, do they open?" Sam asked, indicating a pair of solid metal double doors set in the rear wall.

"Yes. They're locked now, locked from the inside. One of Sebastiano's creatures has the keys. The doors open on ground level. They're used to move the girls in and out of the building quickly, and to bring in food and supplies," Herrera said.

"I detect the beginning of a plan germinating in your head," Remy said, eyeing Sam.

"I've got a few ideas. They're still in the budding stage," said Sam.

Twin sets of spiral staircases stood at the left and right of the under-stage area.

Sam went to one, looking up to where the staircase went through a hole in the ceiling to the stage above.

"Those give the crew quick access to the stage and under-stage areas," Herrera said.

"Can we go onstage?" Sam asked.

"Now? Yes, it is permitted. Outsiders are banned from the stage and under-stage during the auction, however."

"Let's go up."

They climbed the spiral staircase, Herrera first, then Remy and Sam. The staircase topped off on-stage, in a wing of the backstage area. Some crew members were setting up a speaker's stand, nailing boards in place, sawing wood. They glanced incuriously at the newcomers before resuming their task.

The layout was a proscenium arch stage with a semicircular wooden apron extending beyond the frame of the arch, towards where the audience would be seated. The rows of seats were now currently unoccupied, of course.

The Pago opera house was minor and inconsequential compared to the grand concert halls of Europe and New York. It was a vest-pocket edition, a modest jewelbox of a theater. What was amazing about it was the fact that it had been built at all, here in Pago amidst the ragged mountains and high desert plains of the Espinazo.

Exit doors were ranged along the long side walls of the theater. At the opposite end, above the orchestra seats, was a balcony.

"That completes the tour," Herrera said.

"I think we've seen enough," Sam said, looking at Remy, the latter nodding agreement.

"I hope the tour has been inspirational," Herrera said.

"I've got a few ideas that might play. I'll develop them later."

"I will escort you to the exit."

They went down a short wooden set of stairs, one of a pair that were in place at left and right of the proscenium leading down to the theater's hall floor. They followed the center aisle, went under the balcony and through the doors into the lobby and out the entrance, onto the broad portico above the steps.

Sam took several deep breaths, filling his lungs with fresh air. Freedom had never tasted so sweet, after the miasmic atmosphere of the maze of captive girls and their cruel jailers.

"We should meet tonight to make our plans," Herrera suggested.

"We'll be staying in town overnight. Too risky to keep running back and forth to the hideout outside Pago. It might draw suspicion," Sam said.

"Try the Lamplighter hotel. It's cheap and clean. The owner is not one of us so it will lull Don Carlos's spies if you are where they can keep an eye on you."

"We'll give it a go," Remy said.

They made a show of parting—they might be under the watchful eyes of Sebastiano and his agents even now. Remy reached for the gold, taking some gold coins from the pouch.

"Not too much. Sebastiano will take most of it," Herrera said. "But not too little, either. I don't want him to think you're cheap."

"Thanks for looking out for our good name," Remy said dryly, handing the other the coins.

"*Gracias.* Any thoughts as to how to make the fatal strike?"

"Nothing definite yet," Remy said.

"I've got a few ideas I'm kicking around," Sam said. "I see some promising angles of approach. If they work out, they just might bring down the house."

"Good, good!" Herrera said.

"I'll let you know more later, after I've studied on the subject for a while."

"I look forward to it. To act, to strike, after all these years of being ground under the heel of Don Carlos!" Herrera said. "I must leave you now. I'm sure you can find your way back to the *zócalo*. I must give Sebastiano his share of the gold, lest he accuse me of hiding some for myself. This way I can turn out my pockets to prove that I hold back nothing and that I am an honest crook, at least where he is concerned."

Herrera turned, going back inside. No sooner had he passed through the front doors then Sebastiano swooped down on him with open palm and grasping claw. Herrera gave a sickly smile as he dug into his pants pocket and hauled out the payoff for appropriation.

Sam and Remy made their way across the grounds toward the front gate. "That was *hell*, pretending to be a flesh peddler and not giving any of the girls an encouraging word that help is on the way," Remy said.

"We've got to keep playing our parts," Sam said, "until the final curtain."

"Whatever else we do, those girls have got to be

freed. Not just the ones from our side of the border, but all of them."

"That's my thinking, too."

"The others may not get far if they're loosed, but at least they'll have a chance to escape."

"If we do our job right, there won't be many slavers left to bother them after the show," Sam said.

NINETEEN

Tonight's activities required that Matt Bodine trade the gun for a bow and arrows.

Matt was a fine archer. Having grown up among the Cheyenne, he and Sam had had the bow put into their hands from the earliest age. They'd learned to hit the mark, downing game by arrow, from the smallest bird right up to a hulking grizzly bear.

There's no greater skill for an archer than to face an enraged, charging five-hundred-pound grizzly capable of shattering a man's skull like an eggshell with one swipe of its front paw, and bring it down with a few expertly placed arrows. Those arrows had better be expertly placed in the bear's sure-kill zones of the heart and through the eye to the brain, because when the grizzly charges, there's little time to loose more than a shaft or two—those grizzlies are fast!

Matt was an ace bowman, to be sure, but of the Brothers of the Wolf it was Sam who was the supreme archer. Matt's affinity had always been more with the gun. With the gun he was supreme.

Now, though, while Sam was all duded up playing his part as bodyguard to "New Orleans vice lord" Remy Markand in the fleshpots of Pago, Matt had Sam's bow and quiver of arrows in hand, for use against the foe.

That's a switch, thought Matt. *Funny how things work out sometimes.*

It was the night before the day of the auction, Friday night. The Tombstone raiders rode out from the hideout in the butte's hidden box canyon.

It was good to be going into action, having spent a long day waiting for nightfall.

Earlier, shortly after dark, Gila Chacon had met up with his gang outside the hideout.

Along with Paco Maldonado and the other three Guardsmen were ten of the *muchachos,* the rank and file members of the outfit. They were a tough bunch, ragged, hard-eyed, the genuine article of wild and woolly *bandidos.*

It had been decided earlier that the Tombstone raiders and the bandits would act seperately, independent of each other. The bandits were slavishly obedient to the commands of the newly returned Chacon, but were unlikely to work well in concert with a band of gringo gunslingers, even if they had returned their maximum leader to them.

Then again, the raiders were a long way from putting their trust in the bandits. Gila had proved trustworthy enough, but his men were under no such obligation.

Surveying the *bandidos*, Matt was glad that Sam and Remy had taken the machine gun with them on a packhorse when they left the hideout earlier this day before dawn.

The secret of what lay within Markand's crate was known only to Matt, Sam, Remy, Jeff Howell, and Stebbins. Gila was aware that the crate held something besides ordinary supplies. No doubt he would like to get his hands on it, if only to satisfy his curiosity.

Matt could well imagine the havoc that could be wrought should the machine gun fall into the hands of Chacon and his murderous crew.

That's why Sam and Remy had ridden out by themselves in the darkness before dawn, making sure they hadn't been followed. The plan was for them to hide the machine gun in a safe place outside of Pago for retrieval when the hour to strike was at hand. After completing this task, they had then met up with Nando, for the latter to identify Pepe Herrera to them and by his presence signify that Sam and Remy were to be trusted.

Matt had confidence in Sam's abilities to get out of a tight spot, a confidence born of their long experience as adventurers riding together. Had something gone wrong with the plan or in Pago, Matt was certain that Sam would have escaped to spread the alert.

Reuniting with his gang, Gila and the bandits rode off into the night. Their task was to go among the *campesinos*, heralding the news that their long years of oppression under the yoke and whips of Don Carlos was nearing an end.

The peasants would arm themselves with what weapons were at hand. They had few firearms beyond shotguns and single-shot muskets, but many machetes, knives, axes, scythes, sledgehammers, and the like. They must then hold themselves in readiness until the morrow, when they would filter into Pago in small groups by drips and drabs, so as not to excite suspicion among Don Carlos's loyalists until the signal was given to rise and slay the foe.

The Tombstone raiders had another mission. Their target was Captain Bravo and his troops, garrisoned in the Pago presidio. It was the old strategy of divide and conquer. Matt Bodine planned to lure the soldiers away from Pago and out into the countryside, where they would be unavailable to come to the aid of Don Carlos when the crisis had arrived.

A decoy lay close to hand, a ripe plum for the taking. It was the patrol camped out on the river bottom in the eastern plains south of the Espinazo, the soldiers whom the Tombstoners had slipped by without being detected when they came off the Goat Trail.

Victorio and his Apaches had the state of Sonora in an uproar. No one knew where he was hiding out or where he would strike next. Matt was going to put that fear-bordering-on-hysteria to work on the nerves of Captain Bravo.

The idea was to hit the patrol and make it look like the work of Apaches. To carry out the illusion would require a little stagecraft by the use of some unshod ponies and a few strategically placed arrows.

Unshod ponies, for Apaches did not put iron horseshoes on their mounts. Yet only a few such animals were needed, since the Apache was a past master at horse theft, with many if not most of the braves having equipped themselves with horseshoe-fitted horses stolen from Anglos and Mexicans.

The same applied to arrows. Apaches were wizard bowmen, but preferred the repeating rifles of the whites. Some bows were still in use and continued to take their fatal toll during Apache raids.

Nando had rounded up a string of a half-dozen unshod ponies earlier, bringing them to the hideout. He would go out with the raiders to serve as guide. The Tombstoners could find their way to the soldiers encamped by the river, but Nando knew the landscape with the expertise of a local outdoorsman, having at his fingertips the knowledge of the shortcuts, water holes, hiding places, and the like.

Midnight was near when the raiders moved into position among the low round mounds west of the river bottom where the troops were bivouacked. The camp nestled in a hollow beside a shallow river ford. Their fires were visible from a long way off.

It was Friday night and, even though the troops were on patrol out in the field, they were making a big night of it, passing around bottles and canteens filled with tequila and mescal, whooping and hollering. What few sentries they had posted were as drunk as the rest.

Matt and Ed Dane hunkered down behind the

cover of some fallen trees at a vantage point overlooking the camp. Drunk and staggering soldiers were outlined against the firelight.

"You'd think they never heard of Victorio," Ed Dane said.

"Careless of them," Matt agreed. They spoke in whispers.

"Say! I just thought of something—what if we run into Victorio and his men?" Ed Dane said.

"You'll never know what hit you," Matt said, "unless you get taken alive, in which case you'll be plumb out of luck."

"Apaches don't attack at night, though."

"Mostly not. Still, the exception is what proves the rule."

"Them soldiers must think otherwise."

"I reckon."

The moon climbed from the top of the sky, sliding west. The soldiers fell out in a drunken stupor and took to their bedrolls. A sentry sat with his back to a tree, rifle across the tops of his thighs, snoring.

The campfires burned low and smoky. No one got up from their blankets to toss fresh kindling on the fire.

A bowstring twanged, sounding a musical note like a plucked guitar string. Matt loosed an arrow into the sentry's chest. It *thunked* as it hit home. The sentry woke, squirmed, clutched futilely at the shaft protruding from his breastbone, and died, slumping into a heap at the foot of the tree.

His death passed unnoticed by his fellows. The

camp remained undisturbed, no one sounding the alarm.

The Tombstone raiders fell on the camp from all directions, shooting and slaying. It was necessary for the ploy to be a success that no survivors should escape to tell that it was not the Apaches who struck the camp. None did.

It was a massacre. The troops were slaughtered, while the raiders suffered not a single casualty.

Now came the work of planting false clues to make the killings look like the work of Apaches. The unshod ponies were run back and forth, in and around the camp, leaving their tracks.

Matt had slain several soldiers by bow and arrow when the attack came. He shot some more arrows into others of the dead to make the deception look good.

To be really realistic, some of the corpses must be scalped and mutilated, the Apache way, a terror tactic that was a hallmark of theirs. It was nasty work. The men from Tombstone were a hard bunch, but some of them shrank from doing what had to be done.

Not so Geetus Maggard. "Hell, you done killed them dead already. What difference does it make what you do to 'em after they's dead?"

"You do it. It don't sit right with my stomach," Dutch Snyder said. Even under waning moonlight he looked a little green around the edges.

Pima Joe was notably unconcerned about taking a hand in this stern duty. For generations, the Apache had slain, scalped, and mutilated his people of the

Pima tribe. It was fitting to lay this slaughter on the Apaches, further inflaming the wrath of Mexican soldiery against Victorio and his braves. Joe set to work with a will.

So did mountain man Vern Tooker, veteran of countless Indian fights. Among the warrior tribes of the Great Plains, Northern Range, and Southwest desert, torture and mutilation were a given, a way of life. He plied his bowie-style knife with the cool hand and practiced eye of a huntsman skinning and quartering a deer carcass.

"Four legs or two, meat's meat," he cheerfully philosophized.

"I like how you handle yourself, big fellow," Geetus Maggard said. "Not like my lily-livered pardner Dutch, who's off getting sick somewhere."

TWENTY

It was opening night. The Pago slave auction was about to begin in a half hour, promptly on the dot at eight o'clock Saturday night.

A crowd of opera buff swells in black-tie formal wear and evening gowns would have been hard put to outdo the enthusiasm and anticipation displayed by the pack of vice lords and ladies, their bodyguards, and hangers-on, as they came down the aisles to take their seats in the prime center orchestra seats of the theater.

Buyers and bidders, whoremongers and madams, pimps and procuresses eagerly awaited the opening of the curtains for the unveiling of all that fresh, young female flesh destined for the auction block.

Any moment now, the red velvet curtains stretched across the proscenium arch screening the stage would part to reveal the first lot of nubile captive girls.

Close to a hundred-and-fifty favored customers

and their entourages filled plush, maroon-velvet, cushioned seats facing the stage.

Many of the flesh merchants looked like respectable businessmen, indistinguishable from the big city bankers, lawyers, brokers, traders who were the bulk of their clientele. Most were Mexican nationals, but more than a few came from Guatemala, Honduras, Salvador, and even farther south.

Not all were professional flesh peddlers. There were many rich men in the provinces, dons and hidalgoes, masters of great estates, plantations, ranch lands, and landowners whose holdings of necessity isolated them from the comforts of civilization and its alluring honeypots. They hungered for a bit of fresh young comfort to warm their beds and excite their jaded senses, providing diversion from their lonely exile and old wives and mistresses grown shapeless, stinking, and stale with the passage of time. Some came themselves, journeying great distances, making a pleasure trip of it.

Others sent their purchasing agents.

If there were next to no *norteamericano* vice lords here, it was not for any moral reason but simply because the great North American continent supplied them with an ever-fresh crop of new recruits fresh from the farms and factories every season. Besides, the trek to Pago in Sonora was hard and dangerous.

The buyers brought their protectors: strongmen, violent men, gunmen able to protect the large sums of gold and silver with which their principals traveled and traded.

Yet other flesh merchants were out, and thugs glorying in their toughness and ability to protect themselves and their property from all comers.

Women, misnamed the "weaker sex," were well-represented at the conclave, making up between one-fifth and one-quarter of the assembled guests. And why not? The vice trade runs on women—who better to run it than women themselves?

Brothel owners, whorehouse madams, procuresses, some old and ugly, others young and fair, took their seats in the Theater of the Damned. Some, not many, but some, had come up through the ranks of whoredom themselves.

Conspicuous by his absence was the supreme slave master himself, Don Carlos. The *padrón* felt it was incumbent on his dignity as a titled aristocrat and landowner to maintain a certain distance from the enterprise which had brought him wealth, power, and an official patent of nobility.

He was safely and comfortably ensconced at home at his rancho outside town, secure in the knowledge that his punctilious overseer Sebastiano would ensure that the proceedings went aright.

Servers, liveried flunkies, went among the guests, proffering crystal flutes of champagne from silver platters. Few if any of the guests discerned that the "champagne" was in reality sparkling wine. "Real champagne is too good for those pigs," Don Carlos had carefully and confidentially instructed Sebastiano during pre-auction preparations.

Don Carlos's *pistoleros* served as armed guards

posted along the theater's side and rear walls; riflemen kept watch in the balcony.

When one's clientele consists of crooks, cut-throats, and killers grown fat on the vice trade, one must ensure that they maintain proper standards of decorum. The house rules, enforced at gunpoint, were the only law such criminals respected or understood.

The hall buzzed with loud talk, high spirits, and alcoholic spirits. Yet nowhere among the assembled were New Orleans vice merchant Jules Duval, nor his bodyguard, Cherokee, to be found.

Sam and Remy were in the house, if not the audience. Decked out in stuffy formal wear rented that afternoon from a Pago tailor, they had entered the opera house with the other guests when the entrance doors were first opened to receive them.

Gliding sharklike along the edges of the crowded lobby, they slipped downstairs into the under-stage area, where Pepe Herrera conducted them to a hiding place, an unused storeroom on the right-hand side of the corridor stretching the length of the building from front to rear.

Performing his task unobserved by prying eyes, Herrera rushed away to rejoin the stage crew and carry out his appointed duties, both professional and personal.

Despite the formal wear, Sam and Remy were well armed. Sam had a pistol stuck in the top of his waistband at his right hip, worn butt out. His sheath knife hung below his left arm. Gun and knife were covered by his jacket, which he'd gotten in a too-large size to help conceal the telltale bulge of weaponry. Remy, too, had a pistol stuck in his belt, along with the sleeve gun hidden in his right cuff and a derringer in his left jacket pocket.

There were no lights in the storeroom. Sam and Remy waited in darkness, broken only by the wan glow of lights shining through the crack under the door and a slitted vertical crack where the door stood slightly ajar from its frame, open a half inch.

Remy pressed his face to the crack, peering through it, keeping watch on the comings and goings in the corridor. Sam kept watch, too, not with his eyes but with his ears (listening for untoward noises and disturbances), and with his skin (sensitive to changes in air currents caused by bodies in motion and alert to vibrations quivering through the floor).

Remy checked his pocket watch by the sliver of soft light shining through the crack of the open door. "Seven-forty. Herrera is ten minutes late. The auction starts at eight o'clock."

Sam made a noise, acknowledging the other's comment. He remained silent. Nothing he could say would affect Herrera's progress in keeping their appointment.

Remy watched the second hand make its sweeping circuit of the watch dial ticking off another minute, two, more. He grew ever more anxious as the minutes ticked away, each second another turn of the screw drawing his nerves tighter and tighter. He breathed gustily. Sam laid a calming hand on his shoulder.

"It's getting late, just short of seven-forty-five now," Remy whispered. "Fifteen minutes to curtain—"

"Someone's coming," Sam said, quivering with alertness.

"I don't hear anyone," Remy protested. But a few beats later, he did. There was the scuff of shoe leather on stone, footfalls approaching the hiding place. "It's him!"

Pepe Herrera paused beside the door, and coughed. Remy eased the door open.

"Sorry," Herrera said. "Sebastiano was making a bother of himself under-stage with last-minute preparations, making sure that everything will be just so, the sharp-eyed little wretch. I had to wait until he went onstage upstairs."

"Anyone keeping an eye on him?" Sam asked.

"Pablo, one of the stage crew. He's one of us," Herrera said. "We lost precious time. Now we must hurry. Eight o'clock draws nigh."

Sam and Remy stepped into the corridor. Herrera set off toward the rear of the building, the duo following. They walked side by side, shoulder to shoulder, traversing the passage to the under-stage area at its far end. The still air was thick with the rank smell of too much flesh, too much fear.

As they neared the end of the passageway, two men rounded the corner, stepping into view. Guards: One was short and stocky with a paintbrush mustache; the other tall and handsome, glossy silver hair styled in an oily pompadour. They stopped short when they saw Herrera approaching with Sam and Remy in tow.

"Keep going," Sam said from the corner of his mouth, low voiced. The trio continued to advance, not slowing their steps.

Sam took a cigar from his inside breast pocket, biting off the tip and spitting it out, all seeming nonchalance. He ignited a lucifer match, striking it into flame with his thumbnail. He lit up, puffing hard, venting smoke, cigar tip a bright orange disk. The smoke was good, masking the sickly, overbearing fleshy smell.

The guards moved to bar the way, Silvertop smiling, his partner dour. "You must go upstairs, señores. No guest allowed down here now, it is prohibited. The auction is about to start," Silvertop said.

Herrera showed a leer and a sly wink. "These gentlemen are friends of Sebastiano, very generous gentlemen. They want one last look at some of the girls, to be sure their money will be well spent. They have plenty of gold to spread around. . . ."

The sour, stocky man shook his head, unyielding. "The under-stage is closed, señores. You must go—"

Sam thrust the lit end of his cigar into the stocky man's eye, grinding it in with a shower of sparks. The stocky man shrieked.

Remy drew the gun from under his jacket, slashing its short stubby barrel across Silvertop's face. Silvertop staggered, crying out. Remy backhanded him in the mouth, breaking teeth, stifling the other's outcry. Silvertop's hand shot out, closing on the wrist of Remy's gun hand. They locked up, struggling for control of the gun, blood droplets venting with each of Silvertop's explosive pain-laced breaths.

Sam pulled the knife from under his arm, cutting the stocky man's throat with a stroke that came close to decapitating him. Blood jetted as the stocky man fell backwards, crashing to the floor.

Sam sidestepped him, thrusting the knife into Silvertop's chest, stabbing him in the heart. Silvertop died that instant on his feet. Remy caught him, easing him down.

"*Caramba!* The fat's in the fire now," Herrera said, sounding excited by the prospect.

Sam wiped the knife blade clean on Silvertop's pants leg, returning it to its sheath.

Herrera peeked around the corner. "Here come two more!"

Sam heard them coming, his gun already in hand. "Don't shoot if you can—"

The newcomers advanced, in quick time—not running but hustling along, jogging. Round the corner they came, coming up short under the drawn guns of Sam and Remy and the sight of bodies and the blood fast pooling on the floor. The guards' eyes bulged, and their jaws dropped.

Remy circled around to the side of the one nearest him, clubbing him behind the ear with the gun in his fist.

The other guard clawed for his gun. Sam lunged, thrusting the gun muzzle hard and deep into the guard's belly in the soft part just below the breastbone, knocking the wind out of him. He doubled over so that he was bent far forward from the waist, clutching his middle with both hands.

Sam laid the gun barrel down smartly across the back of the guard's neck, knocking him out cold.

"Any more?" Sam asked, not even breathing hard.

Herrera looked around the corridor, and shook his head. "All clear for now."

The two guards were stunned but alive. Sam cut their throats with his knife. "Can't risk them giving the alarm and besides, we don't need any more foes at our back. We're playing for high stakes, not just our lives, but those of the captive girls," he said.

Remy risked a quick glance at his pocket watch. "Less than ten minutes till curtain time," he agonized.

Sam put away the knife and stuck the pistol in the top of his pants, covering it with the black jacket. Remy tucked away his gun in likewise style. They made a right turn at the corner, entering a cross passage that met the long corridor at right angles.

Herrera squared his shoulders, assuming an air of jauntiness and forcing a cocky grin, once more the feisty bantamweight.

Sam glanced at his front splattered with ruby teardrops, blood droplets that had sprayed him when he made his kills. Well, there was nothing for it but to keep on making his play. His dark eyes glittered intently; his face was a mask of stolidity.

Along the cross corridor they went, into the under-stage area and its maze of rooms where the captive girls were penned. Three men loomed ahead, burly stagehands in denim overalls, six-guns in hand.

"Our men," Herrera said quickly.

He, Sam, and Remy joined the others. They exchanged knowing nods, and tight grins.

"What of the other crew members, Sebastiano's people?" Herrera asked.

"In there," one of the stagehands said, indicating the door accessing the big barnlike room directly beneath the stage. "They had an accident. They fell down and broke their necks."

His companions' smiles widened.

"Sebastiano?" Herrera pressed.

"Up in the theater. Pablo will warn us if he starts to come downstairs," said the spokesman for the crew.

Herrera nodded, and turned to Sam and Remy. "We had best secure the girls now."

"Are the back doors open?" Sam asked.

"No, but I have the keys," the crew chief said, pulling a key ring from a hip pocket and holding them up for the others to see, jingling them. "I took it off one of Sebastiano's loyalists after I killed him."

"We didn't want to open up too soon, for fear of guards entering before we were ready," another stagehand said.

"We're as ready as we'll ever be," Sam said. "Open the door."

"Hands up!" Duenna Dulce, the matron assigned to guard the Arizona girls, stepped out of the greenroom with gun in hand, pointing it at the conspirators gathered in the hall outside the under-stage door. A big-caliber horse pistol was held level at her ample hip.

Her eyes were dull black buttons and her mouth a narrow slit with vertical lines at the corners, all set in a brown doughy face. "Ho! What treachery is this? I knew something was afoot," she said, moving forward. "I'll kill the first one that moves."

"She'll do it, too," Herrera cautioned. "Easy, men, easy . . ."

Sam raised his hands along with the others, his right hand stealing to the back of his neck to reach for the throwing knife held on a rawhide cord down between his shoulder blades.

An old woman slipped out of the green room where the American girls were being kept, coming up behind Duenna Dulce. The old one had long silvery hair tied in a knot at the back of her head, a wrinkled birdlike face, and weighed less than a hundred pounds. A withered clawlike hand clutched a clublike lead weight of the type used to secure the rigging, raising it to strike.

"Don Carlos will have you flayed alive, traitors," Duenna Dulce said, smirking.

"Easy," Herrera repeated.

The old one brought the weight down suddenly, savagely on the back of Duenna Dulce's head. There was a crunching sound. Duenna Dulce's black button eyes rolled up in her head, only the whites showing.

The old one was poised to strike again, but it was unneeded. Duenna Dulce collapsed like a poleaxed steer, hitting the floor with a thud of too-solid flesh. Happily, the pistol did not go off.

"Hit her again. That one takes a lot of killing," a stagehand said.

"Not any more. That did for her. She's dead," Pepe Herrera said, bending over the body and prying the gun from her hamlike fist.

"La Vieja, the old woman, a cleaning woman— and one of ours," a stagehand whispered to Sam and Remy. "Her granddaughters were taken and sold on the block."

"Best secure the rest of the women guards now," Herrera said.

"Give me the gun, I know what to do with it," the old one said.

Herrera handed her the pistol. She handled it lovingly, slitted eyes undimmed with age, alight with malice and eager expectation.

Pounding noises came from the under-stage area.

"Someone's knocking at the back door," a stage-hand said.

"Vincente, Miguel, come with me. We'll take care of the women guards," Herrera said. "Hector, unlock the door and see who it is. I pray it is our friends who are knocking."

He glanced at Sam and Remy. "You had better go with them." Hector, the stage crew chief, ducked through the doorway into the under-stage area, Sam and Remy following.

Vincente and Miguel, the other two stagehands, drew their guns and went to Herrera and La Vieja.

the old woman. Gun in hand, La Vieja crossed to the next room where captives were being held, rapping the bony knuckles of a free hand against the door panel.

"What?" a woman's voice gruffly demanded.

"Cleaning woman," La Vieja quavered. The door opened, a burly matron sticking her head outside. La Vieja stuck her gun in the other's bulldog face, backing her into the room.

Vincente went in with her. Herrera and Miguel moved to the next room to continue the process.

Crossing the threshold of the under-stage area, Sam glimpsed from the corner of his eye four corpses heaped in an untidy pile against the wall to the left of the entrance, the bodies of the freshly slain, loyalist stagehands. He, Remy, and Hector rushed to the back door.

"Let's not take any chances," Sam said, raising his gun and flattening his back against the wall to one side of the double doors. Remy did the same, taking up a similar stance on the other side of the doors, so that he and Sam flanked them.

The knocking sounded again, coming in a series of three raps.

"Three, two, one. That's the recognition code—let them in," Sam said.

Hector fitted a key from the ring into the doors, unlocking them. He opened one door, swinging it back against the inner wall.

Outside, five men stood grouped around a wheeled serving cart, three outfitted as guards and two in white jackets and servants' livery. The guards wore broad-brimmed sombreros, ponchos, and serapes of the type worn by Don Carlos's *vaqueros*, the garb of the rancho *pistoleros*, not the uniforms worn by the opera house guards. The sombreros were worn with brims pulled low in front, partially covering their faces.

The waiters wore short black jackets, white shirts and black pants. They were bareheaded, faces in plain view: Juan Garza and Howling Jeff Howell.

"They belong to us," Sam told Hector. Hector opened the other double door wide. "Come in men," Sam said.

Garza and Howell entered first, one pulling and the other pushing the four-wheeled serving cart through the doorway. Its tablelike upper surface held open crates of sparkling wine, set atop a white linen tablecloth whose sides fell almost to the tops of the wheels, screening the underside of the cart. The three guards followed in their wake.

Sam and Hector closed the doors, Sam delaying long enough for a quick scan of the grounds outside. The sun had set, the sky was darkening, though some afterglow was still showing.

The grounds behind the back of the building stretched some fifty yards to an eight-foot–high, iron spear fence. A complex of several small, one-story outbuildings stood in the middle ground to the right. One of them was the kitchen and food storage area, from which the wine and cart had come.

Guards with shouldered rifles marched back and forth along the inside of the back fence. They evinced no sign of alarm or even interest in the proceedings at the rear of the opera house.

The back doors were closed but not locked. The guards took off their hats, ponchos, and serapes, revealing themselves as Matt Bodine, Ringo, and Polk Muldoon.

"How goes it, brother?" Matt greeted Sam.

"Better, now that I see you," Sam said, flashing a grin.

Howell and Garza each took hold of a rope handle at opposite ends of a wine crate, hefting it off the top of the cart, and setting it down on the floor. Polk and Ringo did the same with the other wine crate.

Jeff Howell gripped in both hands a bottom edge of the white linen tablecloth covering the cart. With the air of a stage magician performing a feat of sleight of hand, he whisked off the cloth, baring the underside of the cart.

On a lower shelf stood the Montigny Mitrailleuse machine gun, its stand, and olive-drab canvas pouches filled with cartridge plates full of ammunition.

"For my next trick, I'm gonna make a bunch of slavers disappear," Jeff Howell joked.

"See if you can make those guards along the back fence disappear first," Sam said.

"We already did," Matt said. "We took care of them before coming through the back gate. Those're our boys walking the wall, Curly Bill and Dutch Snyder and some of the others. The rest are inside, too, waiting for the go."

"Bill wanted to come in for the turkey shoot, but I convinced him it was more important for him to stay outside and cover our retreat with the girls," Ringo said.

"The rebels had the serving cart and these waiters' outfits waiting for us, just like we planned. Me and Juan put 'em on and here we are," Jeff said.

"You have made a grave error, my friend," Remy said, solemn faced, holding up a wine bottle.

"I did?" Jeff said, face falling. "What—?"

"Sparkling wine must be served chilled. This is warm."

"Why, you son of a b—, er, that is, you golderned son of a gun, you!"

"Take a look at these appetizers, though," Matt said. He started taking wine bottles out of a crate and setting them down on the floor. Below the top layer of bottles were repeating rifles, six-guns, and bandoliers of ammunition. Polk and Juan Garza pitched in, doing the same.

Remy set the machine gun's tripod stand on top of the serving cart. Sam helped him haul the Mitrailleuse out from under the cart, lifting it and lowering it so that its base support post was fitted into the socket at the top of the tripod stand, clicking into place.

Ringo's twin ivory-handled Colts were holstered on his hips. He picked up a Winchester rifle and a couple of bandoliers from a wine crate, putting the bandoliers on over his shoulders so they crisscrossed his torso, making an X.

Matt hauled out a gun belt with a holstered gun, proffering it to Sam. "Your gun, hombre."

"Much obliged," Sam said, buckling on the gun belt and settling it down low on his hips, the way he liked it.

"Yours, too, Remy," Matt said.

"Thank you, my friend." Remy paused in his labors over the Mitrailleuse long enough to strap on his gun, sticking the pistol he had in the top of his belt on the opposite hip.

The others armed themselves with rifles and bandoliers. When they were done, there were still some extras left. "For you and your friends, amigo. Help yourself," Matt said.

"*Gracias,*" Hector said, quickly possessing himself of a Winchester. With his big, work-roughened hands, he caressed the piece's polished wooden stock and long barrel, then began loading it.

Remy started wheeling the cart with the Mitrailleuse on top of the elevator lift platform directly under where center stage would be. The ammunition pouches lay on the bottom shelf. Juan and Jeff pitched in, lending a hand, rolling the heavily laden cart onto the platform.

Polk Muldoon knocked off the head of a bottle of wine against the wall, loosing an explosion of shattered glass and foamy golden liquid. Brushing the top clear of any glass shards and splinters, he drank long and deeply, draining half the bottle before pausing for breath.

"Don't get drunk," Juan Garza cautioned.

"Drunk? On this sod'ypop?!" Polk said, scoffing. "Talk about 'teach your grandma to suck eggs!'"

"From what I've heard, Polk might be more dangerous drunk than sober," Sam said.

"Yes, but to whom?" Remy said.

"Don't you worry none, Frenchy. Drunk or sober, I never shot nobody I wasn't aiming to," Polk said.

A commotion sounded beyond the under-stage area of stirring movements, and shrill voices of young females.

"I'll make sure things're squared away," Sam said. He went into the hall, Ringo and Hector following.

Herrera and friends had the situation in hand. The duennas had been rounded up and were being herded at gunpoint into one room. There were a half-dozen of them.

They were marched to a supply closet, and shoved inside. It was a tight fit—they were big women and it was a modest-sized closet. Vincente and Miguel put their shoulders to the door to force it shut, cramming the duennas in like sardines in a can.

Hector used a key from his ring to lock the door. Muffled protests and squalls of outrage sounded from within.

"Silence!" La Vieja said, knocking on the closet door with the barrel of her pistol. "A few bullets perhaps will stop your complaining!"

The clamor inside the closet ceased, not a murmur coming from the other side of the door.

"I know how to handle such as these." La Vieja smiled grimly, spicing the word "these" with contemptuous relish.

Open doorways lining the hall were crowded with girls in white nightdresses looking out, talking rapidly in hushed, excited tones among themselves. Duenna Dulce's corpse lay on the floor where it had been struck down, nobody having bothered to move it.

"Where're our girls?" Ringo asked.

"They're all our girls now, John," Sam said gently.

"Point taken," Ringo said with a tight grin. "The American girls, the ones Jones took, where're they?"

"There," Sam said, indicating the room from which Duenna Dulce had emerged.

Ringo went through the doorway, his quick reflexes only keeping him from being brained by a wooden stool held high in the hands of a teenage girl who stood beside the door, ready to club the next man who entered.

"Whoa," Ringo said, sinewy brown hand shooting up to grab a side rail of the stool, arresting its swift downward progress in midair. With a twist of his wrist, he wrested it from the wielder, lowering it to the floor.

"I'm on your side, girls. We've come to take you home," Ringo said, grinning wryly.

Disbelief warred with exultation among the girls in the room. One of them, Rowena Whitman, came from a ranch in the Sulphur Springs Valley outside of Tombstone.

"It's Johnny Ringo!" she cried, recognizing the newcomer.

"At your service," Ringo said, touching the tip of his hat brim between thumb and forefinger.

The others may not have known him by sight, but all knew the name of one of the West's most famous gunslingers. Gasps, squeals, and shouts came up from them.

"Is it possible, can it be true—?!"

"We're saved, thank the good Lord!"

Ringo raised his hands palms out, motioning for silence. "Hush up, you all. We're not out of the woods yet, not by a long shot."

"You're going to have to cooperate and do as you're told to make this thing work, girls," Sam said from the doorway. "A bunch of us came from Tombstone to bring you home. Sorry I couldn't identify myself when I came through here yesterday and let you know what was in the works, but we couldn't risk tipping our hand to the slavers."

He surveyed the young femmes, matching them with the faces he'd seen on Friday during his inspection tour with Remy. It looked like they were all present, but he wanted to be sure.

"Is this all of you? Any others of you being kept elsewhere?" Sam asked.

Several of the girls spoke at once, confirming that this indeed was the full complement of females stolen from north of the border.

"We've got wagons waiting out back for you, but

we can't move you just yet. Some of us are going to stage a diversion to distract the slavers and keep them busy while we move you out," Sam said.

Diversion? That was an understatement, but Sam saw no need to expand on his remark. He went on. "Quiet down, sit tight, and one of us'll be along in a minute or two to tell you what's next," he said.

"Keep your courage up, gals. Don't lose your nerve, and you'll be on your way home real soon now," Ringo said.

Sam nodded to Ringo, who followed him into the hall.

"Johnny Ringo!" one of the girls sighed, a tremulous thrill in her voice.

Sam cut Ringo a sharp side glance.

"Females of all ages and persuasions just naturally cotton to the Ringo charm," Ringo said, shrugging. "Can't help it if I'm famous, Sam."

"Modest, too."

"You're just sore none of them recognized you."

"Good thing they didn't yesterday, or the whole plan might have blown up in our faces. Anonymity has its virtues, John."

Matt Bodine stuck his head through the doorway of the under-stage area, into the hall, looking around. He saw Sam and Ringo, and motioned to them.

"We're loaded up and ready to go," Matt said, "but we need a couple of hands to work the lift."

Sam nodded, going to Pepe Herrera. "We need Miguel and Vincente at the capstan. You and La Vieja will have to hold the girls back until we get the ball rolling."

"How will I know when to start moving them out?" Herrera asked.

"Wait till we come back down. We can cover their flight then. That's the safest way, if 'safe' is a word that applies to a tight spot like this. When the shooting starts, get them going."

"It shall be as you say, amigo. Good luck."

"To you, too."

"And—good hunting!"

Matt and Ringo had already disappeared into the under-stage area. Sam and stagehands Vincente and Miguel went through the doorway.

Remy, Matt, and Jeff Howell stood on the lift platform, with Polk, Juan Garza, and crew chief Hector at the capstan. Ringo, rifle in hand, stood on the spiral staircase at the left wall of the space, about halfway to the top.

The capstan, a wooden cylinder four feet tall and three feet in diameter, stood mounted on a sturdy square-shaped platform bolted to the floor. The platform was open at the sides, making visible the rims of tooth-geared wooden wheels and rods like giant clockwork innards stacked vertically beneath.

Chains ran from the gear work to a set of wheels and pulleys in a block-and-tackle arrangement mounted on the left wall, controlling cablelike rope hawsers that ran up the wall and across the ceiling, before dropping straight down to the sides of the rectangular lift platform below.

At the top of the capstan, a number of wooden spokes jutted out horizontally from the hub, allowing the central shaft to rotate on its axis, turning the gears below and manipulating chains and ropes to raise or lower the platform as needed.

The block-and-tackle rigging enabled a few stage-hands to work the platform.

Manuel and Vincente took their places at the capstan, freeing Hector.

"Two of our men are onstage behind the curtain keeping an eye on things. I will tell them that the time has come for the axe to fall," Hector said. "A time we have been waiting for for so long, fearing it might never arrive." He crossed to the spiral stair-case along the right-hand wall, starting up it, rifle in hand, six-gun in his belt.

Ringo paused, waiting for Hector to ascend and pass the word to his fellow rebels. A moment later, he started up the spiral staircase, with its wooden treads and iron risers and struts, corkscrewing around a vertical central iron shaft.

The staircase shook and swayed under Ringo's tread as he mounted to the top, through a hole in the ceiling—a ceiling that became a floor once he'd gone topside.

Now he stood in the wings.

The backstage area was lit, but not brightly. The curtains were closed, screening the stage from the audience on the other side.

On the side of the stage opposite from Ringo, Hector stood, animatedly talking to another stage-hand. A third stood at center stage where the cur-tains joined, peeking out through a narrow slit between them to keep watch on the comings and goings in the theater hall, ready to sound the alarm should any show sign of coming back behind the curtain.

Seeing Ringo, Hector pointed him out to the stagehand to whom he'd been talking. Ringo raised a hand in greeting, the other nodding.

Urged by Hector, the stagehand started down the staircase, disappearing through the hole in the floor. Descending to the under-stage floor, he crossed to take his place at the capstan.

He, Juan Garza, Polk Muldoon, Vincente, and Miguel stood in the spaces between the capstan handles, each facing the back of the next man before him in his slot, each gripping one of the horizontal spokes in both hands.

La Vieja stood in the under-stage doorway, holding back the girls crowding the halls.

Pepe Herrera stood beside the wall, gripping the wooden handle of the lever controlling the trapdoor mechanism.

Matt, Sam, Remy, and Jeff were aboard the lift platform. Matt and Remy sat crosslegged on the platform, Indian–style, the machine-gun cart between them. Each held the cart to steady it. Sam and Jeff stood at opposite ends of the lift, gripping the twin vertical hawsers rising to pulley wheels set in the floor beside the short ends of the trapdoor hatch.

Remy consulted his pocket watch. "Eight o'clock, showtime!"

Herrera threw the switch, tripping a set of jointed rods and gears running up the wall and across the ceiling to the trapdoor.

A series of solid metal *thunks* sounded as the mechanism shot home. Above, the seemingly solid ceiling parted, hinged hatches swinging open to fall vertically in place, opening a rectangular space in the stage floor.

The men put their weight against the handles, digging in, moving forward, pushing the spoke handles gripped in front of them. The capstan rotated on its axis, turning the intricate clockwork gears and wheels stacked under the platform. They, in turn, hauled in the chain, winding it around the central shaft at the base, heaving at the hawser ropes attached to the lift platform.

With a jerk and a heave, the platform left the floor, rising ceilingward. There was the creak of taut hempen rope, the squeal of recently well-oiled pulley wheels and toothed clockwork gears.

The platform rushed upward through space, swiftly rising up to and through the trapdoor hatchway. It fit neatly in the oblong space, its topside level with the stage floor, with only a hairline crack around the edges to indicate the platform's outline.

Matt, Sam, Remy, and Jeff—and the Mitrailleuse-bearing cart—appeared onstage, materializing as if by magic.

Below, seeing the platform was in place, Pepe Herrera threw the lever home, locking the platform firmly into the stage floor. Not so firmly that the four aboard it failed to quit it as soon as possible, rolling the cart clear of it, too, pushing it downstage towards the curtains.

Handles on the legs of the cart allowed the wheels

to lock in place, freezing them and immobilizing the cart.

"You came onstage like Mephisto the Devil popping up in the opera *Faust*," said Ringo as he joined them, being a man of some wide-ranging culture.

"Our mission is not only to raise hell, but to loose it," replied Sam, himself not unschooled in the realm of the arts.

Remy readied the Mitrailleuse, ramming a cartridge plate into the receiver at the underside of the piece, hitting it with his palm heel to ensure it was properly lodged. Matt stood beside him, carefully studying Remy's actions, fascinated by the gun, absorbed in its workings.

Remy pulled the bolt forward, then pushed it back, engaging the firing mechanism. He set the piece for single-shot capacity.

From beyond the curtains came a hubbub of crowd noises, the rise and fall of loud talk, and bodies stirring.

Matt and Jeff flanked the machine-gun cart on one side, Sam and Ringo on the other. Hector and a second stagehand waited in the wings, manning the ropes controlling the opening and closing of the curtains.

"Ready," Remy announced.

Matt waved a hand, signalling the stagehands. He shouldered his rifle, as did Sam, Ringo, and Jeff.

Hector and his sideman heaved away at the ropes. Curtains parted in the center, the open space widening as twin sets of red velvet curtains rushed away from each other to the sides, baring the stage.

Beyond the proscenium arch, the audience was revealed, 150 flesh merchants, male and female, decked out in gaudy finery, massed up front in the center orchestra seats, surrounded by bodyguards, *pistoleros*, and fawning hangers-on. Their faces were flushed with wine, eyes glittering, all eager and expectant for the show to commence, the bidding to begin.

A hush of silence fell like a death knell on the assembled vice lords as they experienced the shock of recognition. The open curtains unveiled not a clutch of fresh young captive beauties clad only in thin, short, sleeveless, white cotton shifts for quick and easy removal to expose every inch of their intmate nubile charms (made more piquant by tearful eyes, trembling mouths, and quivering chins), but rather, the shape of their own deaths.

Annihilation was nigh.

Oohs and aahs of appreciation and scattered applause were almost all stilled now, though a few slow-witted dolts and drunks continued enthusiastically hammering meaty palms together in heavy-handed clapping. A collective gasp of mingled terror and outrage went up from the audience.

Don Carlos was not a humorous man. It was known he was not given to pranks, jests, and similar foolishnesses. He was all business. No, this was none of his doing.

The pause lasted but an eyeblink, a space between heartbeats stretching out under the monumental strain of awful revelaton, stretching out into eternity.

Then—

Eternity snapped—shattered—as Remy opened up with the Mitrailleuse, the others cutting loose with their rifles.

Remy turned the hand crank, milling out rounds like a butcher working a meat grinder, turning fresh meat into hamburger. He went for the guards first. They were a sweet target ranged along the side and rear walls of the theater.

More were on the rear wall, so he targeted them first, swinging the machine gun on its tripod, sweeping the muzzle from left to right. He mowed down the line of guards like a row of clay pipes in a shooting gallery, and with as little compunction.

Flames bearded the wide, disk-shaped muzzle, spearing from one barrel bore to the next, thirty-seven in all, brass cartridges arching sideways out of the ejector. Guards were spinning, swirling, throwing their arms up in the air as they went down, smearing blood on the wall behind them, a wall progressively cratered by machine-gun fire.

The four riflemen were no less enthusiastic, picking off the guards along the side wall. They fired, then levered fresh rounds into the chamber, and fired again.

Clamor racketed off the walls: gunfire, screams, shrieks. The flesh peddlers in the center orchestra seats were hurled into pandemonium by stark-raving fear. Some threw themselves below the seats to the floor; others tried to flee, tripping each other up.

A lull opened in the clamor as Remy exhausted

his thirty-seven-shot cartridge plate, pausing to reload. A couple of *pistoleros* standing in the aisle near the stage swung their six-guns toward the machine gunner to take him out.

Matt Bodine swung his rifle into play, drilling the gunmen with some well-placed shots. They crumpled to the floor.

Remy reloaded another cartridge plate, the Mitrailleuse resuming its lethal chattering.

Sam Two Wolves focused his firepower on a tempting target he'd spied out the day before while reconnoitering the opera house.

A length of thick hempen rope stretched from a wall-mounted cleat to center ceiling, where it threaded a block of wheels and pulleys to stretch downward to the hub of a chandelier, now a wheel of light dangling over the audience's heads like the Sword of Damocles.

Sam's rifle blasted the rope in the same place time and again, cutting into it above the cleat, which he used as a guideline to concentrate his tight firing group. The rope came partially apart, chandelier lurching downward some few feet before jerking to a halt.

Its frosted globe lamps and strings of beaded crystals rattled and tinkled as the chandelier swayed like a pendulum.

The vice lords below looked up, heads tilted back, necks cording. The rope still held.

Sam took careful aim and fired once more, parting the rope. Loosed, the heavy chandelier plunged floorward, the now-severed end of the rope racing upward, whipping through pulley wheels.

Shrieks of the hopelessly doomed sounded beneath the plummeting juggernaut, only to be cut off by the scythe of the crash. A dozen or more were crushed beneath. Others at the rim were struck down like half-squashed bugs.

Globe lamps shattered, spewing fire, flames licking over velvet seat cushions and gold-braided ropes, setting ablaze those helplessly pinned beneath the great weight.

Carried away by the carnage, Jeff Howell vented a bloodcurdling Rebel yell, its piercing shriek rising to a whooping crescendo—the famous "howl" that had given him the name of Howling Jeff.

His rifle barrel began to glow a dull red as he slung lead throughout the hall, gunning down foes.

Armed guards rushed down flights of stairs to the edge of the overhanging balcony, rifles raised to fire down at the killer angels performing onstage.

Matt Bodine saw them coming, raised his rifle barrel and opened fire.

One guard was hit, causing him to tumble down the balcony stairs in a bone-shattering somersault. Another, tagged, let the rifle fly from his hands. Clutching his chest where he'd been hit, he bowed forward from the waist, and pitched headfirst over the brass balcony rail to fall shrieking into the seats on the floor below, silenced by a sickening crash.

Not pausing, Matt swung the muzzle in line with the next target, squeezing the trigger. A third guard was hit. He sat down hard, dead. Matt picked off a fourth *vaquero* and then there were none, at least not in the balcony.

The vice lords were not minded to return fire, fair fights against armed foes not being in their line. Helpless girls barely out of childhood were more their meat.

Panicked fugitives fled blindly in all directions at once like so many chickens with their heads cut off, tripping each other up. They collided, crashing into each other, fighting madly, tearing, and clawing at one another. The weak and luckless went down to be trampled by those still on their feet.

A bullet whizzed past Ringo's head, so close that its passage lifted his long hair.

The shot had been fired by a tough in evening clothes standing alone between rows of seats.

He missed, but Ringo didn't. A rifle bullet drilled the shooter through the chest, a red carnation of blood blossoming on his ruffled white shirtfront where the bullet had found him.

A figure jumped up from where he'd been crouching behind the seats, darting into the aisle and running madly toward the back of the hall—

Sebastiano.

Sam had been looking for him, but Sebastiano had kept under cover until now.

Sebastiano ran with arms and legs pumping, sprinting on his toes, fast eating up the distance between himself and escape.

Sam shot one of his legs out from under him. Sebastiano fell sprawling.

A fat old bawd overstuffed into a too-tight, green

satin gown and her two bodyguards came hurrying up the aisle. Sebastiano was in the way, so they ran him down, trampling him underfoot.

Sam paused, holding his fire for a few beats. The hefty madam and her two protectors ran on, leaving Sebastiano sprawled on the carpeted aisle, twitching and jerking. Clutching the arm of an aisle seat, he began trying to pull himself up.

The woman in the green dress and her bodyguards were under the balcony, closing on the safety of the lobby door. Sam shot them down, all three.

Sebastiano somehow hauled himself forward and began crawling up the aisle, pulling himself from seat to seat, dragging himself along with one dead leg trailing behind him. Sam shot him in the arm that was pulling him along. Sebastiano went down again and lay there writhing and squirming.

Doors at the far wall burst open, *pistoleros* rushing in, blasting away with six-guns at the men onstage. Matt and Jeff cut them down.

Sam dropped a kill shot into Sebastiano's back, shattering his spine, and turned to other targets.

Fires started by the chandelier downed by Sam were going good now, ripening into a hearty roaring blaze in the middle of the center orchestra seats. A number of small independent fires had combined into one furious conflagration, smoke columns rising from it.

Some of the vice lords were on fire, long red tongues of flame licking greedily over gaudy checked suits and body-hugging gowns, turning the wearers into human torches.

The theater was filling with heat, smoke, screams. Matt Bodine reckoned that he and his fellow revengers had done their part here.

Diversion? The carnage in the theater hall was more than enough. Vengeance was sweet, but the purpose of the mission was to rescue captive girls.

Matt motioned for the others to stand down and begin the retreat. Hector and his fellow stagehand had already gone below to the under-stage area.

Matt and Sam stood side by side, laying down covering fire while Remy and Jeff pushed the machine-gun cart back on the platform.

Ringo stood in the open hatchway of a spiral staircase, waiting for the others to step on to the platform. When they were all in place, he went down the stairs into the under-stage room.

Herrera and the others stood by, manning the capstan, waiting for the signal.

Ringo descended the staircase halfway.

"Take it down!" he shouted, leaning over the rail, hand beside his mouth.

Pepe Herrera threw the lever that worked the trapdoor mechanism, unfastening the restraining bar and clamps holding the lift platform locked at stage level, opening the traps.

The men at the capstan put their shoulders into it, setting the wheel in motion, circling the central shaft.

The lift platform started downward, sinking

through the oblong hatchway. Matt, Sam, Remy, and Jeff sat on the platform to better maintain their balance during the descent. Ropes creaking, pulleys squealing, the shaking, shimmying platform sank through the hatchway and through empty space toward the floor.

It touched down with a bump, Herrera once more working the lever, closing the trapdoors and sealing them shut. No enemy gunmen could shoot down through the hatchway at them, should any of the foe have the presence of mind to do so.

The under-stage rear doors were open, Pima Joe and Ed Dane standing beside them. Gunfire and shrieks could be heard throughout the opera house grounds.

Remy and Jeff rolled the cart off the platform, Remy pausing to reload a fresh cartridge plate.

"That's a powerful piece of ordnance you've got there," Matt said, pausing to reload his rifle.

"Be sure to tell Stebbins that," Remy said, grinning.

"Hell, I'll tell Davenport!"

Sam reloaded his rifle, then went to the rear doors, approaching them from the side so as not to outline himself in the gaping doorway.

"Sounded like hellzappopin' up there, Sam," Ed Dane greeted him.

"I said we'd bring down the house."

"Sure, but what do you do for an encore?"

"Get the girls out of here."

"A lot of folks have the same idea," Ed Dane said,

gesturing toward the open doorway, which framed a group of people gathering outside.

A mixed bunch of townsfolk and *campesinos* was collecting there, with more coming every minute. Many had come with some vain hope of rescuing stolen daughters, wives, and sweethearts—impossible dream now turned into tantalizing reality!

"They're waiting to take their gals home, too," Ed Dane said.

"We won't disappoint them," Sam promised.

Hector was outside speaking to the people, getting them ready for the big breakout. The Tombstone raiders moved the machine gun outside to provide covering fire if needed, Jeff Howell pushing one side of the cart, Polk Muldoon the other. Remy stood at the rear manning the gun.

The crowd parted, letting the Mitrailleuse move to the fore, commanding a field of fire across the rear grounds and gardens of the opera house.

Violent action raged in front of the building, where a mob of townsmen and *campesinos* tore into slavers and buyers fleeing the burning opera house, shooting down vice lords and Don Carlos's *vaqueros* and flunkies as they came stumbling down the front stairs.

Those who survived the gauntlet of gunfire were met by enraged and outraged citizens wielding machetes, knives, axes, hoes, sickles, and the like. They tore into their longtime tormentors, hacking, slashing, stabbing, and bludgeoning.

No soldiers were on the scene. Captain Bravo had taken the main body of his force into the field earlier this day to run down what they thought was a war party of Victorio's Apaches who had massacred a detachment of troops on patrol south of the Espinazo who'd been bivouacked beside the river.

The skeleton crew remaining behind to man the presidio showed no inclination of leaving the safety of the stone-walled fort to venture into the town of Pago where rebellion now ran riot.

The Tombstoners formed a loose arc around the machine-gun cart, securing the rear grounds so the girls could safely come out.

Within the under-stage area, Matt and Ringo and Juan Garza and Herrera began moving the captives into the open air.

American and Mexican girls alike had undergone an emotional sea change from the numbed hopelessness and apathy of captivity to a rising near hysteria at the once seemingly impossible prospect of rescue and freedom looming near at hand.

Matt and Ringo herded the young Americans out in a bunch.

"Move out, girls!" Matt urged, motioning with the gun in his hand toward the open doorway. "Move fast, but stay together . . . move as a group . . . stay with the group . . . don't drop out, don't fall behind. Get separated from us now and it'll be disaster. . . ."

Ringo served as rear guard, coming up behind the femmes to make sure that none strayed or stumbled. The girls went out through the exit into the night.

Herrera, La Vieja, Vincente, and Miguel escorted the larger group of Mexican girls to freedom, streaming them into the back gardens of the opera house grounds.

The crowd of waiting townsfolk and *campesinos* spread out, circling around the combined throng of girls Mexican and American, forming a human shield ringing them.

The burning opera house threw lurid red, yellow, and orange lights on the garden grounds.

The girls found sweet relief in breathing the outside air. Energy? Despite the privations of the ordeal they had suffered, they were now suffused with a surplus of energy, thanks to youth and its marvelous recuperative powers.

On they came, long unbound hair streaming, supple bare limbs flashing, rushing barefoot over flagstoned path and weedy lawn. Once the girls came pouring out of the building, it was like a dam breaking—there was no restraining the flood.

Matt, Herrera, and La Vieja were the last to leave the under-stage area.

The old woman hugged to herself the knowledge that she had accidently on purpose forgotten to free the brutal duenna guards from the closet into which they'd been locked. Better that such should remain behind to perish in the flames as the opera house burned down!

Sam Two Wolves, Polk Muldoon, Ed Dane, Juan Garza, Jeff Howell, and Pima Joe formed a crescent whose center was the serving cart with Remy Markand standing ready at the machine gun.

The crescent moved forward across the grounds toward the back gate, now held by Curly Bill, Hal Purdy, Arnholt Stebbins, Dutch Snyder, and Geetus Maggard.

The crescent was the advance guard, clearing the way for girls and rebel citizens following. Ringo, Hector, and Miguel brought up the rear, watchful lest some of Don Carlos's hard-pressed men screw up their courage for a sneak attack.

This was unlikely. The slavers' primary concern now was to save their own necks and flee the opera house grounds without being intercepted by vengeful rebels.

The Tombstoner crescent neared the far end of the grounds, an open back gate gaping in the eight-foot iron-spear fence bordering the perimeter of the property.

Scattered inside and outside the gateway lay the bodies of men—guards, *pistoleros*—who'd gotten in the way of the raiders and been slain for their troubles.

Beyond the fence stretched a cobblestone street running parallel to it. Parked along the grassy verge bordering the outside of the fence were two wagons, each with solid wooden wheels and high rail sides and a team of horses yoked to the spans. Geetus Maggard sat in the driver's seat of one wagon, Dutch Snyder in the other.

A man with gun in hand fled the advancing

crescent, racing out of the gate, a Don Carlos gunman. Hal Purdy loomed ahead. Both fired, Purdy's shot lancing a line of fire from gun muzzle to the other's chest, dropping him, the latter's shot going wild.

The crescent reached the back gate, Tombstone raiders spreading out to secure wagons and street. The ring of rebel townsfolk protecting the mass of girls within it began streaming out the gate, fanning out on both sides of the street.

Cutting the knot of American girls loose from the others, the raiders moved them toward the wagons.

"Howdy, gals! Your chariot awaits, climb on board," Dutch Snyder roared, doffing his hat and grandly waving it in the air.

The seven femmes from Bear Paw and five Arizona natives clambered into the wagons.

Remy broke down the machine gun, putting it and the tripod in a crate and the amunition in a burlap sack. Matt and Remy loaded crate and sack in the back of a wagon, Remy jumping aboard to mother-hen the piece during the ride.

Matt and Sam watched the freed Mexican femmes, numbering some two score or more, pour into the street, watched over by the rebels.

"Some will be saved, but not all; some of those saved now will fall by the wayside," Sam said ruefully.

"Hard words, but true," Matt said, "but at least they've all of them got a chance, which is more than they would have had once the slavers sold them into whoredom. It's like saving baby rabbits from a flooded warren—all you can do is set them free and hope for the best, even though there's rattlesnakes and coyotes and birds of prey on the prowl, waiting to move in. Man proposes and the Lord disposes, 'twas ever thus."

"Amen, brother."

"Hell, we and our gals are a long way from the border."

"Don't think I haven't thought of it."

Pepe Herrera floated into view, coming to them.

"Here's where we part company," Sam said.

"It has been a good fight, señores. The power of Don Carlos is broken after this night, I think," Herrera said.

"Hope so. But there will be others to try to take his place, and there's still Captain Bravo and his men to be reckoned with."

"When they come, we will be ready for them."

"Take care of yourself and keep your guard up, amigo," Matt said.

"That we will. *Vaya con Dios*," Herrera said. "Go with God."

"And may He go with you."

Herrera waved a hand in a farewell salute, slipping into the tail end of the fleeing crowd, wrapped in the cloaking mantle of night.

A string of horses was hitched to the fence, waiting for the raiders. Matt and Sam and the others mounted up.

Dutch Snyder cracked a whip mule skinner style

over the heads of his team of horses, moving his wagon out, Maggard piloting the second wagon behind.

"Next stop, Tombstone!" Dutch shouted, cracking the whip again.

TWENTY-ONE

Bad news travels fast, disaster comes at a gallop. Three riders bearing word of the opera house carnage raced to the rancho of Don Carlos de la Vega.

The Vega holdings comprised several hundred square miles, much of it well-watered grasslands. The grand hacienda and principal outbuildings were sited several miles outside town. A road ran straight to the walled compound of the Vega rancho.

The main buildings were encircled by a ten-foot-high adobe wall, armed *vaqueros* posted on the ramparts. The road led to the main entrance, a double-doored gate beneath an archway.

Within, the hacienda was ablaze with light. Later, after the auction, Sebastiano and his henchmen would bring the booty to their master Don Carlos, chests of gold harvested at the opera house.

The slave master would demand a full accounting of the business of the night on that same night, including a detailed retelling of the transactions: who paid what for whom, who outbid which rival, and all the other fascinating trivia of the slave mart, of which Don Carlos could not get enough. He took a prurient interest and was hungry for gossip.

He would have liked to attend the auction in person, as had been his practice in younger days when he was still establishing himself. But since assuming the title and mantle of the de la Vegas, he reluctantly had to forego what had once been one of his prime pleasures.

Don Carlos knew that he risked being cheated of his full due by thieving underlings freed from his eagle-eyed supervision. It was a worry offset somewhat by his practice of setting his creatures to watch each other, alert for the slightest peculations.

The opera house violence sent three riders on fast horses hastening to Rancho de la Vega. They wore big sombreros, crossed bandoliers, belt guns, and bell-bottom pants over spurred boots.

Their blistering pace slowed as they rode up to the main gate of the rancho compound, for "none dare enter the precincts of Vega uninvited," as local wisdom held.

They slowed to a halt short of the arched gateway, horses frothy with white foamy sweat.

Challenged by a watcher on the wall as to their purpose, one of the riders shouted back enough of the bad news to ensure that the massive gate doors were unbolted and opened.

Beyond lay a palatial grand house, the hacienda, multi-storied and hung with ornate iron grillework, orange roof tiles scaled like a reptile's armored hide. There were stables, tack room, storehouses, a mill for grinding corn, quarters for the house servants, and bunkhouses for the *vaqueros.*

Most of the *vaqueros* had been sent to town to provide security for the auction, but a fair number of *pistoleros* had been held back in reserve, against the Apache scare occasioned by the massacre of the troop patrol.

A number of *vaqueros* and *pistoleros* idling in the courtyard heard the report that the opera house had been attacked, sacked, and burned and that much of Pago was in armed revolt. Some went to the hacienda to hear more; others went to spread the word to their compadres in the bunkhouse.

The three messengers rode on to the front of the hacienda, stepping down from their mounts.

One wore a broad-brimmed sombrero whose rim was decorated with a round of dangling, little, black pom-pom rebozos. His serape was bunched around his neck and shoulders so that its folds hid the lower half of his face.

He must have been of a shy, retiring nature since he stayed in the background, saying little, mostly nodding vigorously and grunting in assent as their leather-lunged spokesman told the tale to the doorman, gatekeeper of the hacienda.

The doorman was sufficiently impressed to summon the segundo, Don Carlos's foreman and second in command at the rancho. The segundo got the message fast and hurried inside, returning some minutes later with Don Carlos, along with several of the *padrón*'s inner circle of henchmen.

Don Carlos was middle-aged, stocky, balding,

with thin eyebrows, and a well-trimmed brown beard. His face was fleshy, with a bulbous nose and full lips. He wore a custom-tailored brown suit with black braided frogging and trim, a white ruffled shirt, lace cuffs partly covering square, strong, thick-fingered hands.

"Tell me what you know," Don Carlos demanded of the spokesman of the three riders.

"There was much shooting at the auction. Gringo bandits got in killing many men, *vaqueros*, and buyers, freeing the slave girls and setting the building on fire. . . ."

"We heard nothing, no sounds of gunfire," a henchman protested.

"We are too far away to hear shooting in town," Don Carlos said flatly, stating what he knew as fact from past experience.

He looked over the top of the wall toward town. Pago lay hidden behind a ridge, the glow of its lights showing above the crest as a blur. He saw nothing untoward . . . but was that a patch of red firelight shimmering in the blue-black opacity of night? He was unable to tell. One's eyes played tricks, especially at night.

"You saw this?"

"We were not inside the opera house, Don Carlos. Such magnificence is not for such lowly ones as us, but we were outside," the spokesman said. "We heard the shooting, saw the men and women flee in terror. There were many dead, more wounded, much blood.

"Your men were busy fighting, so we volunteered

to tell you, Excellency. We are but poor humble men who wished to do our duty to the *padrón* and the generosity of Don Carlos is known to all—"

"Yes, yes, you'll be well taken care of if your story proves true."

"We raced to be the first to tell you. You see that our horses are all blown out. We worked them without mercy to get here."

Don Carlos motioned for silence, then conferred with his henchmen

"Can it be true? It sounds beyond belief," one said.

"What would they gain by lying," another asked, "the lash, rope, or knife?"

"It could be a trick, a trap," said the first.

"Hold them until we can confirm or disprove their story," Don Carlos said, coming to a decision. "Give them something to eat and drink, but keep some guards on them—discreetly."

"*Sí,* Don Carlos," the foreman said, summoning some *vaqueros* to him. "You men, take these three around to the kitchen and see that they have something to eat."

"*Muchas gracias, señor,* but our horses need a rubdown and toweling. The sweat must not dry on them lest they take a chill," the spokesman wheedled.

"Our grooms will tend to them. Take them away, Joaquin."

"This way," an underling said, the trio following as he led them to the kitchen.

Confirmation was not long in coming. Within ten minutes came another rider from town, one of Don

Carlos's own men—known, trusted. Gunpowder burns, soot stains, and a bullet crease across the muscle of an upper arm added their own mute but eloquent testimony to his account of the sacking of the opera house, though he was somewhat surprised to discover that the tale had already been told.

"But then I stayed behind while there was still fighting to be done," the *vaquero* said somewhat self-importantly.

"Why aren't you there now?" a henchman quizzed.

"Somebody had to give warning."

The men were mustered out of the bunkhouse, guns were loaded and holstered, horses were saddled. A band of heavily armed *vaqueros* formed up in the courtyard.

Don Carlos stood on a patio to give them their orders so he could address the mounted men while looking down at them rather than standing on the ground and looking up at them.

"Go to town. Find who did this and kill them," Don Carlos said. "Take the ringleaders back alive if possible. I want them to suffer before they beg for death. They have questions to answer—who's behind all this? Find as many girls as you can, round them up and bring them here.

"Send some men to find Captain Bravo and hurry him back to Pago to join in the hunt.

"*Go!*"

The *vaqueros* rode out through the gate and onto the road to Pago. A skeleton crew remained behind to guard the rancho. Gate doors were slammed shut and bolted.

Don Carlos stayed behind, of course. The days when he would lead his men into battle were long gone. He was too valuable to risk losing—too valuable to himself, that is. These days, like all good generals, he led from the rear.

The men were paid and paid well to take risks, he told himself. Paid, anyway.

Don Carlos was in a foul mood, not minded to answer questions from underlings about what to do next, mainly because he was unsure about the answer himself. He needed hard answers first. His *vaqueros* would get them in Pago. Once he had the facts, he could better map out a strategy.

Don Carlos closeted himself, sealing himself up in his study with brandy and cigars. Henchmen and servants knew better than to bother him now with a lot of nonsense. When they were wanted, he would summon them. Until then, he didn't want to be bothered.

He steadied his nerves with a glass of brandy, then another while he mulled things over. Whatever the final disposition, it was clear he and his enterprise had taken a hit, a hard hit. Much effort would have to be expended in setting things right. At bottom, it meant he would be spending a lot of money he didn't have.

He had taken a double hit, really. His power and prestige had suffered by virtue of being perceived vulnerable enough to be attacked, and the disruption of the auction meant he would be unable to harvest revenues he'd been counting on since the spring auction six months earlier.

Dead *pistoleros* were the least of his worries. They could easily be replaced for cheap. Mexico was swamped with hungry gunmen, a surplus of them. The opera house was a far greater concern. How extensive was the damage?

Don Carlos lit a cigar. His hands shook so badly that he had to grip one by the wrist to steady it with the other hand before he could bring match flame into play against cigar tip. He puffed hard, venting smoke. He had another brandy to "steady his nerves."

It had been a long time since he had carried a gun. That was what he paid the *pistoleros* for. Now, though, touched by an apprehension long absent from his thoughts, he took a revolver from a bottom drawer of his desk and laid it on its side on the desktop, near at hand.

Time passed, ticked off by the wind-up clock mounted on the fireplace mantel. Each tick fell with a heavy, leaden sound. Twenty minutes passed, thirty.

The night hush was shattered by a violent disturbance. A furious outburst of shots, screams—then, silence.

Don Carlos started violently, accidentally knocking the snifter over, spilling brandy on the desk. He stood bolt upright, snatching the gun off the desk. He was frozen in place, listening.

A ponderous, creaking groan of metal and wood reached his ears; he recognized it as the sound of the heavy front gates of the rancho being opened. A pounding as of many hoofbeats could be heard approaching in the distance.

Don Carlos forced himself to go to the window. He moved stiffly, like a very old man. He lifted the edge of a curtain to look outside. It was a warm night, and the window was open.

His study was on the second floor of the hacienda, the window overlooking the courtyard. A body lay sprawled in the dirt yard, lit by a rectangle of yellow light that shone through a window of the front hall on the ground floor.

A man came into view, one of Don Carlos's men, a guard, running across the platform at the top of the high wall. He ran toward the gate, holding a gun in his hand. He was shouting something. Don Carlos couldn't make out what it was.

A stone staircase on the inside of the wall connected the platform with the courtyard. The guard went halfway down the steps and opened fire, shooting at two men who stood side by side, pulling the gate door inward. It was already open. They were opening it wider.

The shots were loud, explosive. Don Carlos flinched with each report, his hand a claw clutching the curtain which he had parted.

One of the two men at the gate was hit, and went down. The other turned, drew, and fired at the guard on the staircase.

The guard was hit. He cried out, falling off the steps into the courtyard. It was a modest fall, no more than a man's height. He placed his hands on the ground and raised his upper body, groaning.

The shooter who had knocked him off the stairs

stepped away from the gate door for a better shot, pointing his gun at the downed man. The guard raised an open hand in front of his face, shouting, "No, don't—!"

The shooter fired. The guard cried out as he was hit. He flopped facedown in the dirt, arms and legs working. He screamed for mercy. The shooter fired another slug into him, finishing him. The guard stopped thrashing and lay still, motionless. Silent.

The other man at the gate, the one who'd been shot by the guard, was not dead. He got his legs under him and rose shakily, clasping a hand to the shoulder of his other arm as if it had been hurt.

His partner started toward him. The wounded man waved him away, staggering to the staircase. He sat on the steps, propping himself up against the wall for support. He used his good arm to draw a holstered gun. He rested his gun hand on top of his thighs, pointing the weapon at the interior courtyard, covering it.

His fellow holstered his own gun and went back to the gate door, hauling away at it. The door was heavy, made of stout oak planks and beams reinforced with iron bands. The shooter gripped one of the metal flanges used to hold a bar to secure the door and used it as a handhold. He leaned back, digging his heels in, using his weight to help open the door wider.

The drumming of hoofbeats grew louder, nearing. The shooter finished wrestling the gate door open. He stepped back in time to avoid being trampled by a line of riders racing through the open gateway into the courtyard.

They were many—ten, no, twice that. They filled the courtyard, reining their horses in hard. Some of the animals upreared, rising on hind legs for an instant before touching all four legs down.

Hooves dug into the dirt, kicking up dust. The dust cloud climbed out of the courtyard above the walls, looking ghostly in the moonlight.

For an instant, Don Carlos dared hope that his *vaqueros* had returned, turning back from their Pago-bound course for some unaccountable reason, coming to the rescue in the nick of time.

The rescue? *His* rescue!

A second glance was enough to disabuse him of that notion. His *vaqueros* were hard, tough men, professional guns, killers. But this group was of a whole different order of being, a ragged, wild-looking crew.

A glimpse of them through slowly settling dust clouds was enough to tell that. They shrieked, whooped, and fired their guns in the air.

Apaches? No, they wore sombreros and serapes and fired six-guns, looking like outlaws, bandits—

A gang of *bandidos* was what they were, that was plain to see.

What of his men, defenders of the rancho? Where were they? Some began to show themselves, running out of the bunkhouse toward the edges of the courtyard and the spaces between outbuildings, not coming straight on, but scrambling to the sides, dodging, running for cover, snapping off a few quick shots.

They were more concerned with protecting their own miserable lives than doing their job of protecting him, Don Carlos, their paymaster and *padrón*! Worse, their numbers were depressingly few, a sparse handful.

They popped some shots at the boiling black mass of rowdy invaders. Gunfire sparked in the shadows, in thin fiery lines.

The bandits had something to shoot at now and were quick to make the most of the opportunity. How dare they?!

They dared. They were doing well, too, making a good account of themselves, better than that of the defenders. Skilled horsemen, they wheeled their mounts about to exchange shots with the guards, some breaking apart from the mass to charge full tilt at an opponent, blasting away at him.

A few guards stood atop the platform of a long side wall, shooting down into the mass. A bandit was hit, and knocked off his horse. Some of the bandits returned fire at the men on the wall.

Hit, a guard pressed hands flat against his chest, stumbled forward, and pitched headfirst off the rampart, tumbling into a tool shed and falling through the roof, collapsing the structure. The shed came apart, vertical planks and beams falling outward from the center, opening like the petals of a flower.

The pale gray haze of dust was threaded by lines

of light that were muzzle flares from the bandits' blazing guns.

Fresh shooting burst forth from much closer, seemingly from inside the hacienda itself. A house guard stood in the front doorway shooting at the outlaws.

A bandit was hit and fell shrieking from his horse. His foot caught in the stirrup as the horse bolted toward the gateway and outside. The bandit was dragged off down the road, screaming.

A couple of outlaws fired back at the man in the doorway, tagging him. He cried out, falling backwards into the front hall and out of Don Carlos's sight, though not out of hearing. Now unseen, the newly wounded man called out for help, his cries echoing hollowly through the halls.

Breaking glass sounded below as windowpanes were knocked out to allow the hacienda defenders to thrust rifle barrels through the frames, opening fire. Their shots were few, tentative, half-hearted.

Bandits began shooting at the hacienda in earnest, pouring a volley into the front of the house. Don Carlos shuddered, flinching violently from the impact of each hit tearing into the building. Gunfire from within the house, never strong, fell away fast.

A round fired high tore through the window at which Don Carlos stood immobilized. He fell back, tripping over his own feet, still clutching the curtain as he crashed to the floor. The drapes tore loose from the curtain rod, spilling around him in folds.

Don Carlos crouched on hands and knees, fighting loose of the gauzy curtain enveloping him like a shroud. He realized that he hadn't been hit. He released his grip on the curtains. He still had his gun, and he kept hold of that.

Crawling on hands and knees to the cover of his massive desk, he rose shakily on rubber legs to a half-crouch, turning toward the door.

A flickering shadow at the edge of his vision made him look up—a figure loomed in the doorway.

Don Carlos jerked his gun up. A shot sounded, not his, simultaneously with a smashing hammer blow to his gun hand as the weapon was shot out of his hand. It fell to the floor a half-dozen paces away.

Don Carlos screamed, clutching his maimed hand to himself. Broken fingers jutted at odd angles, blood spurts jetted. He staggered back into the desk, its support alone propping him up, keeping him on his feet.

The mystery gunman stood framed in the doorway, a hauntingly familiar figure—where had Don Carlos seen him before?

A line of black pom-pom rebozos dangled from the brim of his sombrero, jiggling back and forth over the stranger's slitted, burning eyes. Serape folds hid the lower half of his face.

His smoking gun was held hip high with seeming nonchalance, giving the illusion that the difficult trick of shooting the gun out of Don Carlos's hand had been tossed off almost negligently.

Don Carlos now recognized the shooter as one of the three messengers, the bearers of bad tidings—the one who'd been the least forward, remaining in the background.

He stepped forward into the room, his gun covering Don Carlos.

"Who are you?!" Don Carlos cried.

The stranger's free hand pulled down the serape, uncovering his face. Don Carlos's cry crescendoed into a peak of terror:

"*Gila Chacon!*"

"The massacre at the opera house was so exciting that we had to race here to tell you the good news. Good for me, that is, not for you." Gila smiled. "The other two? My men, *sí*, but new to the gang. None here know them to recognize them. So obliging of you to open the gates and let us in—*Gracias, señor*.

"But then you were always mindful of the little niceties, Don Carlos. I still carry the scars from our last encounter to remind me. We three took care of the guards you had set over us with the strangler's cord and the knife, so as not to disturb you. So you see, Don Carlos, the Chacon is mindful of the social courtesies, too.

"The other two opened the gates to let the *muchachos* in. I came in through the kitchen, to pay my old friend a visit. It is a meeting I have been waiting for for a long time."

"W-what— How did you get away from the Tombstone jail?" Don Carlos stammered.

"You made a big mistake when you sent your slavers north across the border. I had a rope around my neck—thanks to you, señor—but the gringos of Tombstone wanted their girls back alive more than they wanted the Chacon dead.

"I made a grand bargain with them, my life in exchange for leading them here into your stronghold of Pago so they could destroy you. I put them together with some of the many here who have long had reason to wish you dead. Much as I would like to take credit for your downfall, in all honesty I cannot. I helped load the gun, *sí*, but others pulled the trigger.

"And now the deed is done, the bargain is complete. The gringos have their girls back—and I have you."

Don Carlos's mind whirled with desperate scheming to get him off the hook. "Don't be hasty, Chacon. Think! Before you pull the trigger, think!

"The slave market is a big thing now, taking in much gold. Our customers are some of the best people in the land, the best and the biggest. The richest. I need a partner. You have the men and guns. I have political pull and connections, influence all the way to the highest levels of government. I operate *con permiso*, with permission, do you understand?"

"*Sí*, very much so."

"Then we'll do business together—"

"No. I have something else planned for you, Don Carlos, old friend. . . ."

Gila Chacon was the last to ride out of the Rancho de la Vega, all his men having exited through the gates before him. They left well before dawn. Gila would have liked to have lingered, but he couldn't afford the luxury of indulging himself.

There was still Captain Bravo and his troops to deal with. When they returned in the morning, exhausted from their wild-goose chase searching for Victorio's nonexistent war party they had been duped into believing massacred their patrol by the river, they would find a surprise waiting for them: the Chacon and his band in possession of the town, at the head of an ambush that would tear into them like the fangs and claws of the jaguar.

Gila regretted that the gringos had taken their devil of a machine gun away with them on their flight north. What he could do with such a weapon! He considered racing after them with his men and taking it from them, reluctantly putting aside the thought.

Men such as Matt Bodine and Sam Two Wolves were not to be taken lightly. Nor Ringo and Curly Bill, and all of the others. The least of the raiders was a deadly gun—why, even the bookkeeper could shoot!

It would be madness, too, to charge the machine gun, knowing what it could do, the destruction it sowed. No, best let them go their way and consider it a bargain made and kept.

With men such as those, and a weapon such as that, though, the Chacon could make himself a power in Sonora, perhaps the supreme power in the state, and beyond. Thoughts of other bandits and strongmen who had risen from obscurity to command a nation whirled through his head, opening dizzying prospects. Fate was strange. Who knew but that he and the Brothers of the Wolf might someday meet again?

Only time would tell.

For now, he and his outlaw band and the rebels of Pago had firepower enough and more to shoot Bravo and his men to pieces.

Gila and the *muchachos* did not leave Rancho Vega empty-handed. Saddlebags and pockets were stuffed to bursting with gold coins. Packhorses and mules were heavily laden with sacks of gold and silver plate and jewel boxes filled with precious gems, pearl necklaces, and gold trinkets.

A wagon and several ox carts were heaped high with plunder: firearms, boxes of ammunition, hundreds of bottles of fine wine and vintage brandies, boxes of cigars, heaps of handsome garments, bolts of expensive fabrics, valuable antiques, and much more. Don Carlos's stable of fine-blooded thoroughbred horses were enlisted as part of the caravan of pillaged loot.

The bandits rode out one by one, each afforded an opportunity to bid a final farewell to Don Carlos. Indeed, it was virtually impossible for them not to.

For Don Carlos Mondregón de la Vega hung by the neck at the end of a length of yellow hempen rope, suspended from the center of the archway spanning the tops of the gate posts.

An instructive sight, if not a pretty one. Staring eyes bulged in a swollen purple face, blackened tongue extended, the rope of the noose buried deep in the flesh of the neck.

Don Carlos hung at such a height that the bottoms

of his feet were almost at a level with the tops of the hats of the mounted bandits filing out through the gates. His feet were bare—his expensive custom-made boots had been stolen, too.

The *muchachos* had to duck or tilt their heads sideways to keep from having their sombreros knocked askew by the dangling man's feet. As they passed, they inadvertently seemed to bob their heads in acknowledgment of the generosity of their unwilling host.

Or so Gila Chacon saw it as he sat his horse inside the courtyard watching his men file out, savoring the sight of his deadly enemy Don Carlos suffering the fate he had intended for the bandit chief.

For such was the justice of the Chacon.

TWENTY-TWO

The convoy of Tombstone raiders and two wagonfuls of freed young females rushed north along the Camino Real, through the narrow gorge of La Garganta and out of the Espinazo.

Beyond lay a flat stony plain. At its far end, a wall of mountain peaks was broken by the mouth of a canyon pass stretching north between them. Breaking dawn found the convoy halfway to the pass.

South, a plume of dust showed, closing fast, nearing. It resolved itself into a band of mounted men.

"I make it about twelve, maybe fifteen men. That how you see it, Joe?" Sam Two Wolves asked.

Pima Joe nodded.

"We can't outrun them, not with the wagons," Matt said.

"Outrun, hell! I say let's have it out with 'em and kill 'em," Curly Bill said.

"Can't risk any of the girls getting shot, Bill," Ringo said gently.

"Right, right, of course! What do we do, then?"

"Send the wagons on ahead while some of us stay behind to tangle with the hombres chasing us," Matt offered.

"Now, that's a plan I like," Curly Bill said, flashing a big grin. "I'll stay, of course."

"Me, too," Ringo said.

All the raiders with the exception of Geetus Maggard were eager to stay behind. The Mitrailleuse machine gun would do no good here, where there was vast space for the pursuers to peel off and swing wide, clear of the weapon's field of fire. Then they could converge to hit the convoy's flanks or even outrace it to cut off the wagons.

It was hastily decided that the rear guard would consist of the best mounted pistol fighters: Matt, Sam, Ringo, Curly Bill, Jeff Howell, Hal Purdy, and Ed Dane. The others would escort the wagons to the safety of the north pass.

"I was hoping to be in on the finish," Remy Markand said seriously.

"Once you get to the narrow confines of the pass you can bring the machine gun into play, if they should get by us," Matt said. "I want men I can trust to bring the girls the rest of the way home if we don't make it, men like you."

"I concede the logic of your argument, but I don't have to like it."

"Hell, Remy, you got to solo with the machine gun onstage at the opera house last night. Let the rest of us have some fun, too."

"If that's how you want it, Matt."

"That's how it adds up. Better get moving. Those

riders are coming fast and the girls have to be out of shooting range."

"Good luck!"

The wagons raced north, driven by Dutch Snyder and Geetus Maggard, escorted by Remy, Polk Muldoon, Juan Garza, Vern Tooker, Pima Joe, and Arnholt Stebbins.

Breaking dawn sent long, radiant yellow shafts of sunlight slanting across the pebbly, purple-gray plain. The rear guard formed up in a loose line facing south, toward the oncoming riders. They started their horses forward.

"Damned if that don't look like Black Angus hisself," Jeff Howell said.

"It is Jones, along with his gang and some other jaspers they must've picked up along the way," Curly Bill said.

Black Angus Jones and company had outstayed their welcome in Pago. Being slave hunters, not buyers, and not particularly desirable company to boot, they'd been excluded from the theater hall when the shooting started, allowing them to escape with their lives, guns, and horses, if little else.

Some hours had passed before they realized that the situation had changed irrevocably and Pago was to them a closed book. The Tombstone convoy had a good head start but the wagons slowed them down, allowing Black Angus to catch up with them in the plains north of the Espinazo.

"Let's put them down for good," Matt said.

"It won't be for bad," Sam said.

"Dorado is mine," Ringo said.

"Not if I beat you to him," Curly Bill said.

"Quirt Fane, too."

"Getting' kinda greedy, ain't you, John?"

"First come, first served, Bill!"

The Tombstone raiders spurred their horses onward into a gallop, landscape rushing by in a blur. They were outnumbered at slightly better than two-to-one by the foe.

Sam shucked his rifle out of the saddle scabbard. The tomahawk was stuck in his belt at his hip. White-haired, white-bearded old Nando had told Sam about Dorado and the legend of the golden gun, how it had been forged from the gold mask of an Aztec death-god, how the curse on it protected its wielder from death by gunfire. Sam figured the tomahawk might come in handy for the showdown.

From this distance, he'd let his Winchester do the talking first. Taking the reins between his teeth, Sam levered a round into place and fired.

A rider in the lead of the Jones gang was knocked off his horse and lay where he fell, motionless.

Bullets began whizzing through the air around the charging Tombstoners. Gunshots popped from the onrushing Jones men, puffballs of smoke forming at their gun barrels.

The play had changed thanks to the raiders' bold charge. It was no longer a case of lumbering wagons laden with helpless young women trying to outrun swift mounted pursuit. Now it was all speed, dash, and blazing gunplay on both sides. The seven kept on coming, making straight for Jones and friends.

Black Angus didn't like this so well. The charging foe were pouring plenty of lead into the air, streaming it at him and his men.

A round from Sam Two Wolves's rifle tagged Sime Simmons, riding on Jones's right, their horses pretty much neck and neck. They were so close that Jones heard the thwack of the bullet tearing into Sime.

A puff of dust rose up from Sime's shirt where the bullet entered him. He swayed with the mortal hit and stopped shooting, but stayed upright, shirt turning dark red where he'd been hit.

He sagged, slumping in the saddle like he was melting. The horse's leaps and bounds caused him to fall sideways off the animal.

Black Angus ducked down still lower, trying to cover behind his charger's massive crupper and head, shooting around it with his six-gun. Carmen was on his left, outracing him, a gun in one hand blazing away.

Like knights of old locked in a jousting match, the two lines of shooters rushed straight at each other on a headlong collision course.

Sam's rifle dropped Porgy Best, who went down off the back of the horse as if some giant invisible hand had brushed him off like a gnat.

Matt Bodine, Ringo, and Curly Bill were grouped together, a triumvirate of six-gun fury. Riding like the wind, they blasted down foes like a whirlwind.

Six-guns banged away in a riotous racket of noise, lines of fire lancing the Jones men. A volley of slugs sieved Sonny Boy Algar, shooting his middle to pieces.

Rio Jordan tagged Curly Bill high on the left side, a hot iron creasing Bill's ribs. Another shot took a chunk out of Bill's upper left arm. Bill blasted away, shooting Jordan's face off.

Howling Jeff Howell howled his Rebel yell as his gun blasted away.

Matt Bodine came in close with the reins clenched between his teeth and a gun in each hand, both blazing. He was a better shot with a pistol at long distances than most men were with a rifle.

Two slugs burned down two of Don Carlos's *vaqueros* who had joined Black Angus in his pursuit of the escaped captive girls.

Ed Dane was pounded hard in the right shoulder by a round, rocking him in the saddle. The cantle behind kept him from falling backwards off the horse. The bullet drilled his upper arm, numbing it. The arm dropped to his side, useless. A gun was still in his hand, but he couldn't lift it. His arm wouldn't respond.

Carmen Oliva had winged him, mahogany-red hair streaming behind her like the tail of a fiery comet.

The two opposing forces met at last, riders coming face to face at point-blank range in a blistering mutual exchange.

Jeff Howell's horse collided with that of Slicker

Dupree. Dupree had been enjoying himself until then, a broad grimacing grin of murder-lust contorting his face, baring lots of teeth.

Came the crash, with a terrible sound of horseflesh slamming horseflesh, the horses screaming. Jeff catapulted from the saddle, flung headfirst into the air for some distance. Dupree stayed on his horse, but it went down, pinning him under it and then it was his turn to scream.

Jeff's horse somersaulted, breaking its neck. Jeff somersaulted, too, as the ground rushed up to meet him, but he had better luck. He went into a roll, tucking an arm under him, taking the impact on his shoulder and rolling, rolling and tumbling, going ass over tea kettle, taking a hell of a pounding. He was thumped, pounded, and slammed, thrown for a loop.

Hal Purdy fired into Mort Donegan's torso, so close that muzzle flares caused Donegan's shirt to burst into flame.

Not to be outdone by his rival, Ed Dane filled his good left hand with a gun, shooting at a *vaquero*.

Carmen Oliva raced by, shooting Ed Dane between hat brim and eyebrows. His forehead exploded, hat flying off his head.

Matt Bodine passed between Earl Calder and a *pistolero*. His left hand fired a shot into the *pistolero* and less than an eye blink later, his right fired a blast into Calder.

Calder lurched, crying out, fighting to stay in the saddle.

The two lines passed beyond each other, reining in and wheeling their mounts around for another pass, another murderous go-round.

Dorado turned his horse tightly, sunbeams glinting off his golden gun. Hal Purdy was slower in turning his horse, not much slower but those fractions of a second meant the difference between life and death.

Dorado put two quick shots into Purdy's back. Purdy pitched forward, upper body bowing outward under the bullets' impact as they shattered his spine and then he felt nothing, nothing at all.

He fell off his horse and lay on his side, one side of his face pressing stony ground. He felt nothing below the neck, nothing. He couldn't breathe, the great heaving bellows of his lungs was stilled.

His field of vision took in Ed Dane laying nearby, dead. Well, that was something anyway, Purdy told himself, he'd outlived his rival, if only by a matter of seconds. Blackness gobbled him up and he was dead.

The battlers kept at it, separated by less than the distance of a stone's throw. They closed again.

Jeff Howell stood on his knees, shaking his head to clear it. Quirt Fane charged him. Jeff's hand plunged for his gun, encountering an empty holster—his gun must have fallen out when he took a tumble.

Quirt Fane leaned over in the saddle to one side of the horse, arm extended, gun in hand, shooting. Jeff glimpsed his gun on the ground a man's length away. He threw himself flat on the ground, rolling sideways away from the charge, Quirt Fane's bullets tearing up the piece of turf Jeff had just quitted.

Quirt flashed past. Jeff stopped rolling and snatched up his gun, heaving a heaping holler as he lined up the muzzle for a potshot at Quirt—

Carmen Oliva came at him, firing. Slugs tore into Jeff, knocking him over.

Carmen rode him down deliberately, trampling him. Jeff went under the animal's iron-shod hooves. One struck his head, silencing him in mid-howl, and he knew no more, forever.

The horse's legs tangled on Jeff, tripping the animal up. It fell, throwing Carmen. She landed clear, shaken but unhurt, with nothing broken.

Ringo reined in beside Curly Bill. Bill's upper left arm and side stained his shirt red. "You all right, Bill?"

"I ain't hit bad, John— Look out!"

Dorado charged, hand coming up to level the golden gun on Ringo and Bill. He figured he'd take them both out with one rapid-fire burst, they were so close. Ringo was turned away from Dorado and Curly Bill was slowed by his wound.

Sam pulled the tomahawk from his belt and let fly, pinwheeling the war hatchet at Dorado's outstretched arm with the golden gun held at the end of it. Reflected sunlight from the golden gun flashed in Ringo's eyes, dazzling them.

Dorado went to pull the trigger to burn down Ringo and Bill, but nothing happened. The gun was silent, refusing to fire. Dorado looked to see what was wrong with the golden gun.

There was no gun, no hand either. Sam's tomahawk blade had taken Dorado's hand off at the wrist, severing it. The hand with the gun in its fist flew away into the air.

Dorado stared stupidly at the empty space where his hand had been. There was a neat cut at the wrist. He could see the round-mouthed tubes of blood vessels and the oval ivory disks of wrist bones.

After a beat, the wound began spewing blood, geysering the red stuff, a fountain of it. Dorado screamed.

He looked back, searching frantically for what he'd lost. A few paces off, his hand lay in the grass among the weeds, still clutching the golden gun, the gun all a-glimmer in the sunlight, looking like it was made of molten metal.

Dorado was still game. One-handed, he fumbled for the reins. The horse lurched; he missed his hold and fell off.

Amidst the whirling melee, Matt Bodine and Quirt Fane found themselves face to face. Their horses milled side by side, shying clear of each other.

Matt and Quirt opened fire, cutting loose with six-guns. Matt was a shade faster, his first round tore into Quirt, walloping him, knocking him off balance so that Quirt's opening shot went wild, nicking a hole out of Matt's hat brim.

Matt plugged away, pumping lead into the other man. Quirt was still shooting by reflex as he toppled off his horse, shooting straight up into empty sky—

Dead before he hit the ground.

The wagons and their protectors had reached the safety of the north mountain pass. None of the Jones gang gave chase. Their charge had broken on the rock of the seven from Tombstone.

Remy, Polk, Juan Garza, Pima Joe, Stebbins, Snyder, and even Geetus Maggard herded the girls to cover. Mountain man Vern Tooker lingered outside the canyon mouth, readying his Sharps, a big .50, long-rifle buffalo gun.

It needed reloading after each single shot, but he knew how to make every shot count. Vern had keen eyesight, so he could make out the figure of Black Angus Jones from a long way off.

He sighted on Jones and squeezed the trigger, unleashing a big booming blast. Fate took a hand in that split-second, causing a *vaquero* to ride in front of the outlaw chief and taking the bullet meant for him.

It sounded like a rug hung up on the line being struck by a carpet beater, splattering Black Angus's head and shoulders with a stinging shower of blood droplets.

The *vaquero* was hit so hard it looked like he was yanked sideways out of the saddle.

Vern Tooker swore softly under his breath and started to reload the big .50 Sharps.

Jones knuckled his eyes, wiping them clean, blinking rapidly and repeatedly. The big-caliber shot coming seemingly out of nowhere spooked him, eating up what little fight he had left. The round had been meant for him, blind luck saving him. The Devil's own luck. He couldn't rely on that kind of crazy fluke striking twice.

Black Angus's last charge had taken him off to the side, momentarily out of the action. He looked around, and what he saw was not good. His gang was pretty much done for, along with the handful of *vaqueros* who'd attached themselves to him for the chase.

Jones was whipped and he knew it.

"Time to quit while the gittin' is good," he said to himself. He turned his horse away from the fight toward open space, out of there, away.

Carmen Oliva was on foot, clicking the trigger of what she now learned was an empty gun. She and Jones saw each other. She shouted, waving the gun.

Jones changed course, swerving toward her. He came on as she stood facing him. He leaned out of the saddle, long reaching arm curved like a hook. She dropped the gun, freeing both hands for the attempted save.

Black Angus scooped her up, Carmen hanging on for dear life. He swung her up on horseback, planting her behind him. She hung on tightly, hugging Jones.

He would have liked to grab another horse. There was no shortage of riderless horses around, their riders having been shot off them. But they were clustered in the wrong direction and he was not much minded to stop, not with that big buffalo gun somewhere out there. There was such a thing as crowding your luck too close, even when it was the Devil's own.

Away he rode, Carmen holding on behind. Two or three other survivors, *vaqueros*, also peeled off, arrowing away in different directions.

Dorado's nightmare world had dissolved to a single object, the golden gun.

He crawled to it on hand and knees, each frantic heartbeat sending more of his lifeblood gushing from his truncated wrist.

He was possessed by the conviction that somehow all would be well if only he could lay his hand on the golden gun. It was almost within his reach, inches away. He groped for it with his numb fingers fumbling.

A booted foot stepped down on the gun and severed hand, pinning them to the ground, denying the gun to Dorado.

Dorado straightened up, standing on his knees looking up at Ringo and Curly Bill.

"You ain't golden no more, hoss," Bill said, shaking his head.

Ringo picked up the gun and hand. The fist was closed tight around the pistol grip. He tried to shake it loose, to no avail.

"That hand plain just don't want to let go," Curly Bill said, laughing and wincing. His bloody shirt was unbuttoned. His wounds looked worse than they were, spilling a lot of blood. He held a wadded bandana against the hole in his left arm. His creased ribs were bruised but unbroken.

Ringo methodically opened the severed hand's fingers one by one, prying them loose. The hand flopped to the ground.

The golden gun was clean, unbloodied. It had ebony-wood plate handles on the grip. Ringo held the gun measuringly, weighing it in his hand. He liked the feel of it, its balance and heft. It felt right, like it had been made for him.

Golden surfaces glimmered, alluring, hypnotic. Ringo could see his face reflected in it, distorted like in a funhouse mirror but golden—gold. He smiled.

"Cursed gun, it has been the death of me," Dorado breathed. "It will bring you no joy, Ringo."

"I'm feeling pretty good right now."

"May it bring you the same fate it has brought me, you—" He called Ringo a dirty name.

"You killed Bob Farr," Ringo said, deadly serious now, an executioner formally passing sentence.

"Who?" Dorado rasped, genuinely puzzled.

"Bob Farr. You don't even know who he is, do you?"

"I have killed so many I don't bother to keep track of them—as will you, Ringo."

"You shot Bob Farr in the back at Cactus Patch," Ringo pressed.

"Oh, yes, I hardly recall it. It seemed so unimportant at the time," Dorado said, voice growing faint, whisper thin.

"If not for that I wouldn't be here and you'd probably still be alive. At least, you'll be getting it straight on instead of from behind."

"Shoot and be damned . . . And damned you will be, Ringo, damned by the golden gun."

Ringo fired, shooting Dorado through the heart.

Dorado fell over, dead. Ringo stared down at the golden gun. It felt like a living thing in his hand.

"You'd be safer holding a rattlesnake," Sam said. "That gun is bad medicine."

"Bad luck, you mean?" Ringo asked.

"Something like that." Sam knew the golden gun was evil, a gun of doom. It protected its owner, perhaps, but at what cost? His soul? Aztec death-god magic, blackest black magic.

Sam had beaten Dorado because instead of a gun he had used a tomahawk. The war hatchet had a blade of white man's steel at its head, but its haft was made of wood cut from an ash tree in the Northern Range. The tomahawk had been ritually purified long ago with the smoke of burning herbs, steeped in the smoky mysteries of the sacred lodge of a Cheyenne medicine man. Cheyenne magic had checked Aztec magic.

Sam knew that there was no explaining that to Ringo, their backgrounds were too dissimilar, so he said simply, "Yes, the golden gun is bad luck."

"What do you expect me to do, leave it lay here or throw it away?" Ringo asked, not caring about the answer. His mind was made up.

"I would," Sam said.

"I believe you would at that," Ringo said, and did. But not he. He did not believe, or if he did, he did not care. He was already under the spell. He took an ivory-handled Colt from his right hip holster, putting the golden gun in its place and tucking the Colt in his belt.

"I'll take my chances. I'm not superstitious," he said.

Matt looked around at the bodies sprawled on the stony plain. "We took them, but at what a price: Hal Purdy, Ed Dane, Jeff Howell. . . . It's a damned shame. Nothing for it but to load our dead on their horses and take them home for a decent burial."

This was done, fallen heroes tied facedown across their horses. Stray mounts were rounded up to add to the convoy's string. Black Angus's gang was left for the buzzards.

"If they'll have 'em," Curly Bill said.

"Their epitaph," said Sam.

They rejoined the others in the mouth of the pass and the convoy resumed its northward trek home.

Black Angus Jones and Carmen Oliva were in a tight spot. They had gone east, leaving the gray stony plain behind. They were in a broken land of thin, dry, brown soil, gray-black rock outcroppings and dry washes. No water in sight, except what Jones had in his canteen and most of that had to go to the horse, dribbled out by the palmful for the animal to thirstily lick from his hand. Not a trickling spring or water hole was in view.

There was no going back to Pago, an unhealthy climate for slave hunters now that the power of Don Carlos was broken. That door was closed.

The horse plodded on, laboring. It had had a

hard run north out of Pago through the Espinazo, and the double load of Jones and Carmen it carried on its back wasn't helping.

"I know a little pueblo village about ten to fifteen miles from here," Jones said, "that's if Victorio ain't wiped it out. They ain't got much, but we can get another horse or mule and some food and water, especially water."

"Then what?" Carmen asked dully.

"North, back across the border."

"What's there, a rope?"

"What's here? We're done in this part of Sonora, played out." Jones's voice was a parched, rasping croak, Carmen's, too.

They plodded on, the sun rising, a miserable ride in the mounting heat, misery embittered by the knowledge of defeat. The horse couldn't be pressed too hard. It was already carrying the weight of two. If something should happen to it to cause it to go lame, Black Angus and Carmen would be forced to go afoot in this high desert, paring slim chances down to next to nothing.

A line of low rocky ridges rose in the east. A blur of motion flickered in the corner of Jones's eye, motion where none should be.

A line of mounted men came into view cresting the ridge, eight or more, neat, compactly made, dusty, copper-skinned men with long black hair astride tough. scrappy little horses.

"What, what is it?" Carmen mumbled, rousing from a drowsy torpor.

"Apaches," Jones said. That woke Carmen up.

The Apaches must have been some of Victorio's bucks, Jones reckoned. A raiding party. He turned his horse's head, pointing it north.

The line of Apaches went north along the ridge, keeping pace with Jones and Carmen on the horse. Jones knew they were being played with because, ordinarily, Apaches never skyline. They're too trail wise for that. They're only seen when they want to be seen.

Jones fought to keep calm, to quell the rising panic in him, but what was the point? He found himself kicking the horse in the sides, urging it forward into a lurching run.

The Apaches angled down off the ridge, coming up behind Jones and Carmen. It wasn't much of a chase, not against that overloaded, exhausted horse. The Apaches prolonged it, stretching it out so as to not to end the fun too soon. They fanned out, yipping, howling.

The horse stumbled over a gopher hole, falling and throwing its riders. It rose on all fours, unharmed, and shakily trotted off, one of the braves riding out to intercept it.

Jones and Carmen struggled to their feet, dazed, swaying, groaning. The Apaches closed in, silent once more.

"What do we do now, Angus, what do we do now?" Carmen babbled.

Jones knew the answer to that one. He'd seen what Apaches do to captives unlucky enough to be taken alive. He drew his gun. Only one bullet wa left. He'd forgotten to reload after the fight and there was no time left now.

"Sorry, Carmen," Black Angus said. He put the gun to his head and pulled the trigger, blowing his brains out. He died smiling, his Devil's own luck still holding. Under the circumstances, this was triumph.

"Jones, you dirty coward," Carmen shrieked.

The Apaches formed a ring around her, hemming her in. They sat their horses, faces implacable, eyeing her.

Carmen grabbed the gun from Jones's dead hand, pointed it at the nearest Apache and pulled the trigger. It clicked on an empty chamber. She kept pulling the trigger, squeezing metallic clicks out of the empty gun.

One of the Apaches barked a laugh, and two or three others smiled. They moved in, the ring closing on Carmen.

TWENTY-THREE

On Monday, September 18, 1880, the convoy of freed girls and their rescuers rode into Tombstone, Arizona.

It rode through town, people rushing out of doors to see, throngs of them lining the street, cheering and shouting. Men waved hats in the air, women fluttering handkerchiefs, kids running around yelling and screeching. More than a few excited citizens fired guns in the air, whooping it up.

It was as if a carnival had come to town, touching off a festive mood of celebration. Wagons and riders turned into Allen Street, rolling to a halt in front of the Hotel Erle.

"Great day in the morning!" Colonel Davenport said. Then he started cheering and shouting louder than anyone else.

The church pastor was there, and members of the ladies auxiliary do-good society, crowding the wagons, ready hands reaching up to help the girls down and into the hotel.